TO GAZE

UPON

WICKED

GODS

TO GAZE UPON WICKED GODS

MOLLY X. CHANG

NEW YORK

Published in the United States by Del Rey, an imprint of Random House, a division of Penguin Random House LLC, New York.

DEL REY and the CIRCLE colophon are registered trademarks of Penguin Random House LLC.

Hardback ISBN 978-0-593-72224-4
International edition ISBN: 978-0-593-72476-7
Ebook ISBN 978-0-593-72225-1

Printed in the United States of America on acid-free paper

randomhousebooks.com

2   4   6   8   9   7   5   3   1

First Edition

Art credit: lyotta, WinWin, Maryna Stryzhak, Vector Tradition, SB © Adobe Stock Photos

Endpaper illustrations by June Tran

Book design by Sara Bereta

To my grandparents,
for the stories that inspired this book,
and for always reminding me that if our ancestors
could survive the harshest winters known to man,
genocide after genocide, famine, and war, then I can
survive anything. Memories of you gave me the courage
to keep going, even when publishing this book felt
like death by a thousand cuts.

AUTHOR'S NOTE

I remember my grandfather's tears. The way his voice cracked when he whispered of the ghosts who haunted Manchuria. The demons who stole misbehaving children from their beds to conduct monstrous experiments on. All my life, I thought these stories were mere folklore, passed from lips to lips. Fiction. Made up to scare me into doing my homework. It wasn't until 2020, after my grandfather had sadly passed and I was homesick for China, my chest raw from the grief and sorrow of watching anti-Asian hate run rampant in the land I left home for, did I realize these stories were so much more than what I originally thought.

In my desperation to cling to my grandparents and home, I stumbled across articles of Unit 731, a place that existed in Harbin during WWII, just twenty minutes from where I grew up. I realized those ghost stories that haunted my childhood were never just stories. They were memories, rooted in reality. They were a piece of history, forgotten by too many. So while *To Gaze Upon Wicked Gods* is fictional, its inspirations were very much real. Everything from the abhorrent experiments to the men who tried to play Gods. The horrifying true stories of Manchuria under Russian and Japanese occupation deserve to be retold and remembered.

What happened to the people of Manchuria and the people of China left trauma so harrowing, its survivors could not retell it as history. This was why my Manchurian grandfather and his people wove it into horror stories with sinister traces of the paranormal, ghosts, and demons. These memories of the past became folklore passed down from parent to child as the Japanese denied the existence of Unit 731, denied the Manchurian blood we lost, denied the pain and trauma suffered by generation after generation, interlocked by tears.

My grandfather's stories were seeds, and I hope if he were alive today he'd be proud of the tree that sprouted from those seeds: stories of tribes and Empires, of our people's pain and suffering, of the Siberian wilderness, and of the ancestors who had survived genocide after genocide. How lucky I was to be of Manchurian blood, to have grown up on Manchurian land. He said if our ancestors could survive the Siberian ice, we could survive anything.

I hope if he could meet Ruying, my main character, he'd be proud of her ferocious need to survive. Just like our ancestors who grew up in a time where no one was safe, where people would do anything to survive.

Hunger and poverty. The love of family, that feeling of powerlessness as everything precious to our culture, our people was stripped away, piece by piece because China fought our Western invaders' bullets and planes with bows and arrows. But what if we had more? My grandfather interwove history with demons; I choose to repaint his stories with hope. Because what if the magic of our ancient stories about Gods and heroes were true? What if we had that magic to fight their science?

What if?

What if?

What if . . . ?

To Gaze Upon Wicked Gods at its heart is about many things. It's about the forgotten histories of China's Century of Humiliation, the hard choices one has to make in order to survive a merciless world. It's about an Asian girl who is taught to be quiet, but longs to be loud. But at its heart, it's a story about immigration and its

sacrifices—crossing oceans and worlds, enduring hardship and uncertainty—to give those you love a better life.

Dear Reader, I hope you love this book as much as I do. I hope
you read Ruying's story and see her not as a villain, but as a girl
who loves her family, as a victim of the brutal world she was born
into, doing everything in her power to protect those she loves. Even
if it means forfeiting her morals and working for the enemy—doing
unforgivable things—as long as she can protect her family.

PART 1

天外之神

Gods from Beyond the Skies

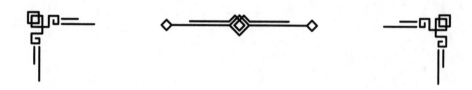

Somewhere between Life and Death exist our two worlds.

One rich with magic.

One rife with science.

Pangu was a paradise,

where magic and humanity lived in harmony.

Rome was a world of another realm,

where electricity chased away the night and engines ran on
fumes.

Our worlds existed in parallel,

separated by a Veil woven by Fate herself,

Until the Romans came like Gods from the sky in their planes
docked with guns.

In the beginning, they greeted us with smiles.

When we awed them with our magic,

they amazed us with their technology

that made the impossible

possible.

A treaty was signed.

The age of a peaceful union.

We thought they were benevolent, kind.

Until—

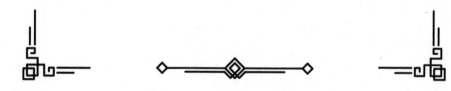

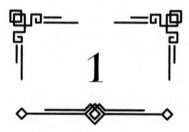

1

THE SKY WAS CRYING AGAIN.

All around me, my world wept. Gray, icy tears caressed my skin, shivering cold in the late-summer heat. With deliberate steps, I passed the Fence that carved my city into halves, guarded by Roman soldiers and their white-knuckled grips on the guns that haunted our nightmares, ready to shoot me down over perceived slights.

I hated these men. Hated their stern, foreign faces and foreign attire from beyond the shimmering portal high in the somber sky that now joined our two realms. A glistening fracture, looming over my broken city like the all-seeing eye of a vengeful God who was not here to love and protect, but to torture.

To inflict unimaginable pain and suffering, as the Romans had for over two decades now.

Every day, I cursed this road, this fence, their loaded guns, and every trace of Rome that marred my world like a permanent stain.

Yet, I still bowed my head for them, still walked this road week after week, under hawk-like gazes, for the drug that killed my sister slowly, but without which she would die fast like a flower cut from the stem. At least with opian, Meiya might live another two, three, or even five years like Father had.

Without it, she might not live through the season.

Some Romans wore disgust and hate clear on their faces. Others wore smirks and lust.

One pursed his lips and let out a sharp whistle that made my spine flinch cold.

Death's magic thrummed quiet under my skin: embers ready to kindle into wildfire the moment I allowed it.

I had no reason to fear these men. Given my powers, I had no reason to fear anyone.

With an arch of my hand, I could dip into Death's realm of stark grays, pluck *qi* from their bodies until only corpses remained. A constant temptation—to take something from them the way they had taken so much from us.

But Grandma had raised me to be cautious. A girl could never be too careful in this age of colonial destruction, where the peace between magic and science balanced at knife's edge.

I could kill one of them—perhaps two or three if I was lucky. But I couldn't kill every Roman who marched this city. Their heads high with arrogance, entitled to claim anything and anyone they pleased.

Though years had passed, memories remained vivid like a fresh dream: the first time I witnessed one of my own slaughtered in cold blood under Roman hands.

I was still a child and Father was still alive and kind as he'd ever be.

It was murder by gunshot, execution-style. And the fingers that had pulled the trigger belonged to none other than their eldest prince—Valentin Augustus. Just three years older than I was, he'd shot a man dead before hundreds of witnesses for the audacity of placing soiled hands on the prince's pristine clothes, for daring to beg him for the pennies he kept carelessly in pockets. Pennies that would enable a father to feed his starving child.

If I closed my eyes, I could still feel my father's shaking hands holding mine, smell the fear that radiated from everyone in that crowd like a foul stench. The very fear that emanated from my own skin the moment I heard that sky-splitting *bang*. A primal thing from deep in my belly.

Evil ran in all Roman veins common as blood, but Valentin Augustus was rumored to be something worse.

The city whispered of his brothers, too.

The middle prince who lived on Pangu soil with Valentin, but no one had ever seen him venture beyond the Fence.

The third and youngest prince, who was a bloodthirsty military protégé and the only prince who remained in Rome as their grandfather's right hand.

Their mighty yet odious grandfather, whose disdain for my kind shaped the politics of two worlds. Whose callous heart doomed my Empire to this bitter fate.

Cruel and monstrous, all of them. Privilege and power fed the evil in these Romans like oil to flame.

So I walked with vigilant steps, hands folded across my torso where they could be seen. Quiet as a mouse, rigid and timid like a ghost drifting away. This was how we were taught to move around them.

Too many stories of trigger-happy soldiers.

Too many warnings from Grandma.

One step out of line and they might slaughter my family in retribution, like they'd done too many times before to the patriots and the martyrs who refused to kneel.

Everyone in this wretched city knew someone who'd died by Rome's vicious hands, playing Gods with their machines and science that had our once great Empire begging for scraps of mercy.

Stories of horror tangled with stories of awe. Whenever they perused our streets, we knew better than to venture too close.

When it wasn't Prince Valentin, then it was some other Roman nobleman or soldier terrorizing our crumbling city. Men who dragged my people from the streets in lust or rage or a twisted combination of both, pulled them into alleys in broad daylight where their terrified screams could be heard by all who passed, yet few were brave enough to do something. And of those brave souls, fewer were lucky enough to live and tell the tale.

路见不平, 拔刀相助. *When you see someone in trouble, you draw your blade and help.*

But what was a blade against a bullet?

What was magic, against science?

What was the point of seeking justice when these vile monsters lived above decency, above rules? Who would punish them? Mortals who lived like Gods, who had such power even our young Emperor Yongle had to lower his head and let them walk all over his dignity . . . just like his father did before him.

How far our great Empire had fallen. From a great beacon of power, shining over the entire continent, to a puppet hung from strings, dancing to Rome's command.

All in the span of twenty-something years.

That incident with Prince Valentin might be the first time I had witnessed a Roman kill us in cold blood, but it wasn't the first time it had happened on our soil.

And it wasn't the last.

Once, an elderly father with a feeble body had tried to seek justice for his son, who had been murdered by a group of drunken Roman ministers because he had dared to look at them with contempt instead of bowing respect—an act of defiance that had cost him his life. That father had bellowed and cried at Rome's gates before the guards shot him down with a swift bullet, then hung his corpse on the Fence for an entire moon cycle.

A formal warning to anyone who dared to disrespect the Roman Empire.

Our Emperor and his city guards and all of those generals and governors who were supposed to protect us did nothing, said nothing.

The Romans could beat us, kill us, do unspeakable things to us, but as long as they returned to their side of the Fence before authorities caught them, they couldn't be punished.

Not like anyone in Jing-City was brave enough to arrest a Roman anyway.

To do so would be war.

And nobody in their right mind would willingly start something so horrific over a few lost lives. The Romans knew their power, and they'd never hesitate to exploit it.

Mortal laws don't apply to Gods: a saying whispered in grief and sorrow.

This might be our world, our home, our land, but the Romans had forced themselves into our lives with guns and grenades and flying machines, with weapons beyond our worst nightmares.

The war that had killed my grandfather almost twenty years ago began and ended right before I was born. For the Romans beat us not in a year, not in a month, not even in a week.

They had beaten us in a single day.

Planes filled the sky like a storm and rained fire and bullets upon the camps where the Er-Lang armies were stationed—a fight unlike anything our continent had ever seen.

And since then, when Rome told us to kneel, we knelt.

For we knew, in a war between magic and science, we stood no chance.

In the aftermath, we surrendered more things than we could count. Nobody knew the full extent of the peace treaty and what our emperor gave up to ensure another war would never take place on our soil.

This was the nature of power. The decisions of Emperors were never relayed to their subjects. So we grasped at every rumor and speculation as our city changed before our eyes. The west half of the capital was surrendered to the Romans, and all of its inhabitants were either evicted or, if they were brave enough to defy the wishes of these cruel tyrants, slaughtered at the edge of the Fence for all to see. And opian—the substance that allegedly sparked the humiliatingly brief war—flooded the streets on unchecked claims of strengthening Xianling Gifts and awakening magic from those who were not born Gifted.

Years passed in the blink of an eye. Babies were born and raised in such times.

Er-Lang Empire existed only in name now. After the late Emperor passed and his last surviving son—three years older than I was, just like Prince Valentin—succeeded the throne, things had only gotten worse.

And while the Romans fashioned themselves as Gods, they refused to answer our endless prayers.

Instead of kindness, we were granted only misery and tragedy. Strings and strings of heartbreak and political upheavals that killed the late Emperor with stress. Though some whispered he had died of an overdose of opian, and had willingly allowed Rome to live beyond the reaches of our laws, had let their sins run free of consequence. All for a steady supply of this supposedly heavenly drug.

Clenching my jaw, I passed a street performer enchanting a small crowd with swirling shadows and honey-sweet words. She echoed the age-old chant we were taught as children: "Somewhere between Life and Death exist our two worlds. One rich with magic. One rife with . . ."

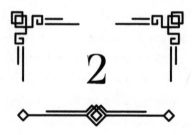

2

I ROUNDED A CORNER, VENTURED down a festive street with clamoring merchants setting up night-market stalls. The scent of street food and candied treats invaded my lungs, made my mouth water.

The Lotus Tower stood at the edge of the Fence, overlooking a row of newly built Roman houses and cafés with signs that proclaimed NO PANGULINGS ALLOWED.

Though they had already annexed half of our city, the Romans continued to take more because they knew they could. Because it seemed no matter how much they took, they would never be satisfied.

And we had no way of stopping them from buying up land, either through legal monetary exchanges or sinister coercions.

Because of this, what used to be the busiest teahouse at the heart of Jing-City now stood tall as a prominent opian den, swarmed with sin.

Inside, under opulent red beams and half-moon archways, the world smoldered with dancing smoke and fluttering silks, transparent on the bodies who wore them. Meaty hands flashed a wealth of jade and gold, their pockets laden with silver. Sweet sighs and warm caressing breaths swirled in the air, tangled with the delicate laughter of serving girls and boys.

I pulled the satin veil tight across my lower face, obscuring all that was beneath.

This was not a place for honorable girls. Too many of Er-Lang's elites frequented its parlors. Words were water, and one rumor could drown a girl's reputation for life. If I wished to secure a good marriage, I had to go unrecognized.

However, Azi spotted me the moment I entered the smoky foyer.

This wasn't my first visit. Or second. Or third. My sister burned through her rations like wildfire, and I counted my blessings that Baihu practically gave me the drug for free.

For now.

Get in and get out. Don't mess this up. I couldn't risk another fight with him. Not when Meiya's life depended on the White Tiger's small mercies.

Azi greeted me with a deep bow, her scant silks slipping dangerously low off bare shoulders. Roman eyeshadow was smeared across her eyelids, and when she looked up through neatly cut bangs, there was a certain allure behind her gaze. But all I saw were the bruises she tried so hard to hide.

She flashed a delicate smile, warm and familiar, and all my contempt and worry faded from existence.

Azi's Gift: trust, comfort. An ability to manipulate emotions. Baihu kept her around for powerful men to open their hearts to and spill forbidden intel to in whispers, to be used as bargaining chips in his games of politics and power.

The Lotus Tower was a hive of secrets and lies, but gold and opian weren't the only things traded here. The right information from the right man was more valuable than an entire city's worth of opian.

"Is he here?" I asked, my words laden with hope.

Baihu spent few days of the moon in Jing-City. Fewer here at the Lotus Tower. Nobody knew where he was the rest of the time, and I didn't care to know. If Baihu wasn't here, then all the better. Azi would give me the drug, and I'd be on my way without seeing him.

There was no such luck today.

Azi gave a subtle nod, and my heart dropped.

"*Qing.*" *Please.* She gestured toward the grand staircase leading up from the smoky foyer where casual customers gathered on red silk cushions, passing long pipes of opian round and round, giggling and swaying like spineless puppets of flesh and hunger. "He's waiting."

I pressed the back of my hand over my nose, less to cover my face than to keep myself from smelling opian's sickly-sweet scent—an odor that never failed to trigger biting memories of Father passed out in the courtyard. Of Grandma crying. Of loan sharks' furious fists pounding down our doors.

This smell made me feel seven years old again. Weeping in the shadows, powerless as strangers carried away pieces of our home. Hunger pinching my belly, the howling winter wind clawing at my skin, numbed and cracked. Father had wasted the money that should've bought us wood for fire on opian until there was nothing left, not even for food.

I shook the memory away. *Focus.*

I followed Azi up the creaking wooden stairs; the melodies of *gu-qin* and imported Roman drums fell away with distance.

We passed latticed doors pasted with paper that offered little privacy from the rowdy laughs outside or the quiet giggles inside. As we ascended the levels, these twisting hallways became quieter and the rooms more private. Sparsely decorated walls were now lined with carvings and tapestries, jade statues and delicate vases— rich pieces of our history that endured wars and changing dynasties only to end up here, decorating a den of smoldering sin. Glass panels and heavy iron doors were installed to protect the secrets of important men, and the rare Roman customers who frequented these halls for its alcohol, for its pretty faces, for the traitors with loose lips whose pockets they lined with gold.

But never for opian.

The Romans knew the deadly consequence of this drug despite the lulling lies they sold to my kind.

Baihu's office was on the top floor. Far from the sickly fumes, tucked away in a secret corner.

Azi knocked three times. "Miss Yang is here."

"Send her in," came the reply.

Azi stepped aside, then grasped my wrist when I reached for the door, her touch firm with warning. "He's a good man. Don't be so hard on him."

No man who touches opian is a good man. Let alone one that sells it, I almost told her, but bit my tongue.

I was a pawn in Baihu's hand, playing his game.

I lowered my chin. Forced a nod.

The door opened. I swallowed my pride and stepped inside the tiger's den.

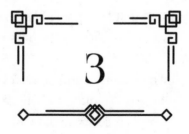

3

Baihu.

The White Tiger.

Clad in a crimson three-piece suit, red as bloodstains—Roman fashion—the man standing across the table from me resembled nothing of the sweet, blushing boy of my childhood memories. The friend, the neighbor, whose sickly mother traded cured meats and pickled cabbage for our rice in the winters. The boy who sat on rooftops with me to watch fireworks at New Year, cried into my arms when his mother grew ill and his princely father grew violent and cruel like my own father.

Of course, at twenty, Baihu was no longer a boy.

Like me, he grew up too fast.

But while I clung to my dignity, Baihu chose to abandon his three years earlier, when he ditched the robes of our heritage and severed his topknot. His hair was now short, styled back in the Roman way. Every day, he resembled more of the false Gods on the other side of the Fence, as if he couldn't wait to shed this skin, erase his past and any resemblance to us from his new, elevated position as Prince Valentin's right hand.

In the eyes of another, he might have been handsome, beautiful: a man handmade and loved by Nüwa herself.

To me, he was nothing but a traitor. One of *them.*

"You're back," he said, voice gentle as a falling feather.

"This is the last time," I told him. "Meiya is going to quit. She's doing really well. Soon, we won't need your charity anymore."

A half smile. "You said that last time." His tone wasn't threatening or malicious. It was innocent, brows drawn as if in genuine concern.

The fluttering in my chest turned into a hard weight. Opian was a toxin, and addicts who tried to quit rarely lived through the pain, the way one's body deteriorated during the withdrawal period.

The odds were not in my sister's favor. And they never will be.

Nevertheless, I believed in her. Meiya was strong and brave. She would survive her addiction.

She had to.

Opian had already taken my father. I refused to let it take my sister, too.

But my faith in her didn't make coming to the Lotus Tower, time after time, any easier.

To say Er-Lang Baihu was a villain would be a stretch. To say he was innocent was a lie. He existed somewhere in between: the gray between black and white.

Once upon a time, before his mother smoked her life away to ease the pain of her ailing body and he sold his loyalty to the Romans for fortune and power, Baihu was my friend. Someone I had once admired. Someone who was noble, kind, loyal.

Not anymore.

"Maybe opian isn't as bad as you think it is," he said, voice cold as unworn silk. "Many praise opian for its ethereal benefits, you know. It also enhances Xianling powers, makes your magic stronger. Word has it the late Emperor himself was a fan."

Frustration was dark crimson. It tasted of ash when I tried to swallow, scorched my throat before clotting my lungs. "Yes, so much of a fan that he sacrificed his only daughter to Rome as collateral when they threatened to halve our opian supply," I retorted, and quickly regretted it.

Beautiful and kind, Princess Helei was the late Emperor's 掌上明珠, *the pearl atop his hand,* the apple of his eye. The person he'd treasured the most in the world. But now she was just insurance, a hostage kept behind their towering fence, to be killed the moment Er-Lang dared to defy Rome's rule.

What I said might be true, but Baihu was the last person I should insult or offend. With the support of Rome at his back, with the ear of the prince, he was basically one of *them.* A God among men. Above the law, above Emperors, above everything. Capable of making my life hell with a snap of his finger.

"That's only a rumor." He smiled. "And even if it were true, so what if Rome asks for collateral to ensure the Empire doesn't stab them in the back, as the young Emperor's many advisors are demanding? You think Rome doesn't hear the whispers in teahouses, know of the letters exchanged in night markets, the Phantom and his scum stirring up trouble, calling for rebellions in rural villages?"

"This is *not* Roman land. They have no right to dictate how we should live." *Those people are right to rebel. To want more, to want better.* But I couldn't bring myself to say the last part. Too cautious of his wrath, too aware of my sister's mortal vessel with its mortal needs for opian.

"And our Emperor does?" Baihu countered, his eyes so sharp, so lethal, I almost flinched under their weight. "Who gave him the right, Ruying? Because he was born from the right womb with the right family name?"

Barbwire words that Baihu had wrapped around himself over and over again, to hide his pain, his sorrow. For if he'd been born from the right mother, if he'd been legitimate, he wouldn't just share blood with the Emperor, but the birthright that would put him in the line of succession. And if Baihu was born royal, had the power to lead, maybe he never would have turned his back on his home.

With his determination and wit, maybe the Empire would be different.

Maybe our world would have been different.

"The days of the old Gods are gone, Ruying. Magic has grown scarcer in recent generations. In their absence, maybe it's time we bow for new ones."

Baihu was right. Even before Rome's descent into our realm, magic had grown scarce over the generations, and harder to wield. The Gift of the Gods slipped from our veins, slowly—among the royal bloodlines as well as the masses. Xianlings became rarer and rarer, and our powers became a husk of what our ancestors' had been. And after the Romans invaded, after they seized the Wucai temples where those born with magic used to train, we grew weaker still. Without the proper tutelage, our magic remained raw and defiant, useless against Rome's bullets.

We can't wait for the Gods to save us. We have to save ourselves, Meiya's words echoed.

My heart ached. But how could we fight against their guns and airships and all the impossible weapons that existed on the side of science?

And what would be the cost of such a war?

The last time Er-Lang tried to stand up against the Romans, tens of thousands perished in a single afternoon. What would happen if we tried to repeat history?

What would we lose?

Behind Baihu, through the open latticed windows, the streets of Jing-City were chaos and beauty. The narrow paths were bustling with people, wild with music, voices, laughter, the sweet melodies of street artists stringing *erhu* and *pipa*. Glowing scarlet red lanterns guided strangers home to their beds, and above it all, the sapphire blue sky of dusk hugged a thousand dazzling stars that shone like crystals.

I imagined Baihu perched there at the window, one foot against the frame and the other resting on the overbite of the tiled roof, patient as a predator. Watching the festivities swirl in the streets below with a possessiveness that he had earned after clawing his way to this position of power.

In the distance, the golden light of the royal palace shone like a second sun at horizon's edge. But the true master of Jing-City, of Er-Lang, didn't live behind towering red palace walls.

The true master was here, and Jing-City knew him as Baihu. The bastard son of a dead prince who was once our Emperor's uncle. He was the traitor who had turned his back on everything and everyone, whose hand now held the pulse of opian—the most precious commodity in all the land.

If circumstances were different, I would have been proud of Baihu and all that he'd overcome. Of all that he had *become*.

His Baba abandoned him. His Mama neglected him. His cousins, the princes, mocked him for being an illegitimate son. People had looked down on Baihu all his life. But he proved the world wrong and now harnessed more power than anyone could possibly dream of, by doing the bidding of those monsters who had made ruins of our lives, our futures.

As our people gasped for breath, Baihu stood taller than ever, clad in the blood money of people like my dead father, his dead mother.

"Do you have it?" I asked, pushing the memories away, changing the subject. It didn't matter who Baihu had been. The only thing that mattered was who he was in this moment, and what I needed from him.

I placed a small silk pouch on the table. Its insides jingled with just enough coins. The bangle I pawned would have fetched triple the amount in plentiful times, but turmoil and instability had made trades hard. The prices of everything once opulent and indulgent were in decline—with the exception of opian. No one cared for jade and gold and glistening silk when their bellies were empty and their homes were stolen. Grandma said that during wartime, a single grain of rice was worth ten times its weight in gold.

I hoped things would never come to that.

But the realist in me knew such a future was inevitable. The only question was how much time did we have left to prepare?

Baihu took the pouch without checking its contents and deposited it in a drawer with the rest of my belongings. Bracelets carved from whole pieces of jade, earrings adorned by pearls, and pendants of solid silver. The only things my mother had left me and my sister. Things he'd kept like souvenirs from when I used to pay him in tokens.

I had switched the form of payment months earlier. It meant the extra effort of going to a pawnshop, but was worth it because it made everything feel less intimate.

Seeing my things stashed away like treasure in his office did something to me. It stirred a feeling that was a mixture of unease, guilt, and . . . something else.

Exchanging tokens was something lovers did.

Baihu and I were not lovers.

We weren't even friends. Not anymore.

Though once upon a time I had wanted nothing more than his affections, than to trade trinkets and breathe warm air in an empty room with him. To have him look at me as he did now, with a gaze so burning it made my pulse quicken.

His lips were thin from holding words back. When we were children, those eyes used to regard me with tender affection. But as we grew older, that tenderness hardened into lust, into a kind of want I'd grown used to seeing in the eyes of cruel men.

But did he want me for my body, or my magic?

Without breaking eye contact, Baihu finally pulled a small parcel from the top drawer of his desk. I reached for it instantly, fingers grazing the parchment before he pulled it away.

He wasn't done with me just yet. "I heard your grandmother is interviewing suitors."

I forced a nod, fake pleasantries. "She wants me to marry soon, before whispers of war become reality."

My father might have lost all that our ancestors had left us, but the Yang name still held weight in certain areas of the Empire. I was a descendant of a legendary general, a family that used to wield military might. The soldiers who had once served under my grandfather remembered his name and saw it as an honor to marry a descendant of the great Yang Clan.

That, and . . .

Baihu arched a brow, the heat of those moon-carved eyes suffocating. "And what do *you* want, Yang Ruying?"

My hands itched to snatch the parcel out from under his claws.

"Do I want to shackle myself to the will of a man and forever bow to his orders?" I nearly laughed. "My mother died giving life to me and my sister because that's what women are expected to do. Grandma is the smartest strategist of her generation, the reason behind my grandfather's military success, and nobody knows her name. Grandpa got all the recognition she isn't allowed to have. The praise and applause and admiration from the wide-eyed girls whom he bedded behind her back, despite all that she did for him. No, I don't want to marry. But my family needs protection. Rome grows greedier by the day, and like you say, the Emperor's advisors are pushing for him to retaliate, to fight. And the Phantom gains more rebel supporters with every one of Rome's transgressions. Too many people have lost too much to Rome, to opian, to our Emperors' cowardliness. Every day, new players materialize in this game of power. Grandma fears war is closer than we realize. I don't blame her."

Baihu took a seat and made himself comfortable, toying with the twine of the parcel. He poured two cups of tea and gestured at the leather chair across the table.

I didn't sit, didn't accept his offered tea, though my lungs delighted at the luring scent of *da hong pao*—a familiar luxury from when my family could afford it. Instead, I stood and looked down at him and pretended I was the man who held the power of an Empire and he was the girl in need of help and mercy.

Death's magic was warm and comforting as it tingled up my arm. Temptation sang like melodies, reminding me that I could force him to his knees if I wished to.

I pushed Death's taunts to the back of my head, remembering Grandma's words.

Magic comes at a heavy price, Ruying. Use it wisely.

"I heard Taohua is back from her military duties," said Baihu, his tone measured and careful, as if testing me. "I remember the two of you used to be inseparable as children."

"Are you scared Er-Lang's mighty commander is here to slay Rome's pet tiger?" I replied, my words sharper than they had the right to be, but I couldn't help myself.

"I think Taohua has her hands full with all the rebellions sparking up across the Empire. Peasants thirsty for blood and justice, ready to overthrow the Er-Lang Dynasty in their rage against Rome." He smiled. "Don't you miss the old times, when we were kids, running around that narrow backstreet between our homes, playing games, singing songs? Don't you miss those carefree days, however brief they were?"

"We also used to hate the world, hate the Romans for what they made of our home," I whispered. "Do you remember that, Baihu?"

"I do. But I also remember how we used to starve, how shitty it was to live not knowing where my next meal might come from as my mother cried and my father got high with my uncle behind their gilded palace walls, so far from our mortal problems. Sometimes I look back on those simpler days, in that street of fallen houses as they slowly became infested with poverty. As money poured from our parents' pockets and into Rome's. The memories of long-ago days of full bellies and feasts on New Year and silk robes adorned with fanciful embroideries, back when my father remembered to entertain his fatherly duties . . . I was twelve, when my father died, but yours died before that, right?"

I was ten years old when my father drew his last breath, because we'd finally run out of money for the opian that kept his *qi* burning bright, and Grandma made a decision that no parent should have to make. Choosing between her son and her granddaughters. In the end, she chose us, and hid every penny and scrap of jewelry she could find from his hungry hands so we might have something to live on. So that her granddaughters might have a chance at a decent life. In those final days, my father would have sold all three of us to the whorehouse if he'd had the strength to drag us across the city.

But at least my father had been kind once.

At least he had been present, however long ago that might have been.

Baihu's story was different. His father had abandoned him and his mother long before he died. Baihu's father might have been of royal blood, but he was selfish and cruel. Once upon a time, there might have been bedtime stories and birthday kisses, but by the time Baihu was old enough to keep memories, he treated Baihu like dirt and treated Baihu's mother even worse. In the end, he decided those coins spent on his bastard son were better off spent on opian and young girls from the brothels.

I knew every single one of Baihu's scars. Just as he knew mine.

"Get to the point," I murmured into the silence, forcing bitter memories from my mind.

"Remember when we were children," Baihu continued, his eyes on me like a tiger stalking prey, "how I used to joke that I'd marry you one day?"

He did used to say such things.

Throwaway words from times long lost, meaningless as the made-up games of our childhood.

I never told him how I used to daydream about us. A happy marriage like the ones from Grandma's bedtime stories. Baihu tall and beautiful as he was now. The kind of husband who would be good to me, love me, protect me. The kind of love that could withstand the wildest of storms.

Now, I laughed at these naïve fantasies. The kind of love that would never exist in real life.

No love was strong enough to withstand the cruelty of the Romans, the chaos and impoverishment that had swallowed our Empire in these past years.

What use was love when I didn't know if we'd have enough food and fire to last the winter? If Baihu's mercy would continue, handout after handout, as my sister struggled to wean herself off opian?

Though a version of me had once wished upon stars for a simple life, a happy family, she had long been washed away by pain and grief. To love was a privilege not afforded to those of us born in these trying times when survival was never guaranteed.

We were products of our surroundings, of our upbringings.

Childhood promises and childhood dreams were like dandelion seeds, scattered by the slightest of breezes.

Baihu would never marry me. But I was shocked he still remembered these foolish things from so many winters past, when his mind should be occupied by other things. Such as how to elevate his position among the Roman ranks, how to exact revenge on the legitimate, noble sons—everyone who had dared to wrong him.

And most important: how to sleep at night, knowing the horrors he was inflicting on his own blood. His ancestors would weep from their graves if they knew the man he had become.

I looked around the room, at the Roman commodities surrounding us. The oil paintings hanging from the walls, statues of jade, delicate vases made by the finest craftsmen. *Dirty money.* Wrapped around Baihu's body, hanging from his neck, adorning his fingers, lacing the very air we breathed. Silver from the pockets of addicts, tears from broken families.

"Things have changed, Baihu," I whispered.

The world has changed. We have changed.

"You're right. Things have indeed changed." The smile fell from his face, and his eyes hardened. I felt the air grow thin around us. "I need your help, Ru."

My stomach twisted. I had anticipated this moment for months.

Baihu was a businessman. He couldn't possibly help me out of the goodness of his heart. He had to have a motive.

"I won't do it."

"You don't know what I'm about to ask."

"What else is a girl like me good for in times like these?" I whispered, the unspoken words hanging between us, magic burning my fingertips. Death's powers grew heavier and heavier with each breath.

A power like mine, in an era as lawless as this, brought more harm than good.

"People have been selling our Empire to Rome piece by piece, street by street, indiscretion by indiscretion, for twenty years now. What's so bad about breaking a few laws of magic? Plus, using your magic isn't against the law."

"But using magic to commit crime is. The last time I checked, murder is a crime, right? Or have the Romans changed that in the last couple of minutes?"

"You have me. I'll protect you. I'll *always* protect you, Ruying."

I don't need your protection. The words curled at the tip of my tongue—an alluring lie. One I wished were true. "If you are so powerful, why don't you kill whoever you want dead yourself?"

"Because . . ." Baihu trailed off. He took a deep breath, tentative with his words.

He didn't trust me.

My ribs gripped my insides tight until I couldn't breathe, my anxiety a heavy tempo at my throat.

I had an idea of who the target might be.

The only thing a man like Baihu coveted but couldn't have. Something that would not only benefit him, but the Romans whom he knelt for.

The Er-Lang throne.

My magic was silent, traceless. I could kill the young Emperor without implicating Baihu or his Roman masters. And with the Emperor gone, there would be a vacuum of power. One that Baihu was perfectly positioned to fill.

A bastard son he might be, but nothing could erase the Er-Lang blood in his veins. And with the might of Rome at his back, there would be little he wished but couldn't accomplish.

Seizing the throne would be easy. Taking candy from a child.

Baihu would finally possess what he'd always wanted: power.

And so would Rome.

Emperor Yongle was months shy of twenty-two, still sheltered and soft-spined for now. But he wouldn't always obey Rome's orders, heed their every warning. Not while he was surrounded by advisors who had counseled three generations of Er-Lang Emperors—men who had lived long enough to remember the glory before the humiliation.

Despite the rumors, I liked to think the young Emperor was smarter than he let on, more capable than anyone gave him credit for.

This mewling cub might one day grow into a beast.

Baihu, on the other hand, would always be their perfect puppet.

All Rome had to do was kill the current Emperor, and it would be the end of Er-Lang as we knew it.

"There's something I must do, Ruying. If you lend me your Gift, I can make it worth your while. Name a price, and I—"

"My magic is not a *Gift*," I snapped.

My eyes fell on the parcel of opian, reminding me that Baihu was no longer the sweet boy whose laughter used to trail mine, whose arms would hold me when I cried.

He was a predator.

A tiger with talons and fangs, one who would turn on me sooner or later.

He owed me nothing and I owed him everything. He was the reason my sister was still alive. Without him—without opian—the withdrawals would kill Meiya as it had our father.

I lowered my head.

"Death's magic is a curse, one that shaves time off my life with each use. You know of its consequences."

"I do."

"Then don't ask this of me."

He hesitated. For a moment, understanding settled over his face like the soft gold of a summer's sunset and I foolishly thought the conversation was over.

The deceiving shine quickly passed, replaced by a dark determination. Gray as a piercing blade, vanquishing the gold with a violent swipe.

"When war comes, chaos will reign, and these laws that protect the Xianlings will cease to exist. You know the stories, Ruying. Of the Qin Emperor, how he tried to conquer the continent with Xianling magic. The way babies were ripped from their mothers to be trained as killers. How Xianlings used to be trafficked for their Gifts. An era of atrocity that only ended when the Gods reincarnated from heaven to defeat the tyrant. But those Gods are gone now, Ruying. No one is coming to save us."

We have to save ourselves: my sister's words. Sometimes Baihu sounded just like Meiya.

I hated that he was right.

I was the girl blessed by Death. This power marked a target on my back. Something people would want to possess, use, exploit. The only thing protecting me from those fireside horror stories of life under Qin's rule was the Empire's law against the trafficking of Xianlings. Another thing that would soon perish if or when war fell like a hammer against this thinning illusion of peace.

I had to make myself small, keep Death's Gift quiet. For if Rome or the Empire knew what I was truly capable of, they would force me to fight. To be the killer I had spent my whole life running from. A monster who hungered only for destruction, trading shards of my life for fleeting magic in the name of a losing war. Fighting for people who would never see me as anything other than a power to be feared, a weapon to be used.

"If you do this for me," Baihu continued, "I can offer you protection. So much money that you don't need marriage to provide for your family."

If I was smart I'd take Baihu up on his offer, do what I must in order to survive.

But the Emperor was chosen by heaven; a descendant of the very Gods who had reincarnated to save the Xianlings thousands of years ago. To kill someone of godly blood was blasphemy, a sin of the highest kind.

After the Old Gods died mortal deaths in their reincarnated bodies, their souls returned to the heavenly realm and abandoned us to fend for ourselves. Their descendants—who continued to rule over the continent despite civil wars and uprisings and shifting borders—became the last thread connecting us to them.

Some believed this connection to be the single thing keeping the gate of energy open between our world and theirs. And if these bloodlines ever died out, this gate would close and magic would perish from our bodies and Pangu would be left defenseless against tyrants and invaders.

If I killed the Emperor, the heavens would curse my entire bloodline to a lifetime of misfortune and sorrow.

Though there were countless legends surrounding the origin of our Gifts, and this could be folktale like any other, no one in their right mind would risk testing its truth.

No one with something to lose, at least.

Despite all that I had lost, I did have one thing left to lose: my family.

I would never test this legend with their lives.

I parted my lips, tried to speak, but words rattled inside my head. Accepting Baihu's offer might be the smart thing to do, yet it was far from the right thing.

Baihu's expression turned soft at my silence. Hesitation as he took in the conflict written all over my face. "You always looked out for me when we were children. Do you remember? Let me do the same for you now, Ruying."

"If you are truly looking out for me, you wouldn't ask this of me." I whispered, eyes on the parcel in his hand.

It didn't matter what I wanted. With opian in his hand and his mercies around my throat, if Baihu demanded my Gift as payment for the drug, I couldn't say no.

I couldn't watch my sister die.

His lips thinned. Shame was quiet and tender, and it sounded like regret when he said, "I know." He rose to his feet, slowly. "Take some time. Consider my offer. Give me an answer the next time you're here . . . And keep in mind that I'd hate to see something bad happen to you, or your family."

My heart stopped. "Is this a threat?"

"A storm is coming," Baihu whispered, as if I didn't already know. "When the Gods died, they left the continent in the hands of their children. And for a brief century, our continent knew peace, knew true prosperity. But here is something they didn't teach us in school. As the eras went by, as some Empires grew richer while others grew poorer, as floods, droughts, and bad harvests plagued pockets of land, our mighty Emperors began eyeing one another. For more fertile lands, for better water sources, for mountains filled with gold and iron and precious metals. Battles and wars were fought and won and lost in the name of heritage and glory and honoring our ancestors when the truth was simpler, more human. They fought not for the Gods, who had long returned to the heavenly realm. They fought for greed, insatiable and endless. They fought for pride. They fought for power. Even before the Romans came, peace was a tenuous thing. A folktale. Er-Lang had always been one of the wealthier Empires, one of the stronger Empires. This is why the other Empires refused to help when Rome orchestrated our slow demise. We had stolen so much from them; it was only fair that a more powerful nation stole from us."

I knew what Baihu was trying to tell me. If the Romans could humiliate Er-Lang like this, Gods knew what they might do to one of the weaker Empires like Jiang with their dwindling magic and whispers of Xianlings being trafficked just like in the times of Qin. Rumors swirled of Xianlings disappearing at our borders. Crimes that would not have gone unpunished twenty-something years ago.

But now we were all too busy looking out for ourselves. How could we care for the pain of strangers as our families starved and loved ones died one by one from overdoses or withdrawals or the general cruelty of the Romans?

"Our neighbors have abandoned us," Baihu continued. "Rome continues to amass power. They've already made alliances with Jiang Empire. Our closest ally before all of this was Lei-Zhen to the north, through Princess Helei's betrothal to their Crown Prince—an alliance that has been fraught ever since Rome took her hostage. Ne-Zha is too far to the west to care for the politics of the east. And Sihai doesn't interfere with the politics of the land. Er-Lang is without allies. We've called for help time and time again from our neighbors, but we are alone. Between Rome's greed, and the Emperor's advisors nudging him toward war, the end is closer than you think. It's time to pick a side, Ruying."

"To live as a traitor like you, or die a hero?" I whispered.

Fight for my country, or betray it.

Er-Lang had stood proud and powerful for thousands of years, but with magic dying in our veins, and those of us with magic unable to train, we were prey ready for slaughter.

Xianlings were no longer safe. Sooner or later, I would have a target on my back. And so would Meiya.

"Pick a side, Ruying." Baihu pushed the parcel across the table.

I grabbed it with both hands before he could change his mind. Our fingers grazed, barely.

Something tender flashed in his eyes. Was it fear? Or was it something else?

"I will think about it," I said. "I'll give you the answer next time I see you."

"Okay." He smiled.

I did, too, and made myself a promise: *There won't be a next time.*

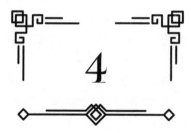

4

I STARED AT MY HANDS. Remembered how it had felt, the first time I killed someone. An accident on the hottest day of the summer. A moment that continued to haunt me, years later. I could still feel shimmers of his *qi* lingering within me. Felt Death's colors, burning.

Baihu's mercy was frayed, hanging by its last threads. What would he do if I turned down his proposition?

If I provoked his wrath, there was no telling what he might do. To me. To my family.

He had the power.

Was the blushing boy I remembered from when life was simple and free still there somewhere? Or had Baihu burned his former self to ashes when he pledged his allegiances to Rome?

The package in my hand was hefty. Enough to last Meiya through the next moon cycle. But was that enough time to wean her off the drug? Withdrawals were dangerous, deadly. An abrupt stop would put her life at risk.

We had to take this slow, give her body the time it needed.

I only hoped I could make this final supply last.

Outside, the sky had darkened from dusk to night. Baihu's office on Lotus Tower's top floor shone like a beacon, unnaturally bright, with its lights powered by humming electricity instead of candle flames.

I savored the sight—because next time I might not leave so easily.

If Baihu wanted to, he could use Meiya's life as leverage. Make sure no one in this city sold any opian to me. Force my hand in the cruelest possible way.

If he did that, I would kneel, do whatever he commanded of me. He knew I would.

I owed Meiya too much to repay in one lifetime. Forget about murder. If Baihu asked my life for hers, I would surrender without hesitation.

If becoming a murderer meant keeping my sister safe, I would do it. But that didn't mean I wouldn't try and find another path first.

"Traitor," I muttered under my breath in a burst of rage. A small show of defiance—one he would never hear.

I hurried my steps. Grandma didn't like it when I got home after dark. I kept what remained of my coins deep in my sleeves, far from the reach of pickpockets, as I brushed shoulders with pedestrians and hollering traders. The night market was crowded with farmers hawking goods illuminated by bright lanterns. The atmosphere was chaotic but comforting. A dizzying array of distractions that helped me forget my worries and smile at the parents wandering with their children, lovers holding hands, friends linking arms.

Under the portal's ambient light and the Fence's shadow, the danger of war staled the air. Yet, happiness found root.

Sparse joys. All that we had left.

In the dark corners, plastered across the crumbling walls and peeling beams, red and black, were posters I had seen a thousand times before. Scattered in the streets, hurriedly pressed onto walls.

But today, I paid closer attention.

Because a few days earlier, I had found a stash of these posters in Meiya's room.

Join the rebellion. The humiliation ends now.

Join the Phantom. Stand on the right side of history.

Across the continent, rebels disguised as martyrs and vigilantes risked their lives by ransacking opian shipments. Small retaliations. Useless in the bigger picture. These rebels, they died, they bled, they drained their magic for brief flames of fame and a sense of justice.

Had the Phantom's promises gotten to my sister? What was Meiya doing with those posters? Was this why she entangled herself with opian in the first place? Had some scoundrel sold her on the narrative that opian could strengthen her Gift, or turn her magic into something it was never intended to be? A killer? Like me . . .

The claims weren't always false. Opian enhanced magic the way oil coaxed flames. But the brighter we burned, the sooner we perished. The effects Rome's drugs had on my people were temporary, and always short lived. Was this the truth she hid from me, the reason she had become an addict of the very drug that had killed our father? So that she could fight for a futile cause?

Heroes die. Cowards live.

Baihu's proposition rang in my ears, hauntingly quiet. *I can make it worth your while.*

Was I a coward, or a hero?

I shook the thought away and kept walking. At the street corner, an elderly lady with graying hair perched on a cart of fruits: hawthorn berries, plums, persimmons, and lychees piled in neat order. Ripe and swollen, brilliant with colors that promised sweet bites.

My mouth watered for the lychees, but Meiya's jutting bones and hollowed cheeks flashed before my eyes, her body so frail and tiny. No matter how tightly she wrapped her robes, the soft cotton failed to find flesh to cling to. One of the more deadly symptoms of withdrawal. It pilfered her appetite for anything other than opian, causing her body to wither away like dust vanishing in the wind.

I reached for the coins in my pocket. Food prices kept climbing, day by day. If the scale of peace finally tipped for war, the prices would go up even higher. What would three women do then, when we could barely survive now?

You should save these coins for a rainy day, my better judgment urged. But my sister deserved a treat. A splash of sweet in these never-ending bitter days.

Tomorrow she would have gone ten days without opian—the longest since I had found out about her addiction. She deserved something to celebrate this small milestone. The hawthorn berries were expensive but worth Meiya's smile. Maybe in that moment she wouldn't hate me so much and we'd be the people we were once more.

Sisters.

Best friends.

Money and fruit exchanged hands just as a loud gong tore through the air.

"Gather around, gather around! Ladies and gentlemen, I am about to change your life." A young man in black linen robes hollered from the wide streets of a crossroads up ahead. Around him, a wide-eyed audience gathered in a circle. "Does anyone here know an opian addict?" he called.

I sighed, knowing where this was going—another false antidote. One thing this city had never lacked were lies that preyed on the vulnerable.

First, they sold us opian with deceptions of longevity and miracles of granting normal people Xianling magic, or making Xianlings stronger, enhancing our magic to godly heights. Now, grifters sold lies to the addicts who could no longer afford this deadly drug and its sickly highs.

The smart ones walked away. The desperate ones stumbled forward to ask the price. Hope was precious, and some would pay anything just to hold its beating wings for a few seconds.

I hurried away without paying the man heed and was at the edge of the market when a haunting melody made me pause for the second time tonight.

There, under the arches that marked the end of the market, knelt a girl in gray, muddied clothes, an *er-hu* in her lap. Beside her, a slender, limp hand peeked out from a long bamboo sheet, skin pale and translucent as rice paper, blotted by dark veins.

I didn't need a closer look to know what was under that sheet, and why this girl was here.

Another life, stolen by Rome's drug. There one day, gone the next.

Meiya's face flashed behind my eyes, and I shuddered. Beside the girl was a wooden board with the words 卖身葬母. She was selling herself to pay for her mother's funeral.

My throat closed, and grief welled fast inside me.

Keep walking, I told myself. *She's not your mother. This doesn't concern you.* Girls like her littered these streets day and night. I couldn't help everyone I met.

I could scarcely help myself.

In Jing-City, beggars were considered trouble, to be avoided at all costs. Better to take those extra steps than to risk being mistaken for a saint. But a young man not much older than I was stood proud before the girl, listening to her play with his head high, eyes closed in appreciation of the lilting melody she wove from the weeping strings.

Skin pale and hair dark, with soft curls cropped short against his face. Even from a distance I could tell he was handsome—though not in the way Pangu was used to. Strong nose, pillowed lips, arched brows, and rounded eyes. His features were sharp as the chiseled statue Rome gifted the late Emperor when they first arrived, displayed in the square near the palace—*Caesar Augustus,* one of Rome's legendary rulers from thousands of years ago. Their first Emperor.

Something about this young man's face reminded me of that statue.

I didn't realize I was staring until his eyes met mine, pale green as prized jade.

Tailored fineries draped his body. A midnight-blue suit with glistening cuff links; a gold watch wrapped around his left wrist; several rings adorning his fingers. Everything about him—from the way he dressed to the way he stood—announced power and wealth.

The boy was Roman. If his face wasn't indication enough, the dirty money settled it.

When the song was over, he leaned down and gave the girl a single gold piece—enough to bury her mother ten times over.

Envy surged, quick and burning. Envy for the girl's newfound fortune, and the dizzying privilege resting in the palm of his hand. That silk pouch of his held more gold than I would see in a lifetime— *our* gold, stolen from the limp hands of my kin.

Overwhelmed with glee, the girl *ketou*'d to thank him. She knelt and bowed until her forehead hit the gravel so hard that I heard the echo of skull. The louder you knocked your head against the ground, the more respect you paid the person you bowed for, and she bowed for this Roman like a mortal would a God.

Wide-eyed and confused by our custom, the young man quickly set down the pouch to help her up. "You are going to hurt yourself."

One of our traditions clashing with theirs, and a lifetime's worth of gold sat forgotten at his side, inconsequential.

I stared at it.

Baihu's hard, merciless eyes.

Meiya's soft, withering breath.

Grandma's hunched back, the legs that seemed to shake when she stood for too long.

A spoiled Roman boy who probably had everything in life handed to him wouldn't miss the pouch at all. But in my hands, it might be the difference between life and Death.

Step-by-step, I inched closer, lured by desperation. With this kind of money, I wouldn't have to rely on Baihu's mercies, wouldn't have to marry a man I didn't love just to provide for my family.

All my life, Grandma had taught me to be cautious.

This was not me being cautious.

What happened next, happened fast.

Cold silk at my fingertips. A solid chest colliding against my shoulder. A hand tried to grab me, but I must have been faster because in the next moment I was running, clutching the heavy bag of gold against my chest, elbowing past the crowd and into the shadows of twisting alleyways.

The Roman yelled for someone to stop me, but nobody did. Half of the crowd would have done the same if they were in my shoes, and the other half just didn't want to get involved in someone else's mess.

Gasping for breath, I bolted through the backstreets like my life depended on this escape—because it did. In Jing-City, crimes against Romans carried automatic death sentences.

No exceptions.

No hesitation.

I'd just committed the ultimate crime, and if I—

Something pounced on me. A rough hand grabbed me by the throat and propelled me toward the ground. Gravel scraped the palms of my hands raw with blood, burning red under the torn sleeves of my favorite robe. I tasted copper in my mouth, heard my elbow crack against stone, my attacker's body heavy on top of mine as I gasped for breaths that wouldn't come. I barely had time to turn and see him winding his fist back, ready to strike.

"I'll teach you filthy savages a lesson for stealing from—"

I didn't want to kill, but I couldn't say the same about this Roman and his rabid hound of a guard.

I grabbed the guard's hand, the one gripping my throat like a falcon's claw. My Gift didn't require skin-to-skin contact, but Grandma said it would help me control it.

"I'm sorry," I choked.

I could count on one hand the number of times I'd actually used Death's magic, though the temptation was constant. A whisper in the back of my mind that I always pushed away, the tingle in my hands I tried so hard to ignore. Every second of every day. After the Accident, after the first time I realized how easy it was to untether

souls from their mortal bodies, I promised myself I'd only use my
Gift if it was life or death.

This was life or death.

And I didn't want to die.

So for the first time in years, I stopped fighting the luring im-
pulses that haunted my every waking thought.

Like a stone sinking under pressure, I fell into Death's embrace.

A warmth familiar and soothing as coming home.

Colors bled away as I slipped between worlds, until everything
faded to shades of black and white like that of a water painting,
starkly in focus. Gold was the only other color that existed, in the
shimmers of the *qi* that resided in all things and bound mortal souls
to mortal bodies. Delicate yet taut, I rolled my fingers over the puls-
ing currents of glistening gold dust and *pulled*.

Everything unraveled. Energy poured into my hands, rushed
through me like ocean tides that nearly knocked the air from my
lungs. Then it began to spread, tingling through my veins like the
heady wine Father used to drink to calm his sorrows right before
they turned to rage. Like the opian I had pressed to my nose once
when I was still a child. To try. To sate my unquenchable curiosities
for the substance on the tip of everybody's tongue.

This feeling was like that, but better.

So much better.

A symphony roaring in my skull, trembling in my bones. This
feeling was beyond mortal pleasure, beyond anything the realm of
the living could ever offer me.

The high took hold of me for a mere moment before his bellow-
ing cries pierced the alleyway, echoing off ancient stones.

Something burned in my chest, growing hotter and hotter as
Death's magic tore *qi* from his body and pulled it into mine.

Fast, too fast.

I tried to make it stop, to control it, but magic was a weapon I
had never learned how to wield.

Sweat beaded my skin. Color drained from his face, and his eyes went dull. His wail grew hoarse as I devoured his energy with one hand and fed it to Death with the other. My body was a mere vessel, converting energy from the world of the living to the world of the dead.

"Stop!" he cried. "Please!"

Whoever said Death was painless hadn't met me.

I felt his *qi* depleting, his soul untethering.

This is enough! I wanted to yell, to make everything stop. I tried to pull back, but Death had other ideas. Magic clung to the man like a beast who would not give up its feast, starved for more *qi*, more energy, more everything. Death continued to inhale the dusts of gold, faster and faster, even as I fought to let go.

The Gods gave you a Gift for a reason. You were born to kill, child.

"Help!" the man cried. "Please!"

Are you a hero, or a monster?

"Please stop!"

At the last moment, just as his *qi* grew muted and hazy like a wilting flower, I pushed him away, his body limp and lighter than it had been.

I struggled up on shaking legs.

The man was going to live, slithers of energy clung to him still.

Mercy.

I had shown him mercy. More than he would ever give me.

In Er-Lang, magic wasn't taboo, but using magic to commit taboo—such as thievery or attacking a Roman—would earn me a trip to the executioner's block.

I wasn't ready to die yet—not when I had so much to do, so much to live for.

But before I took off running, I caught a splash of green at the other end of the darkened alley.

"What are you?" The gasp was low, tinged with both fear and wonder. The Roman whose money I'd stolen stood on the other side of the alley, watching. He gazed upon me with astonishment, as if I were some sort of marvel he couldn't believe existed. A gun in his hand, finger on the trigger.

I expected him to shoot me.

He didn't.

Instead, he smiled. A wide, beautiful smile that touched his enraptured eyes, and held me there for a second longer than I knew was safe.

He raised his free hand, as if waving me forward to talk.

I wasn't a street rat dumb enough to fall for his tricks.

When the rest of his guards rushed into the narrowed path, he immediately held up his hands and cried, "No guns!"

He wanted me alive.

I stumbled back, tried to gather my magic, but there was an ache in my muscles, a shortness of breath in my lungs. I wasn't used to mobilizing my powers in such quick successions, and my body had already been pushed to the brink of exhaustion after that run.

I tried to reach, but his *qi* was slippery in my hands. Resistant, stubborn. A man who had too much to live for to be swayed by my ill-practiced magic.

Shit.

I was about to turn and run and hope for the best when a slender shadow bolted into the alley and knocked the closest guard out with a single punch.

She was barely taller than I was, with a slender frame too fragile to take down a man twice her size so easily.

Then I saw her delicate face and enchanting smile.

"Taohua?"

"I can't leave you alone for two seconds, can I?" she hissed and took my hand. "Run!"

I didn't need to be told twice.

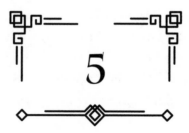

5

WE DASHED PAST BUZZING STREETS and murmuring alleys to a quieter part of the city. East of the palace, where the courtyarded manors were sizable enough to hold larger families. Before the Romans
came, this used to be one of the most affluent parts of the city,
bustling with shops that specialized in calligraphy and antiques,
with long lists of wealthy clients.

Now, these courtyards were packed full with squatters and generations of families under the same roof. Paint crumbled off the
walls as the street of my childhood fell to ruins in slow motion.
Most of the families who had lived here when I was a child were
dead now, either killed by opian or by the debt collectors who broke
down their doors and looted their homes.

Panting, Taohua and I dodged into a darkened corner several
streets from my home and waited for the sound of footsteps chasing
after us. When we heard nothing but the rumble of the city and our
pounding hearts, I laughed.

Death's hunger clung to me still—painfully so. A sense of want
that only draining currents of essence from living souls could sate. I
drew deep breaths. Death and all his temptations were constant,
but after so many years I had learned to ignore them.

Deep breaths.

Soon, it would all fade into the background.

I had done enough. I had gotten away. There was no reason to take more.

得饶人处且饶人. *Show mercy when you can.*

Something Grandma had taught me. I was the one in the wrong. I had stolen from the green-eyed Roman. And judging from the weight of the pouch in my sleeve, it was a hefty sum.

Enough that I wouldn't have to worry about food and fire when winter came.

Laughter rippled at the edge of my lips. I had done it. I had robbed a Roman and lived to tell the tale.

Taohua, on the other hand, didn't share my humor. "What did you do?" she snapped, her eyes cold and hard and full of accusation.

I held up the pouch. "Something Grandma will skin me alive for when she finds out."

Her eyes went wide. "Ruying, if you need money, you can come and ask me. These coins aren't worth your life. The Romans could have *killed* you. Gods know what would have happened if I wasn't by chance walking past and recognized you."

The wise words of a concerned friend who had never experienced the pain of poverty, a drunk father with hate in his heart, harrowing winter nights without firewood, and the fear of not knowing where your next meal might be coming from.

The daughter of a renowned general, Taohua had never known some of my and Meiya's basic worries. Though Grandma did her best to keep us afloat, to keep Meiya and I sheltered, it was hard not to notice the bleak meagerness that Father had left us.

I forced a smile, then checked the streets one last time before stepping out of the shadows.

Taohua followed me. "Ruying, answer me. Why did you do that? You—"

"I didn't think you'd be back before the New Year," I interrupted, a blunt change of subject.

Taohua's face fell.

She got the message.

Two years earlier, Taohua had joined the army as the second female commander in Er-Lang's history, after her older sister, Tangsi. Now, she spent most of the year away, following her father and sister on campaigns across the Empire. She'd endured all sorts of grueling training in order to prove herself as a woman worthy of power in the military ranks. She knew which battles to pick, and when to relent because her opponent was too stubborn to be persuaded.

Even with her Gift of inhuman strength, it was a hard thing to convince men that a woman could be their superior, unless she was ten, twenty times better than everyone around her. Unless she was without flaws. As a warrior, a leader, a conversationalist. And so, Taohua drove herself ceaselessly toward perfection. This meant no time off, no rest. Her responsibilities were her life.

Everything else came second.

Including her family. Including her best friend.

I hadn't seen Taohua since the New Year, more than six moons earlier.

"It's only for a few days. My father sent me so that Mother would have at least one of her daughters home for her birthday. I'm heading south again in a few days."

I smiled. "Is it true your father wants to promote you to general, give you a battalion to train and lead?"

Taohua and her sister were tasked with quieting the rebellions rumbling in the south, where unrest grew too loud to ignore as Xianlings vanished from their beds and disappeared from their morning walks. Stolen or killed or something else entirely, I didn't know.

I didn't want to know.

But their cries for answers were impossible to ignore. Mothers and fathers, orphans and distraught families desperate for their loved ones to be found. Some claimed it was Jiang's traffickers, while others claimed it was the Romans.

This was the exact sort of turmoil the Phantom wanted in order to gather more recruits willing to risk their lives for freedom.

"I also heard that you've fought the Phantom's rebels and won? Not once, but twice? That's an incredible feat," I added in the face of her silence.

For three years, General Ma, Taohua's father, had hunted the Phantom on the orders of both Rome and our Emperor, but he had nothing to show for it—a rare mark of incompetence from a celebrated leader—which only added to the Phantom's strength and power.

Rumors in teahouses suggested Rome's patience was wearing thin. There had been too many skirmishes between the Phantom's rebels and Roman soldiers.

In the beginning, Rome had seen the Phantom as someone of small significance. A fly, buzzing in their peripheral awareness. But in recent years, he had grown into a genuine threat.

Apparently the Phantom had already attacked Rome's armory twice this year. And twice they had failed. The rebels wanted guns; they wanted the very science that made Er-Lang kneel in fear. But such heists were not so easy. The Romans understood the might of their own weapons and guarded their armory well. Painfully so.

Again, Taohua didn't reply.

She forced a smile, uncomfortable, neither confirming nor denying anything. She was hiding something. Like me, Taohua was stubborn with her secrets.

"The people call you a hero," I continued.

Finally, her lips twitched.

"You went from a general's docile daughter to a hero whose name will be carved into history—an honor once reserved only for men. One day, people will sing songs of your conquests and recite poems in your name the way they do for Peng Yuefei and Wei Xinling."

"Maybe this is how far our Empire has fallen," Taohua whispered, with a bitter laugh. "Even girls like me are allowed to lead, allowed to be remembered. I just wish my success wasn't built on the pain of so many. If magic weren't slipping away, leaving the army in desperate need of Xianling soldiers, the court never would have granted me and my sister the chance to fight. If the rebels weren't furious over the state of our Empire, and our Emperors didn't kneel so easily . . ."

"It doesn't matter how you came to these titles. The important thing is that you will be remembered. As a hero," I said, my heart prickling with an all too familiar feeling.

I was proud of Taohua. Her honor and glory were all earned.

I had once wished for the same thing.

In another life, maybe I would have joined her as a soldier, become a general like my grandfather and his grandfather before him. Learned to hone Death's magic and put it to more noble uses.

But not in this life.

Not when I had a grandmother and sister to protect.

In this life, I sought no glory.

Only survival.

For myself, and those I loved.

Still, something unpleasant brewed in the pit of my stomach.

Envy.

Hate.

Feelings I was ashamed to feel.

We'd both dreamt of becoming heroes as children.

Taohua was brave enough to chase after this dream, while I wallowed in fear of too many things.

When I looked at Taohua, I saw the woman I'd always hoped to be and hated that she could pursue what I could not.

"It's incredible how much has changed since you joined the military," I whispered.

"It certainly is." She smiled. "I guess I'm too strong for bullies to pick on now. Do you remember how kids used to chase me down the street, throw rocks at me, because they blamed my father for Rome's invasion and their parents' addictions? They used to say if he were a better general, the Wucai temples wouldn't have been burned, and we wouldn't have had to carve out half of our city for the Romans to demolish and inhabit."

"They'd chase you up to my doorstep, see me, then run the other way."

"No one dared to make fun of me when you were around."

No one was brave enough to cross the girl blessed by Death.

This was how Taohua and I became friends. I protected her from bullies, and she shielded me from the loneliness after rumors spread that I was a monster, after I killed . . .

I shook the thought away.

Taohua didn't need me for long, of course. A couple of years after we came into each other's lives, Taohua found her own Gift of strength. Though she stayed delicate like an arching willow, her magic made her strong. She outgrew her need for my protection like an old robe.

But she never outgrew me. Never discarded me to find better friends, safer friends, like I expected her to.

Like she should have.

"Now," she said, "are you going to tell me why you stole that Roman's coins?"

I fell quiet.

With gentle fingers, Taohua examined the wound beneath my tattered robe, red with blood from when the guard attacked me.

"Ruying." Her tone was firm with authority, sounding too much like the mother I'd never known. A slow warmth seeped through me. Between looking out for Meiya and trying to help Grandma, I could no longer recall what it felt like to have someone looking out for *me*. "Tell me the truth, please."

I didn't say anything. Meiya's addiction wasn't my secret to tell.

"Fine, be like that." Taohua sighed. "What a coincidence, though. I was actually on my way to see you before I saved your life from a bunch of Romans with guns." She took out a silk handkerchief, unfolded to reveal the jade hairpin I had pawned off months earlier. One of my favorites. One that had once belonged to Mother. "I saw it in a shop window and remembered you have one just like it. Now you have two."

Taohua's lies were so easy, so flawless, I almost believed her. The last few times I pawned off jewels for Meiya, her family's servants brought them back as gifts to the family. Again, in the guise of completing a nonexistent collection.

Taohua never outright asked why I was selling my things. She didn't ask for my gratitude, either.

"Thank you," I murmured, taking the silk-wrapped gift from her.

A quiet settled over us.

We approached my home, the decaying walls dirtied with age and crawling with vining plants trying to devour it.

Taohua's face was empty, but I felt the distaste rolling off her. "Is it still just you, your sister, and your grandmother who live here?"

"Just us." It was frowned upon for women to live alone without men and without guards. But it had been years since Father had passed, and we were fine. Hells, even when Father was alive, he didn't offer us much protection. "I can look out for my family. Death didn't bless me for nothing."

"But who's looking out for *you*, Ruying?" Taohua whispered, sisterly instincts breaking through the cracks of her armor. "Something bad is coming. I can feel it brewing like a storm. If you are in trouble, Ru, tell me. I will help you in whatever way I can. I promise."

No.

Not this time.

I couldn't tell Taohua what had happened to Meiya. She would never agree to help me buy opian. She would hate Meiya, and possibly hate me for letting my sister get involved with the drug. Her father had strongly opposed letting opian into our world from the moment Rome introduced it.

Plus, those posters I found in Meiya's room? The Phantom's propaganda? She would arrest Meiya on the spot if she knew.

"I'm fine," I lied. "You worry too much."

Taohua smiled but said no more about it. "I should get going. Mother wants us to eat dinner with all of my aunts and uncles today. Like a family. She demands that I bathe with scalding water and pray to our ancestors to wash away the *sha-qi* of the battlefield before I'm allowed near anyone. You know how superstitious she is."

Sha-qi. Deathly energy. Something that would follow me always if it were real. As a child, I wondered if this was the reason I found it so hard to make friends—if like prey sensing danger, those kids sensed the *sha-qi* within me.

Father had believed in *sha-qi,* too, when he was alive. Though his way to get rid of *sha-qi* was to lock himself in his room with a hefty amount of opian.

General Ma, Taohua's father, was the youngest of twelve children, sold into the army at just nine years old so that his parents could feed his siblings. Back when my grandfather was still alive, he had nurtured and trained General Ma from foot soldier to the leader he was today. Promoted him battle after battle, groomed him to take his place as general because he didn't see such talent in his own son, my father.

Father had hated General Ma for as long as I could remember. Because Grandfather had believed in an orphan boy more than his own son.

"Ru, you know you can come to me about anything, right? If you are ever in need of help, I'm here. No matter what. We are friends, family, *sisters*. I'm here for you."

"I know," I murmured. Her sympathy made me uneasy. A quiet reminder of my powerlessness. The difference in our statuses and situations.

While a small part of me did want her help, these thoughts were embers among snow—quick to kindle, quicker to perish. Some called it pride. Others called it independence. Whatever it was, this thing that kept me from asking for help, it was as much a part of me as my cursed Gift.

"Be careful, Ru. There have been more reports of kidnappings at the edge of the capital. More and more Xianlings are reported missing every day, and most of them are addicts. Strange things are happening across the continent."

"What kind of things?"

Her eyes darted left and right before coming close to whisper in my ear. "I've heard reports of corpses washed up on the shore, their blood drained, their bodies like shriveled husks. There are storms brewing in the south, and rumbles of Sihai trying to sign another peace treaty with the Romans . . ."

I clutched the bag of opian hidden in my sleeve tighter to me. Meiya was waiting. Still, curiosity got the best of me. Knowledge was power and Taohua knew so much from her father and sister. The kind of military and political secrets most only heard in forms of speculation and rumor.

I spoke with carefully chosen words. "They say the court is torn between those who call for rebellion and those who wish to kneel deeper and deeper into the ground until the Romans have their foot at our necks."

"Because the consequence of submitting is far less dire than that of war." Taohua echoed the sentiment shared by too many, not just in court but among the everyday peasants who just wished for survival and an illusion of peace so they could go about their days. "The elder men of court have witnessed Rome's powers firsthand. If the late Emperor had not surrendered so fast, bowed to all their demands, Rome would have burned the capital to the ground. And what's to say—"

"But they didn't," I said. "There has to be a reason. Something that they want from us."

Her eyes shifted.

Which side was Taohua on?

Which side was the right side?

Should we stay on our knees and let them continue to humiliate us, or should we fight? Was freedom even worth fighting for when our opponents were as mighty as Rome?

"Is your mission in the south related to this?" I continued. "Everyone in the Empire knows of the unrest at our borders. Rebels calling for independence. From Rome. From the Er-Lang family. They think our Emperor weak. What do you think, Taohua?"

Was she there to quiet the rebellions, or was it something more complicated?

Again, she was quiet, eyes flittering over everything but me. Her lips thinned, tension at her jaw. Words bitten, held back.

Baihu and I weren't the only ones who had changed over the years as our world faded to a version of its former glory.

Once upon a time, Taohua and I used to tell each other everything. Our deepest secrets.

But now, a canyon divided us.

It felt as if everyone I held dear was slowly drifting away. Despite all the powers at my fingertips, there was nothing I could do to pull them back and keep them close.

I looked down. Her silence was all the answer I needed, all the answer I would get. There was no point in pushing when she clearly didn't want to share. And what use did I have with such secrets anyway? It wasn't like I had the power to change things.

I was just a girl, suffering like everyone else. I held no chips in this game of power. The only thing I could hope for was mercy.

Survival.

Such simple wants in eras of peace. Such impossible dreams in times like these.

"The Phantom is causing trouble, disrupting opian routes and getting in the way of things," Taohua reluctantly added after the pause. "But Pangu's enemy has always been Rome—whether the Five Emperors of the continent realize this or not. And if they are too cowardly to fight for their own kin, maybe it's time we take our destinies into our own hands."

"And what of—"

"Ruying? A word of warning. The less you know, the better—though you might believe otherwise. You can ask me these things, but never ask them from anyone else, do you understand?"

I nodded, heeding her advice, grateful for the sliver of information, of power, I had received.

The Phantom's supporters grew day by day. Not just in the outer villages now.

They existed here in the cities, hidden in plain sight.

Rebels ready to fight. Martyrs ready to die.

My eyes drifted up the house to the second floor, where Meiya's bedroom was, then back to Taohua. "Be careful."

"I always am."

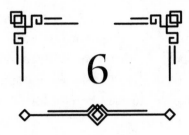

6

I SNUCK THROUGH THE HOUSE using the hidden corridors that once helped servants move between rooms without being seen. It'd been a long time since our house last saw servants. They all left when Father gambled away the fortune our ancestors left us.

Father might be dead, but the consequences of his actions, his entitlement, his debts, remained.

He used to blame his mistakes and his addiction on Meiya and me being girls. He used to shout that if we were sons, if he had someone to carry on the family name, our family never would have fallen from grace. He used this as an excuse to beat us. For years, he took out all the grief and hate he had for himself, on us.

Some days I missed him. Some days I was glad he was dead. Some days I wished I had killed him myself.

Grandma told us it wasn't his fault. That he had suffered, too; that we should try to understand and forgive him because he had lost his wife.

Mama died giving Meiya and me life.

Was this why Father hated us?

Clenching my jaw, I made a quick dash for my room on the second floor, hoping to change into clean robes before anyone saw me. I didn't want Meiya or Grandma to see my bloodied sleeves and worry.

But when I pushed open my bedroom door, I was greeted not by the tidy room I'd left behind but a violent wreckage like the aftermath of a hurricane.

Clothes strewn across chairs, my bookshelf toppled over, all of its contents spilled out onto the ground. Stray pieces of paper and books were flung across the room. Broken bronze mirrors, and vases. I stifled a gasp when I saw that Grandfather's inkstone—the most valuable thing I'd ever owned—lay cracked on the ground.

Immediately, I grabbed the silk pouch, afraid it might vanish.

The Romans. That man must have sent guards to follow me, and now—

Where were Meiya and Grandma? What if they'd chased me home? What if—

"Meiya! Nai-Nai!" I cried and was about to race out of the room when I noticed the shadow of pink and white kneeling on the floor, half-obscured by my overturned bed, next to the alcove where I had hidden a stash of opian.

No.

Meiya's shoulders trembled as she cried quiet sobs, hand clasped over her mouth. She'd made herself so small, half-concealed by the overturned floorboard, that I almost didn't see her.

My heart eased. I let out a breath and closed the door behind me.

Grandma couldn't see Meiya like this. The longer we hid this secret from her, the better. She had gone through enough heartbreaks. She didn't need another reason to shed tears.

This wasn't the first time I'd come home and found my room overturned by Meiya in her quest to find the stashed-away opian. But this was the first time she had succeeded.

She must have been desperate this time. Luckily, there wasn't much left.

"Meiya?" My voice was gentle, hesitant, as if approaching a wounded animal. "Are you okay?"

"Do I look okay?" She glanced up, her eyes bloodshot, her voice cold and nonchalant in a way that reminded me of Father before his worst moods.

The calm before the storm, Meiya and I used to call it.

When I knelt at her side, she didn't look at me, her gaze downcast on the white powder dusting her robes, her jaw clenched like she was ready to punch a hole through the floor.

I wanted to cry and remind her of the progress she'd ruined, but such words wouldn't help her now.

Meiya brushed her tears away. I knew what she was thinking. As a child, she had hated our father for giving in to his addictions time after time.

"It wasn't supposed to be like this," she whimpered. "I was supposed to be better than this. Better than Father. I thought—"

"You thought you were the exception to the rule," I finished for Meiya when her voice broke.

At this, my sister began to sob.

I no longer wanted to ask why she started using the drug.

A part of me already knew.

It was for the Phantom, his clans of Ghosts, and promises of liberation and freedom from the Romans.

Meiya wasn't like me. She couldn't resign herself to silence. Meiya wanted to fight, use her Gift that could both amplify the Gift of others and heal those who were wounded. A Gift of kindness, more powerful than anyone gave her credit for—than she gave herself credit for.

Meiya thought witnessing Father's demise firsthand would make her different from the other addicts.

But addictions don't work like that. For I knew opian's coaxing melodies, heard it between every heartbeat. Familiar as air filling my lungs, the pattern of soft blue veins running up the back of my hands, the curves and slopes of my knuckles when they tightened into fists.

Opian and Death's whispers were more similar than they were different. Both dangerous acts with haunting highs.

How could I blame Meiya, when most days I was only one impulse away from giving in?

We both had our demons, my sister and I.

But while I'd grown used to these deadly urges, had lived years trying to ignore their melodies, Meiya was different. Her body was dependent on opian. A sudden withdrawal would be too much of a shock to her system. Weaning someone off opian was like balancing a blade by its sharpest edge; difficult, but not impossible.

When there was a will, there was a way.

There had to be.

"We will get through this," I told her and tried to reach for her hand. But Meiya pulled away before skin could touch skin. Something I had expected.

Back when Father was still alive, when his screams filled the house like an ever-present monster, we used to comfort each other with silence, and the gentle touches of our hands. Back then, no matter how bad things got, we were never alone because we always had each other. We promised we would always love each other even if Father didn't.

Too much had changed since we were children, powerless to stop Father's rage.

The whole world had changed.

We had changed.

In the past few months, a chasm had divided us. We were once two halves of the same person, but now we stood on two opposing sides of a canyon.

"I'm sorry," she murmured, looking around at my upturned room, the opian that dusted her robe like specks of crystal. "I—"

Her voice broke.

I knelt a little closer but didn't try to soothe her with warm words or hugs. I knew my sister too well. My sympathy would only make her angrier.

This was all that I could do, be close and remind her that I was here. No matter what kind of trouble she got into, no matter how much she hated me for my cowardliness, she was my sister.

I'd always protect her.

I loved her. Even if she no longer loved me.

"Talk to me," I whispered, begged, *pleaded*.

She wouldn't even look at me.

The shimmery white powder in her lap was fine like sugar, though I knew it was anything but sweet. I brushed specks of opian off her lap and gathered them in a bowl, salvaging the scraps for a later date.

When I left this morning, I'd been hopeful. Meiya was doing so well. I thought the end might be near, and that this would be the last time I had to ask Baihu for handouts.

I was wrong.

The road to recovery was long and arduous, and we were nowhere near its end.

Unconsciously, I patted the pouch of gold, and thought of that green-eyed young man. *This gold might be a drop in the ocean for you, but it will change our lives. If we meet again in another life, I promise I'll pay you back.*

"Grandma is going away tomorrow," Meiya said after a long pause. "Up north this time, to interview more suitors for you."

There was a cold, unfamiliar tone to her voice. Hopelessness. She didn't say it, but I knew she was scared of me marrying a bad man like our father.

I inched a little closer to feel her warmth and pretended that we were still the sisters who told each other everything.

Her blood was my blood. Her soul was my soul. I feigned a smile. "Grandma will find me a good match. Someone who can provide for you and Grandma, keep us safe from the Romans and the looming war."

I tried not to think of the consequences of this protection, the sacrifices required of women on our wedding nights.

For my family, I would give up anything and everything.

"Safe?" Meiya echoed, her tone shivering cold; it pressed against my bleeding heart like an icy blade. When she looked at me, there was no love, only disappointment. "Open your eyes. The Romans won't stop their rampage until they swallow Er-Lang whole, until they have swallowed the *continent* whole! The worst is yet to come. Stop being a coward and—"

Meiya's furious, righteous voice cracked. Her eyes watered, hope dimmed like a candle nearing the end of its wick. Her face scrunched in agony, in disappointment, in disgust. She tore her eyes away as if she could no longer bear the sight of me. I wanted to inch forward, hold her hand, comfort her, say something to make her feel better . . . but I couldn't.

Because the one thing she wanted right now was something I couldn't give her: vengeance, and justice. My magic, surrendered to the Phantom, my allegiance with the rebels she conspired with.

Because it was futile. They couldn't fight off the Romans.

Magic was mighty, but bullets were just as mighty, and twice as fast—and didn't shave hours from their lives to wield.

If rebellions were of any use, Er-Lang wouldn't be in this decrepit state. Our people wouldn't be going hungry, kept out of our own streets. Shops run by our own kind proudly displaying ROMANS ONLY signs on specific days just because those tyrants demanded it. Because while the Romans wished to explore our cities, eat our food, enjoy our culture, stories, history, they wanted to do so without having to be near us. As if we were rodents, or dirt unworthy of being stepped on by their shiny leather shoes, polished to a disgusting shine.

The Romans thought themselves our conquerors.

And they might just be.

"I don't want you getting involved in these dangerous things," I whispered.

If I couldn't give Meiya what she wanted, then I would give her what she needed.

I would keep her from the Ghosts who whispered senseless hope in her ears, convinced her that these small rebellions would make a difference when all they did was anger the Romans further, pushing us closer toward the inevitable war.

My sister wanted to be a martyr.

I'd die myself before I let anything bad happen to her.

"You can't tell me what to do," she spat.

"Meiya, I will find a good husband and get married, and we won't have to worry about money or Rome or—"

Her laugh was a screeching rattle of the lone coin at the bottom of an empty jar. "Do you think I care about these things? And do you really think that getting married like a good little girl will solve everything? The Romans play nice now because Emperor Yongle is bowing to their commands. But soon they will want things the Emperor isn't willing to give. What happens then? A life on our knees is no life at all. We have to fight, slay the beasts before they grow too powerful to be stopped."

Meiya spoke as if I didn't understand.

Though I didn't want to admit it, I understood everything she said. This was why I had to marry. Find a good man of a good family far from the chaos of this city, far from the territories that Rome claimed with rampant zeal.

None of this was about preventing the inevitable pain. It was about giving my family the chance to enjoy what little peace we had left. A remnant of normalcy before we lost it all. Grandma had lived through enough heartbreaks to last a lifetime; I wanted her final days to be peaceful. I wanted her to be happy. I wanted her to see me get married, the Yang Clan's name returned to a shadow of its former glory so that she could face my grandfather in the afterlife with pride.

I wanted to give Meiya a chance to be young, to have a few more years of doing what she wanted before she got dragged into the bloodshed, as all of us inevitably would.

My twin, my minutes-younger sister, who had done so much for me.

"Meiya, I—"

She shoved me away when I tried to touch her. "You are a coward."

Coward. Death's magic burned at this word. I sneered. "Maybe I am a coward. But I am a coward who will do what it takes to keep us safe! Now forget this rebellion bullshit and change into some clean robes. I don't want Grandma seeing you like this."

Meiya stomped to her feet. I couldn't bear the way she looked at me. Resentment so torrid it left the love she once had for me in ashes. A look that would forever haunt my worst nightmares.

Then, in slow, raspy breaths: "I may have disappointed Grandma, but at least I'm not like you, Ruying. I know freedom is worth dying for."

I clenched my jaw, my heart beating at a tempo too fast to be healthy as frustration built and built inside me.

"You are wasting your time."

"What?"

"The only reason the Phantom and his rebels have survived this long is because Rome doesn't see them as a threat. Their numbers and influence might grow day by day, but if they keep poking the beast, they'll be crushed like a cockroach at Rome's feet."

Meiya's eyes sharpened to daggers. "You want to know the real reason I took opian? I took it because I wanted to be strong. Like you. So strong that nothing can hurt me again. Because Death chose the wrong sister to bless. If I had your powers, I'd make Er-Lang proud. I would fight for what's *right*. I wouldn't let this precious Gift waste away like rotting fruit. I wouldn't let my kin live on their knees, bowing to monsters who have no right to call themselves Gods."

The smile I forced tasted bitter. "Do you really think so highly of me? Think my pitiful magic can make the difference you want to see in the world? I'm only one person, Meiya. I can't change anything. I can barely take care of our family! Why do you think I'm letting myself be married off to a stranger who will find me repulsive as soon as he learns of my Gift?"

"Don't have the power, or don't *want* to have the power?" Meiya backed away. "If I were you, born with Death at my beck and call, I would be everything Mother wanted her daughter to be. Brave and courageous, a hero worthy of songs and ballads. This was why she named you Ruying, isn't it?"

The brave, my name meant. I swallowed the lump in my throat. "I'm not your hero, Meiya. Don't waste your time on the Phantom's lies, either. Nobody has the power to save or destroy our world. *Nobody.* And if I were really that strong, do you think we'd still be here?" I gestured at the broken home around us.

"You're right. Maybe you are not the hero I once thought you were."

Meiya slammed the door behind her.

I remained where I was in silence, the bag of forgotten hawthorn berries heavy in my sleeve.

I knelt and swept up the remaining dust of opian into my hand. Meiya would quit her addiction. I would make sure of it. But for the time being, she still needed this drug that was so damn expensive.

Nonetheless, today's bag would be my last from Baihu.

I refused to get involved in this fight or its politics. Because once I was in, there would be no coming out. I might not care about this failing Empire enough to risk my life and save it, but I would not be a traitor, like Baihu.

Not unless it was my only option.

This was the last shred of dignity and courage I could offer my sister.

She will understand in time, I told myself. *She will be grateful, one day. And she will know that I did it all for our family.*

Still, as I stared at the mess around me, I began to cry.

I wanted Meiya to run back into the room, hug me, and tell me that she loved me, understood why I had to be like this. She was beguiled by the Phantom's lies, but someone had to be the realist here, see the world for its dangers and do what was necessary to keep us safe.

Meiya didn't come back.

She didn't apologize.

I cleaned up the mess and hid the new stash of opian somewhere safe before drying my tears.

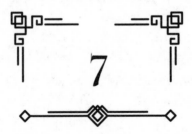

7

I WENT DOWNSTAIRS TO WASH the berries for Meiya. Angry though she might be, she still had to eat. Over the last few moons as we tried to wean her off the drug, Meiya had lost so much weight it made my chest tight, seeing her hollowed cheeks and empty eyes.

The kitchen was tucked away in the corner of the courtyard. Our home used to be bigger, sprawling rooms and gardens and grand halls to entertain guests. Most of that was sold off, piece by piece, to keep us afloat in the wake of Father's death and the debts he left behind. Now all we had left was this tiny section of crumbling rooms, just big enough for the three of us.

When I was little, this kitchen used to bustle with people, noises and sounds. Grandma ordering cakes, Father demanding dinner for his important guests, Meiya and I scurrying beneath feet, peeking over the tables and reaching for a lotus bun or red-bean cake.

Now it was cold and quiet.

I washed the berries, placed them in our best porcelain bowl and dusted them with the precious sugar we could rarely afford—the sugar that Meiya loved—and took it up to her room.

I knocked. When she didn't answer, I didn't push. I left the bowl by her door, hoping she'd see it later.

Night had darkened the sky. I went back down to the kitchen to make dinner, and found Grandma hunched over the cutting board, unsteady on her feet, chopping vegetables with a dull knife. It might have been the dim light, but I swore I saw tears in her eyes when I entered.

"Nai-Nai," I whispered, taking the knife off her. "Let me."

"It's okay, I can—"

"*Let me,*" I repeated, helping her to the chair across from the long table.

She didn't protest, just scooted the chair closer, watching me with glassy eyes. Her face was a mask—one that even after nineteen years I still couldn't read.

After the money ran out and the servants left, Meiya and I took on most of the chores, despite our age. Grandma wanted to help, but she'd gone from the daughter of a wealthy father to the wife of a wealthier man. All her life, she'd never had to lift a finger. Asking her to wash her own clothes, cut meat, and make food so far into her twilight years felt . . . unfilial.

She protested. We insisted.

Meiya and I were kids then. We couldn't exist without her. If anything had happened to her, we would have been orphans, prey in a merciless city with a hunger for pretty girls and rare magic.

The Romans' portal lurked overhead like a silent promise. A tear in the sky, its quiet glow ominous.

They said demons were from hell, but none of us could have guessed that hell opened from the skies above, not from the ground beneath. And this time, Nüwa wasn't here to mend the sky. The old Gods had abandoned us, and magic grew weak in our veins.

Baihu was right, my gift was a target on my back. Without Grandma's protection, her wit and intelligence that turned copper into silver, small trades that kept us afloat, Gods knew what might have happened to Meiya and me.

"I wanted to make you girls something tasty before I go north tomorrow to interview marriage offers for you," she murmured, her voice raspy.

I smiled. "It's the thought that counts, Nai-Nai. Let me do these things. You know how your bones ache when you stand for too long."

Once I put the vegetables on the fire, I helped her to her feet and we went out to the courtyard. The kitchen was too hot, too smoky for her lungs.

Autumn crept into the gold of the leaves, but it wasn't yet cold. The evening air was crisp and tonight's sky was clear. Grandma often observed the stars and the moon the way scholars read proverbs. *The Gods have scattered our futures in shimmers and sparks between the stars. We just have to be patient enough to seek them out.* Something she always told me as a kid. Another one of her superstitions.

I helped her down onto the stone chairs then knelt at her feet, massaging the taut muscles of her leg. I tried to look up, seek the same futures she claimed to have found, but the only thing I saw was the slash across the sky—the pale, incandescent light of the portal that marred our heavens. A permanent mark that disturbed everything, even the stars.

In the daylight, the portal was barely visible. A mere glisten high in the sky like a distorted slant of light. But as the night darkened over the city, the portal became harder to ignore. Its light occasionally flickered like the stars, and its shape changed, constantly. Some nights, the portal looked so small it seemed to be shrinking—as if the portal itself knew what the Romans were doing was wrong and wanted to close itself and lock them out.

A plane, small as an ink blot against the deepening indigo sky, passed through the portal in a subtle ripple of light. In that moment, I could have sworn the portal disappeared for a fraction of a second, its edges rippling when it reappeared in the sky.

According to Grandma, those planes used to come and go once a moon when the Romans first arrived—something our people used to marvel at. But by the time I was born and old enough to hold memories, they were already passing through once a week. Now, we saw them disturbing our skies daily—or perhaps several times a day.

I'd always wondered what they transported inside those flying machines. What were they taking, and what were they bringing back? If they brought anything back.

These aircrafts didn't dock in the city, but on a section of land the late Emperor granted Rome as part of the treaty. A permanent piece of Roman land on Er-Lang soil, as long as our two nations were at peace, where they could do whatever they wanted.

As if the Romans didn't already do whatever they wanted, whether they were on their land or not.

Though I had never been, never seen it with my own eyes, I had heard the stories passed between the gossiping aunties like bargaining chips. They whispered of a place far outside of the city and how it was haunted. How the buildings emitted strange smoke and a foul stench day in, day out. They whispered of the towering metal fences charged with electricity, and the ghostly howls that could be heard deep in the night.

I swallowed the unease in my belly. What happened there was none of my concern. The only thing I should spend my anxieties on was here and now.

My family.

Our survival.

The coming winters that would bring snowy nights and scarce food supply and inflated firewood prices as the people of this city kept dying and money was hoarded by the wealthy and kept out of our hands. We rented out old sections of our home to desperate tenants packed into cheap rooms, but how could they pay us when most of them could barely feed themselves?

As if sensing my paranoid thoughts, Grandma put a hand on my head and stroked my hair. "You're a good kid, Ruying. If your father could see the woman you've become, he would be so proud of you." I pretended to smile. Like I cared what he thought of me. "Keep an eye on your sister when I'm gone, okay? I'm worried about her."

I waited for Grandma to say more, to tell me she was suspicious that Meiya was taking the same drug that'd killed Father, but she didn't.

Either we were doing too good of a job of hiding it, or Grandma knew and didn't know how to face it.

I wanted to tell her that if she was worried, she should talk to Meiya herself, but this wasn't how our family dealt with problems. We painted paper over the cracks and pretended they weren't there. This was how we lived our lives: knowing, never saying.

Just like how we'd never, *ever* talked about Father's death. Never talked about the bruises that haunted our skin when he was still alive.

In the quiet starlit glow, I rested my head on Grandma's knees as she caressed my hair. I savored this moment, fearing the day this cruel world would take her from me. Or the day I would be taken from her, once magic had depleted my life's source and my life was cut short by the very Death who bestowed my sinful powers. "When will you come back?"

"In a week or so," she replied. "I know you don't like the cold, Ru. I don't want you to marry so far away. I—"

"I like the north," I told her. The farther north we were, the farther we'd be from the capital and the Romans. The north might be cold and desolate, but it would be safe.

At least for a while.

North was where the icy mountains guarded the people because the land loved its children and its children loved the land that was soaked with their ancestors' blood and cradled their ancestors' bones. The folks of the capital thought the northerners flesh-eating savages, but I knew otherwise.

Grandma knew otherwise.

Her grandfather had once been a child of the north. Though he had sacrificed his banner name for the cruel mercy and soft grains of southern lords during a once-in-a-generation winter storm that froze the land barren, he kept the stories of our ancestors close to his heart and passed them down between fireside meals.

And the northern land would always be kind to its children, even if the winter flashed its fangs and bared its talons.

I hoped this was true. That despite generations spent away from its soil, the land would remember us, love us, and protect us as the legends foretold.

I wasn't superstitious, didn't believe in lore and myths. But this one, I believed.

Because even my cold heart needed hope, needed something to hold on to. A safe place. A fantasy of a place where my family and I would be safe and happy and free from the traumas and terrors of Rome's looming shadow.

"I'm sorry," Grandma whispered, her fingers soft in my hair.

I knew she meant these words. For she understood what it was like to marry a man she'd never met, stuck in a loveless marriage as a pawn in a game of power where she had no control over her own fate.

She'd never wanted this life for me. If circumstances were different, if she had the power, I would choose my own marriage, forge my own destiny. Fall in love. *Decide* what I do and do not want from my life, and whether I want to marry at all.

But these were cautious times. Freedom was a luxury few could afford.

The days grew darker and darker as the winter approached. My family wasn't what it used to be, and in order to survive the storms ahead, sacrifices had to be made.

"*Nothing good ever comes of unprotected girls in wartime,*" she whispered, her tone grave with guilt and shame. "I would know. I've lived through too many of them at your grandfather's side."

She never spoke of the things she'd seen, and I didn't want to know. The horrors of my imagination were enough.

For our family to survive, she had to sacrifice one granddaughter to save the other. If it wasn't me, Grandma would have married off Meiya.

I'd rather die than let a man touch my sister. Even if he was handsome, kind, everything one could dream of, Meiya wouldn't love him. She'd never love a man.

I pressed a gold coin in Grandma's hand. "Take this," I said. "The journey north is long and arduous. If you need to stop at an inn and rest, or get something to eat, don't make yourself suffer to pinch pennies."

She stared at the gold coin. "Where did you get this?"

"I stole it. From a Roman." There was no point lying to my grandmother, who was too smart to be fooled. Who seemed to know everything—even the secrets I hid in the deepest crevices of my heart.

"*Yang Ruying*, how could you—"

"I saw a chance and I took it, Nai-Nai. I'm not sorry. The Romans take enough from us, every day. I shouldn't feel guilty for taking something from them. That young man won't even miss it."

Her eyes watered, and her lips trembled as rage boiled beneath her skin, tainted by fear. "You could have died."

"But I didn't." My eyes fell to my hand. Grandma had forbidden me from ever using my Gift again after that day at the bottom of the waterfall, when I discovered its existence.

She didn't think I could control it.

And she was right, I couldn't.

But Death had given me this power. I had the right to use it when it pleased me.

Right?

I was strong, powerful. Why should I suppress this part of me in order to make the world more comfortable?

"Can you still sense . . . *it*?" she asked. She could tell I'd used my magic; she could always tell.

Grandma said she could smell magic in the air. Sometimes, I think I could, too.

I lied and shook my head.

Some days, I controlled Death; other days, I felt as if it controlled me. Bloodlust sang under flesh, always.

Some days, it was harder to ignore than others.

Mortal laws don't apply to Gods. With Death's powers, I could be a false God, just like the Romans. Take *qi* as I pleased, drain innocent people of their life's essence, and decide who lived and who died as if I were Death incarnate.

Which, in some ways, I was.

"You shouldn't use your Gift," she said after a pause. "Magic comes at a price, Ruying. Each time you use your magic, your *qi* perishes with it."

"I know."

There were two types of Xianlings in this world: the cautious ones who used their powers sparingly, and those who abused it without care because if we were all going to die, they might as well have a good time.

Power was a dangerous temptation, violence an intoxicating rush. Those who could resist its pull were rare. This was why most Xianlings didn't live long enough to grow old, see the world, or sample the mortal pleasures life had to offer.

Those who thought Xianlings lucky because we were born with magic had no idea what it was like to live in our bodies, and the burden of control we had to carry.

Every second of every day.

Those born without magic thought magic made the world easy. They always failed to remember that magic came at a great cost. How the brightest of matches often burned out the fastest.

"Promise me that you won't use your Gift again." An order, not a request.

I couldn't make that promise.

In Jing-City, everybody had an enemy. Everybody wanted somebody dead. Whomever I married, once they discover the scope of my Gift, how easy it was for me to kill their worst enemies undetected, they wouldn't let such power go to waste. Their family would want to use me like a weapon, and it was demanded of a wife, a daughter—any girl—to follow the orders of her male superiors.

I'd have no choice but to obey. I'd heard whispers that soon the Emperor would force Xianlings to enlist in the military and train as soldiers. I was a blade; it was only a matter of time before someone forced me to kill.

If I married well, to a man who could support my family, at least they would be taken care of.

Right?

Dying young was something I'd long accepted. There were things I'd never experience, like growing old with someone I loved. The luxury of having enough time to bear children and watch them grow into adults—if my husband could stand my monstrous abilities enough to touch me. If my future mother-in-law would let me go anywhere near my own child . . .

Could I even have a child, with Death and all of its hunger rumbling inside me? Or would it suck the life from any seed that dared to sprout within me?

My time was capped, and the end might be sooner than I realized.

Every second was precious, which was why I intended to live for as long as I could.

And buy those I loved some happiness with what little time I had left.

Grandma left the next morning as she said she would.

Meiya didn't eat the berries I left by her door.

The hawthorns stayed ripe outside her room till bugs smelled the sugar and attracted rodents, who made off with their sweet flesh.

8

As a child, I felt blood before it was spilled, saw Death before he came. As I grew older, these senses only grew stronger. Like how animals sense storms before they arrive, I sensed bloodshed before it happened.

Three days after Grandma left, I dreamt of Death's icy breath.

In my dream, I saw Jing-City from above, as if through my patron's all-seeing eyes. The capital slumbered in darkness, broken by rivers of scarlet cast by lanterns red as blood.

Tonight, they weren't the only things that were red.

Something inside me coiled and twisted. Panic surged. A sharp, rising tide inched up my throat.

Men marched through the night, slipped into houses unheard, knives gleaming in their hands.

The Phantom, was my first thought.

Then I looked closer, at their foreign attires and the guns strapped to their backs.

Romans. Taohua's warning echoed.

I wanted to laugh. I shouldn't be surprised. Rumors had long swirled that it was the Romans who stole Xianlings from our beds like the traffickers who had existed during the Qin Emperor's reign from a thousand years ago. And like smoke without fire, rumors rarely came from nothing.

But why?

The Qin Emperor had wanted Xianlings to build his army with magic, so that he could conquer more land. But Rome already had science. What use did they have for magic?

A silent, yellowish smoke followed the Romans into every home, lulling its inhabitants to sleep, but it couldn't sedate everyone in time. So when wails ruptured the night, so did the gunshots. Colors exploded. Bullets tore souls from paling bodies, and they drifted up from streets to skies in a wash of vibrant hues.

So many they illuminated the dark.

Run, ordered Death.

I woke with a jolt, panting. It took a moment for reality to sink in, to realize the screams in the distance were real and not a lingering aftertaste of my dream.

The glow of red flames and shadowed chaos flickered through my papered windows.

Get out! Death's voice came sharp and fast.

Now.

I scrambled to my feet, hastily grabbed my robe and the pouch of stolen gold, before slipping into a pair of boots.

Jing-City was under siege. The swords and iron-tipped arrows of its city guards would only hold off Rome's swift bullets for so long. I had to get Meiya out of here and find somewhere safe before they found us.

Grandma's warning rang like a bell. *Nothing good ever comes of unprotected girls in wartime.*

Something tingled at the edge of my senses.

I closed my eyes and dipped into Death's world of black and white to see what my mortal eyes could not.

Three shimmering silhouettes advanced toward my home, slipping in through the peeling red doors.

Panic boiled to fear. I had to hurry.

When I slipped into Meiya's moonlit bedroom, I didn't dare to light candles for fear of attracting unwanted attention.

"Meiya!" I breathed, trying to shake her awake. "We need to leave. Come on!"

She didn't move. Her skin was hot to the touch, searing like blazing coal.

Skies. I couldn't remember the last time a fever had set in so fast. Her withdrawals were coming faster and faster now, just like it had before Father—

"Meiya!" I said urgently. "*Please*, wake up!"

As if sensing my distress, my sister stirred. Her fingers twitched, and her eyes fluttered. "Ru?" A murmur. She hadn't called me Ru in years now. Her eyes peered open, dazed, not quite seeing me.

"I'm here." I let out a shaky laugh, relieved. "We have to go. *Now*. I'll explain everything later."

I tried to help her up, but Meiya's eyes closed again.

I heard the intruders in the hall below, rounding the courtyard, kicking open one door after another. Searching and searching and searching. For something to break. Something to take. It was only a matter of time before they found us. "Please, Sister, wake up." I tried again, but it was no use.

When her hand went limp in mine, I let her go. Even if I managed to wake her, she'd be too weak to run.

I wasn't Taohua. I wasn't strong enough to carry her.

Only one of us would survive the night.

I curled and uncurled my fingers, letting magic hum through me like a familiar symphony. I wanted to reach out and drain *qi* from the intruders until their bodies fell as corpses dead and cold, but they were too far, and my magic was too raw, untrained.

I had spent my whole life suppressing Death's powers, never using it outside of dire situations. I knew I wasn't strong enough to take on all three men.

But I had to try.

With a shaky breath, I took in Meiya's sullen face and her beautiful, moon-carved eyes. It was so easy to forget we were twins.

Grandma used to say when we were born, Meiya had been small
enough to fit in the palm of her hand. Because of this, Grandma
almost named her Mingzhu. For 掌上明珠. *The brilliant pearl at the
palm of her hand.*

It wasn't until after I discovered my Gift that we realized why
Meiya was so small, when I'd been so healthy.

I was a parasite, a leech. Even as a baby in our mother's womb I
was stealing both Meiya's and Mother's *qi*. I had tried to kill them
both.

I was the reason our mother had died.

Meiya was the reason we'd lived.

I took life away. Meiya gave it back.

A giver and a taker.

Yin and yang.

Father hated both of us for Mother's death. But he should have
hated only me.

Meiya was innocent. Yet I let her hide me in cupboards when
Father was in his dark moods. Let her face his wrath alone because
I was too scared to protest.

I was as cowardly then as I am now.

Tears stung the back of my eyes. I owed my sister too much.

I always had.

Nineteen years of debt. From the moment we were born, I owed
her my life.

It's my turn to take care of you, Meiya.

I popped open the floorboard under Meiya's bed and laid her
down in the alcove Grandma had prepared for occasions like these.
She always thought two steps ahead—the intelligence behind our
grandfather's success—and taught us to do the same.

Meiya groaned, an inaudible murmur slipping past unconscious
lips, delirious in her fever.

"I'm going to take care of this." I leaned down, placed a kiss on
her forehead. "You'll be safe. You'll be okay. Take care of yourself,
Meiya. *Remember me.*"

I placed the pouch of gold in her soft hands, then pushed the floorboard back into place.

I calmed my breathing, tiptoed down the servants' stairwell, magic ready at my fingertips.

I saw the intruders just as they exited Grandma's empty room, moving toward the staircase that led up to my and Meiya's rooms. Cloaked in crimson uniforms, armed with guns and ammunition, wearing boots too nice to belong to common criminals.

Making no effort to keep quiet, I bolted from my hiding spot. When they saw me, smiles bloomed on their faces, painted ghostly white in the moonlight.

"I've found her," the one at the front said into a device at his collar before raising his gun.

I ran as fast as I could. I had to lead them away from Meiya. Anything to protect my sister.

I tried to remember what Taohua had taught me about magic, about the art of battle.

Like a tiger, pounce for the throat. Aim to—

I ducked when the first gunshot rang like thunder.

Two bullets zipped past my ears, brief flashes of color at the edge of my vision, fast like shooting stars. I twirled out of their way like Taohua taught me. The trick was to stay in motion. It was easier to kill a sitting duck than a moving one.

It'd been years since I'd practiced dodging arrows, and bullets were much faster. Either these men were bad shots, or they weren't shooting to kill. They wanted me alive.

I shuddered to think of why.

I'm not going down without a fight. I wasn't a whisper of the wind, or a willow who bent to the will of the sun. I had to hunt them before they hunted me.

If these traffickers wanted to touch my sister, they better think twice.

I threw out my magic and, with an arch of my hand, *qi* slammed into me like a swarm of fireflies searching for a new home, climbing up my arms, bringing heat, tingles. Their beating wings sent energy surging through me, making me faster, stronger, and rendering everything sharper.

Grandma said my magic was a doorway between this world and the next. Each time *qi* flowed through me, it felt like I was being carried by a chariot of ten thousand horses. A sweet rush like the high after a sprint: muscles aching, heart pounding, lungs burning for air, my whole body weightless like that flying sensation when a rope swing reaches its greatest height. A moment where gravity ceased to exist, where *everything* ceased to exist except this ethereal, glorious feeling.

But as these stolen energies sang loud in my veins, I shuddered to think of the consequences.

Twice in five days.

Once my body got a taste of power, Death's taunts always grew louder, harder to push back into the background.

I would have to worry about that later, though.

First, I had to get through tonight.

When the first man collapsed into a motionless heap—not dead, just knocked out—I quickly moved on to the man running next to him. But this one's energy was angry and stubborn as a wrought noose. It refused to heed and clung to its mortal body no matter how hard I called for it—a man who really didn't want to die.

Without skin-to-skin contact, my grip on his *qi* came loose. Magic was a muscle, one I had hardly used. If I had practiced, trained, I might have been able to stretch it further and control it better than I could now.

It's too late to think of what-ifs. I gave his energy another pull, and this time it was enough to make him stumble, lose balance. His falling body caused an avalanche of skittering feet with the man behind him. They hurled toward the ground, snarled by one another's limbs.

I ran faster. The faded red of the courtyard doors was in sight.

Taohua's home wasn't far. The general's mansion was patrolled by guards and surrounded by soldiers. If I could reach—

Pain exploded down my spine as something sharp punctured my neck.

A bullet? A needle—no, a dart.

My muscles went numb, collapsed under my weight as my body folded into a tangled mess, crashing toward the ground. Sand and pebbles peppered my skin red, reopening the barely healed wounds from four days earlier.

The dart was laced with poison that dripped cold under my skin, as heavy as sinking stones, making me want to sleep.

I tried to keep moving, my eyes on the red door. I dug my elbow into the ground, jagged rocks cutting into my skin.

I crawled, forward and forward.

Almost there.

I was so close.

So.

Close.

"Aren't you a handful," somebody said, crunching gravel behind me before grabbing me by the leg. "Let's go."

Meiya's safe, I tried to tell myself when their rough hands hauled me up. This was all that mattered.

My sister was safe, and she was going to live.

PART 2

Veni

Vidi

Vici

I came

I saw

I conquered

9

Something didn't feel right.

I woke with tears in my eyes and half a scream in my throat. The world came into focus with slow, shallow breaths. Stark rays of white muffled by storm gray, a husk of shadows by the time it spilled through the narrow opening, touched my lashes, illuminated these four walls in ashen tones.

The clang of chains and never-ending cries rang sharp in the air. People begging for their lives.

"Let me out! Please!"

"The Gods will damn you for this!"

"Please! I have a family! I have a daughter and a mother and . . ."

Some of the cries were in our language. Some were in an accented attempt of the Roman tongue. Grandma made sure to educate Meiya and me in both, just in case. Language and communication were talents that might keep us alive if our worst nightmares bled into reality.

Upright, I rubbed my thudding temples. The rush of heartbeat was too loud in my ears.

Buried beneath dirt and molded stone, the cell was a dingy cube barely big enough to fit a bed and a metallic toilet. Misery drenched the walls and blood rusted the ground. The stench of urine and vomit permeated the air, making my stomach lurch.

I rolled my shoulders, my senses returning in slow stages. I had no idea where this place was, and there was only one way to find out.

Closing my eyes, I reached for Death's simmering magic. If I could push it out, I might get a better view of this prison, see all that my mortal eyes could not.

But, for the first time, the barrier between the living and the dead didn't crumble at my touch. I pushed harder, hands reaching far into the air, fingertips searching for warm and shimmering cords of *qi*.

Of *something*.

Please, I thought. *Let me in.*

Nothing happened.

Then I saw them. Twin metal bracelets, thin and narrow, clamped around my wrists like a second skin. Humming with something I didn't understand, frigid to the touch. They choked my magic like fists around a throat.

Zhentian iron was my first thought: a legend used to scare Xianling children. A creation capable of repelling magic, invented by the Qin Emperor during the Great War to protect himself against the Gods. Back when Xianlings were both feared and exploited.

Could it be?

I ran a finger along its length. No, these bracelets weren't products of magic. They buzzed with a low current of science, a subtle vibration against my fingertips when I tried to gather magic into my hands.

I turned them around, looking for a lock, the slightest seam. I would pry them open with my bleeding nails if I had to. Anything to get these monstrosities off me.

"I wouldn't try that if I were you." The voice made me flinch, reach for Death's Gift by instinct. Again, it eluded my commands. A man stood beyond the narrow window of my cell, baring a smile like the glint of a dagger, honed by malice. "The best minds of Rome designed those things. A science far beyond the comprehension of you simple creatures. No Xianling has ever broken out of them."

The man looked me up and down like I was a piece of meat he couldn't wait to taste. I tightened my hands into fists until nails dug into flesh. I wanted to gouge those vicious eyes out of their sockets so that he'd never look at another girl like this. I wanted to sink my hands deep into his chest, tear life from him dust by dust until he screamed—

I remembered him.

A flash of pale eyes, green as jade. The young Roman master whose gold I'd stolen: This was his guard. The one who'd tackled me, the one I almost killed.

I shrank back, fear rising in place of magic.

I didn't get a good look at his face that day, but I recognized his deep, menacing voice and the rough way he snarled each word through half-clenched teeth.

After I had unleashed Death on him, I'd left him half-dead. There was a paleness to him still, a visible exhaustion under his eyes, the slightest silver streak at his temple. His once supple skin was now papery and thin. I didn't know how old he was, but there was a weathered age to him now, despite those young and furious eyes.

At least he was alive.

If our positions were swapped, if he were the one who held the powers of Death in his hands, I wasn't sure if I would have walked out of that alleyway that night. The Romans held no mercy for the people of Er-Lang. We were rodents in their eyes, puny creatures at their feet. My death would have been insignificant. I doubt I would have been the first Panguling he'd killed.

The worst part was even if he had wetted his hands with my blood, choked me till there was nothing left against that ancient stone path, he wouldn't face consequences.

Would never pay any form of price for my murder.

At my silence, his smile deepened, as if deriving pleasure from my capture. "Such a pretty little thing. I'm going to especially enjoy killing you."

"Wait," I called before he could leave. "Where am I? Why am I here?"

He paused but didn't turn to face me. "You will soon find out."

And with that, he was gone.

10

TIME PASSED IN SLOW AGONY.

Without daylight, there was no way to keep track of time. I slammed the bracelets against the walls, over and over again. Tried to pry them open until my fingers were crusted with blood. I cried out until my throat was scraped raw. Nobody answered me. There was no way to communicate with the world outside, no way of knowing where I was, or what had happened back home.

Had Grandma returned from the north? Did Meiya survive that night unscathed? Was the attack a onetime thing, or had events progressed? Were we already neck-deep in war with Rome?

If so, what would happen to my sister, my grandmother? I tried to coax answers from the guards, but they wouldn't look at me, much less talk to me.

This might be the scariest part of all: not knowing.

When the guards did regard me, it was with hatred and disgust.

So I stopped screaming, and didn't fight or complain when they handed me bland foods through the narrow opening of the cell. I didn't cry, didn't beg for mercy. I conserved my energy and ate everything they gave me to stay strong.

I knew a thing or two about merciless men from my father. The more you begged, the more they enjoyed hurting you. I preferred to keep quiet and rob them of that satisfaction.

Small victories.

This would not be how the girl blessed by Death died. Not as a martyr or a traitor, but nameless on foreign lands, far from those I loved.

I would survive at all costs. And in order to survive, I had to play by their rules. Wait for my chance.

The harrowing wails of my fellow inmates continued, day and night, at all hours. And in the beginning, I was grateful. They kept me alert and vigilant as I waited for a chance to break free, fight, defy Rome's ballooning ego, and save myself against all odds.

That chance never came.

After a while, exhaustion won. I curled small on the center of the bed to keep warm and fell into nightmare-racked slumbers.

In the end, I grew used to their cries, a melody that haunted even my dreams.

The guards came and went through the corridors, sometimes to shove new prisoners into old cells or drag old prisoners out to make those cells new again.

Those who were taken never returned.

I didn't know where they went. Whether they were alive, or . . .

Such a pretty little thing, that guard's words rang like thunder heralding a storm. *I'm going to especially enjoy killing you.*

I clenched my hands tight, thought back to my last conversation with my sister: that argument. The things she had said, which I knew she didn't mean. I would not let those words be her last memory of me.

Meiya would never forgive herself if it was.

I would not let Grandma go through the pain of burying her granddaughter after she had already buried her son. 白发送黑发, 不孝之道. *Letting the white hair bury the black hair was unfilial to the highest degree.*

I would not do that to Grandma.

I—

"Let me go!" A familiar voice. "Do you know who I am?"

No.

It couldn't be. It wasn't her. She wasn't here.

"Taohua!" I yelled, scrambling to the narrow opening they used to give us food and water just in time to see the guards dragging my friend through the too-bright corridors, kicking and screaming.

"Ruying?" she gasped. "Ruying! Help! Help—"

"Shut up!" The guard who had her by the arms fumbled with the device in his hand, and Taohua's whole body convulsed into a violent seizure, her limbs flip-flopping like a fish's dying effort to liberate itself from its captors, to return itself to the serene ocean.

"Taohua! Taohua!" My hands clawed through the tiny opening, as if I could reach her, as if I could somehow pull myself through the confined space and get to her. Help her. Save her. Like I had done when we were children. Like she did for me over and over again, after we'd grown into teens. "Please, let her go! Take me! Take me! Take—"

Pain bolted up from my wrists, shuddered through my whole body until I was heaving for breath on my knees. I didn't realize I was crying until I choked on my sobs.

Taohua . . .

"Behave," someone on the outside snapped, and slammed shut the small window. My only source of light.

I pressed my hand against the icy, metal door.

I was nobody.

Nobody would miss me. But Taohua was somebody. She was the daughter of a general, a commander of the Er-Lang army. Her presence would be missed, investigated. Even if Rome wanted to, they couldn't take Taohua so easily. Not without motive. Not without a reason worthy of conflict, worthy of war.

The green-eyed boy flashed before me again.

The Romans were getting bold, attacking the capital like that. But were they bold enough to steal the daughter of Er-Lang's most esteemed general?

Then a more chilling thought occurred to me.

Was it my fault Taohua was captured? She'd helped me get away that day. Was this revenge?

Was he the reason we were both here?

If so, who was he?

聪明一世，糊涂一时. *Intelligent and cautious for a lifetime, it takes a second of stupidity to unravel it all.*

What had I done?

11

IN DARKNESS, TIME PASSED EVEN slower.

I wept.

It was my fault.

It was all my fault.

They gave me food, but I had no appetite.

If I was the reason Taohua was here, then I had not only ruined her life, I had brought her to hell.

I broke everything I touched. I had killed Mother, killed the childhood friend who had his whole life in front of him. I had hurt so many people, and now I might have killed Taohua.

My only friend.

I slammed my hand against the grime-soaked walls until my knuckles were crimson with blood. Until I felt nothing but frost-laced numbness, a burning kind of hatred one could only feel for themselves.

I never should have let myself befriend her, let myself believe I was worthy of friends, of love. If I had stayed away from her as I knew I should have, maybe Taohua wouldn't have helped me at the night market, wouldn't have put herself in the sight of that Roman boy and his cruel, cruel eyes.

I whimpered, hugged myself close. I stayed like that for a long time.

Until a tap sounded at my door.

Until a voice drew me back from the darkness that threatened to consume me.

"Ruying?"

Baihu?

I opened my eyes. Was this real? Was this the beginning of another nightmare, right before the monsters started to chase me?

The narrow metal slot creaked open, and light poured into my tiny cell once more.

I looked up.

A familiar pair of brown eyes, dark hair cropped short. I blinked twice to make sure it wasn't a trick of the light.

"Ruying, are you okay?" he whispered, and pressed a hand through the opening.

My heart thudded into rhythm once more.

No. This had to be a dream. I was hallucinating. There was no way someone like Baihu would show up in a place like this.

Still, hope grabbed me by the throat and threw me against the door.

He took ahold of my hand to keep me upright, and I grasped his like a lifeline. Tears were warm when they touched my cheeks, just like Baihu's hands.

It was real.

He was real. This was real.

I was so happy I wanted to kiss him.

"Taohua," I choked. "Help her. She's here, too. Help her, please. She—"

"She's alive," Baihu whispered. "The princes were impressed by her Gift of strength. They've decided to keep her alive, for further observation."

"Help her," I whimpered. "Get her out of here . . ."

"I'm trying." His hand continued to squeeze mine. His face was caught somewhere between relief and terror at seeing me, like I was a reality he didn't want to face.

"Is my sister safe? Has my grandmother returned from the

north, does she know I'm alive? Where am I, Baihu? Has Rome declared war? What happened to those who got dragged away? Why has no one come back? Where is Taohua? She's alive, but is she okay? Is she safe? Please, Baihu, I don't want to die . . ." Words poured out in one rushed breath before I could stop myself. All the haunted sorrows and manic questions I had kept inside in an attempt to stay strong, to keep myself together until I found a way out.

"They are fine. And I won't let anything happen to them, or you," Baihu reassured me, his hand squeezing mine in emphasis. "I'm here. Nothing is going to happen to you. This is the Roman side of the capital. And those who are taken from their cells, some of them are killed, but if the princes believe them to be useful, they will be left alive. At least for a while longer. Show them your powers when they ask, Ruying. Let them witness what you're capable of. That's the only way to survive here."

"Why are we here?" I asked again, though a part of me already had an idea.

Baihu's eyes darted from left to right. This wasn't a safe place to talk. "It doesn't matter why you're here. What matters is that you *shouldn't* be here. That entire raid never should have happened. There was a pact between the Empire and Rome. Only take those who would not be missed, keep to the rural villages so the Emperor can 睁一只眼，闭一只眼, *keep one eye open, and one eye closed.* Your name never should have been on that list. None of this was supposed to happen. You were never supposed to be on their radar. Antony wasn't supposed to—"

Everything went cold again.

I tore my hand from his, the thudding of my own heartbeat all I could hear as the fog of excitement cleared. His words sank in slowly with the chill.

My eyes trailed down. The window was just wide enough for me to see his light blue blazer, tailored and immaculate. Crisp white shirt. A silk tie adorned his throat.

This wasn't the attire of a criminal on a heist, but someone who *belonged*.

He had walked through these corridors, right up to my cell, without anyone stopping him.

"You knew?" I demanded.

All at once, I felt like a fool for not realizing sooner.

Of course Baihu knew about this. He wasn't the Er-Lang Baihu of my sunlit childhood memories anymore. He was the enemy. A boy who'd sold his soul to the Romans.

"You knew this was happening, and you didn't do anything to stop it." Not a question, but a statement. I had always known Baihu was a traitor. The whole of Jing-City knew he was a traitor.

Yet a part of me had thought, had *hoped* . . .

I laughed at my childish naïveté. At my audacity to hope in a world like this.

I stepped back, let the shadows consume me once more.

My ears rang with the cries that tormented these walls, the pleas into the silent void that never garnered replies. Our Gods did not answer us because they were no longer around to hear us.

Under Rome's iridescent portal, ever growing like the torn sky of Nüwa's legends, we were at the mercy of another kind of God entirely.

Footsteps sounded in the distance.

Baihu's attention jerked up. "I have to go, Ruying. But I'm going to get you out. I promise. Just wait. Give me time. *Please*. Trust me."

He pulled the window to a close, and darkness swallowed the world whole until I was left alone with the screams of my own blood. Hunger, desperation, fear, and hate burned like nothing I'd ever felt before.

I sank against the cold ground, my knees tucked under my chin.

Just wait. His words rang with the ever-present cries.

12

BAIHU DIDN'T COME AGAIN.

The cold numbed my senses, the days bled into one, and I wondered if Baihu had really been here or if he were a mere figment of my imagination. Down here, trapped in darkness with nothing but my thoughts for company, I couldn't be sure.

Maybe I'd imagined the whole thing.

Maybe I was losing my mind.

After days, weeks, months, years, or eternities, I stopped waiting.

No one was coming. Hope's fluttering wings stopped beating.

Waiting for someone to rescue me was useless. If I wanted to escape, I had to rescue myself.

Amid the darkness, I conjured a plan from Grandma's teachings.

Grandma's intelligence, my ancestors' determination, and the force of my will: These things were not Gifts from the Gods. They belonged to me. And no matter how hard the Romans tried, they could not steal what was mine.

I didn't know how much time passed before the guards opened my door and escorted me through a series of glaring corridors.

With every step, I bit down the urge to fight. I wouldn't let fear or ambition get the best of me. I would wait. Bide my time. Until a chance presented itself.

I would survive. No matter what, I would survive.

With or without magic.

I kept my eyes open, built a map in my head, made a list of places to run, to hide. Just in case.

They led me through a pair of iron doors that opened to reveal a dimly lit, cavernous room. At its center was a giant glass box, bigger than the courtyards of even the wealthiest of ministers.

The hall was spacious and airy, with domed ceilings that climbed so high they must have been built by giants, not mortals. Curved seamlessly in a way Pangu architecture had never managed. Beautiful sculptures stood atop mighty columns, carved in such vivid detail the fabric on their bodies looked like it might tremble under the slightest breeze. Men in armor and children with wings, dusted in gold that glistened under light. Everything was a marvel to behold, capable of stealing my breath if my body didn't sense danger from all sides, my fight-or-flight response activated to a degree I'd never experienced.

Because this time, I didn't have Death at my side, didn't have the invisible weapon that had protected me since my first heartbeat.

Baihu's words echoed. *Show them your powers when they ask, Ruying. Let them witness what you're capable of. That's the only way to survive here.*

The far wall held a glassed-off balcony. High above everything, its inhabitants overlooked the arena like emperors and kings. Arrogance curdled in their smirks.

The two men at the very front of the balcony made me pause. Pale and beautiful, clad in velvety suits embroidered with gold, red fabrics draped elegantly across their shoulders and down their backs like the capes of battlefield heroes. Though I doubt these men had ever done anything honorable or heroic. My eyes focused on the one to the left, the sharp features and dark curls, eyes of—

My heart caught in my throat like a silk ribbon, moments before snaring into tattered pieces.

Eyes, green as jade.

The boy from the night market, whose money I'd stolen.

The slender laurel wreath nestled in his dark curls was all I needed to know. The second prince of Rome. *Antony Augustus.*

And the man next to him, a face I recognized from my nightmares: Valentin Augustus. The first-born son of their late father.

While his brother's reputation preceded him, Antony Augustus was the opposite, quiet and elusive. The city whispered the reason he never left their side of the Fence was because he was disgusted by our kind, thought Xianlings a crime against nature. But not all rumors spiraled from truths, it seemed.

That kindness in his eyes when he placed a heavy gold coin in the hands of a desperate girl, and his look of awe and astonishment in the alleyway when he witnessed my magic, were far from disgust.

If anyone was disgusted by my people, by our magic, then it was his brother. Whose tally of victims grew longer and longer from the smallest of transgressions. Of the years Valentin Augustus had spent in my realm, not a single kind act—rumored or otherwise—came to mind.

When the younger prince's eyes drifted in my direction, I looked down quickly, hid my face under falling hair, hoping he wouldn't remember me.

I'll always protect you, Ruying . . . . Baihu's promise. But how much were his words worth against a prince of Rome? He said he could protect me, but even his powers had limitations. 狐假虎威: *Mighty as Baihu was in Jing-City, he was nothing but a fox flaunting the power of a tiger.*

Those two young men high in the balconies, they were the real tigers behind Baihu's fox.

I cursed myself for not heeding Grandma's warnings to stay away from the Romans. If I had kept myself small and stayed out of trouble, maybe none of this would have happened.

Maybe my name never would have ended up on Rome's list.

Arrogance and desperation had propelled me to steal that night. Now I must pay with my life.

I clenched my hands until nails bit flesh. I pressed the bracelets against my sides, rubbed them against my clothes, tried to work them loose for just a sliver of magic. Something to protect myself with.

But like fetching water with a wicker basket, it didn't matter how I struggled against the bracelets; magic did not flood back.

With Death's magic, I was a force to be reckoned with. A girl to be feared. Someone who didn't have to bow for the whims of any man.

Without it? I was just a girl.

Alone.

Lost.

Afraid.

No match for these men. No match against Rome.

They ushered me to a boxed-off waiting area just outside the glass arena. From this vantage, I saw the girl inside. On her knees, crying.

Translucent skin, hollowed eyes, dark veins that laced her hands—an addict. My heart lurched. *Meiya.* My first thought. Then, upon closer look, I realized the girl was too small to be my sister, her features too soft, like tender dough that had yet to be molded into shape.

"Your Gift is water?" a tall, slender man with an electronic tablet in hand asked from the balcony.

The girl was shaking, weeping. "I don't want to die," she whimpered. "Please, I don't want to die."

The words echoed in my heart.

A bowl of water was brought into the glass box. "Show us your talent. Impress us with your magic. Earn your right to live," the man replied, nonchalant. No sympathy. No emotion behind those deep-set eyes.

Then her bracelets beeped. A sharp yet beautiful sound. I leaned closer to the glass, eyes wide, afraid to blink because I didn't want to miss any of this.

The girl raised her hand, and water began dancing in midair to the will of her magic, like transparent serpents twisting and distorting. An ability to bend water.

Useful, but common.

Magic was bestowed randomly, and Gifts varied in startling magnitudes. By the will of the Gods, our Gifts were often as unique as we were, as the lines of our fingertips. This girl was born with the ability to move water, but another might be able to freeze water, another might evaporate water, and another might possess the ability to draw water from thin air. And somewhere out there was a rare talent who could do all four, if not more. There was no telling what someone's power might be, and what they might be capable of, if provided the right training.

No two Gifts operated in the same way, obeyed the same rules. This was why nobody knew how much *qi* burned with each use, not until a Xianling's dying breath.

My attention shifted up to the balcony—specifically, to the princes. From their impassive faces, they thought the same as me.

The older prince gave a subtle, almost annoyed shake of his head. The man typed something into his tablet.

The girl was dismissed without so much as a word.

"Wait!" she cried when guards entered the glass box and pulled her away. "Where are you taking me? What's going to happen to me? Please, I don't want to die! I don't want to—"

She was dragged through a pair of metal doors that opened and closed with a sound like swooshing ocean waves, her voice died in the distance.

My insides went tight, my ribs closing in like a clenched fist. I didn't know what awaited me on the other side of those doors. Something told me I didn't want to find out.

"Next!" the tall man cried.

The next Xianling was another girl, a little older than I was. Tanned skin and crescent green eyes that were sharp and alert, as if excited to be here. She kept her head low, but not in fear.

"My Gift is plants," she offered before the Romans had the chance to ask.

The older prince arched a brow at her boldness. Then, half a smile. With a wave of his hand, a soldier brought a pot containing a tiny, half-wilted sapling into the arena.

Her bracelets beeped once the soldier had safely stepped outside, the glass door closing behind him, locking her in. I noticed the sword at his hip, the card at his waist that opened and closed the doors, and the device with the ever-changing surface. I didn't know how it worked, but I knew whenever the tiny blue button at the top was pressed, the bracelets beeped and magic was returned to the intended person. Such a small thing, barely the size of his palm, quietly slipped into his pocket between uses.

The girl placed a hand on the dried branches. As promised, the wilted plant straightened and greened. Two heartbeats later, it was bursting with flowers, growing small, red berries under a now thick foliage.

Both of the princes smiled this time.

The elder prince gave a subtle nod, and the girl's face bloomed like a peony of spring, bright and luscious in elegant beauty.

The soldiers escorted her through another set of doors, made from a dark wood, on the other side of the arena.

When they opened, I caught sight of a wide corridor and an open window.

Blue skies, just beyond it.

13

"NEXT!"

A soldier pulled me forward.

I can walk. A string of furious curses burned my tongue, but I swallowed every one. Eyes on the ground, I stepped into the arena, and was immediately blinded by the stark white lights etched into the ceiling. The world outside of the box dimmed into near nothingness. Still, I noticed how one of the shadows high in the balcony straightened.

Antony Augustus.

The elder prince gave him a look of curiosity. Whispered something I didn't hear. Then he frowned, ever so slightly.

Prince Antony remembered me. He had to. The only question now was whether he planned on granting me a quick end or keeping me alive just to torture me.

I had stolen from him. I had committed a crime. A man like him, born in the lap of privilege, raised on entitlement, had probably killed for less.

I meekly bowed and did what was expected of me, what would please them the most. The easiest way to get someone to lower their guard is to present yourself as submissive. It was better to be underestimated than overestimated.

Grandma had taught me this.

Hold your breath, strike when they least expect it.

"Your power is Death?" the eldest prince asked. Curiosity turned into a skeptical crease between his brows.

I tensed. This was the first time I'd heard his voice. A deep sound, like thunderstorms and tidal waves. There was danger in the way he looked at me. A nonbeliever. Someone who feared what they didn't understand.

Too often, fear inspired violence.

I straightened my back. At least I had their attention.

"Show us what you can do," the prince added when I failed to provide a response. A snap of his fingers. Two soldiers dragged a young man out through the metal doors where the unwanted Xianlings went and threw him into the glass cage with me. "Kill him."

I jumped when the bracelets made a sharp *beep*. A sudden chill swept over me, and the magic returned so fast I almost lost my balance as colors regained their usual sharpness and Death's powers hummed deep in my bones once more. A murmuring heat as *qi* gathered at my fingertips, begging to be plucked. Memories of power, of Death's weightless high lingered in the back of my mind, urging me to give in, take just a little, to remember what it felt like to be strong, *powerful,* even in this room where I was no better than a caged animal.

You are the girl blessed by Death, a voice whispered from within me. *You could be a God if you simply . . . gave in.*

I curled and uncurled my fingers, relished how the warmth of Death chased away the cold of fear.

I dared to look up; the princes watched with eager anticipation. The eldest prince's face was a hound thirsty for blood, eyes animal-bright, while Prince Antony was calmer, stern in his gaze, unreadable. Neither was more comforting than the other.

"Kill him," Prince Valentin commanded from the balcony. "Kill him, or I will kill you."

Magic burned. I wished I could reach up and wrap his *qi* around my fingers like phantom threads, pull and tug until he bellowed with the horror so many of my kin must have felt within this monstrous cage. But there was something about these glass walls that constricted magic the same way the bracelets did.

At my silence, the guards around the cage tensed. Hands reached for the guns at their hips, ready to take me down if I didn't comply with the wishes of their prince.

"*Please,*" the boy begged through his gag. "Please, I don't want to die . . ."

He was young. Nearly the same age as me, if not a year or two younger. His skin was pale, his hair inky, his eyes red from crying. I saw the face of the first boy I had ever killed in those dark pools, brimmed with terror and tears.

"I don't want to die. I don't want to die . . ." He wept and wept, face scrunched and red as he shrank back.

"Me neither," I whispered as I moved closer. Step-by-step.

Ten soldiers were stationed around the glass box, each armed with swords and guns. That was too many eyes, too many bullets that could kill me over the slightest disobedience.

My attention darted to the wooden door, and thought of the blue skies just beyond it.

If I'm fast enough . . .

"Please." The boy kept on begging, kept on crying. His desperation made me want to cry, too.

He begged as if I had any say in this.

He begged as if I could let him live . . .

I didn't have such power. I was as helpless and trapped as he was. Surrounded by the might of science, my magic at their mercy. A mere ripple in the ocean.

The walls pushed in around me, my heart pounding at my throat, making me want to vomit as magic gathered hot at my fingertips.

Kill him. I could hear Death at my ear. *Show them what you can do. It is the only way to survive.*

"I'm not a God," I told him as I closed the distance between us. Pressed my hand against his cold cheek. Colors bled away until all that remained were a mirage of gray and the golden light of his *qi,* fluttering like silk strands, like the luring strings of a beautiful instrument begging to be played. "I can't save you. I can only save myself."

This is life or death.

I forced myself to think of blue skies. My sister's guilt. My grandmother's tears.

I couldn't die. Not without saying goodbye.

"I'm sorry," I whimpered, then *pulled.*

An ear-splitting shriek.

His energy fought me harder than the rest, indelible and resilient. Desperate to live.

I'm sorry I'm sorry I'm sorry I'm sorry I'm sorry I'm sorry I'm sorry I'm sorry I'm sorry I'm sorry I'm sorry I'm sorry I'm sorry I'm sorry I'm sorry . . .

The boy sank to his knees, a puddle of urine forming at his feet.

I pulled harder, and a current tore through my body, feral as ten thousand beating wings, all but knocking me off my feet as it raced into Death's arms.

Something else slipped through my fingers, too. The boy's energy took something from me just as I took from him. Fragments of my life, minutes and hours, shaved off with every offering to Death. Nothing in life was free, or without consequences.

Magic gave with one hand and took with the other.

My chest quaked as his light dulled, and his shrieks quieted. Faint shades of his soul began to surface, a color somewhere between blue and green. I had taken enough. Any more and he would die.

The men above us watched in marvel.

Tears burned my eyes.

Enough. I pulled back before the last flicker of life bled from him.

The boy fell, unconscious. The men above us clapped—a thunderous applause, excited by the prospects of their shiny new toy.

The bracelet beeped once more, and soldiers marched into the box to take his body away, to escort me through the far wooden doors.

I let them come close. When one placed a hand on my shoulders, I pretended to sway on my feet so that I had an excuse to lean into his warm body, slip my hand inside the pocket, and palm the remote that controlled my fate.

The Gods gave you a Gift for a reason.

I looked up at the princes' elated faces. I could smell their hunger, hear their insatiable greed rumbling, as they pictured all the ways they wanted to use me against my own people. Terrifying thoughts that made me want to rip this monstrous power from my veins, kill the beast beneath my flesh and bone so nobody could have it.

You were born to kill, child. Death's voice. *It's about time you stopped running from your own potential, Ruying. Embrace it.*

Now that Rome knew what I could do, they would never let me go. They would make me the killer Grandma had always feared I would become.

"Please!" the half-conscious boy mumbled. "I don't want to die . . ."

Me neither.

With that thought, I pushed through the tears, the fears, the stunned guards too distracted by the murmuring of a supposedly dead boy, and ran.

A click of the button and the bracelets fell silent, allowing magic to flood back.

"Don't shoot!" somebody shouted as I dove past the guards who reached for me, stealing an ornamental sword in the process. To my relief, the thing was sharp and real and not just for decoration. "I want her alive!" Another guard bolted for me. I ducked under his arms and swung my sword upward at his throat the way Grandma had taught me.

Metal carved open flesh and veins, and blood poured down raw, hot, and pungent as it devoured me. My stomach heaved, and bile climbed up my throat.

I forced my body to keep moving as I tore the card that controlled the doors from his waist.

I'd clean the blood off later.

First, I had to get out of here alive.

14

Loaded with stolen energy, I found my body lighter and stronger as I dashed through the doors and down the echoing corridor, so fast I felt like I was flying toward the blue skies on the other side.

Freedom was cold, fresh air filling my lungs, more delicious than anything I'd ever tasted.

"Get her!" somebody bellowed from behind.

The corridor was guarded by two men; both startled when they saw me. Wide eyes took me in, surprised and confused.

Before they could snap into action, I pushed Death out and called for their *qi*, pulling hard. One of them stumbled and fell to his knees while the other man's energy remained stubborn, holding on to life with everything it had. He reached for his gun just as I swung my sword, slashing a sharp line under his jaw, deep enough to draw blood and inspire panic, but not enough to kill. Something Grandma had taught me many years before. A skill she hoped I would never have to use.

Keep running, I told myself when the man collapsed like his friend, clutching his throat, blood pouring fast like a river.

Killer. Killer. Killer. These mocking words rang in my ears. *You were born to be a killer.*

Those scholarly books about magic said it was like any muscle, one that would strengthen only with exercise and use. Already, I could feel it pumping warm and tingling, infusing my body with energy until I was drunk with power.

The fables were right; magic was truly an intoxicating rush. Finally I understood why Xianlings died young. Why people threw away years of their lives to linger in this exhilarating high. Why Meiya couldn't pull herself away from the clutches of opian.

This was power. *True* power.

I smiled. As Death himself intended. As I was born to—

A shot pierced the air. A bullet whizzed past, missing me by an inch.

Bang. Another gunshot.

I pushed my legs faster, reaching my hands out. Freedom was so close I could smell it, feel the—

I cried as a bullet tore through my right thigh and sent me tumbling. One shaking knee collided against the hard ground just as somebody grabbed me by the throat and smashed my face against the cold tiles. I gasped for air, but it only made him shove me harder, until I couldn't breathe.

I caught a glimpse of his young eyes and sullen face. The soldier whom I had almost killed at the night market. *Not you again.*

I reached for magic—seconds before something zapped through me and tore Death from my fingertips.

My magic vanished, just like that.

The bracelets tightened, and a sharp, burning pain shot up through my bones. The same pain I had felt in the cells when I first got there, when I had tried to claw my way out of that hellish space to save Taohua. I didn't want to cry, didn't want to give them the satisfaction, but the next second, all I heard was my shrieking voice. My body convulsed like a dying fish, like Taohua had when she refused to behave. My head banged against the stone-cold floor, jerked and thrashed so violently I thought my bones might shatter.

This might be the end.

"Filthy mudlings," the man who held me spat at my face. There was bloodlust in his eyes, for revenge and for pain, to pay back everything I did to him at the night market.

My insides tightened. I hungered for magic, hungered for the power to snuff out his life like a candle. *I should have killed you when I had the chance.*

But all I managed to choke out was, "I don't want to die," an echo of that boy's pleas. Without magic, fear quickly replaced courage.

My vision blurred. I couldn't concentrate on anything but the shuddering pain.

It felt like I was being burned alive.

I shouldn't have run. It was stupid, it was—

In the distance, there was laughter.

The eldest prince came to kneel before me, a remote in hand, wheat-blond curls framing his face. A victorious grin slashed his face from cheek to cheek. A face so beautiful, yet deadly.

He's going to kill me.

The prince laughed, a finger caressing my bruised cheek. "You thought it would be that easy? Who do you think you're up against? We are not like the puny traffickers of your world. We are *Roman*. We are the masters of science, and we are your new Gods."

The prince snapped his fingers, and a soldier handed something to him.

A syringe.

I recognized the incandescent contents as liquid opian, the newest drug of the Lotus Tower.

"Time to teach you a lesson, little girl. A talent like yours might be too rare to be killed, but I also can't keep you around like a liability." Then he leaned in closer and added, in a quiet whisper, "Especially when Antony has already claimed you. A weapon such as yourself at his side? I can't let brother dearest have everything he wants, can I? Don't worry, this doesn't hurt. Quite the opposite; it's going to feel good. So good you'd rather die than live without it."

"No!" I tried to shout over the pain, tried to writhe myself free from the soldier's giant hands, but he was too strong. Without magic, I didn't stand a chance.

No.

Please no.

I knew what the drug had done to my father, what it had done to my sister. Once I was under its influence, I'd never be able to break it. Opian would become all that I craved, all that I knew. The rest of my life would fade to nothing. I'd become Rome's toy. I'd . . .

I wept.

"Please, don't. I'll behave. I'll do whatever you tell me to. Just don't . . . *please.*"

"You should have thought of that before you tried to run." The elder prince placed a hand on my throat, pressed the icy tip of the syringe against my jugular. I could smell its sickly-sweet fragrance. Fear burned my insides like acid, tears pooled against the marble floor, the vicious tempo of my drumming heart pounded in my ears. "What a shame. Such a pretty little face. Maybe I'll have some fun with you before I send you to the labs."

"Valentin," a new voice interjected, stern, firm. "That is not necessary. I told you, this one is mine."

A sneer, but the prince's hand relaxed, the pain stopped, and the chilling needle of the syringe was removed from my throat. "She's too dangerous like this. If we don't make her an addict, who knows how we'll be able to control something like her, *Brother.*"

"That's up to me to decide. Not you. I have use for her, and I want her lucid."

The eldest prince, Valentin, gave his brother an incredulous look, but relented. "Keep a close eye on her. I don't want her causing trouble around the city. And if anything happens because of your foolish mercy, know that I won't hesitate to report it to our grandfather."

Prince Antony flashed a slow, calculated smile. "I expect nothing less from you, *Brother.*"

15

THEY LOCKED ME IN A cell, surrounded by walls dark with mold, the only light that bled in was the artificial electrical ones, making it impossible to mark the passage of time. They didn't send a doctor to check the slow-bleeding bullet wound on my thigh. I made makeshift bandages out of the rags they called clothes and tried to be careful. Hoped it would heal. But without proper medicine and treatment, an infection soon nested itself around the raw, pus-filled flesh. Heat crept up my body, flushed my face until I was drowsy and weak.

In and out, I breathed, consciousness ebbing and flowing like shallow tides. I prayed for my body to heal itself, prayed for a chance to live. Prayed to the Gods I no longer believed in, prayed to any God who would listen . . . Even those I hated.

This would not be how I died.

Through the dark, I kept breathing, kept opening my eyes, kept repeating my name, remembering where I was. I made myself picture the people who would miss me if I died.

Meiya.

Grandma.

Taohua.

Perhaps even Baihu, in his own, twisted way.

"I'm not going to die." I forced the words into the bitter air. *I am the girl blessed by Death. If I intend to live, nothing can stop me.*

Were these truths to be believed or words of hope, destined to shatter?

Death might be my patron, but he owed me nothing. To him, my life was just like any other: a fruit waiting to be harvested. Whether I'd live long enough to swell with the sweet juice of life or be tragically picked sour and early like too many Xianlings before me was a question only he could answer.

Time passed. I kept praying, kept reminding myself of all the reasons I had to live.

When footsteps sounded, I knew a God had answered my prayers.

But he wasn't the God I wanted.

"You're alive." Pale green eyes regarded me through the iron bars that kept me caged like an animal.

Antony Augustus. The second prince of Rome.

Was he here to gloat, to delight in my pain? Was this the price of daring to steal his gold days, weeks, maybe even months earlier? Time slipped through my fingers like water. I had no recollection of how long it had been since I was taken. All I knew was that it felt like an eternity of torment.

"You know, all of this would have been a lot easier if you hadn't tried to escape and severely injured some of my guards in the process," he said, looking around the cell. "I didn't want us to start off on the wrong foot. My father used to tell me we attract more bees with honey, so this wasn't how I wanted our second meeting to progress. But you left me no choice after that little escape attempt."

"What are you doing here?" I asked, my voice wispy.

"Is that how you're going to greet me? You should thank me after I forced my brother to spare your life, not make you an addict. I've seen what opian does to your people, how they lose themselves in its borrowed bliss, the hunger that devours their minds. Once you get a taste, it will be all that you crave, all that you can think about. The addiction will make you forget your name, forget your family and friends, everyone who loves you and everyone whom you love. I've watched the strongest of warriors turn into performing monkeys, dancing to my brother's whims."

"Are you here to kill me?" I didn't have time for whatever game he was playing.

He chuckled. "No."

"Take revenge?"

His head tilted, and amusement twinkled in those pale eyes. "No, unfortunately. Though you did steal a lot of money from me. If this was Rome, I could put you in jail for a very long time."

"I *have* been in jail for a very long time," I murmured, gesturing at our surroundings.

"I can make it longer if you insist on making things harder for yourself."

My lips creased, though not with a smile. "I know. In Jing-City, you can kill me with your bare hands and not suffer a single consequence, because you are a Roman. And I'm not."

"You don't like me."

"Should I like you?"

"I saved you from my brother."

"You saved me because you didn't want me to become his weapon. You said it yourself; that drug would have consumed me. I would be a dog, willing to lick the boots of whoever gives me my next dose, wouldn't I? And a dog who is not loyal is not a dog you'd want around."

A shadow of a smile. "You are smart."

"Did you assume I was stupid?" I retorted. I strained not to tell him that I was raised by one of the smartest women Er-Lang Empire had ever seen, the woman behind one of our most decorated generals, before history forgot his name. "Tell me why you are here."

The smile deepened. "I'm here to offer you a chance to live. You want to live, don't you, Yang Ruying?"

I swallowed the lump in my throat, and my heart beat a little too fast when he said my name, so gentle, so benevolent.

More than anything. The promise of life lured me, but I refused to let him know. "At what price?"

A throaty laugh that was somewhere between an exhale and a sneer. "Do you know why you're still alive?" He came closer, wrapped his arms around the cell bars, and watched me like a hawk would prey. But I wasn't his prey. Not yet. There was something he wanted from me, which meant I wasn't powerless in this exchange. The playing field might not be level the way he'd engineered it, but at least I had something.

A single bargaining chip. One I would play to my full advantage.

"Tell me, Yang Ruying, what are you willing to die for?"

My sister's smile, my grandmother's warm hands, cupping mine. I straightened. "You are asking the wrong question, my prince." I spoke slowly, words sweet. He would like a docile victim. Grandma had also taught me how one caught more flies with honey than vinegar. Too bad I didn't want flies. I wanted this false God's beating heart, clutched in my hands.

"What is the right question, then?"

"You shouldn't ask the girl blessed by Death whom she'll die for. You should ask her whom she'll *kill* for."

Again, his head tilted. I had his attention. "Letting you live isn't enough?"

It was, but I was greedy. I wanted more. If he desired my magic enough, he would give me whatever I asked. I just had to present the deal in a way that made him think he had the better end of the bargain.

"No, it's not enough. Especially if I have to betray my people, my land, my Empire. Death is a powerful kind of magic, one that comes with unfathomable responsibilities. In the wrong hands, a Gift like mine can ruin worlds."

A monster like him, or his brothers, would use it to burn Er-Lang to ashes.

I eyed his strong yet elegant arms, casually looped through the iron bars, without fear of what I might do to him.

"You think highly of your magic," he said.

"You've seen what I can do. If you're smart, you would, too."

"Are you bargaining with me?"

"So what if I am?"

That smile grew wicked across his face. "I don't know what you want, but I know what you *don't* want: to watch your sister and grandmother suffer for your foolish stubbornness."

My heart jerked at the mention of my family. "Are they alive? What did you do to them?"

"They are alive and well. And whether they continue to remain alive and well, that is dependent on your cooperation."

"You're blackmailing me?"

"So what if I am?" The prince licked his lips. "Two can play this game. I don't know who you think I am, but in the words of your people, 我不是省油的灯. *I am not a lamp that will save oil for you.* I'm not someone so easily manipulated."

I was surprised by his perfect pronunciation of my language.

Across Er-Lang, many of my people learned his language, but few of his ever learned ours. Especially not those of the nobility. Of power. They had translators for a reason.

"It wasn't hard, asking around about you. A trip to the pawnshop you frequent was all that was required to learn everything there is to know about you, your grandmother, and your sister. The fallen descendants of a once glorious clan. When you and your sister were—"

"I swear, if you so much as touch a hair on her—" His words were a trap, and I had run right into it. When I jumped to my feet, a shot of burning electricity buzzed through my wrists. I fought back a wince when my body was sent crashing against the stone tiles and I landed on my bad leg.

I bit back the tears. I would not cry in front of him. I would not cry in front of any of them.

"That's not fair," I snarled, noticing the small remote in his hand.

The pain subsided slowly, but something lingered like an aftershock in my muscles.

"Life isn't fair, darling."

I should know better than to fight with a prince who could kill me as easily as snapping his fingers. Yet, here I was, foolish as ever. Playing with the tiger's whiskers, tempting Death.

I wanted to kill him. I wanted to reach out of this cell and grab him by his shirt and smash his pretty little face against these stones to see how he liked it.

Anger festered like slow-spreading poison, curled between my ribs like tiny serpents, writhing tight. Even without Death's temptations at my ear, his hunger haunting my every thought, I wanted to make this man whimper, make him fear, make him weep as he begs for his life.

This prince who saw himself as something superior, who looked down at me with that stomach-turning smirk, deserved the Death I carried.

I will kill him, I promised myself. *I am the girl blessed by Death, and I will see this man on his knees before me. I will be the reason he dies.*

But these bracelets of science around my wrists, the lack of magic in my veins, and the fever in my leg told a different story. It would take a miracle for me to walk out of this cell alive, much less kill a prince of Rome.

He sighed. "Relax. I have no interest in your sister and will continue not to have interest in her if you do as I say. I don't want to hurt you. The sooner you stop fighting me, the easier things will become."

"You mean as long as I submit to you, do as you say like a trained dog who barks on command?" I sneered as my body finally collapsed to the ground, worn to the point of exhaustion.

I had no power in this bargain, even if I had something he wanted. Nothing would stop him simply taking it from me.

I had nothing.

I *was* nothing.

"You don't have to be here, Yang Ruying. I can change your life if you'd let me. Nice quarters. Your family safe and provided for. Food, shelter, more money than you know what to do with. I can give you everything you've ever wanted, make great things happen for you, for your family. There's so much more to life than struggling to survive. Don't you want that?" He looked around the tiny cell, his voice became quiet and soothing when he continued. "I want your magic, something you can grant. And you want the survival of your family, something I can make happen. I assume your grandmother has told you plenty of bleak stories, warned you of the dangers that lurk in darkness? An elderly lady and an opian addict won't survive the hardships ahead."

Tears pricked like tiny needles behind my eyes. I held them back, but desperation was heavy, and it pulled me down like a drowning current.

My heart bled because his cruel reminders were true.

War was barbaric and violent. To protect my family, I needed him more than he needed me.

"Your proposition?" I asked, finally lowering my head in defeat.

His smile turned dangerous. "A deal that will benefit us both. I'm not Valentin. I don't want Pangu and all of its inhabitants burned to ashes to build a second Rome on stolen lands."

I frowned, incredulous. I had expected the young prince to have his eyes on something more trivial. Like power, or the throne. I had expected him to ask for the murder of his brother, or Er-Lang's young Emperor, or even the Phantom. "You want to *help* us?"

"I want to save both our worlds. And in order to do that, yes, I need your help."

"How? I know nothing of your world's politics, and I have no power, no influence in mine."

"You might not have status, but you have something much more valuable: magic. My brothers have supporters in Rome, but I can take care of politics on that side of the Veil. What I need is someone who can eliminate any triggers of war on *this* side."

"You want me to kill the Phantom?"

The prince shook his head. "The rebels calling for Er-Lang to rise up are pesky, but revolutionaries have existed at every point in history and have rarely toppled Empires. They are not a threat. At least, not yet. What I'm concerned about is the Emperor."

The new Emperor was young, his mind malleable. "So you want me to kill the advisors who are influencing him?"

A slight tilt of his lips, half-impressed, half-surprised. "You might be a little too smart for your own good, Yang Ruying."

My lips thinned. Killing the ministers and the advisors who wished for Er-Lang to stand up against Rome's tyranny would only prolong Rome's rule over us, give them time to amass more power and plant their roots like a parasite around the Empire's veins, sucking life out of us like vengeful demons.

I closed my eyes.

But he had a point, in a way. It would prevent war, keep peace balanced at knife's edge for a little longer. It would give Grandma the chance to live out her final years in some semblance of normality.

A life on our knees is no life at all. But Meiya was wrong. A life on our knees was better than Death.

"I know you don't like me, but trust me, I am the best option you have right now."

I sneered. "You Romans are all the same."

"Maybe in your eyes we are. And maybe there's nothing I can say to make you trust me, but I want to keep Pangu safe from those who wish to exploit it. I have watched enough people suffer to last a lifetime. I can't watch Rome's greed poison your world the way it did ours. I don't want us to be enemies, Yang Ruying. I can be your ally if you'll let me."

His words were sweet, but I knew politics. I recognized lies when I heard them, saw manipulation when it clouded my eyes. I knew better than to trust a Roman. "A man like you won't be satisfied by the happiness of *other* people. The survival of my world isn't all that you want, right?"

An arched brow. He leaned forward, eyes fixated on me as if I were a poem he longed to decipher. "What kind of man do you think I am, then?"

"Someone who is ambitious. Someone who is selfish. Someone who wants to topple his brothers and claim the throne for himself. This is the oldest story in the book. Pangu has princes, too. I've heard enough stories about these games of power between entitled young men and their egos to recognize it."

A shrug, feigned innocence. "So what if I want power? What better way to protect our two worlds than by becoming the ruler of Rome? To have your family under the protection of the most powerful man in our two realms sounds ideal, doesn't it? I can covet power and wish for peace at the same time. Ambition and morality aren't mutually exclusive."

"But if you fail, your brother will kill me *and* my family."

"If Valentin inherits the throne, your family won't be the only ones who'll end up dead, I can assure you. The whole of Pangu will suffer for it. But at least we won't be lonely in the afterlife. Am I right?"

I hated how he had an answer for everything, and how everything he said had its point.

"良禽择木而栖, 贤臣择主而事," he continued. "*Wise birds nest on the branch of strong trees, and wise minds serve under strong masters.*"

I didn't like the way my people's proverb poured from his lips with such smooth cadence. "You know a lot about Er-Lang's literature."

"If I'm here, then I should take the initiative to understand your people, your culture. 知人知己, as your people would say it. *Know others like you know yourself.*"

He was calculating, smart. Not someone I wanted as an enemy.

Because if he could give me power, he could also take it away. Build me up then tear me down with a snap of his fingers. If I took this deal, I would live by his mercy, exist as a sword at his side, a puppet to be commanded.

Heroes die. Cowards live.

In order to do the right thing, to be on the right side of history, I first had to survive.

"I have three conditions."

"Go on."

"Magic has a price. I can only kill so many people for you, and I—"

"Our agreement isn't forever. Only until I've amassed the power I need to convince my grandfather of a better solution, or until I'm named Heir. Whichever comes first."

"And if I die before that happens, you'll still take care of my sister and grandmother in my absence. Think of it as compensation for my death."

"Scared I'll stab you in the back?" he said with a laugh. "Such a promise is given. Stay loyal to me, and I'll be loyal to our agreement. What's the third condition?"

"I want you to let Taohua go."

"Taohua?"

"The girl who fought your men at the night market. The daughter of General Ma."

"The girl warrior?" He hesitated. "Why?"

"What's more important, her Gift or mine? Which power is rarer?"

To ask for what wasn't given was a bold move, but I couldn't just forget about Taohua. She had helped me too many times to count. This was nothing compared to all that she'd done for me.

"Very well, I will see what I can do," he said.

"No," I replied. "I don't want you to try. I want you to promise me that you will let her go home, and no one will ever touch her, or her family, again."

The edge of his left eye creased ever so slightly, as if amused that I was bargaining with him. Finally, he nodded. "Very well. As you wish."

I tried not to grin, not to laugh, and instead hid it all under a gratified exhale.

"But first, I need to make sure you're worth this bargain," he continued.

"Why? You've seen my Gift with your own eyes. You know what I'm capable of."

"Yes, I know the strength in your magic, but what about you?"

"What about me?"

"Are you strong enough to wield such magic? Because all I've seen so far is weakness, hesitation. You spared Dawson's life, and you spared that boy in the glass cage. You even spared the guards, who would have done anything to kill you. You've shown mercy at every turn, as if you were afraid of your own potential, of all that you could become. I need to know whether that is merely kindness or a form of weakness. Can you wield the extraordinary Gift that has manifested within your body, or are you just a girl given more than she can handle?"

My jaw tightened. I didn't say anything because he was right. I had shown mercy—even to the soldiers, whose throats I had made sure to cut just deep enough to hinder, but not deep enough to mortally wound.

Death was cruel, and it was permanent. I didn't know those men. They might work for the enemy, but that wasn't a reason to kill in cold blood.

So I didn't.

Yet it seemed even these small mercies were luxuries I could no longer afford.

"Rome isn't like Er-Lang, Yang Ruying. We don't keep what's obsolete just for the sake of it. If you're not of use to me, I will dispose of you without hesitation."

"Then how do I prove myself to you?"

A slow, deliberate smile. One that sent shivers down my back.

Stupid question.

"We are going on a trip to your side of the city tomorrow, after my doctors fix you up."

"I don't think my wound will heal in a single day."

"Oh, honey, you have no idea what kind of scientific marvels exist on my side of the Veil, do you? You won't be fully healed, but you will be up on your feet within hours." He leaned closer once more. "Do as I say, prove you're capable of following orders. Once you're one of us, I will show you a whole world of impossibilities in time, my darling."

"And if I can't?"

His eyes turned warm, kind.

Was this warm, flickering mercy real, or was it part of an act?

"Let's hope you don't have to find out."

16

WAR HAD NO MERCY. I came from a long line of generals and soldiers, raised by one of the greatest strategists of her generation. I knew this, better than anyone.

The privilege of being able to choose was something I'd never possess no matter how Antony Augustus tried to convince me otherwise. Not really.

I'm not betraying my people, I told myself. *I'm protecting them. There is a difference.*

There *had* to be a difference.

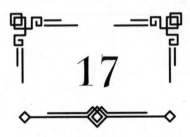

17

My city wept. For its missing, for its dead, and for the survivors who marched on in the wake of tragedy and loss. Apparently only seven days had passed since Rome's men raided the capital and took me in the night.

It felt like seven years.

Xianlings were scarce before the reaping; magic had slipped from our veins generation by generation. Now, the city had fewer than ever. And without magic, what weapons did we have against the might of science? My sister wanted to fight, but with what? With hope and optimism and beautifully bloomed words that inspired revolution?

Such fragile things, too easily shattered under Rome's bullets.

Tears stinging, I watched my city mourn through the tinted windows of Antony Augustus's car: a sleek construction of metal and glass, slithering like a serpent between narrow streets. Crowds parted for him like oceans parting for the dragons of legends. Mortals kneeling in his presence, as if he were something to be worshipped.

My hands lay clenched in my lap.

Our once noble magic. Our once imperial history. They felt so small and insignificant now, things that only existed in Grandma's stories.

Acceptance sank, storm gray clouded a once cerulean sky.

"If only they knew how close their lost loved ones are . . ." I whispered, watching mothers howl for their children on the streets, orphans with half-drawn sketches search for parents.

"They would die if they tried to breach Roman grounds and take back what they've lost. Valentin will kill anyone who leaks this information." In other words, if I wanted to live, I best keep this a secret.

"Does the Er-Lang Emperor know?"

Antony was quiet for a beat. "He keeps one eye open and one eye closed. 睁一只眼，闭一只眼, as your people say."

"So he chooses to do nothing?"

"He is wise for choosing to do nothing," Antony retorted. Defensive.

"What hold do you have over our Emperor?" I asked him the very question I had asked the sun and the moon and our beautiful, fractured sky a thousand times before. "Your people continue to commit atrocities against mine, while our Emperor sits idle and does nothing. Why?"

The prince's smile was slow, beautiful. Achingly so. The smile of a demon, smug with the kinds of secrets someone as insignificant and lowly as me would never know.

Watching him made my blood boil, so I tore my gaze away from both him and the horrors beyond the tainted glass.

Monsters.

The Romans were truly monsters.

As if reading my mind, Antony turned to me, eyes gentle and warm as if hoping for me to see something in him that didn't exist. "Like you, we do what we must to survive."

Maybe these words were meant to inspire sympathy, dilute my anger, but the only thing I felt was my blood burning hotter. "Which part of this can be justified as *must*?" The words slipped from my lips before I could stop myself, before I could break this anger into manageable pieces and tuck them into their own separate compartments where they wouldn't cause trouble. "Why did you take us? What does Rome want?"

The prince said nothing. His silence marked the end of our conversation.

The car stopped, and our doors opened.

I stepped out and faced the red gates of the Lotus Tower, its lanterns bright even in daylight.

"There are a few things I need to take care of," the prince told me as we entered, not by the main entrance but through a doorway nested in the shadows of a nearby alleyway. Narrow and dark, hidden from sight. The door opened onto a well-lit stairwell, one of polished wood and vivid red carpet. "Dawson, take Miss Yang to the suite. I will be there as soon as I'm done."

Dawson was the guard whom I almost killed at the night market. Did he follow Prince Antony everywhere he went? If so, just my luck that Prince Antony's shadow was a man who so clearly wanted me dead for almost killing him.

Too bad he couldn't touch me. Not while I had the prince's favor.

Not while the prince needed my magic.

Wordlessly, he led me through the corridors to a private room on the top floor, high above the foyer and all of its iniquities.

The world felt quieter up here. Tranquil, almost. So far from the sorrows and the grief of my people.

The space was neat and beautiful, with Roman-styled furniture instead of ours. Velvet chairs, tables of metal and thick panels of glass. The door closed behind me, and I was alone once more.

A pause.

I listened, surveyed the space. Then I bolted for the window and pushed it open.

I could jump out and run. But where would I run to?

Home? The prince would know to look for me there. If I went home now, I would only bring Death to those I loved.

No matter how desperately I longed for home, for my loved ones, I couldn't risk it. Not with demons hot on my heels.

I'd made my choice. I had dared to bargain with a Roman, and now I had to pay the price.

The door slid open with a soft swish. "Ruying?"

I looked up, thinking it was the prince coming to join me. But when I turned, I saw Baihu, his face ghostly pale.

He flinched when our eyes met. Then they watered, so full of concern my heart almost broke there and then. "Are you okay?"

Tears welled. How badly I wanted to run into his arms, bury my face in his chest, feel the warmth of him wrapped around me, and cry, *Help me!*

"We don't have much time," he whispered. "I asked Antony here as a decoy, we—"

Before he could finish, the door opened once more and Prince Antony walked in. Ever-observant eyes darted between us. "The two of you know each other?" His voice was smooth, the perfect performance of unaware innocence.

"No," I said before Baihu could respond.

The prince smiled. He walked right up to me, touched my cheek with his fingertips and brushed away the stray tear I didn't know had fallen. "You may leave now," he said to Baihu, without taking his eyes off me. "Leave the documents with Dawson."

Baihu hesitated. But in the end, with one last longing gaze, he turned and left.

I bit back the stinging behind my eyes. I refused to shed another tear. Not in front of Antony.

As soon as Baihu was gone, I pushed the prince away.

He laughed. "Come, sit." He gestured at the table, made himself comfortable, then pushed the window open farther. A breath of cold air engulfed the room, along with the bustling noises of the street below. "You know, for a genetically advanced species with unlimited magic at your disposal, one'd assume your civilization to be something more impressive, more advanced. Yet, everything here is so simple, the way my world was a thousand years ago," he mused. "I guess when you have magic, things like technology and scientific discoveries wouldn't be high on your list of priorities. Instead of creating tools to solve problems, your people simply used magic. A convenience in the beginning, but detrimental to your growth in the long run."

I followed his eyes, scanned the civilians with their eyes still wet from all that we'd lost. The smell of smoke lingered. In the distance, I could hear chaos from the direction of the Fence that separated our side of the city from theirs, separated children from mothers.

Cries for justice.

Cries for help, not knowing that these false Gods would never help us, and were in fact the ones inflicting our torments.

"You almost can't blame my people for what we are doing," Antony continued. "Fighting machine guns with bows and arrows? Isn't it hilarious, how unbalanced our positions are? Nature has a preferred order, you know. Evolution. If you don't evolve and keep your place in the food chain, then you get eliminated."

My jaw tightened. 落后就要挨打. *If you fall behind, then it is your fault when they beat you to a pulp.* Another saying that echoed between these ancient, mournful streets.

I couldn't tell if the haughty way he spoke was part of his nature or if he was deliberately needling me. "Just because we don't engage in science, it doesn't mean we are any less intelligent," I said, my words cold and venomous—a quiet reminder that my people weren't always the sickly prey for him to mock as he pleased. "Maybe the reason we don't have your weapons of mass destruction is because we've never needed them. Perhaps, despite our own greed and wars, we are not as far removed from our humanity as you are."

His eyes narrowed, expression half-annoyed, half-amused. "And where is this magic now? I've lived in Er-Lang for almost three years and, aside from you, nothing has impressed me. I came to Pangu expecting to have my mind blown, to kneel at the feet of some superior species. But as it turned out, *we* are the Gods *you've* knelt for."

"If you think so little of my world and my people, then why don't you leave?" I dared to ask. Half taunt, half genuine question.

Everyone knew how the Romans had arrived, everybody knew how they had forced themselves into our lives and stayed not as guests but as feared tyrants on our own lands, but nobody knew what they had stayed *for*. Endless speculation and rumors circulated behind cupped hands: how the Romans were here for our gold and silver and jewels and grains. Others said they were here for our magic, all those workers recruited from rural villages with promises of better lives and gold. A life of luxury in a world that didn't possess magic, where they'd be revered and worshipped. All of those wide-eyed dreamers and desperate seekers, taken back to the Roman side of the realm, never to be heard from again.

Or, was it something else altogether?

Like you, we do what we must to survive.

The Romans wanted something from us, and it wasn't the political alliance they had claimed over two decades ago.

Perhaps if we knew what it was that they wanted we could get rid of them without inciting a war. A peaceful solution—one that would spare my homeland from ruin.

To my surprise, the prince's face softened. "You are angry."

"Of course I am. Those people you are insulting are my ancestors."

A pause, then Antony nodded. "I'm sorry. I spoke without thinking. I should have considered your feelings."

An apology? From a prince of Rome? I blinked, unsure if I had imagined it.

He quickly looked away, and whatever guilt I saw vanished, just like that. "Your people's magic used to be stronger, I heard."

"Yes, our magic has been . . . *weaker* these past generations. Xianlings are becoming rarer, too. Not just in Er-Lang, but across the continent."

If we could return Er-Lang to its former glory, perhaps one day the Romans would be the ones kneeling—for us.

"Why?" he asked.

"If we knew why, your people wouldn't be here." *If we knew why, I wouldn't be here, entertaining your ignorance,* I wanted to add.

His lips tilted at the corner. "You lack control."

"That's because ever since your people burned down the Wucai temples and the Monks disappeared there has been no one to teach us how to properly harness our Gifts."

"I heard, once upon a time, that people used to fear Xianlings. Hunted you, even. That this is why the Wucai temples were established, to teach Xianlings how to control their magic, so that magic and humanity could exist in harmony."

He was right.

If I were born in the warmer days before the war, before Rome's intrusion, I would have been sent there. Learned how to harness Death's magic under proper tutelage and guidance, so that I might one day control it instead of fear it.

"How did you learn to use your powers, then?"

"Through books. Through my grandmother's tutelage. Through a sheer will not to die."

"That's all?"

"That's all."

He nodded, considering. "I've already seen your Gift at work, so let's try something else today." He scanned the crowd. "See the tall man in blue, with the broken nose and the scar across his left brow?"

"What about him?" I spotted the person he was talking about. An average-looking man with bronze skin and big hands, a slight frown as he leaned against the beam of an opposing building, a bun in his hand. From his linen clothes and muddied nails, I assumed him to be a laborer on his lunch break. Someone who slung bags of grain before shop fronts.

"I want you to kill him."

I flinched. "Why?"

"Your job is to do as I say, not ask questions." Antony handed me a gun and made me point it down at the hustling crowd below. My chest suddenly felt constricted, my ribs closing in on me until every breath became a struggle.

I stared at the man. A stranger. Someone whose life I knew nothing of. Someone who didn't do anything wrong except catch the wrong eyes at the wrong moment.

Every time I'd used my powers, hurt people, it was because I had to. Because it was them or me. But this? This was different. Down there, that man didn't do anything to deserve this.

"I can't," I murmured. "Not like this."

"You will have to get used to killing innocent, perhaps even good people, if you want to work for me. Don't make this harder for yourself. I need to know I can count on you if I'm to make you my ally. Trust me, Ruying, if you don't pass this test, you won't like what I have planned next."

Though his expression was hard and focused—what you'd expect of the cruel prince my world had imagined him and his brothers to be—his eyes were anything but. Patient, wet; he looked at me like a pleading boy. As if he were telling the truth, that he didn't want me to know the consequences of disappointing him.

My hand shook when I raised the gun, tried to aim it down at the man who was a stranger. Who could be someone's loyal brother, someone's doting father, someone's beloved son, someone's lifeline.

But he could also be hateful, a fruit rotten from the inside.

I thought of my own father.

Finger on the trigger, I wanted to pull, to fire the bullet and let all of this be over.

But like always, I hesitated.

From the corner of my eye I watched Antony watch me. What would happen if I turned the gun on him? What would that do?

Nothing. If I so much as touched a hair on a Roman prince's head, it would mean Death for not just me, but everyone I loved.

"Do as I say," he repeated in warning.

I tried to focus, tried to will my body into obeying his command. "No," I said. "I can't."

Antony sighed, disappointment and resignation clear across his face. "I really hoped you wouldn't fail this test."

"I'm not going to kill an innocent man over nothing! Show me one of your enemies instead."

"That's not what I'm asking of you."

"But who am I—who are *you*—to decide who lives and who dies down there? We are not Gods. We cannot treat other lives as flowers to be plucked from a field."

His eyes hardened. "Aren't we?" With that, Antony took a second gun from his holster and fired. "With your powers, you can be anything you wish to be. Even a God."

A brief beat of stunned silence. Then . . .

Screams.

Antony closed the window before I saw the bloody aftermath. He snatched back his gun, forgotten in my clenched hands. "And for your information, that man *was* one of my enemies. He is a follower of the Phantom. He and his little group of rebels have been spying on me, plotting to steal weapons from Rome's armory. An offense my brothers and grandfather won't stand for in the slightest."

"You said you want to save my world. How is killing those who wish to defend Pangu going to save us?"

His smile was slow, deceiving. "That information is classified. And my trust is a privilege you have to earn, Ruying."

Something inside me shivered. "And why should I trust you?"

He pointed the gun toward me. "Because I can kill you. Anytime I want." Then, his mouth broke into a grimace. "Sadly, you failed your test."

"You didn't clarify—"

"I want a killer who can follow orders, not a girl who wants to know the backstory of every target she's handed." The frenzy outside grew louder with the thunder of rushing feet.

Chaos.

Terror.

If these things had a sound, it would be this.

I stared at the gun in his hand, wondered what it would feel like to kill without consequences. Magic came at a cost, but guns and bullets? Payment was not required for such violence.

Was this the reason Romans were the way they were? Why Antony could be so cold? Because consequences were a foreign concept? Something that had never directly impacted him, at least. All he had to do was pull the trigger, and Death would handle the rest.

Maybe instead of years of life, a part of their soul was taken with each person murdered, until they were nothing but a husk of a being. Monstrous and cruel.

If I obeyed his commands, became the weapon he wanted me to be, would I one day grow to be just like him?

I closed my eyes.

"You can be so powerful, Ruying, if you just accept who you are."

"Not everyone wants power."

"Not everyone wants power . . ." he echoed, then laughed. "You say that now, but once you get a real taste of power, you will do anything to keep it. Mark my words." The prince rose to his feet and offered me his hand. I stared at it. The same hand that had killed a man so easily. "Come. I'll make a killer out of you before sunset."

I swallowed the lump in my throat and tried to quiet the screeching cries inside my head. My breathing was shallow, my heart in knots.

I didn't want to do this. I didn't want to help him.

Yet . . .

I took his hand, let him help me up. His skin was warmer and softer than I had expected.

These didn't feel like the hands of a killer.

But I guess mine didn't, either.

"I thought I'd go easy on you. I thought we were more alike than you realized, and you'd be easy to mold. Clearly you need more of a push than I had previously thought. Don't blame me for what happens next. I've warned you."

"Where are we going?"

"You'll see soon enough."

18

THE CAR SLOWED TO A stop, and I gazed up at a familiar sight. Peeling red walls, a pair of splintered doors, rusting knobs.

Home.

"Why are we here?" Immediately, my attention fell on the gun Prince Antony polished so lovingly in his lap, gleaming in the late-afternoon light.

"I've told you," he said. "I'm going to make a killer out of you before sunset."

I tried to open my mouth, tried to protest, but no sound came out.

Instead, my eyes darted between the doors of my home and the sleek black cars of Roman guards who trailed Prince Antony like shadows. Armed and dangerous. My heart shuddered to think what might happen if I pushed him too far.

The prince noticed my silence. "It seems I've finally found a way to quieten that sharp tongue of yours."

"Leave them out of this!"

"In conflict, there will always be collateral damage, Ruying. The sooner you learn this, the longer you'll live."

I dug my nails into my legs to keep myself from doing something I'd regret. "*Leave them out of this,*" I repeated.

"Be a good student and I won't touch a hair on your sister's pretty little head." The prince kept polishing his gun. "If you're not a good student? Well . . ."

He didn't have to finish the sentence.

I drew a shallow breath, and that too-familiar sting gathered behind my eyes again. I could feel the serpents between my ribs hissing again. I hated this callous prince with everything I had. I hated his disrespect for life, his arrogance, and the ruthless lengths he'd go to get what he wanted.

I hated his everything with my everything.

"There are snipers all around us, ready to shoot if I give the order. If you fail this assessment, then—"

Everything happened so fast, I didn't know what I was doing until I had his gun, ice cold, in the palm of my hand, its barrel pressed against his temple. "*Leave them alone,*" I repeated one final time.

To my surprise, instead of cowering, a crooked smile inched its way across the prince's face.

His eyes met mine, without fear. As if daring me to prove my words.

I gripped the gun tighter. "Call off the snipers!"

"Or what?"

"Or I'll show you how much of a killer I can be."

"Do it," he whispered without taking his eyes off me, his body too close to mine in the confined space, his voice a taunting rasp.

"What?"

"Do it. Kill me. Pull the trigger."

I froze. Was he calling my bluff?

"Kill me, Yang Ruying. Pull the trigger, and I'll let your family live."

"What are you saying?"

"Kill me. Show me the lengths you would go to protect those you love. I ask again: Do you have what it takes to be a real killer?"

He had planned this. I had walked right into his trap.

He began to count. "Five."

I couldn't kill him. There was no telling what his guards would do to me and my family if I did.

"Four," the prince snarled, his eyes vicious and taunting. "Three—if you don't kill me first, I might just make your family pay the price for your weakness."

My finger twitched.

"Two—you don't want to know what happens when I get to one."

I pulled the trigger.

Click.

Nothing.

The chamber was empty. Of course it was empty. Antony Augustus would never play with his own life like this. He was provoking me. He wanted to see how far he could push me.

With a crooked smile, he snatched the gun away and placed it back in his lap.

"I like you, Yang Ruying. I was just like you once—naïve about the world and its brutalities." His fingertips brushed my chin, slowly traced the edge of my jaw. We were so close his scent engulfed me like a hungry tide of ocean salt and sandalwood. "It takes courage to kill, but it takes power to spare a life. I admire you for your magic, your restraint, and most important . . ." He grabbed my throat, thumb pressing hard against my jugular. "I like that you are not above fear, above love."

He pushed me away, loaded a bullet into the gun, and pressed it against my head this time.

I stopped breathing.

I waited for the inevitable. I had threatened him, almost killed him. He would never let me live after this. I had defied him at every turn. Even if he wanted my magic, he couldn't keep someone this dangerous at his side.

He would pull the trigger, and my life would end. For nothing.

My family wouldn't be safe in my death, and the world wouldn't remember a girl called Yang Ruying as a hero or a villain. I'd be just another life taken too soon by Roman hands. A cry into the dark, never to be heard.

"If you *ever* pull something like that again, I won't hesitate to end you, your family, and everyone you've ever held dear. Do you understand me?"

Biting back tears, I nodded.

"*Do you understand?*" He repeated, louder this time. "Answer me!"

"Yes," I whimpered, "I understand."

I expected Antony Augustus to smile, to gloat in triumph at my defeat, but instead he sighed, brows tight as if in guilt, in sorrow. "I told you that you wouldn't like my plan B. Your power is exquisite— and you are beautiful. But there are plenty of pretty things in this world. Don't think for a second that I, Antony Augustus, am someone who sees a pretty girl and loses his head or grows soft. If I were like that, I would have been killed a long time ago, and Rome would never meet its greatest ruler. I like you, Yang Ruying. I admire your magic and your will to survive and everything that makes you dangerous and untrustworthy. But you are disposable, like everything else in my life. Back home, we have a saying: Don't bite the hand that feeds you. If you follow my orders, I can promise you safety and prosperity. If not? Well . . ."

Click.

I flinched. Too scared to speak, too scared to even breathe.

"I will kill you. And when I do, I won't give you the courtesy of counting to five. Do you understand?"

"I do."

"Good. I think you're ready for your assessment." With a wave of his hand, the driver reignited the engine. The car hummed back to life.

"I'm not going to underestimate you, and you need to stop underestimating yourself."

19

COBBLED STREETS BASKED UNDER WANING summer heat. The Roman half of Jing-City was another world compared to ours. Tightly packed terracotta homes had long been obliterated in favor of widely scattered manors with glass windows, iron doors, and manicured lawns.

But instead of bustling streets and lively laughter from these grand establishments, I saw only vacant residences and vacant shop fronts, empty as the heart of their invaders.

As a child, I'd always wondered why the Romans chose to frequent our side of the city, those shops they thought themselves too good for.

Now I knew.

These houses weren't homes. Everything felt like a ghost town of failed ambitions, eerily quiet.

Hollowed shells of concrete coated in pristine white. A marvel, beautiful to behold, but for these streets to be called a city they would need people, life. The kind of flurried movement and laughter and crowded warm air that existed only on our side of the Fence.

Seeing Rome's half of the city derelict and lonely, I didn't feel smug or pleased. Instead, a creeping fear nestled against my belly. A multitude of houses meant the Romans had plans to fill this place with their own people, but they were delaying.

Waiting.

For what, I was too scared to wonder.

Military men in uniforms patrolled sparse avenues unarmed, with none of the bulky guns so commonly seen guarding the Fence.

No scowls. No glares. Just kind and polite nods when the prince's car cruised past like a shark gliding in cold waters—a decency reserved only for their own kind.

"Most Romans who live here are either diplomats, politicians, military officers, business men, or the family of such people. Rich people. Important people," the prince said in a lecturing tone. An explanation I didn't ask for.

"Powerful people, then. Just like you," I said, my voice still small and shaky from what had happened not twenty minutes before. Everyone on this side of the Fence were people I should stay away from. Be careful of.

Though these streets exuded peace and beauty, a girl like me would never be safe on this side of the Fence. Never be respected, or viewed as an equal. Unless a prince was at my side, a master watching over his tightly leashed pet.

"Like me," he echoed, quietly. There was an edge to his words, a fleeting emotion: there one moment and gone the next. Too quick for me to unravel and make sense of. "Most of these houses are still empty, despite my grandfather's invitations to move more people over."

"Did they refuse because they are afraid of us?" I remembered Grandma's warning from when I was a little girl.

The fence was built to protect the Romans.

From whom?

From us, she'd whispered. *From you.*

"No," replied the prince. "Not entirely, at least. It's a big decision, leaving behind all that you've known, all the safe familiarity, for something new in a faraway land."

Or maybe they were afraid of witnessing the horrors their people had committed against mine. The ruin of a civilization. The hungry and the destitute who roamed our streets because they'd evicted half of the city from their homes in their quest to build these hollowed houses over the ashes and bones of our sorrows.

For their pleasure.

One side of the city dazzled under electricity while the other wallowed in darkness. To make room for their spacious parks and cobblestoned roads, what remained of our city was squished and crammed to accommodate the lost and the broken, businesses stacked on top of each other, flimsy new additional floors added to ancient buildings. Makeshift beds in corridors, homes cracked and divided into sections to make room.

While half of the city shivered in this empty abandonment, the other half, far from the taunting electric glow, felt only grief and rage.

At night, kids pressed up against the Fence, tiny hands reached for the glimmering lights, enchanting and golden—so close, but never close enough to touch.

I cast my eyes to the skies and wondered what the capital had looked like before the Romans came and built their empty buildings high with ivory-white columns? Had it been beautiful, as Grandma said? I bet it was. More beautiful than anything Rome could ever create. They said Jing-City used to be a place of magic—both figuratively and literally.

Now that magic was dying, and what was left in its place was a gray hopelessness that tainted everything like a heavy layer of dust.

I snuck a glance at Prince Antony from under my lashes. Was it easy, ignoring the human consequences of his people's brutalities? Safe and sound on this side of the Fence as their drugs and soldiers brought my Empire to its knees?

Seven days earlier, the people of Er-Lang had watched our capital burn, had witnessed the abduction of our kin.

For what?

What did the Romans want from us?

We passed small shops, places for them to eat and drink and dance and shop for daily necessities and small trinkets. The few establishments they had here for such activities were as small as they were lifeless, like everything else on this side of the Fence. To seek real joy, they had to cross the Fence, to our side. Where they wanted our music and art and bustling culture, but not us.

On the corner of the street was a mother holding her toddler's hand, waiting for the car to pass. Did these people feel guilty for what they were doing to us? Had they even seen the devastation on the other side of the Fence, where my people continued to mourn in garb of bone-white for those stolen during the raid?

Empty graves. Families that would never find closure. The horrors of that night would be passed down through the generations as folklore—if we survived long enough to see another generation.

Er-Lang was an Empire that had thrived for hundreds of years, a paradise where magic and humanity had lived in harmony—mostly. But Rome had managed to make a mockery of us in just twenty years. Slowly but surely, one violent act at a time, they had shoved our honor and legacy into the mud and built homes and lamp-lit streets over our ruins.

I could still hear my people's shrieks echoing in the streets, the cries of rebels brave enough to protest against the Romans, the desperate prayers of Pangulings who still saw Romans as Gods—somehow, someway—kneeling at their gates and praying for miracles.

Our world withered under storm clouds, while theirs thrived in the sun.

I closed my eyes, swallowed the lump in my throat, and tried to shake dark thoughts from my mind.

The car slowed at the center of the Roman sector before a building both magnificent and opulent. It didn't take a genius to know this was where the prince resided.

A heavy breath. I followed Antony out of the car and ascended the stone steps. The house's interior was as grand as its exterior. A foyer of splendid stained-glass windows and gilded furniture greeted us. Its ceilings bore intricate paintings framed in gold, each scene flowing into the other, as if retelling a story I didn't know. It was breathtaking, like too many other things I had seen from this haunted half of the city.

I'd never seen the inside of Er-Lang Emperor's imperial palace, long hailed as the most beautiful place in the world. But I struggled to imagine something more beguiling than this. Everything here was elaborately decorated, wastefully lavish. Shimmers of gold could be seen in every corner of the house.

More of a statement than a home.

We are better than you, it bellowed. As if the princes were over-compensating for something.

"Why are we here?" I asked.

"Follow me." The prince led me toward a pair of electric doors.

We stepped into a small metal box that descended deep below ground. As it turned out, the manor was even bigger than it appeared on the outside. Hidden in the belly of the beast was a complex underground network of corridors, illuminated by Rome's violently bright lights.

Antony stepped out of the metal conveyance, and I followed. He walked with slow, measured steps beside me, and I could feel his eyes on me the whole time, lips twitching as if there was something he wanted to say.

"Wait." The word finally emerged when we arrived at the end of the corridor, before a grand set of iron doors. "This is your final task today. Whether you live or die is dependent on how you behave next."

"You want me to kill someone for you?"

"I want you to prove to me that you are worthy of the tasks I want to bestow upon you, that you are the person I have been looking for. The ally I need at my side. Prove this to me, because I don't want to kill you, Yang Ruying." There was a quiet fear to his words when he spoke. A softness. As if he were a man confessing something he didn't want to be heard. In this moment, I wanted to believe his words, see him as someone other than a prince monstrous in his greed. "When my father died and Grandfather gave me the task of governing this city, I made a promise to my father that I would protect this land with care, just as he had. And that means rooting out any sign of rebellion, any reason my grandfather or brothers might use to justify war. I promise I am not the man you think I am. I am nothing like Valentin, or my grandfather, who unleashed those bombs and missiles upon your world just because he could. I want the same thing as you, Ruying. Peace. It is our common goal. The one thing we both want. The one thing *everyone* should want."

Peace . . . Such a tantalizing word. One that felt like fiction, the one thing no citizen of Er-Lang had known since Rome's arrival. "They say war is inevitable," I replied.

"Not me. I believe war is preventable, but I cannot do it alone. I need you. A silent assassin who can take pieces from the board without anyone noticing, without suspicion or accusations that would spark conflict."

I thought of the telltale signs of trauma I'd left on his guard, Dawson, after the night market. The sallowed skin, the dimmed eyes. "My magic isn't completely untraceable."

"It is enough," he replied. "It is the closest thing to untraceable that I have found so far." Antony pushed the door open, revealing an echoing room, similar to the arena where we had been judged just days before.

A glass cage stood at the center of this room, too, though smaller than the last one.

But like last time, there was a man inside. Long-limbed and sharp-eyed, metal bracelets around his wrists.

My prey.

20

THE FIRST LIFE I TOOK was also the first boy I'd ever kissed.

Seven years old, in the twilight of summer, the neighborhood kids hid from the heat under crisp forest leaves, green as fine cuts of jade. A creek burbled down a mountain's edge, spilled into a sparkling waterfall that carved a chilling lake at its foot.

Sometimes we dared each other to jump off the waterfall. The climb up was steep, but the thrill was worth it. Memories of those summer days were dazzled with laughter, promises of forever, and dreams of growing up.

That evening, there was no laughter, no promises. Only tears and a haunting shade of gold against a backdrop of winter gray. What should have been a harmless prank ended as something that couldn't be undone.

Most children didn't inherit their parents' Gifts, and some didn't inherit magic at all. Hushan was one of the rare few who had. He was the son of an ocean merchant, and his ability to manipulate water would be useful when he took over his father's business someday.

Even as a boy, Hushan was so confident in himself that I thought he was invincible. He made everything seem so easy. There was nothing he couldn't do. If he had grown up, maybe he would have become the hero my world needed in this time of chaos. Someone who would lead and fight, a martyr whose blood would change the world. Someone brave enough to die for what he believed in.

The opposite of me.

Maybe that was why I liked him. His easy smiles, kind eyes.

An offered hand, and I followed him up to the mountain's edge while our friends paddled in the water. Up there, far from the noise, his lips brushed mine, ever so gently, and I felt fire melt against me. Tingles like pins and needles showered my body, except there was no pain—only joy, relief. His lips were velvet petals, his touch was gentle. But when the boys jumped out from behind the trees, their cheering laughter a sudden explosion, I startled.

The cliff's edge was wet and I slipped; my body toppled off the edge. In that terrifying moment of freefall, I tried to grab something, *anything,* and took Hushan with me.

Bare skin against hard water and rough stones, our flesh peppered red. Hushan laughing. The fall was quick. Done and over in one heart-stopping second before the icy waters swallowed us whole. If things had ended there, it would have been any other day. Grandma would have scolded me for putting myself in danger for a kiss, warned me of the immaturity of boys.

Everything would have been another memory to be forgotten.

But things didn't end there.

My body hit water. I tried to propel myself up toward the surface, but something pulled me under. I fought the water, hands clawed for the rippling light. Surface. *Air.*

But something pushed me down, hard. A force too strong for an idle lake. A current that felt like the magic of ocean waves.

"What are you doing?" I heard my sister's panic.

Laughter burbled through the water from above.

I wasn't laughing. I was drowning. My lungs were burning.

"Hushan, stop!" Baihu's voice.

I clawed for air. Searching, *praying* for something to grab onto, to pull me back up. When the world fell to shades of black and white, I thought I was going to die, but a flashing cord of gold shone bright overhead like starlight through the darkest night.

"Stop, Hushan! This is going too far!"

It was beautiful, and it called to me.

Do you want to live, Ruying?

I reached until fingers wrapped around the light. In a desperate need to breathe, I pulled at it like a lifeline—anything to get out of these waters.

Something rushed through me like the collapse of a dam. Warm, comforting as a hot bath on the coldest of winter days, enough to melt fear into courage. Raw energy ran through my veins, flooding strength into my body.

It had always been about this, the most addictive part of my Gift. Though the adrenaline that came with stealing *qi* and letting it course through me was beautiful, otherworldly, deep down I knew this was what I wanted more than anything else.

To feel invincible, *powerful.* To know that when I wished for bad things to happen to bad people, it was not as simple as a desire, but a manifestation I could make happen as easily as snapping my fingers. An impulse I would fight with my every waking second, but to be the girl blessed by Death meant I had *power,* even if it was deadly and cruel. And to be a girl with power was rare. I was born the property of my father, doomed to live and suffer and die either the property of a husband or of a son like my mother had, like my grandmother would have if she didn't bury my father first.

However, in that moment under the waterfall, I did not yet know these epiphanies. In that moment, I only wanted one thing and one thing alone.

To live.

Rattled with fear, I held tight and made the rippling light my anchor until I broke the surface and gulped up thick, comforting air.

The current slowed. The light dimmed to nothing.

The laughter died.

When I looked around, Hushan was floating, face down in the water, his body still as a limp willow leaf.

There was no blood.

Somebody screamed. It could have been me; it could have been any of the kids standing at the water's edge.

When the healers came, they said Hushan died because he'd exhausted his Gift.

Some people believed the healers' words, but I knew the truth.

Maybe it was the trauma of losing a friend, or maybe it was because somewhere deep down those kids knew what I was capable of, but everyone stopped hanging out with me after that.

They still called for Meiya to go play, but not me.

It was fine. I made a new friend after that.

Taohua: someone who never judged me for my mistakes, or feared me for the monster within, this Gift I didn't ask for.

Later, I learned there were few records of Xianlings born with Gifts like mine. None of them were good. None of them lived long lives.

Monsters in flesh. Destined to ruin.

I deserved the guilt and shame I carried, and all of the pain this world threw at me.

21

"ONLY ONE OF YOU WILL walk out of this cage alive today," the prince whispered, his words bitter with promise. But his eyes were warm, pleading, just like in the Lotus Tower. Then he leaned close, his breath bringing a warm rush of tingles down my neck, his lips a gentle brush against the shell of my ear. I shivered. "I want it to be you, Ruying. Don't disappoint me."

He placed one hand on my shoulder and the other under my chin and forced me to look at the bloodied man inside the cage.

My opponent's eyes were feral, wild. He was as desperate to survive as I was. A symphony of want deep in our bones. Neither of us would let the other one win in the name of mercy, nor morals.

"He's a Xianling. Multiplication. A rare talent, but he's served his purpose now. It's time for him to go."

"He's served his purpose? Is this a glimpse into my future? Would you feed me to your next killer once I've served my purpose?"

"Maybe," he replied, eyes hard. "Maybe not. Don't give me a reason to want you dead, and I won't hurt you."

Antony's hand released me.

Dawson escorted me to the cage and pushed me in.

Bloodied and bruised, the young man swayed ever so slightly. Now that we stood face-to-face, inside inescapable glass walls, I took notice of his eyes: sharp and unblinking. A serpent ready to strike. The kind of focus that signaled danger, required caution.

Multiplication? A rare power indeed—one I'd only heard of in books, in stories. Xianlings, capable of dividing their bodies into two, three, even four different versions of themselves. A power this unique, one'd think the princes would want to keep him around. Why force him to fight? Even if he had served his purpose—whatever this meant—a talent like his was a good addition to Rome's armory. He was worth more alive than dead.

Wasn't he?

"Don't hesitate," Antony's voice echoed through the speakers. Advice or warning, I couldn't tell. "Death would not grant you this power if he did not intend for you to use it. This is your fate, Ruying. Don't run from it. Embrace it."

He sounded like my sister.

Silence fell over the cage.

Our bracelets beeped.

Science stopped humming, and magic flooded back in a visceral rush.

Kill him, a voice inside demanded, urging me forward as Death's magic grew hotter and hotter like abandoned hay out in the summer sun, ready to ignite.

My fists were clenched tight at my sides until nails bit flesh.

I remembered Grandma's soft prayers to our ancestors in the dark of night. *No one should have all this power. Please, help my granddaughter. Release her from this grotesque Gift.*

My ribs grew tighter. I didn't want to disappoint Grandma, didn't want to become the killer of her nightmares.

But a savage smile spread slowly across my opponent's face. "I'm going to enjoy this. The prince will be awfully upset when I kill his new pet," he whispered before lunging at me with bloodied hands.

I dodged, just barely.

Kill him, Death snarled.

My opponent tried for a right hook, going for a knock-out hit.

Magic burned, fierce like a wildfire inside my veins.

No mortal gets to decide who lives and who dies.

I dove to the ground, then rolled into a crouch. Hands in fists, I was about to run when he multiplied himself into two, with a grunt like a beast torn in half. *It hurts him. His power hurts him.* Before I could do anything with this realization, the duplicate grabbed me by the throat and held me immobile against the tiled floor.

Only one of you will walk out of this cage alive today.

"I don't want to hurt you!" I choked.

He didn't listen. Fist tightened around my throat until I couldn't breathe.

Kill him, Death demanded. *End this fight before it begins!*

I blinked back memories from beneath the waterfall all those years ago.

Power was addictive, just like opian. Every time I gave in to these sinful urges, I feared I might not be able to stop. With every submission to Death's magic, a piece of him followed me back into this realm and his claim over me grew stronger. And the voices, the temptations, grew louder and louder, like ghosts haunting my every breath.

Every moment, I craved to relive those highs, relive that exhilarating rush, that feel of power, of *control.* The fear in my victims' eyes. To know that I was strong, that I was *dangerous,* someone who should be feared . . .

His grip tightened. Darkness blotted my vision. I scrambled for balance through the tilting motions, tried to get back to my feet, but his double held me down.

I heard laughter above me.

"This Gift of a lifetime is wasted on such a weak, cowardly girl." My opponent's voice pierced the echoing gray and my blurred vision. He grinned as if he'd already won the fight.

Kill, or be killed.

The multiplication slammed his boot down on my head, hard rubber against the flesh of my cheek. Pain exploded, sharp and thudding, and pressure filled my skull as if I were underwater.

I tasted blood, my head ringing.

"We don't have to fight just because he wants us to," I tried to say. "We are not Rome's puppets."

I tried to push myself back up a second time, but he swung his feet at my stomach and kicked me back down.

"I thought the Girl Blessed by Death would be harder to kill, but it turns out you're nothing but a coward."

Kill him! Death bawled through the spinning world.

"Death should have blessed a man, someone who is worthy."

I spat out the blood in my mouth. "I *am* worthy."

With that, I reached out and *pulled.*

I wrapped my magic around his *qi,* and this time I didn't hold back. Golden energy flowed through me fast like a rushing river. That delicious warmth, nectar filling in my broken fractures until mortal wounds faded. My body rejuvenated—an act of charity from Death. Like the keepers who rewarded their bees with a little honey, Death was a kind master. *Qi* passed like water through a gate most times, but occasionally he'd leave a little extra in his wake, healing all wounds, flesh or bone.

Death needed me just as I needed him. The stronger I was, the stronger he would be.

The multiplication collapsed against the ground, eyes rolled back and fading into oblivion until only his true self lay slumped on the ground.

I should have stopped there, pulled myself back from the edge as his *qi* faded to nothing. His life still quivered under my hand, the last struggles of a dying animal.

I could almost feel his soul untethering from his body. *You have taken enough,* I tried to tell myself. *This is enough!*

But I didn't stop.

Only one of you will walk out of this cage alive.

I tightened my grip and felt something snap.

I want it to be you.

22

WHEN THE LAST DREGS OF life left that man, something inside me died with him.

When his soul untethered from his body, I closed my eyes to shield myself from seeing the color of who he was—an experience that always left a bitter aftertaste. A brief vision of the life unlived, of what sort of man he'd been before I cut his life short. Of all the joy and sorrow I'd stolen.

A connection too personal, too haunting.

Sometimes when forced to face the consequences of one's actions, it was easier to look away.

Like a house of cards caving in on itself, I collapsed and broke into a fit of sobs.

Another life, I had taken another life. And with this life, Death and all of his violent delights dug himself deeper into my soul, generating more cracks beneath the good-girl façade I'd tried so hard to keep up for Grandma, for myself, for those who saw me as something monstrous beyond recognition because of the Gift I never asked for.

A hand touched my shoulder, warm.

Then another. Before I knew it, someone had drawn me into their embrace. A safe place of tenderness to hide from the cold of everything else.

In silence, Antony Augustus held me tight, as if doing so could hold all of my broken pieces together, keep me whole against the cascading gray waves of hate striking me like an ocean striking at crumbling cliffs.

Deep in my bones I knew everything about this moment was wrong.

Leaning into his touch was wrong, wrapping my arms around him and clinging to him for life was wrong.

But I did it anyway.

"It's going to get easier," he whispered, his lips brushing my temple. "I promise."

"How would you know?"

"Because it did for me."

23

LATER, AS THE GUARDS CARRIED the body out, I sat at the edge of the cage, back pressed against the cold glass.

Tender-eyed, the prince positioned himself beside me, our bodies so close I could feel the warmth radiating from him, but not close enough to touch. Skin and skin, separated by this tiny breath of space that divided us like a canyon—one we'd never be able to cross.

"He was dying. My scientists said he wouldn't live through the month. Even if you didn't kill him, he'd still be dead in a matter of weeks," the prince said quietly. He observed me for a moment, then offered a small white pill from his pocket. "It'll help with the—"

I didn't give him the chance to finish before I threw the pill on the ground. I didn't want his medicine or his solutions of chemistry and science.

I wanted to feel this pain.

I had to.

I'd just killed a man. If I shaved these hard feelings to nothing like Antony, like the Romans, then what separated me from the monsters of our ancient folklores? From *them*?

Murder was a sin, yet Antony didn't even blink when he pulled the trigger from the Lotus Tower. I couldn't let that kind of non-chalance engulf me. I had to feel this pain, drown in it. Suffer and cry and let the guilt eat me up. Let it be a constant reminder that everything I did here was wrong.

The last tether between me and my former self.

To the girl Grandma raised. The sister Meiya saved.

"He deserved to die." Antony spoke after the pause, his voice a delicate breath, raspy and soothing like a stroking hand against a shivering spine. "He was a bad man. The rich son of a rich man. A lowlife who took from the weak, terrorized innocents, and got away with it because he had a father who paid off every problem and swaddled him in privilege. You did the world a service, killing him. Sometimes we have to do bad things for good reasons. Sometimes, we must make sacrifices for the greater good."

"I'm no better than he is," I murmured. Even now, my hands hummed with *qi* and power.

"The two of you are not the same." When Antony looked at me, his eyes held mine with a gaze so intent, so gentle, I felt like I was talking to a different man. A boy the same age as me instead of a prince who cradled my life in his hands, capable of crushing me as easily as a bug. Our shared moment from inside the cage lingered like a permanent stain.

His pale eyes glistened with subtle patience, understanding. As if he saw me—the real me. The girl who was both tempted and terrified by what she could do, could become, if she let her worst instincts take over.

"That man did bad things because he wanted to, because he *liked* it. You are different. You do them because you have to. Like me."

Was he trying to make me feel better?

I want to do bad things, too—a truth I couldn't bring myself to confess. *Every day. Take what I want and not apologize for it. Make those who sneered at me kneel, make them shriek in fear* . . .

Rage simmered, a constant flame.

I tucked my knees under my chin and hugged myself tight, as if doing so could hold everything together for a little bit longer.

"How does it feel?" he asked.

I shouldn't talk to him, shouldn't linger in this moment with this villainous man, our bodies so close I could feel the heat of him singeing my edges. His scent of ocean salt and sandalwood. But my chest was hollow, and his words delicate and comforting and warm like liquid gold, filling the cracks of my fractured heart.

"Do you want to know the worst part?" I whispered into the dim room. A confession of sorts. Uttered under the judgment of this unworthy God. "I like it. That feeling, when life passes through me, it is the best feeling I've ever felt. *Will* ever feel, perhaps. Once, when I was young and curious, I'd stolen a taste of opian, lured by your people's claims and boasts. A substance so heavenly that even the Gods from beyond the sky sing its praises? But when I inhaled it, its high was nothing compared to the high of Death. I like the way energy gathers at my hands. I like knowing I can kill whomever I want, whenever I want. Death is beautiful, but he is cruel. His whispers haunt me, knowing that with each heartbeat I long for this feeling."

"But you resist it. Because you think that is the right thing to do? What a good person should do?"

"Yes."

"And most days, you don't want to resist."

Something hot gathered behind my eyes. Tears. More tears. I closed my eyes once more so that the prince wouldn't see me cry. "The only thing that keeps me from giving in to this desire is my fear of dying. Xianlings who give in to the temptation of magic live short lives."

"Are you sure that is true, and not a lie those who do not possess magic tell those who do? To keep them leashed, to exert some power over those more powerful?"

"What do you mean?"

The prince looked away, his eyes suddenly distant after this un-expected intimacy. He had more to say, but only silence followed. Our shared moment, beautiful as the embroideries Grandma used to sew, came apart, snarled into halves, barely held together by tangled threads.

A heartbeat passed, then another.

Antony placed a hand over mine: warm, strong. "I know how it feels." An echo of what he had said inside the cage.

"Do you?" My voice came out harsher, crueler than I intended. "You must have killed so many people at this point that murder is as easy as breathing."

A slight smile at his lips. "Contrary to popular belief, I do feel things. I feel guilt, and regret, and shame, and doubt constantly. I question whether I'm doing this for the right reasons, whether the ends justify the means. I feel just as much as you, as anyone. I'm simply better at hiding it from the world. I'm a prince, trying to prove himself worthy of a ruthless throne. If I show weakness, my grandfather will cast me out. I would lose all my value to him. And if I lose value, then I cannot help my people. I cannot help *your* people." His hand squeezed mine, as if we were allies, friends. "It will get easier, over time. Even if it doesn't stop hurting, you'll get better at pretending it doesn't hurt."

"Why are you telling me this?"

"Trust is a two-way street. I want to trust you and want you to trust me in return. Something that won't happen unless I show you my cards, let you see the man under the armor."

"Why?" I whispered. "As long as you have my family's lives in the palm of your hand, I will obey your every command. You don't need my trust. You don't need me as your ally."

"But what if I do? What if I see the pieces of you that you don't want the world to see? All the demons that dwell in the shadows of your consciousness, Death with his inviting words at your ear . . . What if I look at your demons and see my own reflecting back? Someone who's terrified to one day be seen as a villain, to exist on the wrong side of history?"

My heart lurched at his words, plucked from my darkest thoughts. He spoke with such conviction that I feared he could see all the hideous parts I had hoped to hide under soft-spoken words and ladylike smiles. Every day since the waterfall, I fought with the magic inside me, fought with my spiteful urges. "What if we *are* on the wrong side of history? No one should have all this power."

"But you *do*, Ruying. Forget about the lies they tried telling you. Power is worth having. One might say it is the *only* thing worth having. If you accepted yours, you could make men kneel at the mention of your name. I can make you so powerful that no one will ever hurt you again."

His words were a seductive melody. They coaxed me close, my heart fluttering.

Power meant different things to different people. To me, power meant safety, stability. The opportunity to indulge in joy without fear of tomorrow. Power was being able to protect those I loved. Power meant I could punish those who wronged me. A life free of consequences, just like the Romans lived.

But just because I could have something didn't mean that I should.

"Do you know why I chose you as my ally in this fight?"

"Is that what we are, allies? To call us allies, we'd have to be equals. And nothing about this—about you and me—feels equal."

"If you wish," he whispered, "we *can* be allies. I *want* us to be allies. If I didn't, I never would have saved you from Valentin when he tried to inject you with opian."

I blinked. "If *I* want us to be allies? Do I have a choice? And don't try to manipulate me. You saved me because you covet my magic. You want me as a weapon. Nothing more."

Antony smiled, shook his head. "During my time here, I've met many Xianlings who possess impossible Gifts. My brothers and grandfather all believe the more powerful the Xianlings are, the more they need to be controlled. But I've seen too many lose their sanity to opian. I don't want you to be another lifeless shell, a body without a mind. I want you, not as a puppet on a string, but as someone who stands beside me."

"Why?" His words lingered on my skin, lyrics to a melody that felt so genuine they seemed to fill the chasm between us, drew my beating heart closer to his.

He was a prince of Rome. He had no reason to lie to me.

This didn't mean I could trust his words, however.

"Because of your eyes. That first time we met, the way you looked at me, as if you needed me. Desperation drove you to steal the gold. I should have been angry, but I didn't blame you for it. Because I had done the same when I was in your shoes, once upon a time."

"In my shoes?"

"I wasn't born a prince, Ruying. I was born on the streets of Rome, to parents who had nothing to their names—street rats doing everything they could to survive. But it wasn't enough. I was young, desperate, and hungry. I came to the attention of my adopted father, the late Heir of Rome, the same way you came to my attention. I stole from him, the way you stole from me. A pouch of gold. I was a little more elegant about it, of course. I plucked it from his waist, then walked briskly into the shadows before I broke into a run. By the time I made it back to the underbelly of a high-way bridge, where my family shared shelter with others, I thought I had gotten away with it. Until that night, when the prince showed up with his men, guns in hand. He offered me a choice. Turn the gun on myself and pay for my crimes or kill those I loved for a chance at wealth, power, and status. A life as a prince of Rome instead of as a nobody who had nothing, who would forever be nothing."

My heart juddered to a stop. "You killed your parents?"

Antony's face was cold, unreadable. "The Augustus family believes in talent over everything. Their dynasty is built on meritocracy, and the throne is not always passed from blood to blood. My grandfather feared Valentin wouldn't be able to shoulder the weight of an Empire when he grew up. Hence why my father had to find a spare. Just in case. And ever since that night, I have spent every second trying to prove my worth to my grandfather. But it seems I'll never be enough . . ."

I watched him inspect the scars of his past heartbreaks ever so casually, as if discussing the weather. Distant and somber, but I caught a flicker of pain in his eyes, a thin layer of tears misting his gaze.

"At least I didn't go as far as my father, didn't make you kill those you love to prove yourself to me."

"And you don't want me to. If I can kill my family for power, I could kill you just as easily. You want someone who wishes to survive, wishes to be more than whom they're born to be, but not someone as ambitious as you—cold enough to do everything and anything to get what they want."

The way Antony looked at me changed in that moment. "I don't know if I like how smart you are."

"And I don't know if I like how wicked *you* are."

The tension at the edge of his lips turned into a deep, genuine smile, then an indulgent chuckle that shocked his body, making our shoulders brush. I could feel the heat radiating off him, so close. A part of me wanted to lean into him the way I would Grandma, Meiya, Baihu, Taohua, with all the childhood tenderness that made the world seem less cruel.

I didn't. "So you're not a prince?"

"Not by blood. Though I like to think that I've earned this title over the years by endless contributions to the Empire, and my grandfather agrees. Otherwise, he wouldn't place so much power in my hands. Still, blood is thicker than water. My grandfather respects me, values me, but he doesn't love me the way he does Valentin. This is why Valentin has power over me. Why the commanders and politics of court sway his way more often than mine."

"Because they think he's going to inherit the throne. Willows that bend to the wind," I mused. "Do you think your grandfather will pass the crown to him?"

"I think power belongs to those who are brave enough to seize it." A diplomatic response. "But a ruler is nothing without his people. One day when I rule over Rome, I don't want to inflict more pain on the innocent. I have known suffering. I've seen it through my own eyes, felt it cold in my bones, through the bruises that marred my body. I've heard it in the whimpering of my mother when she sacrificed her body to protect me from the gangs of men who took what they wanted, when they wanted it. I've heard it in the sobs of my father as he knelt for strangers, begged for pennies so he could afford something, anything, to feed me when my malnourished body grew sicker and sicker. I don't want more people like us in the world, born to suffer because nobody cares about the poor and the broken."

His voice cracked, just a little. A breath of silence as he straightened himself, as he blinked away the mist in his eyes.

"This is why I rarely venture beyond the Fence. Not because I am disgusted by your kind as so many like to assume, but because I am ashamed." His voice was quieter when he continued, like the sharing of a secret. This was a man who had lived most of his life needing to be strong, to be ruthless, and here he was showing me the cracks in his armor. The angles from which I could hurt him. A predator rolling over to expose the soft of his belly. This was him extending an olive branch, attempting to earn my trust. "I know what it's like to suffer. I see my birth mother and father in the face of your people every time I walk the impoverished streets of your city, and I remember. Where I came from. What life was like, being one of the gutter rats that the world pretended not to see. How it felt, to be desperate and hungry and angry—so angry. At the world I was born into. At the cards I was dealt, and the life I was forced to live. I understand your rage, Ruying. Because once upon a time, I lived it. Before I was given this fancy crown and fancy title and fancy clothes, I had begged for pennies like so many in this callous city are forced to do. Unlike my brothers, I was not born with a silver spoon in my mouth, and I cannot turn a blind eye to the hardship of so many innocent people."

"But how can I trust these words? How would I know, if you become Emperor, that you'd be different?"

At this, a smile danced at the edge of his lips, and his hand reached across the distance between our bodies like a gesture of peace crossing all that divided us and our two worlds. "How can we trust anyone? 人心隔肚皮, as your people would say. *Our hearts are all separated by the skin and flesh of our individual bodies.* I cannot hear your thoughts and you cannot hear mine. All we have is faith and trust that the other will not lead us astray."

"Will you lead me astray, my prince?"

"I will lead you to glory. I will lead you to the life you have always wanted. I will lead you to a better tomorrow. Not just for my world, but for *both* our worlds. A war between magic and science will benefit only those who live their lives in high castles, far from the ground where violence will shatter lives and rob good people of their futures. It will make the orphans and the impoverished easy targets for greedy men. I meant what I said that day in the dungeons, Ruying. I want to save both our worlds. Not just Rome."

Save both our worlds. "What does Rome need to be saved from?"

Antony smiled. A secret. A wink. "Like I said, I'd rather we were friends. Allies, not enemies. The less you hate me, the easier it'll be to trust me, like me, be loyal to me. If it makes you feel better, every life I intend you to end deserves to die in some shape or form, as they'll eventually cause chaos and bloodshed if they are left unattended—like weeds devouring an immaculate garden."

"And why should I believe in you over your brother? You speak of peace, but how? You said your trust needs to be earned. Have I done enough to deserve an honest answer?"

At my words of defiance, Prince Antony didn't get mad, didn't lose his temper as I once thought he would. His eyes remained tender and indulgent, watching me with intrigue and wonder. "Valentin wants a war. Your Emperor's advisors want a war. I'm the only thing keeping my grandfather from giving in to temptation and invading Pangu with every weapon of mass destruction that we keep in our armory. I've convinced him that we can use science to reach an agreement that everyone can benefit from—a concept that will lose its appeal if Er-Lang keeps retaliating. Those men I need dead? They are the people pushing your Emperor to attack and chase us out, or followers of the Phantom hellbent on chaos and revenge. My grandfather is many things, but tolerant has never been one of them. There is only so much I can do to hold him back from retaliating."

I paused. Would an attack on Rome be so terrible?

Magic was a force of unfathomable degrees, after all. What if we rebelled, caught them off guard, and won?

"Apocalypse looms on the horizon like a storm cloud, waiting to strike. A war between magic and science might end us all," Antony continued, as if reading my thoughts. "If you don't believe me, there is something you need to see."

His hand took mine, and pulled me to my feet.

Through a set of locked doors, he led me to a dimly lit room. Press of a button, and lights hummed to life row by row, ghastly white rays over dark gray mechanics.

My heart caught in my throat, a ribbon snared midair. A deep breath, then another, as I took in the sight before me: the endless weapons stacked on metal shelves. Guns. So many guns. The sort I had seen in the streets, slung over Roman shoulders, as well as ones I'd never seen before.

If these were important enough to be kept hidden behind closed doors, then they must be deadly. Creations of science that Rome didn't want us to know existed.

"Earlier, you asked what hold my people have over your Emperor. Well, here is your answer. This is one of our many armories across the city, across the Empire. One of these guns can kill a dozen Er-Lang soldiers within a minute."

"Capable of slaughtering even the deadliest of Xianlings before they get the chance to harness their magic." I echoed what Grandma taught me.

"And that isn't all. These guns are nothing compared to the other weapons we have ready." Antony led me to a heavy steel table at the center of the armory. A tap of his finger, and the surface came alive as an electric screen. He typed something into the system, and an image of a plane came into view—the kind I sometimes saw flying between our world and theirs through the portal in the sky, except much smaller. "Fighter jets." His hand swiped the screen. "You were born after the war that took place between Rome and Er-Lang. I was, too. But unlike you, I have seen videos of what happened. Footage from the fighter jets before they struck your armies and blasted all those good, kind men into gobbets of flesh and splintered bone. The scientific creations of my realm are beyond what anyone from your world can ever imagine. One of our bombs exceeds the powers of ten thousand of your rarest Xianlings, than ten thousand of your so-called Gods. You should thank those Gods that the late Emperor bent his knee before my grandfather unleashed these on the civilians of this city."

Antony grimaced. A hint of 不忍 between his brows: a future he *couldn't bear to imagine.*

He swiped at the screen and the image changed to another object, sharp and slender. I had no name for it. "Missiles: One of these can wipe out half of Jing-City in a heartbeat. My grandfather almost used it on Er-Lang during a disagreement with the late Emperor years ago. He threatened to send a fleet and wipe out your Empire and all of its inhabitants. My father was the one who talked him out of it. Despite everything, he was a good man, my adopted father. Or at least, he'd tried to be. Like me, he'd hoped for a solution that would both save my world and relinquish yours from our tyranny. He didn't want to see innocent people die, either."

The late Heir of Rome, who had passed years earlier. Nobody knew why. This was Rome's internal affair, something beyond the grasp of even the capital's most gossipy aunties. "I assume the same cannot be said for your grandfather?"

"My grandfather wants results. He's never been one to consider the collateral costs of his goals, as long as he gets what he wants. He was raised in a different time, my father used to say. When war ravaged our world, Rome was under attack from all sides—land and sea, against the other superpowers of our world. All fighting for the same finite resources. The wars raged for decades. Our family's right to rule was challenged over and over again. We lost lands, claimed lands, and forced others from their capitals, then lost our capital. So much happened; so much was lost. My grandfather lived through an unfathomable amount of trauma—memories that shaped who he is today, someone who will do everything to protect his home."

"My grandmother went through a lot of pain, too," I retorted. "In fact, I'm pretty sure every Er-Lang child who grew up under Rome's shadow had lived through some form of unfathomable pain, yet none of us threatened to eradicate entire empires from the map."

"His actions in Er-Lang are tame compared to what he's done to enemies on our side of the Veil," Antony replied. "Which is to say that if a war breaks out between our two worlds, there will be no going back. You will not survive, Ruying. Er-Lang will not survive. Not if my grandfather intends to destroy all who disobey." His hand reached out once again, warm fingers cradling mine. He looked at me with the same focus, now tinged with a desperation that was beautifully out of character. A man pleading for me to listen, to heed his warning. Just like in the Lotus Tower earlier. "I am not a butcher like my grandfather, dropping missiles on civilians to extinguish rebels. Nor will I ask you to kill innocent people out of petty greed or any twisted desires for power and false superiority like my brothers. I'm a surgeon, and I intend for you to be my scalpel, cutting only where it's needed, to root out the instigators of this war not just for Rome, but for Pangu as well. For both sides of the Veil. To save the many, we have to sacrifice the few. You can hate me all you want, but please understand that your world needs me. Help me help Pangu. Let me find a way for us to coexist."

I drew a shallow breath.

Again, I thought of my sister and grandmother. How disappointed they'd be if they saw me under the command of a Roman prince, betraying our Empire for a chance to live like a dog at their feet.

I would be no better than the traitors we used to curse at. Than Baihu, whom I'd rolled my eyes at and scorned—as if I had any power to judge him.

I wanted to do the right thing, so badly. But every path before me felt as wrong as it felt right. And maybe that was the point. I wanted too many things, and they were ripping me open at my already frail seams. Between being a good person and surviving, I could only choose one.

"To preserve peace, we have to make sacrifices," the prince continued. "The world doesn't exist in black and white, or right and wrong. Sometimes, to survive, we have to do our best. And sometimes bad things must be done for the greater good."

Like murder.

"This isn't a permanent solution," I whispered.

"You are right, it isn't. But apocalypse is coming, and this is the best solution I have. The best solution this Empire has."

"Apocalypse?"

"My grandfather grows impatient with the progress here in Pangu. He wishes to see results."

"And what are these results?" Then, a little louder, though still only a whisper of courage. "What is it that you seek from my world?"

Antony's eyes turned sharp as his serpentine smile. He was too smart to fall for my simple traps. "My point *is*," his voice was a quiet lull, but every word held authority and they demanded to be heard, to be feared. "Members of my family wish to see not just Er-Lang but the whole of Pangu destroyed to make way for Rome. They are trying to force my grandfather's hand. One year, if not less: That is all we have before he makes his final decision. Ruying, if you want your world to survive, you must trust me. Do as I say, help me make things right, convince my grandfather that war is uncalled for and that maintaining this tedious peace is the best option for all of us."

"Why do you care so much about whether my people live or die?"

"Because my father loved your people. He loved this land with all its culture and breathtaking beauty. The mountains and the rivers, the forests so green they can't possibly be real. Everything about your world is the opposite of the gloomy cities of metal and glass Rome has known for too many generations. Now that he is gone, I must carry on his legacy, protect this world and all its wonders in any way I can."

"Even from your own grandfather?"

"Especially from my grandfather."

"Why are you telling me this?" Even though his hard-kept secrets remained close to his chest, this was still too much to be casually revealed without leverage.

"So that you know the gravity of this situation. So that you know when I say I need your help it is the truth. Do you trust me?"

"No, but what choice do I have?"

I closed my eyes.

Forgive me.

INTERLUDE

Moments Between Shores

DEATH

THE GIRL WAS SLENDER AND slight, malnourished from years of poverty. She moved like a shadow between the realm of the living and the realm of the dead. Fingers plucking *qi* from bodies with care, with precision.

Delicate, gentle.

The last mercy she could offer the unfortunate souls her prince wished to eliminate in this precarious game of power.

One by one, she untethered them from mortal bodies, let them flutter into the ether. She did so in silence, in sorrow, in desperation. Because if she did not do as her prince commanded, what would happen to her family? What would happen to her?

For a girl blessed by Death, she feared dying more than she should have.

Perhaps it was because she had glimpsed the other realm, felt the never-ending nothingness that existed beyond the veil that separated the living from the dead.

Yang Ruying didn't want to die. She had too many things she wanted to do, too many people she had to protect.

For Meiya, she thought to herself. *For Grandma.*
For survival.

THE GIRL

MID-AUTUMN'S EVE BROUGHT WITH IT the familiar scent of moon-cakes and fireworks. Under the falling night, I moved in silence, quiet as winter's breath while festivities roared in the distance. A skill taught by my grandmother, a woman of foresight and too much caution.

Though she had never wielded a sword, never learned how to kill, she was still the eldest daughter of a great general before she became the wife of a greater one. She had watched her brothers spar as children, before they grew into men and one by one lost their lives on the battlefield. She had read the martial handbooks her father kept in his study, had watched her husband teach her son how to fight, how to best a man in just three moves.

Grandma taught us these things not for us to be killers, but to make sure we knew how to protect ourselves. After Father died, our house fell from its former glory, spiraling with our crumbling city into certain doom.

My grandmother was intelligent and brave, had all the qualities of a great man. But she could never protect us the way her father and husband and son had once protected her, which meant we had to learn how to protect ourselves.

Because even my deadly Gift was not enough.

Grandma remembered the stories told by her own mother; then rode beside my grandfather and witnessed the horrors of war with her own eyes. She knew how precious strength and speed and the ability to slip into shadows were for girls born unprotected in turbulent times.

I was luckier than most, in many ways.

I was poor but cared for.

I was a girl without choices yet I had the power to break rules and forge my own path as Death Incarnate if I wished.

If I possessed the courage.

If I did not fear my own potential.

Stay within the lines this world has drawn for you, stay quiet and careful, words whispered to me in warning. Words that kept me shackled while I tried to make the best of bad situations, time and time again.

This is me making the best of a bad situation, I told myself as Death tugged me through the alleyways, as the hunger in my chest grew harder and harder to ignore.

The murders began with men who had hideous pasts.

Traitors.

Heartless killers.

The sort of men who were so desperate for power and fortune they wouldn't think twice about selling out their own kin.

These were the Pangulings who sang Rome's praises, who sought to supply the enemy with weapons and Xianling soldiers. Men who wished to exploit war for their own gain, to climb into bed with these wicked Gods from beyond the skies to get ahead not just in this generation, but for all generations to come.

Then came the good men. The men whose sins were not so easy to define. The good men who wanted good things but through means that clashed with Antony's plans or threatened to tip the scale which kept peace and war balanced precariously. Whose incautious motives I sometimes understood too intimately. Whose noble courage and optimism reminded me too much of my sister.

These were the men Antony offered in quiet, without reason, without explanation. But I knew. I always knew.

I feared Antony's silence more than his words. The thinner the files, the more I knew I shouldn't follow through with the orders.

But I always did, always let my fingers dance and summon dusts of *qi* from their bodies and into mine.

When I felt these good men perish under my hands, it was almost impossible to bear.

I closed my eyes, tried to shake the thoughts away.

Focus.

This is my duty now, I reminded myself. Everything I did was for the greater good.

For peace, however fragile it was.

Antony had reminded me time and time again that I had to be subtle. If anyone found out that I was behind these strange deaths, he might not be able to protect me without political upheaval.

As tensions ran high, too many people were out for themselves and their own motives. Antony had to be careful with every move if he wished to avoid war, avoid conflict. Because every misstep could one day be used against him.

The Pangulings weren't the only ones who felt as if we walked on thin ice.

It turned out Gods knew fear, too.

As evident in the long list of names Antony wanted me to dispose of.

My target tonight was the leader of a small rebel group plotting to steal artillery from the Roman armory.

I snuck into the wine-house where he spent his last moments in silence between crowds. In a darkened corner, pouring himself one last drink before what he knew might be a suicide mission.

Head low, my face shielded under messy hair and the plain clothes of a street rat looking for her next meal, I moved closer and closer until I felt the hum of his *qi* against waiting palms, close enough to heed my call.

A motion of my hand, and he collapsed to the ground.

Energy filled me, delicious as finely aged rice wine.

Another tug, and his soul fled deep blue from his limp body.

I tried to look away, but not quick enough.

Just like that, all illusions of the high faded.

His soul was sharp and cold, like a jagged piece of ice scratching down my insides. With a slight taste of salt, like the tears my world had grown too used to shedding, and the fragrance of the chrysanthemums neighbors offered to grieving families. The suffocating scent of smoke, from the money we burned for father and grandfather and mother and the great-grandparents who had died before I was born.

Just like that, I knew more than I wanted. His life had been one of sorrow, of mourning—like too many of the men I had killed lately.

Pain and rage consumed him, until there was nowhere left for hope to flourish.

Only desperation.

The men who had nothing left to lose were always the most dangerous.

Everyone we know has lost someone to the Romans: a saying that rang in my ears as the drunken crowd continued to drink, to sing, to bellow, to cry.

They would mistake the corpse in the corner for another man trying to drown his problems. No one would know he was dead until later.

I slipped out without anyone noticing.

He was a bad man, I reminded myself when I tasted the tears.

But even as I thought it, I knew it was a lie. He was not a bad man, just one who had run out of roads. One whose hardship and loss had soured into ruthlessness . . .

The sacrifice of the few, for the longevity of the many.

These men wished to rebel against Rome and incur their wrath in the process. By eliminating them from the board, I was prolonging peace so that my people could have a few more years to enjoy nights like these. Moon cakes and rice wine and lanterns and children in new winter coats running free and happy and giggling in their childhood innocence. For they did not know of the apocalypse that loomed on the horizon as members of the Roman senate urged their monarch to unleash the full wrath of their military upon us.

Soon, all of our happiness and joy might become cinder and ash, memories of a time that once was.

"我不求荣华富贵," I whispered into the cold evening air. "我只求奶奶和妹妹安度余年." *I don't wish for prosperity or wealth; I only wish for my grandmother and sister to live out their lives in peace.*

I tried not to look at the kids in threadbare clothes.

The homeless who slept frozen in dark corners.

The families who huddled to keep warm.

The parents who begged on their knees for pennies to feed their starving children.

The parents hawking their own kids so they could buy another dose of opian.

Familiar sights. But now, when my eyes grazed over these pin-sharp anguishes that splintered into heartbreak, all I saw was Antony. His childhood. How he had grown up as one of these starved children once upon a time in another world.

He knew their pain, and refused to turn a blind eye to their suffering just because he could.

There was kindness even in the wickedest of Gods. And all who were monstrous were not monsters.

Like me.

Like him.

Maybe Antony was right, and we were more similar than I wished to believe, wished to see.

Both born with great powers, therefore burdened by a greater responsibility to use those powers wisely.

The world doesn't exist in black and white, or right and wrong . . . Sometimes bad things must be done for the greater good.

I could only hope this wasn't forever. That one day soon Antony would ascend the Roman throne and change things for the better.

I hoped when that day came, these people would still be alive to see the sun shine on our city once more.

A world where we could walk with our heads held high.

A world where the privilege of the Romans wasn't built on the suffering of Pangu.

Hope was a grand thing, but not an antidote. It didn't make the killings any easier.

I cried over good men, just as I cried over bad men.

These icy waves of needle-laced self-loathing washed over me, pushed me further and further from the lights of the distant harbor. So distant I felt like I could never turn back.

To my surprise, Antony met my weakness with kindness.

When the tears fell, he always placed a hand upon my shoulder then held me.

Always, he held me—through the shame that was heavy as damnation, drowning me in its shivering depths.

Those arms were comforting and strong, and they felt like an anchor whenever I was tucked safely within—the only thing that could shield me from the maddening waves. Even as the water climbed higher, as I did all I could to stay above the tides on my tiptoes, he was the only thing that tethered me to my fraying sanity.

When summer eves darkened into winter dusk, he became my only source of warmth. The only place where I could break down, over and over again. The only person I could talk to and be heard, understood.

Without shame.

Without judgment.

Antony didn't hate me like my sister, didn't look at me with disappointment like my grandmother.

When the prince looked at me, he simply saw me, for me.

"Everything is going to be okay," he murmured. "You are doing the right thing. *We* are doing the right thing. Trust me."

Each time he said this, it made me want to believe in him.

I knew it was wrong, but I couldn't erase the desires that burned under my skin, couldn't snip away the traitorous part that wanted to lean against him, to be held tighter in his arms for moments longer. Bury my face in him and not think of the consequences of my actions, of the faces of those I had killed.

All that they could have done with their lives. The future where those men had lived instead of me and maybe changed the world as Meiya dreamt in her grand fantasies.

Guilt chewed at me like vultures over a corpse.

Shame wrought a noose around my throat, too tight to breathe.

The voices I tried so hard to ignore. The things I pretended not to see, not to know, not to think of.

And yet . . .

By doing Antony's bidding, I was helping him amass power, putting him steps closer to the Roman throne, where he could enact change and rule more benevolently than his grandfather.

I wasn't selfish. I wasn't a traitor to my people. I did this to protect my family, yes, but in the process, I was also protecting every other family who called Er-Lang home.

For if one day Antony ascended the Roman throne, he would do better by us.

Antony would do better . . .

He had to.

Because Er-Lang would not survive a war between magic and science. In a few months' time, if his grandfather decided to invade my realm instead of letting the status quo continue, it would be the end of everything.

The end of Er-Lang.

The end of us.

Apocalypse, as Antony had called it. There would be no place to run, and no place to hide.

I feared that day.

I feared for the lost souls that would swarm these streets, if there were any streets left after Rome rained hellfire upon the capital like they did all those years ago in the one-day war that had killed my grandfather.

A life on our knees was better than Death.

Better than an Empire in ruins. Better than corpses littering these streets with no one left alive to bury them.

This era of détente was only temporary. If men like the ones I'd killed kept provoking Rome, kept giving the Roman Emperor a reason to fight, to retaliate, then these last dregs of stalemate would soon perish, too. Everything would fade to dust, swept away by the winter winds.

This was why I had to walk this path with Antony, why I followed his orders without question.

Even if my stomach knotted with nausea.

There were no right or wrong choices in times like these. There were only ways to make the best out of bad situations . . .

This land had seen too many tragedies already.

Please, no more.

PART 3

卧虎藏龙

Crouching Tiger, Hidden Dragon

24

TIME SWEPT ME AWAY IN its embrace. Death haunted my every breath.

Days passed with the seasons, and in the blink of an eye, six months perished between taut fingers. When the leaves withered and snow fell, a part of me died with them.

In the six months since my deal with Antony, my tally of sins now trailed long and far—forty-eight innocent lives whom Antony perceived as threats against Rome and Er-lang.

Their faces tormented my dreams; their blood stained my hands like the juices of rotting berries, scarlet and crimson. I dipped these in water a thousand times, but Death wasn't something that could be washed out so easily.

"Only the powerful get to protect those they love," I repeated Antony's words as I watched my childhood home, the newly painted red doors gleaming in the sunlight.

Vendors hollered and snow crunched under horse-drawn carriages in the distant morning market. Festivity lingered in the air, days after the New Year. Scent of gunpowder was still sharp from fireworks, and festive decorations remained slung across the streets. Despite the horror and trauma of Rome's raid six months earlier, joy found a way to break the weeping frost like a stubborn spring sprout.

Not only had my family's door been repainted since the last time

I was here, three weeks ago, but also the walls had been cleaned, the weeds plucked. Gazing from the shadow, I no longer saw the withering remains of a fallen house, but the stronghold of a prosperous family—as prosperous as we were allowed to be under Roman influence, at least.

I didn't want them to know where I was and what I was doing, so Antony funneled money into Grandma's hands through small trades, made sure every penny returned to her tenfold.

Antony had also offered to move my family somewhere safe, quiet. Far from the watchful eyes of Valentin and all the danger that came with being Antony's assassin, ally, friend—whatever was between us. But Grandma would never leave this house she had built with my grandfather, where she had raised her children then watched them die one by one. My father was the only child who survived to adulthood, and even he had died in her arms, years later, leaving her withered and gray and all alone in this world trying to take care of two little girls.

This was our home. *Her* home. Three generations of the Yang clan had lived here; she wouldn't abandon our legacy. Six months earlier, she might have left if war came to her front steps, but not now.

I knew her too well.

Because if she left, how would I find them again? This was the only home I'd ever known, and until I came back into her arms, she would stay until her bones ached and her body frayed. Stay until her last stolen breath, waiting for me.

Always waiting, waiting, waiting, for her little girl to come home.

And if Grandma wanted to stay, I would do everything in my power to make sure she could, to keep her and this house safe.

Around me, snow melted slowly; the sun climbed higher into the pale blue sky. We were at the cusp of spring, yet winter's last breaths clung to the cold air like an Emperor not ready to give up his reign. Even in my fur-lined coat, I shivered, feet slightly damp inside leather boots, half-sunken into slush as I tried to hide from prying eyes and anyone who might recognize me.

When I heard clicking hooves and the slow-rolling wheels of a carriage, I tucked myself deeper into the shadows. My bare hands gripped the ice-covered wall of the alley until I caught a brief glimpse of Grandma's silvered hair and Meiya's dark locks.

远在天边, 近在眼前. *As far as the edge of the sky, but close enough to be right before my eyes.* I could reach out, touch them if I wished . . .

I bit back the too-familiar sting of tears. Despite getting everything I wanted, all I did these days was cry or hold myself back from tears.

I should go, but I couldn't tear my eyes away.

They were my family. My home. The one place where all the twisted pieces of me made sense. I felt safety in Antony's comforting arms, but that feeling was nothing compared to home. Compared to sitting at the dinner table with Grandma and Meiya. I leaned into Antony's touch because I knew his power and how he could protect me. Here, with my grandmother and sister, we protected each other.

When my sister helped Grandma down from the carriage, I held my breath and clutched the wall harder. These winters were getting colder, and Grandma's bones grew more fragile with each passing year. She was at the age, aunties say, if you fall down once, you never stand right again.

My heart writhed at the thought of Grandma hurting herself and me not being there to take care of her.

What if by bargaining with the enemy, I had forfeited my right to be at my grandmother's side for her twilight years, her last moments?

This was a thought that frightened me more than Death, more than my own powers, more than the ghosts who haunted my dreams, demanding vengeance.

But if those I loved got to live long and prosperous lives because I was a traitor spilling the blood of kin for the enemy, then this was a price I would keep paying.

I was already neck deep now in Antony's bid for power, his dream of a better tomorrow.

It was too late to turn back.

"Careful," Meiya urged as she helped Grandma from the carriage. Color had returned to my sister's cheeks; the dark veins gone from her fingertips.

The supply of opian Antony discreetly put into the hands of my sister was just as addictive, but didn't damage the body as much as the regular kind. Still dependent, still a bargaining chip in the palm of his hand.

Small mercies.

There was a red puffiness to her eyes. She'd been crying, losing sleep. Both she and Grandma had been restless in their search for me, in their—

The pain came sharp and sudden. I felt blood coming before the gags and the heaves. Before my insides burned as if seared by sizzling oil, and my knees caved under me, numb and cold.

I ducked behind the wall just in time, hid in shadows and mud where nobody would see. I threw up one, two, three mouthfuls of blood. Discolored and thick, congealed in a way blood shouldn't be.

It's starting.

I'd heard stories of Xianlings who'd exhausted their magic, but I never thought it would happen so fast. I wiped the red with the back of my hand, careful not to get it on my coat sleeves—an old habit from when nice things were rare and had to be treasured.

A deep breath, then I pushed myself to my feet. I had to go. I shouldn't have stayed this long in the first place. A glimpse: This was the promise I made with myself each time I came. Yet each time I lingered longer than I was meant to, than I knew was safe.

More than once, I had stumbled forward, longing to dry my grandmother's tears, run into my sister's arms, step back into my old room, climb into my old bed as if no time had passed. As if the Romans had never taken me that night.

Days ago, when Lunar New Year came and went, it was my first one not spent with family.

Instead, I spent it east of the Empire, in a border town nestled between Er-Lang and Lei-Zhen, where an imperial advisor with the Emperor's ear spent the holiday in his hometown with his mother, his wife, and two small children. A boy and girl with sweet, dimpled smiles and eyes full of stars. Laughter that radiated happiness when they ran into their father's arms.

The official had been a kind man who gave money to the poor and advocated for the weak. A rarer trait than people liked to admit as tensions between Rome and Er-Lang grew more strained by the day. Most people were too busy looking out for themselves to care for others.

I'd scaled the walls, perched outside of his window as he tucked his children into bed, then reached into the room, gently, to take his soul while he slept.

A kindness I only offered men who truly didn't deserve to die.

Which were most of the men Antony asked me to kill these days.

New Year was a time to eat dumplings, light fireworks, plaster walls with red calligraphy, and be with loved ones. I should have been home with my sister and grandmother, not taking a father from his children, a husband from his wife, a son from his mother. And his children . . . They shouldn't have to wake up on New Year's Eve to find their father's corpse.

"I'm not the Ruying they loved anymore," I reminded myself. My hands were stained with too much blood.

Even as my feet teetered, even as my heart was pulled by the yearning of ten thousand burning suns for home, for my family, I couldn't bring myself to step into the light. Grandma wept for her stolen granddaughter, but this grief would be nothing compared to the pure hatred and shame she'd feel if she ever knew what I'd done, what I was doing, to keep her and Meiya safe.

Antony had fulfilled all of his promises. He had given my family the protection I'd asked for, secretly lined Grandma's pocket with enough riches that they would never have to worry about food or shelter or firewood for winter again.

And with the power of a Roman prince at my back, I was free to do whatever I wanted, go wherever I wanted . . .

Just not home.

This was the path I chose. I would walk it until my feet bled, until magic killed me, until Death took me to the eighteenth level of hell to repent my sins, or until I saw Antony sitting high on the Roman throne and this world a better, safer place under his rule.

25

Before each job, I recalled Antony's orders. *"Make it traceless, a death of natural causes. A stroke or a heart attack, whatever people want to call it. As long as nobody knows what I am doing."*

The target of today's mission was a merchant with a loud voice, causing trouble where he shouldn't.

I waited outside of his house. Our shoulders brushed when he passed, then I reached out with Death's magic.

Two steps later, his *qi* began to dim, his breathing labored. Five steps later, his body collapsed among the crowds, hitting the snow-frozen ground with the *thud* of a thrown sack of rice.

Nine steps later, a woman screamed.

I kept walking. Death's gray world faded in slow progression; colors bled back with every step that carried me farther from my victim.

It took eighteen steps for everything to return to its natural hue.

These days, I noticed how colors returned slower and slower with each kill. A subtle reminder of the price of magic.

When I reached a corner, I leaned against the alley wall to steady myself.

Blood trickled down my nose.

The Gods gave with one hand and took with the other.

Forty-nine.

26

Antony was right.

The killing got easier.

I hated that he was right. Hated that, with every murder, my morals crumbled and numbed to the point where guilt no longer brought tears to my eyes.

Conquer your fears, or they'll conquer you, I told myself to justify the person I had become.

Someone my sister and grandmother would be ashamed to know.

Someone *I* was ashamed to be.

I felt like an hourglass, some vital essence trickled out with each mission.

Antony's list of enemies was never-ending.

My life, waning.

What would become of me when these mortal sands came to a stop?

With a deep breath, I pushed myself off the wall. Dawson was waiting for me at the Fence. I'd lingered too long at my home, already running late. I was about to step out of the alley when a narrow figure blocked the light.

"Ruying?" A voice that pulled my heart to a stop.

Meiya.

When my sister stepped into the alley's mouth, the world fell away and my beating heart became the only audible sound through the thundering silence.

I caught my breath, lips parted and closed like a fish gulping air, trying to find the right words. She wasn't supposed to be here. She wasn't supposed to see me. Yet . . .

The tears fell before I could stop them.

"Meiya." I whimpered her name, so comforting and melodic in my mouth. "I've missed you. I—"

My sister stumbled back when I approached her, apprehension in her eyes. Her gaze fell to my hands, to the thin strips of metal around my wrists.

A frown. Disappointment slowly twisted her face.

"So, Baihu was right."

"Baihu?" I stood straighter. I had not seen Baihu again after that day in the Lotus Tower with Antony. "What did he say to you?"

Meiya looked left and right, checked our surroundings before she slipped deeper into the shadows of the alley.

I followed her.

Always, I followed her.

My heart thrashed like a caged animal, and I wondered if she could hear it.

The sky was darkening. Dawson would wonder where I was soon. I had to get back before he got impatient and came searching for me.

The last time I had returned from my mission too late, he'd used the cuffs to send those painful electric shocks through me for almost five minutes as a warning. I couldn't let Meiya see me go through that kind of pain.

"You promised you'd never use your Gift again after Hushan," Meiya murmured once we came to a stop. I couldn't help but notice how she inched away from me, as if she couldn't bear being this close to me. "You once told me that magic is not a Gift, that no mortal should have the power to decide who lives and who dies. It was just an excuse, wasn't it? You have no problem using your Gift, just not for Er-Lang, not for your own people."

Her sharp eyes were razors, each look of disgust a cut at my already bleeding heart.

"Unless it's a life-or-death situation," I corrected.

"That man who's just died did nothing to threaten you, yet you killed him."

I flinched. "You have no proof that I killed him."

"I'd know your magic anywhere, sister. I know *you*. Don't think just because you hid behind some wall that I won't see you. Why are you doing this, Ruying? Why are you hiding from us? Do you have any idea how much Grandma—"

My breath hitched. "You didn't say anything to her, right?"

"And break her heart all over again?" She laughed. "I'm not as cruel as you."

"A lot has changed, Meiya. I know you don't like what I'm doing, but trust me, it's for the greater good."

She sneered, her face vicious even as tears welled in her eyes. "You know, when Baihu told me that you had betrayed us and started working for the Romans, I thought he was lying. I thought: Not *my* sister. She would never do something like that. Not *my* sister . . ."

"It's not what you think. I'm doing this for you! For Grandma! For Er-Lang, and for—"

"How can you say that when you are literally out here, murdering our kin, our people?" Meiya snapped, teeth bared and feral in her rage at Rome, at the world . . .

At me.

I swallowed the lump in my throat. Piece by piece, I told her the events of the past six months, how I hid her under the floorboards and let myself get caught to protect her. The cage, the cuffs, the exhibition, and my failed escape.

Then, Antony's offer.

When I was done, there was silence. Then my sister shook her head. "Do you remember what Grandma told us when we were young and had just discovered our powers?"

I did. "Power means responsibility."

"The Gods blessed us with magic so that we can protect those who can't protect themselves."

"I didn't ask for this *curse* of a Gift, Sister. None of us did. But I am doing everything I can to protect those who cannot. Prince Antony is a good man. By helping him seize power, I am preserving peace. There is an apocalypse coming, and if we—"

"Open your eyes and look around, Ruying! The people of Er-Lang—of Pangu—will never know true peace as long as Rome holds power over us. We can't turn back time and reverse our ancestors' mistake of trusting them, but it's not too late for us to get back what is lost. This world belongs to us. This *land* belongs to us, soaked with the blood of our ancestors, held up by their ancient bones. The Gods blessed *us* with magic, not the Romans. They might think themselves mighty, conquerors like the Qin Emperor, but the Romans have no claim over this land. We can't let them rule *our* city like some wicked Gods from beyond the skies. We have to do something. We have to *fight,* Ruying."

I thought back to the armory Antony had shown me. Rome's fighter jets and missiles, the destruction they could inflict upon our world with just the touch of a button. "It's not that simple, Sister. What makes you think we'd stand a chance against Rome and their science? Their planes and ships? You don't know the things I've seen. You've never felt science drain magic from your body." I held up the cuffs as a demonstration. "And I hope you never will."

Meiya's eyes narrowed, stubborn. "Science might be strong, but magic can be stronger if we are willing to harness our powers and give it our all."

"A war of magic and science might end *everything,*" I echoed Antony's words from months earlier.

"If it's a miserable death either way, I'd rather die fighting for what I believe in than die on my knees as a coward. We owe our

ancestors this much, don't you think?" Meiya leaned closer, her
expression suddenly soft. "If you want, the Phantom can—"

"No," I cut her off before she could finish the thought. "Antony
will kill me the moment he doubts my loyalty. I can't put you and
Grandma in danger like that. And if you were smart, you wouldn't,
either."

Right thing or not, I would offer Death my own life before I let
harm come to my family.

Blood drenched my hands, and magic was killing me slowly. The
only solace I had left was knowing my family would outlive me,
safe under Antony's protection long after I was ashes and bone.
Their safety was more important than everything, even above safe-
guarding peace.

"Ruying," Meiya whispered, hope shining in the dark eyes that
mirrored mine. "You are the girl blessed by Death. You can burn
the world to the ground if you wish to. Mama named you *Ruying*
because she wanted you to be brave. Even with her last breath,
Mama believed in you. Make her proud, Sister. Be the hero our
world needs."

"I *am* doing the right thing," I protested. "I'm protecting you
and Grandma, and I'm protecting peace. Not all Romans are bad,
Meiya. Some of them are—"

My sister's laugh was a knife that drove right into my chest.
Chilling, bitter with hatred and barely restrained fury bubbling too
close to the surface. "No Roman is good, Ruying. Look at what
these demons have done to our world! A Roman prince whose
wealth and privilege are built upon the bones of our people is not
going to help us. He's one of *them,* and you are just as bad if you
turn your back on your own kind to serve him like some dog."

I flinched at her words, nausea turning in the pit of my stomach.
"You don't understand. He's different. He wants to help and he's
not like his brothers. He's *good.* I know he is."

"I can't tell if you are too naïve for your own good, Ruying. Tell
me you're not stupid enough to believe in his lies."

"It's not all black and white, Meiya. If Antony becomes the ruler of Rome, he will be a good monarch and will bring peace to our two realms."

Resentment trampled hope as Meiya's eyes turned hard and cold as this long winter. "There will never be peace as long as their people walk our world. Look around, Ruying, at how the Romans treat us. Things will only get worse the more power they accumulate. *Please,* see the longer we idle the—"

"No. I can't."

Meiya flinched, and my heart shattered at the sight. Ten thousand broken shards slicing open my chest, sharper than any blade—though everything bled beneath the surface where she would never see. "Peace is sacred, and it is worth every sin I've committed and more. Sometimes, we must make sacrifices for the greater good. The path to a better world isn't built on good intentions and righteous dreams. Sometimes, peace is paved on the withered corpses of terrible, terrible deeds."

A grimace tugged my sister's lips. "Maybe you're just using all of this as an excuse. Maybe the real reason you serve that Roman prince is because you're spineless. Just like Father. And like Father, the only person you care about is yourself. Your name and Gift are wasted on you."

"Meiya, trust me," I tried to say, my words desperate to pull her close so that she could see things from my perspective. But Meiya kept her distance, refused to be reached. I felt that insurmountable distance between us again.

"We are Gifted for a reason, Ruying. When we have this kind of power but willingly waste it, that's when bad things happen. And they happen because of us."

"Meiya—"

"Don't you *dare* say my name!" she spat. "I will say this one last time. If we don't stop the Romans, then the kind of life left for us won't be one worth living. If you want to protect me, protect Grandma, then you'll help the Phantom to overthrow Rome and everything they stand for. Help us make the sun shine on Er-Lang again. This isn't just what Grandma and I want. It's what Mama would have wanted, too."

"I'm sorry, Meiya. I can't."

"Then you are no sister of mine." Her lips curled into a chilling smile. Tears gathering in her eyes. "Mama would be ashamed if she could see the kind of person you've become."

I watched Meiya walk away.

She didn't look back.

I knew my sister. Once Meiya decided on something, nothing in this world could change her mind.

In her shadow, I fell to my knees.

For the first time in a long, long time, I let myself wonder whether I'd made a grave mistake.

High above the city, the portal flickered, just for a moment.

27

THE ROMAN SIDE OF THE city breathed opulence, but all that glittered was not gold. The stationed soldiers shot me wary looks when I approached the Fence, their grips on holstered guns a little too tight for comfort. It didn't matter how many times I entered and exited these gates; the response was the same. Disgust and contempt were clear in their eyes.

A lump in my throat. I tried to swallow, over and over again, because I had to. To protest and cause a scene would mean Death.

Not mine, theirs.

I flashed them the badge that signaled my right to pass the Fence and walk their streets.

The guards exchanged a glance.

"Yang Ruying?" They checked my name, but before I could respond, my bracelets hummed to life and magic was stolen from me once more.

A ritual each time I stepped into their world. It didn't matter how much Prince Antony valued me; they couldn't let a Xianling walk their streets unchallenged.

"You are late." Dawson stepped out from behind them, that annoying remote in his hand.

"The roads are slippery," I replied, doing my best to keep my tone vacant. My sister's words still echoed in my ears, the constant lashings of a merciless whip, shredding my heart bloody.

I couldn't let it show. I couldn't let Dawson know what'd happened.

Though Antony had never said I wasn't allowed to see my family, it was better this way. If he knew Meiya's allegiances, there would be trouble. Not for me, but for her.

"Well, walk faster next time." With that, Dawson's thumb stroked the remote lovingly, and an excruciating jolt of electricity bolted through my body, like flesh being ripped from bones. Like the teeth of ten thousand blades tearing me open all at once.

I bit my lips. The pain intensified, sang louder and louder, but I wouldn't give him the satisfaction of watching me scream.

"You know I can kill you," I snarled when, finally, the pain subsided.

He buzzed me again, the shock even more painful than the last time. "Not while I have this in my hands."

One day, I'm going to finish what I started six months ago at that night market. How I wished I'd killed this vile man when I had the chance.

I didn't tell him this; didn't tell him anything. He wasn't worthy of my words. He wasn't even worthy of my magic. When I killed him, I would shoot him with the guns Antony had taught me to use. The shot would not be fatal, at least not immediately. I would not grant him a quick death. Not before I would bind these cuffs to him and make him taste my pain.

When I refused to scream for him, Dawson rolled his eyes, interest lost. He turned on his heels and I trailed behind, keeping distance between us.

I hated him. Hated the unnecessary violence he inflicted with twisted merriment just to keep me in check—though I rarely overstepped the boundaries Antony set. Yes, I'd teetered at their edge each time I said something Antony didn't like, but Antony never punished me, never raised his voice, never got angry.

He merely smiled at my unwise words—something I didn't know how to decipher.

Dawson? He hated me. I wasn't sure whether he hated me for my Xianling blood, the fact that I was not of his world, or because I almost killed him once upon a time.

The beauty of Rome's gated city, nested inside the slow-beating heart of our capital, was a sight few of my people had ever witnessed.

The Pangulings who had such privilege were often important officials with loyalties in Rome's pockets, or royals born with power and influence—the sort of status that benefited Rome in some way. I tried not to think of the Xianlings stolen from their beds, now trapped beneath in the city's intricate dungeons. Those who had no idea they were on Rome's side of the city and would never see these ivory buildings and marble arches.

Nobody would have thought the daughter of a fallen house could be a member of this exclusive list of visitors.

Yet here I was.

If Father could see me now, would he be proud or ashamed? He'd probably see it as an accomplishment if I were a boy, and an act of treason because I was a girl. This was how things had always worked.

Boys with power were admired—legendary heroes worthy of songs and poetry to remember their honor. Girls with power were painted as malicious, evil, because we wanted more to life than birthing children and following duties. Chasing dreams was forbidden, and *love* was a word we'd never truly understand.

Memories of a sunlit Baihu flashed before my eyes, the kind eyes and gentle smile of our youth. Wandering thoughts of where he was and how he was doing crept back like they always did.

These past few months, our lives had existed in parallel. When I walked on this side of the Fence, he was kept on the other. I couldn't tell whether this was a coincidence, or if Antony purposefully kept us apart.

Our last moment in the Lotus Tower lingered, the way Antony's attention had darted between Baihu and me, suspicion a creeping mist beneath pale jade eyes. I remembered the slightest grimace of his lips, a fleeting display of irritation at seeing Baihu and me standing so close.

What would Baihu think if he saw me now?

I used to mock him for being a traitor. And in the span of a few months, I'd come to embody everything I used to hate about him. Out of options and out of hope, condemned to a smear of gray against this grand canvas. I could only hope that despite everything, choosing to side with Antony was the right thing. That he would fulfill his promises of mercy and kindness.

I am doing the right thing. I tried to reassure myself as my sister's words drifted back into consciousness like the lasting echo of a slammed *gong* that refused to quiet.

Antony was good. He was kind. I had faith in the future he envisioned. One where the Romans and Xianlings lived in harmony. A future where war wasn't necessary and peace, precarious as it was, could be prolonged and maintained.

I had faith in Antony.

Because I had to.

Because the alternative was too horrific to consider.

I would not let Antony's brothers win. I would not let them sit high and mighty on their throne of bones and slaughter my people like a herd of winter sheep.

War.

Bloodshed.

Apocalypse.

A life on our knees was no life at all, but a war between magic and science might be the end of everything as we knew it.

Meiya clung to her hopes and her righteous words of martyrdom, but change was not so easily enacted.

Not when our opponents held the might of ten thousand Gods in the palms of their hands, capable of unleashing a storm of weaponry that would bring hell to the land I called home and destroy everything the eye could see.

These rebellions would only anger them further, push war closer to our shores.

I pulled my coat tighter. The eerie quiet of these empty streets made it feel colder than Er-Lang's half of the city, where streets bustled with people and the warm sounds of laughter. Here, there was nothing but loneliness and hollowed regret painted as superiority and grace.

Once upon a time, when the treaty was first signed, when the late Emperor was still alive, the Fence used to be farther west.

Then, the Romans asked for more land, more space for their city to grow, so they could move more people over. Our Emperors, both current and past, agreed without a fight each time. This was why people called them puppet Emperors. For they held no power, not while most of their court were in Rome's pockets, or wished to be in Rome's pockets.

Power shifted right before our eyes and there was nothing we could do to stop it. Back then I thought the same things—that our Emperors were cowards who had sold us to Rome in their fear.

Now, I knew this was not true.

They were strategists. They were biding their time. If they had not conceded to Rome's every demand, the city would have burned, and everyone with it.

How could our bodies of soft and fragile flesh overpower machines of war so monstrous that survivors of the one-day war still wept in fear every time a plane crossed our sky?

They were strong, and we were weak.

This was evolution.

Conquer, or be conquered.

The soldiers who patrolled the streets frowned at the sight of me. At my face and my clothes, worn to blend in with my side of the city. But even if I tried to wear their clothes, walk like them, talk like them, they still saw through my façade. Heard the twang of accent I tried so hard to erase, the subtle mannerisms that yelled *imposter*.

At least with Dawson leading me, I wasn't stopped every few steps by soldiers who questioned my right to be here.

The few Romans who passed us kept their distance. In fear or disgust, I wasn't sure. The metal bands around my wrists marked me as Other.

I hated the way they looked at me, hated their ignorance about everything their debauchery and reckless joy were built upon: the blood and bones and intergenerational trauma of my people.

Yet I craved acceptance. To have them look at me as they would their own. For them to see me not for where I came from, but as someone special, powerful beyond mortal dreams.

I wanted them to look at me as Antony did.

With respect.

With reverence.

With tender kindness that granted me the warm feeling of safety that so few people had ever made me feel.

I wanted them to see my Gift as something wondrous instead of dangerous.

Because no matter how many times they whispered and pointed, grimaced in distaste or hollered that I wasn't welcomed on Roman land—despite an invitation from their prince—the pain in my chest remained.

Antony had kept his promise. My family was safe, and my pockets were full of gold. I no longer worried about the winter cold or hunger. And every bad thing I did, every man I killed, kept this city breathing, the hearts of its people beating.

Blood stained the very hands that also kept war from marching these streets.

I was doing the right thing, yet I was sadder than when I had nothing.

A drop of wetness kissed my cheek.

The sky was crying again.

28

DAWSON STOPPED AT THE DOOR when we reached Antony's home at the top of a hill that overlooked both halves of Jing-City. He didn't have clearance to enter whenever he wished, but I did.

I flashed a delighted smile over this tiny victory.

Antony's home was just like the city. Opulent and ostentatious but barren of warmth, accompanied by an echoing kind of silence that made me feel sorry for him. He claimed he liked to be alone, so these hallways held few guards. This was a lie. He kept his home sparse of people because he didn't trust anyone who was not himself.

Any of these guards could gather his secrets and report them to his brother.

It was isolating, the life of a prince who wished to rule.

Every time I came here to report my missions, there was not a single visitor.

Which was why the chime of glasses caught my attention.

I stalked toward the source of the sound. The library with its door slightly ajar.

I peeked inside.

The person I found was not Antony but Prince Valentin, alone in the mahogany room, watching Jing-City through high windows, tapping his wineglass against the window in a rhythmic motion. His jaw was tense, and his eyes were hard as he stared at the city beyond—a shade of want in his eyes, a kind of hunger that couldn't be satisfied.

I frowned and was about to slip away when he turned and spotted me. "Care to join?" he asked in a marble-smooth voice, raising the glass in his hand. "I hate drinking alone, and my brother seems to be taking his sweet time coming home."

I hesitated, checking behind me to make sure I was the one he addressed. Valentin never acknowledged my existence after the time he tried to inject me with opian. I was shocked he remembered me.

The clock ticked. It was barely noon. Too early for alcohol. Though one might argue it was also too early to commit murder, and I'd done just that.

"Come," he whispered, voice deep and velvety. Confidence and charisma dripped from him, thick like honey. Antony said Valentin was a good negotiator. I could see how even the toughest of Er-Lang officials could be talked into submission by a voice like that and a face so alluring. "I won't bite."

There was a redness to his cheeks. This wasn't his first glass of wine.

Drunk men had loose lips.

With cautious steps, I approached and took a seat on one of the bolster chairs with carved arms and supple cushions.

The Romans knew how to live their best lives.

These halls were illuminated by electricity, not candles. Their water was boiled by machines and their fires were instant. The Romans didn't have to work for anything on their side of the Fence. Everything was readily available, there at the touch of a button.

"What's your poison?" He gestured at the table of alcoholic beverages, which bore labels I didn't recognize. I wasn't a fan of alcohol. I didn't like the fuzzy way it made me feel, the slowed reactions and numbed control.

"Whatever you're having," I told him.

Valentin poured another glass of wine from the same bottle—a liquid so dark it was almost the color of blood.

When he handed me the drink, I waited until he took a sip before drinking. The wine was strong, and sweeter than I had expected.

"I heard you've been killing people for my brother."

"For Rome," I corrected him, repeating the answer Antony had taught me. "I heard you've been terrorizing the young Emperor," I added after a beat, watching Valentin with the gaze of a tiger sizing up her target.

The prince was on the verge of drunk, and this was the most vulnerable I'd ever seen him. Knowledge was power, and I couldn't waste this chance to steal his. All I had to do was get him to lower his guard and . . .

"That's hardly a nice thing to say," he said with a chuckle. "Someone has to fix Antony's mess."

"What mess?"

Valentin laughed. "My brother likes to play the role of saint, make fun of me and Cassius for our ways, but he is as cold and reckless as the rest of us."

"Cassius?"

"Our other brother."

The youngest Roman prince. The military protégé who had never passed through the portal if rumors were to be believed. The one who had stayed at their grandfather's side all these years.

His most trusted grandson.

"Did you not know there are three Roman princes?" Valentin's lips were loose indeed. "Me, the only biological grandson. Antony, the kid-genius plucked from the gutters. And Cassius . . . My grandfather's dearest Cassius. The last surviving heir of his closest confidant. After his family passed, my grandfather adopted Cassius as his own, putting him in the line of succession in case Antony and I both turn out to be unsatisfactory." A chuckle. "Did Antony not tell you any of this? How many secrets he must keep from you. I bet you have no idea, do you?"

My chest suddenly grew tight at his taunt. "What else is there?"

Again, the prince laughed. "Have you met the Er-Lang Emperor yet?"

I liked how he said *yet,* as if someone like me had the right to hold court with the Emperor of Er-Lang whenever I pleased. "I haven't met him, but I've heard he's very handsome," I replied, letting him change his subject. I would guide him, but subtly. Make him comfortable, coax rambling secrets from those lax lips.

Prince Valentin swirled his drink, watching the dark liquid dance in his glass. "He's an interesting man, Emperor Yongle. He's nothing like what your people paint him as. He's calculated, careful. He's also a broken man who lost his father, and whose only remaining sibling sits in our dungeons as a hostage." The slightest of frowns; Valentin almost looked sad.

I leaned forward. Could a monster like him be capable of remorse?

The Prince fell quiet. His eyes were far away, his attention elsewhere. "Your world is beautiful. It reminds me of my grandfather's photographs from when our world wasn't so polluted. Back when our Earth loved us and didn't try to drive the human race to extinction with pandemics and famines and droughts and floods. I envy your people, you know. How lucky you are to be loved by your world."

I had no idea what he was talking about, but I held on to every word, memorizing every little shift in his tone. There was a secret here, and I would decipher it sooner or later. "Tell me about your world," I coaxed. "What's it like?"

"Not unlike yours, I guess. Our skies are blue, and our grasses are green. The air here is cleaner, though. My father used to praise your world for its mountains and its rivers when he first crossed the portal. What's the saying your people use? *Qian shan, rui shui?* Pale mountain, green water?"

Qing shan, lü shui, I almost corrected him. "Do you miss your world?" I continued. "How long have you been here?"

"A long time. And yes, I miss it. I dream of home every day. Just as I dread it."

"Why?"

A shrug. An exhale just short of laughter. "My brother and I can't leave until we get our grandfather what he wants. And he—" The prince stopped himself. Like a man startling awake, his eyes yielded into focus, then shook his head as if trying to pull himself out of this drunken haze. A sly grin. "I almost said a little too much there, didn't I?"

Don't be sorry. Keep talking, I thought, smiling politely. "Not at all."

Valentin set his drink down, rubbed his temples. Something glistened in his eyes. "I don't know what's gotten into me today."

I knew the face of a haunted man when I saw it. Were those drunken tears, or ones of genuine shame and guilt?

It felt wrong, seeing Valentin like this. The role of a guilt-stricken prince was Antony's to play. I didn't expect to see someone like Valentin so wounded and unguarded—a side of him I didn't think existed, so far from the cruel prince my city's rumors had painted him as.

From the merciless killer I remembered as a child, the killer who had yawned at our torment.

When a tear escaped his left eye, I sat a little straighter, resisting the urge to offer him the handkerchief in my pocket.

This man is evil incarnate. He doesn't deserve my sympathy.

"Tell me, Yang Ruying, what do you think of us?" he asked suddenly.

Cautious of the thin ice beneath my feet, I hesitated and weighed my answer. "I don't know. What do you think of me?"

The prince shrugged. "A clean and accurate shot, every time. A weapon designed to kill with minimum collateral damage. So beautiful, so lethal, like a jeweled dagger. I almost wish I'd gotten to you first, made you mine before Antony laid his claim to you. Who knows, maybe you'll come and work for me once my grandfather tosses Antony aside. I don't like not having the toys I want."

His eyes were sharp and sober all at once. He wasn't as drunk as he'd led me to believe.

I almost smiled. There was the Valentin I knew him to be. "Would that really happen?"

"What?"

"Would your grandfather really cast Antony aside? If you truly believe that, you wouldn't hate Antony so much, right? Are you bitter that your grandfather pays more attention to Antony than he does to you? Trusts Antony more than his own blood?"

A clench of his jaw, a narrowing of his eyes. "I don't like it when my prey talks back to me."

"I'm not your prey." I was his brother's secret assassin. Even if he wanted to hurt me, he couldn't. Not while I remained under Antony's protection.

"Not *yet*," he murmured. "My grandfather should have killed the lot of you and forced this land into submission years ago. But my idiot father dreamt of a reality where our two worlds could coexist. He forced my grandfather to show mercy to you savages. Antony is a coward, just like my father. Rome needs a man with the backbone to save it, not a saint who ponders the rights of people who are not his to govern."

"Save it? From what?" I asked. I was so close to the secret now.

"Our Gods." He laughed. "Our nonexistent God, whose name is Mother Nature. She punishes us for our sins. Day by day, year by year. Our dying world. It would be so easy if we could just take over yours. Fly some missiles and bombs over the cities and kill the lot of you."

If it weren't for the bracelets and their murmurs of science, my magic would seethe under my skin at his words. This time, I might just give in to Death's temptation. Deliver punishment to a man who deserved it.

But if I so much as touched a strand of hair on his head, I would never walk out of here alive.

"Antony thinks he has a better solution with his science and never-ending experiments," Valentin continued. "But what our people need isn't more science. We need a second chance. Somewhere safe and clean, free from our vengeful planet. Your world has everything necessary for this new beginning. Raw minerals, land, and oceans. We could build factories, dump our garbage, mine your oils. All the things my world can't withstand anymore . . ." A drunken giggle. "I'm right. My grandfather knows I'm right. Trying to reason with simpletons like you is a waste of time. Sooner or later, he will see the light. Know that the only way to save Rome is to destroy Pangu."

I ground my jaw tight so that he would not see me flinch. Antony had told the truth, at least. He wanted Rome to show mercy, while others of his world wanted apocalypse, annihilation.

Burn everything to the ground, and my people with it.

Even without Death's taunt at my ears, I wanted to make Valentin Augustus bleed for these words. For his arrogance and hate and his rotting, cruel heart. I wanted to remind him that despite all that they claimed, the Romans were not Gods. Not really.

Beneath that façade was flesh and blood.

They were mortal, just like the rest of us.

Yet I plastered on a smile, nodded as if I agreed. A savage who was their pet, seduced by their lies. When, in reality, I was plotting fifty different ways to end his life.

Antony's missions suddenly felt more important than ever. One day, when Antony finally ruled Rome, I would ask him to let me kill his wretched brother. And it would be glorious.

Unlike Dawson, Valentin's death would be worth the lost seconds, minutes, or even hours of life.

But at the same time, for a brief moment, I wished I could experience the world as Valentin Augustus did, just once.

Born into privilege, lulled into a belief in his own grandeur by all the people who wished to use him for their own gains. Valentin's needs weren't really needs. Aroused from entitlement, they were a mirage sewn by the conviction that he could have whatever he wanted, however he wanted.

Footsteps sounded in the hallway.

Prince Valentin smiled. "Good. Brother dearest is finally home. I'd hate for him to miss this."

A cunning tilt of his mouth, the glint of a syringe from his suit pocket, and memories of our last encounter came like a flood, sweeping me back to my feet and propelling me to run.

He lunged for me, and I grasped for Death by instinct, but the bracelets kept my magic in chains behind phantom cages. It didn't matter how hard I clawed at those bars, magic was wispy as spider silk, coming apart in my hands, impossible to hold.

So I dodged instead, hoped the combat skills Taohua taught me were enough to protect me. I might not be as strong as she was, but I was fast, and my body moved by instinct even without Death's ever-present tutelage.

But Valentin's legs were longer, his movement fluid and prepared. From the moment I walked through the doors, he had been planning for this.

"I said I'd make you my prey, didn't I?" he said with a sneer when he grabbed me by the collar, the syringe dangerously close to my throat.

Without Death's help, I had to get out of this the old-fashioned way. Hand balled into a fist, I swung at Valentin with all my strength and rattled him off balance for a second. Enough for me to break free.

Out of everything Valentin Augustus thought he knew about me, I doubt he had anticipated that I could fight, that a girl could writhe from his clutches.

When Valentin stumbled, I took the opportunity to kick him in the chest, knocking him off his feet. The needle of opian flew from his hand. I was tempted to run forward and grab it, inject the murky liquid into his veins instead of mine. So that he could get a taste of his own medicine, know the pain he'd inflicted upon too many of my people.

"What's happening?" Antony's voice interrupted before I could give in to my dark desires.

I tried to swallow the rage bubbling at my throat.

"She's too much of a liability for the Sihai mission," Valentin spat as he pushed himself back up.

The corner of his mouth was specked with blood from where I'd punched him.

I wanted to smile.

Good.

"She's feral, just like the rest of them. That magic of hers is too powerful to be left untamed," Valentin continued, spite hard in his every word. "That little—"

When Valentin took a step forward, so did Antony, physically placing his body between us to shield me from Valentin, who raised a brow in confusion. "What are you doing?"

Antony pushed me farther behind him, as if hiding me, protecting me. "Ruying works for me. I don't need your interference. You have no right marching into my home, attacking my—"

"Your what, Brother? Your ally, friend, lover, whore, or whatever she is? Because you are clearly bewitched by her. Don't forget what my grandfather taught you. Don't forget who *you* are, Antony. Who she is, and what we are here to accomplish."

At these words, Antony's eyes went hard. "Heed my warning, Valentin. I will allow this only once. If you ever come near Ruying again, you don't want to know what I'll do to you."

"You're going to regret this," Valentin said with an ugly laugh. "Mark my words, this little minx is going to be the death of you."

"That's up to me to decide, *Brother*." Antony placed a hand on my shoulder. "I trust her."

Valentin laughed. "Why?"

"Because I do."

29

THE SOUND OF GUNSHOTS NO longer made me flinch, and the re-coils no longer knocked me off balance.

I had been an unwilling student when Antony first decided to teach me how to maneuver the weapons of his world, but he was a patient teacher. My aim got better and better with each practice until bull's-eyes were no longer strokes of luck.

Weeks earlier, I had joked that in another six months the student would surpass the teacher, and Antony's smile had bloomed with pride like peonies unfurling for the summer sun, warming my in-sides with a splendid glow.

These days, my smiles mirrored his at every opportunity. And his gaze lingered on me, always.

The curiosity and bitter wariness of our first meeting had long since melted. Now he looked at me with a tenderness that was worlds removed from the prince I met all those months ago.

I felt it not only in his eyes, but in the ghost of a smile that danced at his lips' edge. Genuine smiles—not the forced kind to charm advisors and merchants who wandered in and out of his of-fice presenting problem after problem.

A fragile affection, but affection nonetheless. One I hoped would be enough to save my sister if he found out her allegiance to the Phantom.

If he hadn't already.

Antony's eyes were all-seeing. He just rarely said the quiet parts out loud.

I pulled the trigger. Another round of bullets thundered into the room, but none of them found their marks. I was distracted. Memories of my last encounter with Meiya continued to rattle like the lingering hum of a monastery bell, haunting my every thought. And when I closed my eyes, I could still see Valentin's vicious sneer lunging for me with a needle of liquid opian in hand . . .

As if reading my mind, Antony broke the silence. "I'm sorry for how my brother behaved."

I almost smiled; cheeks flushed and heartbeat suddenly fast. When Antony's voice turned gentle and his words turned indulgent like this, it made me feel like he was on my side. Like he would always be on my side.

And after so many years of being made the enemy by my sister, being feared by my grandmother, being left behind by Baihu and Taohua . . . This was a welcomed feeling.

"And I'm sorry for attacking him," I replied.

"Don't be. He deserved it."

"Thank you."

"For what?"

"For taking my side. For not letting him inject me with opian months ago." *For sticking up for me. For believing in me.*

His lips twitched, an almost-smile. "If you were an instrument under opian's lures, then who would argue with me every day? Who would roll her eyes when I say something stupid?"

I shrugged. "Dawson? He seems brave."

"No one on either side of the Veil is as brave as you, Ruying."

My cheeks warmed. He didn't mean that.

I wasn't brave.

Far from it.

If I were brave, I wouldn't be here. My sister wouldn't hate me. Grandma wouldn't be weeping with worry because I was too ashamed to face her, to tell her that I was still alive.

She was better off thinking I was dead than finding out what I had done.

"Nothing in our contract forbids you from going home to your family, you know," Antony continued.

I stifled a gasp. "You knew?"

How?

Was Antony spying on me?

He had said I was alone during my missions because Roman soldiers couldn't be seen near the site of the murders. But what if they kept a closer eye on me than I had previously thought?

What if they had overheard my conversation with Meiya? What if he knew she worked for the Phantom? Would he—

"Relax," Antony replied, sensing my panic. "I'm not spying on you, but I do have guards around your home. This is part of our deal, isn't it? You take care of those I want dead, and I take care of those you want alive. Though recently, I've been receiving curious reports of a strange girl lurking outside of the Yang home like a stalker . . ."

He cocked a brow at me.

I lowered my gaze.

"Go inside if you miss them that much. You might not care about standing out in the cold for hours at a time just to catch a glimpse of your sister and grandmother, but they would if they knew. I'm not stopping you from going home. Your grandmother misses you; you know this. She won't give up hope of finding you, even after all this time. And something tells me she won't give up until she either sees you at home or sees your dead body."

Was that a threat?

Old habits die hard.

I stood alert and cautious, the ice beneath my feet paper thin.

"Go home and tell them you are alive, at least," Antony added.

I gripped the gun tighter, its familiar weight an unexpected comfort after many months of practice. I turned my attention back to the targets and pulled the trigger.

One bull's-eye, narrowly brushing the center, while the other bullet holes were dotted around the outer sheet.

"If my grandmother knew about our deal—what I'm doing to make sure she and Meiya stay safe and warm and full-bellied through these long winters—she would prefer I was dead."

"You don't know that."

"Yes, I do." Three words so quiet as if they didn't want to be heard. "Plus, why do you care? Shouldn't you be glad that I'm keeping my distance from them? The farther I am from those I love, the more unlikely it is that I'll change my mind, turn my back on you."

"Not if it means hurting you in the process." There was that softness again, an earnest concern, a rare slip of his steely mask that had become more and more frequent as the months passed.

Was this real, or was it manipulation disguised as care?

When I looked at him, my heart felt full from his attentive gaze. So full that I feared it was all in my head. Or maybe he was playing me for a fool. Lies to weave over my eyes so that I saw the world from his perspective, handed my loyalty and my magic to him on a silver platter.

Mama would be ashamed if she could see the kind of person you've become. Meiya's words echoed again. Cheeks flushing for the enemy, my heart beating too fast like a traitor.

Lips parted, I waited for the prince to say more, tell me the words I so desperately wanted to hear—that my family would love me no matter what. That I was doing the right thing, that all of this would be worth it when he ruled Rome and returned my world to its former self.

He didn't.

Antony wasn't one to make promises he couldn't deliver.

I was about to reload the gun when his hand fell over mine, warm. Our fingers laced, ever so slightly. "I'm sorry for dragging you into this," he said, words as tender as I felt.

"Me too."

Two words no louder than a breath, yet it was enough to make this mighty prince flinch and recoil. His hand tightened around mine for a moment before releasing it, lips parted like there was something he wanted to say before he clenched his jaw and bit down on the unspoken thoughts.

There was always something left unsaid between the two of us.

We held back our words like armor and shields, kept secrets on both sides. Despite whatever was growing between us, neither of us trusted the other enough to be honest or vulnerable.

But the more time we spent together, the kinder he was to me, the more comfortable I grew around him, the more I believed that I could hurt him.

Just as he could hurt me.

If not worse.

I could break his heart.

Could he break mine?

We were allies, not friends. And certainly not anything more.

Despite his beauty, despite all the ways my heart raced whenever his skin kissed mine in the faintest of grazes, we could not be anything more.

We were of two different worlds, two different statuses. We had no future.

To believe otherwise was foolish.

Though he made promises of us being equals and allies, we both knew Antony had the power to break my heart worse than I could ever break his.

The moment held its breath. "She's lucky to have you, your sister. What I wouldn't give to have someone like you in my life. Someone who would sacrifice so much, just to protect me, love me."

Wouldn't Valentin do the same for you? The question died on my lips, a stupid thing to ask.

Antony and Valentin were rivals before they were family. Even if they were blood brothers, thicker than water, nothing would outweigh the heavy temptation of power.

Valentin had made it very clear what he wanted most in this world. And it had nothing to do with family.

"How old are you?" I asked instead.

From his arched eyebrow, the question caught him off guard. "Twenty."

Just a year older than I was. "I thought you were older."

"Why? Do I look like a handsome old man?" he teased, eyes twinkling. In moments like these, buffered by laughter, it was easy to forget who he was, who I was. The world that divided us. The war that would tear us apart if we could not achieve the peace we both sought.

"No," I said, thinking back to the way he'd drawn his gun on me in that car, months earlier. The coldness of his eyes, the subtle cruelty that would always haunt me, so different from the tenderness he showed me now. Which was the mask, and which was the reality? "You just seem wise beyond your years."

"Because I'm ruthless in my pursuits?" he offered.

I didn't reply. A silent admission.

"My father said the same thing when he adopted me. That I'm an old soul, someone who has what it takes to get things done. Ruthless in my want, callous in my quests. I'm not ashamed of who I am. I'm capable of bad things—*terrible* things. 铁石心肠, one might say. *A heart of stone.* You would be, too, if you were raised like me." A pause. His attention turned back to me, unwavering. "Do I scare you, Ruying?"

Yes. A whisper in my heart, one that I couldn't bring myself to admit, because it would feel like a betrayal. But to myself or him, I wasn't sure.

When I didn't reply, Antony took my silence as answer.

A dip of his head.

"Are you scared of me?" I asked in turn.

"Yes." His reply felt like a stab to the chest, a pain that ripped flesh from bones, as if Death himself had passed through me. He took a step closer. "But not in the way you think. I fear you the way mortals fear Gods. Forget what you've been taught, Ruying. There is nothing monstrous about you. Quite the opposite. I think you are a marvel to behold. And in the words of your people, 我三生有幸, 遇到你. *It is with the luck of three lifetimes to have met you.* To witness the power you hold . . . You have no idea of the wonder it strikes in me each time. The people of Pangu may call my kind Gods, but that's not true. You are the real God here. Your power is meant to be worshipped, Ruying. You deserve to be feared. When I look at you, I see a girl who refuses to let herself reach her full potential. And I wish to show you how, if you'll let me. If you'll trust me."

Trust. A simple word.

Did I trust him? *Could* I trust him?

I wanted to. So much that it scared me.

Antony was so close, the heat of his body was warm against mine. The scent of him. Ocean salt and sandalwood, enchanting as a spell. If I wished, I could press my lips against his. I could taste him, and he could taste me.

If I took a single step forward, he would kiss me.

I knew he would.

I let go of the hand I didn't realize still held mine.

"Do you hate me, Yang Ruying?" he asked when his hand fell.

"No." This answer came easier because it was a truth I didn't need to hide. I didn't hate him. Not anymore. Not now that I knew the human beneath his princely façade.

"Good." The slightest twist of his lips. "I don't have a lot of people I can trust, on either side of the Veil. Not my commanders, not my brothers. I don't even think I trust my grandfather, who is the reason I'm still alive. I trusted my birth parents, my adopted father, once upon a time. But they are all gone now. Talking to you is comfortable because I know you will always tell me the truth. Because I know you'll understand what the others cannot. How it feels to be selfish, to *want* all that the world had stolen from us, denied us. You will do anything to survive, just like me. You know desperation. You know hunger. I see myself in you. An equal I didn't expect to find in another."

His words were a heavy symphony that played to the tempo of my heart.

He was right. I did know these feelings—they were the needles that pricked at my morals, the gravity that pulled me toward him all those moons ago.

Because even if Antony didn't want to protect my people, I would be here, forsaking my country and kin for a more selfish need to survive, to protect those I loved.

For my family, I would gladly forsake the world.

"We are not equals," I teased. "I can kill someone without touching them. Can you?"

"I can command armies and wipe out cities if I wish. Can you?"

I pressed my lips together, bit down the almost smile. "I am no God, and neither are you."

"You are, to me."

"History isn't kind to those who see themselves as Gods. To those who try to *play* Gods."

"No, history isn't kind to *mortals* who play Gods. But there is power and ambition inside both of us, and we shouldn't be ashamed of that. We are strong and brave because we can make the decisions others cannot. Sacrifice the few for the many. Make a lasting change in both our worlds."

"Murder in the name of peace," I echoed, then gathered the question I knew I had to ask at some point. "Tell me, if you become Emperor, would you return Rome to its own world and let Pangu return to its former self?"

Leave, like the last twenty-something years had never happened?

Could he truly resist the temptation of greed, unlike his grandfather, and allow my world to return to its former glory?

Antony didn't respond immediately. Then he said, "I don't think we can put that particular tiger back into the box. But I do want our two worlds to come to an agreement, solve things with as few casualties as possible."

"And what is it that Rome wants from Pangu?" The question that had been on my mind from the moment I met him. Why were they here, and what did they want? Fragments had slipped from Valentin's drunken lips that day, but not enough. Theories, without truth as an anchor. Plus, how far could I trust Valentin's words? Maybe he was trying to throw me off, trying to distract me and create friction between me and Antony.

I wanted an answer, and I wanted it from Antony.

But all that he could offer me, was silence.

Just like that, the melodies that sang between us came to an abrupt stop. His wordless reply was a warning. A line in the sand, one I must not cross a second time.

He changed the subject. "Your last job was the most discreet kill yet. Well done."

I forced a smile like I was proud, like I longed for his approval. "How many more?"

"Not many." *Not many, not many* . . . He always said *not many.* "I have your next assignment ready."

"When?" I set down the gun.

What would Meiya say if she knew all of the wasted opportunities—the times I could have killed Antony Augustus and chose not to?

If she were in my place, would she hesitate, remember how assassinating a prince of Rome would put my life and Grandma's life in danger? Or were hate and revolution all that mattered to her?

"We leave in five days. I will give you a full briefing when we get there."

"*We?* You're coming with me?"

"No. *You* are coming with *me.*"

"This must be some mission then, to have his highness grace the crime scene. Where are we going?"

"Sihai's capital. The City of Donghai."

Teahouse gossip rang in my head like the stolen souls that still clattered my nightmares. "Donghai," I tested the word with my own voice, in case I'd heard Antony wrong. "The rumors are true, then?"

They said Sihai and Rome were scheming to sign a treaty that would give them immunity if Rome waged war on the rest of the continent.

"That depends on the kind of rumors you've been hearing." With a tilt of his chin, Antony slipped on his princely mask and the closest thing I had to a friend in this lonely city vanished, just like that. The air between us grew bitter cold with formalities once more. "If you are talking about Rome and Sihai signing a separate, new treaty, then yes. The rumors are true."

I shouldn't be surprised. Pangu's last treaty with Rome was decades old, signed by the five Empires of the continent. It was meant to last ninety-nine years. But after everything that had happened to Er-Lang, unrest simmered among our neighbors. The other Empires feared they might become Rome's next target. Now that the world knew the dangers of opian, Rome might not be able to weaken Empires with drugs the way they had with us, but they had other methods, I was sure.

Visions of the armory flashed before my eyes. Grandma's stories of the embarrassingly brief war that had killed my grandfather.

Sihai choosing this moment to sign a separate treaty with Rome meant only one thing.

"Everyone is out for themselves now."

Antony no longer looked at me. "My grandfather is being swayed. But as long as I have breath in me, as long as I have my grandfather's ear, I won't let them burn Er-Lang to ashes and dust. Even if I can't stop him, I will protect your family as promised. The people you love will be safe, come hell or high water."

I tried to smile, tried to seem pleased while shame gnawed at me, its fangs razor sharp, tearing me apart from the inside. I stood a little straighter. "What's the plan, and who's the target?"

"I will give you the full briefing when we are in Sihai. For now, you can take a few days off and enjoy yourself—whether that be visiting the finest food stalls the city has to offer or standing outside of your home some more. Just make sure to layer up if you do."

I knew when I was being dismissed and was about to step back and leave when Antony's hand suddenly brushed mine, ever so gently. As if asking me to stay, just a little bit longer.

"Wait." A quiet word that tugged everything to a stop. His eyes were so fragile as they fluttered around the room, looking at everything but me. "I think this is long overdue."

He pulled a small remote from his pocket, the one that controlled my cuffs, and pressed a button.

I flinched, braced for pain by instinct.

Instead of the electric shock I had gotten so used to, my body was met with the tingling of magic, flooding back into my senses.

"I know how much you hate being apart from your magic, how it leaves you hollowed in its absence. Like I said to Valentin that day, I trust you. With my life."

I didn't know what to say. Of all the small mercies he could possibly bestow me, this was the least expected. And it wasn't a small mercy at all. This was huge. A privilege no other Xianling under the princes' command had.

In Rome's eyes, Xianlings were dangerous. For us to exist on this side of the Fence, our magic had to be locked up when not in use. "What will Valentin say if he finds out?"

Antony shrugged. "I don't plan on telling him. Do you? And this is for you, too." He passed me a badge, embossed with the Augustus family crest. "This badge is an extension of me, Ruying. It will give you unfettered access to all of the Roman establishments here in the city, and the next time you pass the Fence, no one will dare to question you. If anyone ever looks at you the wrong way, just show them this badge. If they don't pay you the same respect they would me, it will be treason."

My jaw fell slack. How did he notice this grief prickling beneath skin? How closely he must watch my every move, every sorrow. "Thank you," was all I could say.

"Go get some rest." Antony took one last step toward me so that his lips were against my ear, his breath warm on my skin. "In the meantime, I will let you in on a little secret if you promise not to tell anyone. History is a melody sung by the victors. Truths and lies are what *I* make of these chords. Stay loyal to me, and I promise the world will remember you as a hero, forged in this war of magic and science. Because, come fire or storm, I'm going to win this game of power, and I can give you a legacy that will outlive you. A name to be whispered for thousands of years to come. Your wildest dreams. Everything that you've ever wanted."

Hero.

Legacy.

To be remembered was something my father had dreamt, something my grandfather and so many of our ancestors had dreamt before history forgot their names.

Once upon a time, I had wanted these grand and fanciful things, too.

I had wanted to live up to the suffocating weight of my name, all of my mother's hopes and dreams that she gave her life to bring into this world.

But this was before my father turned to opian for his sorrows, before my city crumbled in front of my eyes, before I knew what it felt like to starve, to freeze, to fear.

After that, I only wanted to protect those I loved. Guard what little peace was left so that my grandmother would not live to see another war. Even if she did, as long as I had the favor of a Roman prince on my side, she would be safe.

As long as Antony held power, so did I.

30

THAT NIGHT, I DREAMT OF the past—memories of spring, golden sunlight cut through sprouting leaves.

Father led Meiya and me through the bustling morning market, his hand so warm as he held mine, let us pick out anything we wanted for breakfast. My basket brimmed with fresh lychees and the beautiful osmanthus cakes I so loved but Grandma never let me eat because they were too sugary. Meiya had two sticks of tanghulu in her tiny hand, taking turns nibbling each one. Men in silk robes stopped us on the streets and greeted Father with bows and pleasant smiles, talked of court politics and the dwindling wars.

The sky was cerulean blue, no longer blemished by Rome's portal high in the sky. No planes or helicopters, no Fences and sectioned-off parks, no shops that held ROMANS ONLY signs.

This was when I knew it was a dream, a beautiful scenery of make-believe that was too good to be true.

I shouldn't indulge in these impossible fantasies. They would only break my heart more when daylight came, but I didn't care. I clung to the dream and danced with my sister, relishing her smiles, my father's kind eyes, and the life I should have lived if only the Romans had left us alone.

A smile bloomed on my lips just as violent thunder shattered the mirage into ten thousand pieces of fractured porcelain.

Vibrant colors dulled; spring turned hot. A burning summer stale with screeching cicadas and buzzing flies.

Father passed out in the foyer, empty jars of alcohol rolling at his feet, drunken mumbles of justice and honor.

I rushed to his side, tried to help him up, but he pushed me farther and farther away. He barked and yelled about how it was my fault, and Meiya's, that Mama was dead, that our house had fallen to ruins.

"*Sons!*" he howled. "*She should have given me sons!*"

When he raised his hand, when his fingers curled into a hard fist, I stumbled and ran, hid in the cupboards and hoped not to be found. From the shadows, I watched him bawl and weep, ceramic jars smashed against the stone pillars carved with our ancestors' glory.

Later, when he was quiet and tired, he staggered to his knees and gazed up at the shimmering portal that watched over the city like a God regarding his subjects, or a hunter waiting to taste its prey.

Wine slowly turned to pipes of opian.

The same men who greeted Father with smiles and asked for favors turned their faces when they saw us in the streets, sneering at the 败家子, *bastard, no good son,* who squandered and gambled away generations of respect and fortune. Everything our ancestors had built with their blood and youths and endless sacrifices rotted away in Father's reckless hands until there was nothing left for winter coal and watery congee.

Another crash of thunder.

Storm clouds drowned out the light, and the next thing I knew Meiya was pushing me into cupboards to hide. Clutched by fear, I cowered in darkness, let my twin sister face Father's wrath alone.

Even as a child, Meiya was braver, stronger.

And I, a coward.

They said our Gifts were not a manifestation of our souls, but I sometimes wondered if our souls were manifestations of our Gifts. Was it a coincidence that Meiya was blessed with the magic to heal, amplify life, and I the power to take life away?

A giver and a taker.

A healer and a killer.

A martyr, and her cowardly sister.

I succumbed to my wickedness, my temptations, my selfishness while she stood tall on the side of the righteous. Even if it meant enduring sorrow and pain and sacrifices beyond her tender age.

Meiya's disappointed face flashed, the way she'd flinched when I'd tried to reach her.

You are no sister of mine. You're no hero. You're just another cowardly traitor.

Her words echoed as the world turned darker, darker, darker, until I stood under a gray sky, staring at the ashes and ruins of the city I had once called home.

The portal that connected my world and Rome ripped open and glowered red like—

I jolted awake, my skin covered in a sheen of sweat.

A dream.

Just another dream.

31

MY APARTMENT WAS SITUATED ON Rome's side of the Fence—the top floor of an airy building a brisk walk from where Antony lived. Lavishly decorated yet eerily empty, the building was intended to house more people who never came.

I didn't complain. I liked the space, and the quiet solitude felt like bliss on most days, except when my head buzzed with too many thoughts.

I was told I could decorate my apartment however I wanted, but I didn't want much. Just a bed and a wardrobe and a few chairs on the small balcony that overlooked Jing-City in the distance. A haunting view of festive lanterns constantly reminded me of the path I'd chosen and everyone I had turned my back on.

After the dream, I woke with tears in my eyes and got dressed quickly, pulling on a dark robe and tying my hair up into a topknot encased in a silver *guan,* set by a hairpin in the fashion of men. It was always easier to travel Jing-City in the clothes of a man than the clothes of a girl.

Though there was a cook at Antony's home who would make me anything I wanted, even the delicacies of my world, and plenty of fanciful cafés on this side of the Fence, I was too tired to deal with the silence and the wary stares today. I wanted home and I wanted comfort. I wanted a bowl of black-bean noodles from Father's favorite stall, the one he used to take us to back when we had the coins for such luxuries.

Antony's badge worked like a charm and finally, I passed between the two halves of this city with ease. The day was sunny, the air was fresh—a brief moment of warmth after a long winter of bitter gray.

I pushed all of the guilt and shame and hard-to-bear feelings to the back of my mind.

I was so tired of pain and responsibilities. I just wanted a few moments alone as a normal person, to eat some of my favorite foods and not worry about war and Rome and Er-Lang and whether I was making the right choices. I—

A little boy in a tattered linen robe ran into me with a force that almost knocked me off balance, my feet stumbling to right themselves. Years of poverty-inspired caution focused my mind as I felt my body grow lighter; the pouch of coins at my waist gone.

A thief.

I wanted to smile, remembering memories of how I'd used the same move on silk-robed men before, even foolishly tried to steal from a seemingly harmless Roman who turned out to be a prince.

I glanced up. The fleeing boy was bone thin, and anger perished before it had time to form. I didn't need those coins. I could make another trip back to my apartment, fetch more coins and buy a new pouch. But for him, that money might mean the difference between life and Death.

It wasn't worth it.

I was about to walk away when the little boy stopped suddenly and looked back, dark eyes signaling something.

He wanted me to chase him.

I frowned but followed.

He led me to the Lotus Tower. This gleaming beacon of desire and sin with its interior of silk and beauty that felt like it was from another lifetime.

In the darkened alley beside it, I saw a figure clad in a crimson suit the color of dried blood watching me with a cold, stern gaze.

Baihu.

A subtle tilt of his head, a motion of his hand. He flashed my stolen purse.

I stepped into the alley, pulled by a lingering instinct from the days when I would have trailed Baihu like a puppy wherever he went. This man who was once my friend. Someone I thought I could trust.

Still, I gathered magic close at my fingertips.

Just in case.

We walked through the same iron door Antony had used the last time we were here. The same dimly lit staircase, except this time we went all the way to the top, and it led us straight to his office. The one I'd visited hundreds of times, now a lifetime ago. Memories from easier times, from harder times. From when I was tormented not by the ghosts of my sins, but the constant fear of winter, of my sister's addiction, the fluctuating prices of opian and rice, and the ever-present whispers of war.

The last dregs of my mother's jewelry, the pennies that rattled in my pockets when even a single summer berry felt like a luxury.

Now, I was warm and safe, as were my sister and grandmother. I could eat lychees by the handful, even in winter. Oranges and watermelons and mountain plums, all of the treats of my childhood that we could no longer afford after my father wasted away the fortune granted to our house on our ancestors' broken backs and blood spilled on battlefields.

Noble sacrifices.

What would they think if they knew how I had sold my dignity, traded my pride?

A traitor, just like Baihu.

Now that I walked in his shoes, I understood.

Morals were fiction. If given the chance, everyone would make the same decisions we had.

Between survival and honor, I chose survival.

Heroes die. Cowards live.

The talons of my own dark acts clawed at my chest, but this was the path I had chosen. The path I would continue to walk, no matter what happened. Because what choice did I have?

What choice did any girl have in times like these?

"You look well," Baihu greeted me, as if no time had passed.

At the sound of his voice, these blood-stained months faded like powders of blush washed away by tears.

My eyes took in the office—a place I had once despised because it was built on the blood money of our people.

Now my hands were red from the same blood.

Six months ago, I had shamed him for being a traitor, not knowing I would soon follow his footsteps with a trail of ghosts at my heels. Stolen lives and stolen futures.

"What do you want?" I asked.

He'd lured me here for a reason. If he had wanted us to catch up, he would have sought me out months ago.

His face was somber, and hesitation hung over his sharp features like dark clouds that heralded storms. "I need your help," he said as he closed the secret door behind us, his voice low and eyes hard, two violent flames burning, burning, burning.

"You said something similar the last time I was here."

"It's the same target."

"I'm surprised he's still alive."

"That's the thing, you see. I don't want him dead. I just need him . . . *removed* from the equation. But when your target is constantly three or four steps ahead of you and every other player, catching him off guard isn't so easy. It seems kidnapping a prince of Rome is a challenge."

My attention jerked up. "*What?* Have you lost your mind?"

"Nope."

"Forget about kidnapping, if you so much as touched Antony or

Valentin without permission, they could kill you for treason! Do you—"

"I'm a spy, Ru." Baihu's confession sent my frantic thoughts crashing like a carriage pushed off the roads. A stomped haze of dust clouded everything. I couldn't think, couldn't breathe. "I'm a spy, and I need your help."

No.

"Is this a trap, to assess my loyalty to Rome? Did Valentin put you up to this?" I demanded, searching the room for more hidden doors, cameras, Antony or Valentin behind the curtains, ready to catch me out. Days ago, Valentin had told Antony that I couldn't be trusted. Did he ever stop and consider perhaps the tiger he kept at his side might be the first to turn on him?

"This isn't a joke, nor is it a test. This is serious, and *we* need your help." I saw the truth then, the desperation behind his eyes. Something that couldn't be faked.

I thought back to what my sister said in the alley. *Baihu was right.* "Meiya knows?"

"Meiya has known for a long time now. It wasn't just childhood nostalgia or . . . personal affection that drove me to help you obtain opian," he whispered, his voice made so brittle by guilt it could almost break.

"So you've been lying to me. All this time?"

"I didn't have a choice, Ru. I lied to everyone. I had to. For Er-Lang. For Pangu. For the young and the old—for everyone who can't protect themselves from Rome's insatiable greed that tears at our world like a starved beast."

He reached for my hand, and I was too stunned by what he was saying to pull away. The warmth of his skin enveloped mine, familiar and comforting and frightening all at once.

"Why are you telling me this?" I murmured. "I can turn around and sell you out to Antony, right now. Do you realize that by telling me this, you've risked everything you've built?"

"I do."

"Then why?"

"Because I have no other choice, Ruying. I need your help."

I closed my eyes. "The target?" I didn't need to ask. I already knew.

If Baihu needed my help, then the target had to be someone he didn't have easy access to. Someone who happened to be the one person I needed alive.

"Antony."

Though I already knew it would be him, I still flinched at the sound of his name. "No." The answer came too quick, too easy.

"Listen to me, Ruying."

"I won't kill him."

"You are our only hope. I've seen the way he treats you. He trusts you. He lets his guard down around you, and grants you the kind of access nobody else has. I don't want him dead, Ru. Just . . . *weaker*. Vulnerable. Contained, for a little while. *Please*. You are not doing this for me. You are doing this for Er-Lang, for Pangu, for our people. For *Meiya*. We need to turn the tide of this conflict before it's too late. We—"

I pushed him away. "Why Antony? Why not Valentin? Unlike his twisted brother, Antony is actually on our side."

"He's Roman. No Roman is ever on our side. You have no idea what Antony is like behind closed doors. Valentin might be bloodthirsty, but Antony is no saint. In fact, he's just as sinister as the rest of his family, even if he pretends otherwise. He calls you his equal, but have you noticed how the two of you always converse in Roman, and he only speaks Pangunese when it suits him?"

"No," I fought. "Antony is different. He wants peace, he wants to protect our people. He is good. And if anything happens to either Antony or Valentin, their grandfather won't stand for it. It would cause a war, Baihu! Is that what you want?"

As soon as the words were out of my mouth, I realized this was the point—why he'd pledged his allegiance to the warmongering prince and not the one who wanted to solve problems, bring peace at whatever cost.

Baihu's gaze turned cold, his face unreadable. "War is better than genocide. Do you think the Roman monarch hasn't strategized on how to completely destroy us when the fight comes, isn't preparing vast armies while our people sit in naïve hope that the treaty and a constant bending of the knee can hold peace? My cousin is a coward. The same goes for every Emperor who rules this continent, claiming to be a descendant of Gods, promising to protect us with their holiness."

A life on our knees is no life at all: my sister's words. No matter how hard I tried to shut out her voice, Meiya's words plagued my thoughts, picked at my already frayed beliefs and slowly unraveling morals.

I knew resolution when I saw it. Baihu was stubborn. If he believed in something, then he believed with his whole being, until his last heartbeat.

"Is that what you believe in, or are you echoing what the Phantom taught you?" I asked.

If Emperor Yongle was the puppet everybody claimed, he would never send a spy into our enemies' midst like this. He wouldn't have that kind of courage. Plus, despite Baihu's royal blood from his father, he held no love for the Er-Lang Dynasty and thought his late father a worthless drunk undeserving of his name and titles.

If Baihu wasn't working for the Emperor, then it could only be one other person. The same person whose lies Meiya reverently believed in. The man who'd built his entire existence on the promise of war and uprising and a revolution that would bring justice back to Er-Lang.

The Phantom.

Baihu tensed at my accusation, like a bow pulled too tight, its arrow aimed at the jugular of its prey, debating whether to fire.

A muscle ticked in his jaw like doubt. "Yes, this is what I believe in. And yes, I work for the Phantom, if that's what you're trying to ask."

I stiffened.

The Phantom was a man of whispers and legends, conjured from shadows and fear, shrouded in mystery. Nobody knew what he looked like behind his iron mask. Some said he was like me—an orphan who'd lost everything because of opian. Others that he was a man of royal blood, a martyr ready to die for his country. And still others that he was a warmonger, rebelling to sow chaos and reap profit.

Baihu was the last person I would have expected to be lured by the Phantom's words. In my eyes, the Phantom was nothing more than a hoggish man using turmoil to his advantage. A manipulator who rallied troops and supporters with rage and false promises. A parasite, just like the Romans.

A power-hungry opportunist, hankering for status in calamity.

Baihu took a step forward.

I took a step back.

In this moment, he towered over me in a way he never had when we were kids. Up close, I realized how tall he'd become, how his well-formed muscles strained against his suit. The dark of his lashes. The cherub boy of childhood memories had long faded from the man standing with his angled jaw and honed edges sharp enough to cut.

I held Death close. Baihu would never hurt me, but there was danger in the way he looked at me, violence a steady tempo to his breathing.

"War will come whether we like it or not. If we don't make the first move, then by the time the Romans have readied themselves to fully invade, it will be too late."

"No. If Antony inherits the throne, if he—"

"Don't try to sway me with his lies of the greater good." Baihu's face twitched into a frown. "Antony is just as vicious as his brother, as his grandfather. I know you, Ruying. You are too smart not to see through his lies, but you have allowed yourself to be lulled by them anyway, because you are scared of the truth. Because you're too scared to admit that you're doing this for yourself."

I straightened, made myself meet his stare, chin tilted and eyes hard to show I wasn't afraid. And for the first time, inside this office, it was true.

I wasn't afraid.

Death's colors stained my hands. If I wanted to kill Baihu, this childhood friend, the man I had loved once upon a time—might still love if we were different people in a different time—it would be easy.

"So what if I am? There is no sin in wanting to live, in wanting a better life for those I love."

"It is if you are murdering our kin in cold blood in exchange for this protection, for all of the luxuries Antony spoils you with. It wasn't hard to win your trust, was it? All it took was locking you in a dirty cell with a festering wound, then in he comes like the self-aggrandizing savior he so likes to pretend he is. A prince from their world's fairy tales, here to protect you from all the monsters who lurk in the shadows. Meanwhile, you have no idea the most dangerous monster of them all is beside you, for he is not hideous or terrifying as the world loves to portray wretched souls to be. No. He is beautiful, with a face that could be mistaken for a God's. All of his lingering stares and whispers of admiration are like lullabies, soothing your fragile ego because no one had ever said those things to you before. Because you have convinced yourself that you don't deserve to be loved. Is your self-esteem so low that you'd let the enemy prince woo you just because you think he sees something in you that no one else can? Do you hate yourself that much, Ruying?"

My heart stopped beating. Baihu's words were a bucket of ice poured down my back. 一针见血. *One prick of the needle to see blood.* Baihu had known me for too long, understood me too well.

Like my sister, he knew how to hurt me in ways no one else could.

"I'm not your martyr, Baihu," I said, the only words I could manage.

"Have you forgotten every insult you've hurled at me the past three years? How you taunted me for being a traitor? Now that our Empire needs you, you choose our enemies over your own people?" he cried, his chest panting so fast I thought he might break.

He was upset, livid, and he had every right to be.

His accusations were all true, every word a blade that plunged into my chest, tearing open flesh and splintering bones. I deserved every ounce of the pain.

While Baihu lied in the name of freedom, my treacheries were real. My crimes were unforgivable—sins I'd never be able to atone for.

I knew this.

I had known this from the moment I exited that cage and took Antony's hand. I could force myself to look away and convince myself otherwise, but no one ever outruns the truth.

"All for what?" he continued. "For your sister and grandmother? Two lives, against the world?"

"Those two lives *are* my world," I snapped. "The Gods have abandoned us completely, Baihu. Heroes die, but cowards live. And I intend to live."

The blood of my kin was the blood of my soul. Their survival was the same as my own. When Death's magic carried away the last fragments of my *qi* and my time in this mortal realm came to an end, I would continue to live on in the memories of my sister and grandmother.

That would be enough.

Baihu chuckled, shook his head. "You really have no idea what Antony is like, do you? What he's done? What he and his scientists are *doing* to our people?"

"You're right. I don't know what he's doing, not in detail. And frankly, I don't give a damn. This is *my* path, *my* grave, *my* decision. I believe in Antony. I believe if Er-Lang wants to survive, we need Antony alive. We need him on our side. And *I* need him to keep those I love safe."

"The Phantom can protect your family as well," Baihu said. "Antony isn't your only choice."

I laughed. "Can he? After all the wonderful things he's done, do you think I'd trust that warmongering psychopath? It was his preaching that convinced Meiya to start using opian. All of this *started* with him. All of my pain and hardship and the fears that keep me up at night started when he made my sister an addict, so she could what? Become stronger? Risk her life for him like you do? I won't let my sister die. I'll rip out my own heart before I let *anything* happen to those I love. The Phantom can't protect them. He can barely protect himself, hiding behind his believers. If Antony wanted, he could track down the Phantom and kill him as easily as squashing a bug."

"The Phantom didn't start all of this," Baihu whispered. "Rome did, when they unleashed opian on our people, when they tore open the sky and invaded our lives like demons from the eighteenth level of hell!"

I sighed, looked out of the window, at the bustling streets below, the tiled roofs of the city I had always called home. A city that had burned to ashes in my dreams, and its history and people with it.

"What if the Phantom loses?" I asked. "What if you are on the wrong side of history, and Rome is destined to win this war? What happens then?"

"Don't you think freedom is worth fighting for, Ruying?"

"You haven't seen the things I've seen, Baihu. Freedom is only worth fighting for when we have a fighting chance. Otherwise, it would just be a senseless sacrifice for a hopeless dream. We have all heard the stories of that one-day war from twenty years ago. How easily Rome defeated us. Nothing has changed since then. If you wish to rebel, then you will spark a war we are not going to win. To survive, I must stand on the winning side. And if that side is Rome, then I'm sorry. I can't help you. But I won't rat you out, either. This is the only mercy I can offer you."

"I won't go easy on him just because you are on his side."

"Take your best shot, Baihu. Just remember, if you are set on hurting Antony, then the two of us will have to be enemies from this point on."

"What do you see in him, Ruying? Is he really worth turning your back on everything you've ever known?"

"He's not worth it. But his ideas, his dreams, *are* worth it. Peace is worth it."

My family's survival is worth it.

"He is wicked, Ru!"

"We are *all* wicked, Baihu," I snapped. "We all do what we must to survive."

At this, Baihu's fury faded. Disappointment overtook him. His pain hurt me as much as it hurt him.

Finally, I had become the monster he once promised he'd never see me as. "Do you actually think Antony likes you? He might mean the alluring things he says, the praises he sings, but at the end of the day, you are just a toy to him. Antony has been like this for as long as I've known him. He loves shiny, beautiful things that excite his curiosity. What he feels for you is much the same. You are many things, Ruying, but you are not foolish. He doesn't love you. A man like him will *never* love you."

"Goodbye, Baihu."

"Do you ever wonder what happened to the people who didn't pass the Exhibition? Do you know what they are doing to our people in—"

"I don't know. And quite frankly, I don't care."

"Fine. *Leave.* Go back to your prince. Keep lying to yourself. But remember this, Ruying: If you are not with us, then you are against us. And you are the one on the wrong side of history."

32

THE SUN ROSE AND SET. Days later, right on schedule, we sailed for Donghai on a Roman warship big enough to swallow cities whole. It pierced the crashing waves like a knife sliding through satin. Wind slashed, brutal and violent, against its giant metal body, as if the ocean itself wanted to push the monstrosity from its waters.

If this was another ship, the ocean might have succeeded—flipped us over and filled everything with gushing water. But Roman ships ran on engines built by science. It didn't yield to wind or storm. The ocean could struggle with all its might, and the Roman ship would continue to pollute and destroy until it reached its destination.

The wind raced through my hair, beat at my clothes. I clutched tight to the iron rails as Donghai City grew closer and closer. Sihai Empire's capital was a series of islands laden with jade-green forest, scattered across a silken tide of impossible blues, lined with beaches of silver. Swallow-tailed buildings and eight-sided towers climbed high into the sky, vibrant in their hues of rustic red and ancient gold.

Beyond the city, pale shadows of mountains loomed tall like giants. So magnificent in height they melted against the sky and clouds like quiet Gods guarding over their worshippers.

A thousand years ago, after the Great War that eradicated the Qin Empire, the people of Sihai carved images of the Gods and the name of every man who'd died during the war into those mountain faces to commemorate their ultimate sacrifice for the continent, for Xianlings, for freedom.

Throughout history, too many had tried to dictate the lives of those born with magic, to force us down paths of destruction and sacrifice for their own selfish goals.

Not unlike what Rome was doing now.

Except this time, there were no Gods coming to save us.

My conversation with Baihu continued to ring in my head.

What if he was right? That we should rise up and fight, even if it might cost us everything? What if he was telling the truth, that beneath all of his grand visions, Antony was as monstrous as the rest of them?

Antony wasn't of Pangu blood. He didn't care for this land; he had no loyalty to us beyond a lingering respect for his late father's wishes. He could change his mind easily.

Turn his back on us in the name of power.

As long as that portal was open. As long as the Romans were here, Er-Lang would always live on its knees. And maybe one day, the entire continent would kneel and weep like we did.

And then one day after that, all traces of Pangu might be erased from the land, replaced by towering Roman buildings and Roman streets and Roman voices.

I closed my eyes, tried to tune out doubt, push away the morbid visions of Er-Lang blood coating my hands, the wrath of the Gods long passed clouding the skies, my sins bleeding into history and poems, my name mocked for thousands of years.

Monster, I heard their tortured chants, a sound seared into my mind. *Monster. Monster. Monster . . .*

"A penny for your thoughts?" I startled at Antony's voice, sudden and close, his breath warm against the brutal winds as he came up behind me, sending tingles down my neck.

"I'm pondering the magic of science," I lied too easily, gesturing at the boat. "What other impossible things are your people capable of? What other kinds of miracles exist on your side of the Veil?"

And the most terrifying thought of all: What else were they hiding from us? I tried not to think of that war room, the videos of planes and missiles and bombs that could level cities in a heartbeat. Visions from a nightmare, a piece of hell they stole from the demons beneath us, I was sure.

"Nothing is impossible in the name of science," was Antony's answer.

"Once, my people thought nothing was impossible in the name of magic, too. But your people proved us wrong."

天外有天. *There is a sky outside of the sky, a world outside of our own.* No matter how powerful, how strong and miraculous magic was, Rome and their science still trampled us when our forces clashed. I touched the bracelets at my wrist. They were no longer humming, but if I crossed a line, provoked Antony in a way he didn't like, would he push the button and steal my magic once more?

If a real war erupted, would Er-Lang stand a chance, or were we doomed from the start?

"Here, this will warm you up." Antony passed me a porcelain cup of milky brown liquid. "Hot chocolate. Try it, I think you will like it," he said. "When my father was still alive, we used to drink it whenever the weather was bad, which was often in our world. Especially after the polar caps began to melt."

I didn't know what he was talking about, but I took a sip. True to its name, the drink was hot, and sweet. I'd never tasted chocolate—a Roman delicacy too expensive for anyone but wealthy opian dealers and the royals to indulge in—but if this drink was any indication of the real thing, I might like it.

"What do you think?"

"Meiya would like it, too, if she were here." With this thought, I set the drink down and forced myself not to take another sip. If she couldn't be here to enjoy this drink with me, then I shouldn't enjoy it, either. As children, we shared everything. Twins of the thickest blood. That wouldn't change. Even if we stood on different sides of a brewing war, nothing could tear us apart.

Not for me, at least.

"So what's the plan?" I asked, knowing this conversation was inevitable. "Who's the target?"

"When we arrive, I'll play the part of an attentive prince, there to sign the treaty on behalf of my grandfather, and you'll pose as my guard." He moved a little closer, stern gaze pinning me down. "Then, after the treaty is signed, I'll need you to kill the Sihai Emperor for me. And make it look natural."

I blinked. The Sihai Emperor? "You can't be serious? He's signing the treaty; he's going to be Rome's ally. Why would you want him dead?"

"I have my reasons."

"But he's the *Emperor*!"

"An Emperor is a man, just like any other, Ruying."

"No. I don't know how Rome works, but in Pangu, it is sacrilegious to kill someone of royal blood. The Sihai Emperor rules the four oceans. He is a direct descendant of Pangu's oldest Gods, the dragons!"

Antony's lips twitched as if my words were a joke.

"My ancestors claimed to be descendants of Gods, too. Of Jupiter and Neptune and Pluto. Zeus, Poseidon, and Hades. Our Gods had many names and variations, and according to our legends they had many children, yet there is no magic in our bloodlines. I am a mortal, as were my ancestors. Not all who claim to be descendants of Gods tell the truth, Ruying."

Anger boiled. My hands clenched into fists until nails bit bloodied half-moon marks into skin. "You might not believe in your legends, but I believe in mine. Magic may not flow in your veins, but it does in mine. As far as I'm concerned, the Sihai Emperor is a descendant of the great dragons. He's not like the other men you've sent me to exterminate."

A subtle nod, Antony's sight fixed on the horizon. "I've read up on Pangu's histories, but they read more like fables. Do you honestly believe the Sihai Dynasty are descendants of dragons who once ruled land and sea, only to give up their unfathomable powers to take on mortal forms?"

"They gave up their dragon forms because they envied us."

"Why would Gods envy *us,* with our brief lives like bursts of violent flame, here one moment and gone the next, easily perished and easily forgotten? Insignificant as an imperceptible grain of sand against the vast, endless beach of history? Fiction, woven as truths. The Gods of your histories don't exist, and neither does magic. There is only science. Magic is merely a form of science we don't yet understand. Abilities like yours are likely the result of genetic evolution, as were the abilities of those warriors who had liberated Xianlings from the Qin Emperor. Mortals, pretending to be Gods reincarnated in mortal form to rally support from those who wish to believe in something bigger than themselves."

"Why do you want the Sihai Emperor dead?" I asked calmly, through half-clenched teeth. My insides were burning from his accusations, his know-it-all tone, trying to explain my world, my Gods, my history, *my* magic back at me. As if I knew nothing. As if I were just a child who needed to be educated.

I never questioned his beliefs, so what gave him the right to question mine?

"The Emperor is signing the treaty with you," I added after a long breath. "That makes him your ally. You should want him alive, not dead."

Antony fell quiet, still as carved marble except for his curls, tousled by the ocean wind. It wasn't my job to cast doubt on his plans—something he'd made all too clear.

But it shouldn't matter how he held power over me, over this land. My people's culture, history, beliefs, the stories that shaped our identities, were ours to own, to criticize, to interpret as we pleased.

Not his.

Never his.

A long stretch of silence.

Antony rarely got mad when I told him what I felt. In fact, there was always a twinkle to the way he regarded me when I stood up to him. He liked the idea of someone who offered honesty instead of someone who cowered to tell him what he wanted to hear.

But these days, I feared the ice beneath my feet as I ventured farther from shore, from home, from who I was. One of these days, would I take it too far, say something he wouldn't find charming?

"How is the Emperor any different from the other men you've killed so far?" Antony mused.

"We will go to hell if we kill a descendant of the Gods."

An arched brow. His eyes found mine. They were not brazen with impatience as I'd expected after overstepping the fine line that separated us. Instead, they were tender, as they too often were these days, regarding me with such affection that my heart ached.

Because in moments like these, his feelings seemed tangible, real. Something I could reach out and claim if I wished.

Just one look from him, and my belly wrought itself into knots, my heart pounding like war drums.

He moved closer, until our chests almost touched.

I wanted to touch him, to lean forward and see if he would kiss me. To see if this tenderness was something that existed only in my thoughts, or if it was real.

What if Baihu was right and Antony was simply fascinated by me, by my powers?

What if I was as pathetic as Baihu had said? Fawning over the first man to whisper kind things to me, mistaking his polite words for real affection, thinking that he understood me?

I wanted to so badly believe that Antony was as good as he said. But what if . . . ?

"I'm certain these are lies made up to protect the ruling dynasties' grip on power. A clever lie, but a lie, nonetheless," he whispered slowly, still too close. "But even if it were true, so what? If we go to hell for this, at least we will go together. After all that we've done, we are both bound for hell anyway, don't you think? What's a little more blood on the ledger?"

I looked away, took a step back. "Tell me why, at least."

"The why is not part of our deal." An amused lilt still glossed his words, but I felt the ice getting thinner and thinner.

"I—"

"Remember who you are, Ruying," he said finally. "I do not answer to you."

A chill swept through my bones; the coldness enveloped me. Just like that, I was reminded that no matter how kind he appeared to be, Antony Augustus and I were separated by worlds.

We would never be equals.

Perhaps Baihu was right. I had no idea what Antony was capable of, and it would be foolish to provoke his wrath or tempt a flame I couldn't control.

He's like the sun. The closer I fly, the quicker he'd burn me.

"I . . . I'm sorry." A placating apology I wasn't sure I meant.

"And I'm sorry, too, for what I just said about your histories and lore." He sighed, shaking his head. "And in regard to why I need the Emperor dead . . . I keep secrets, Ruying. It's part of my job as a prince. I hope I can share one or two of them with you, one day."

Me too.

"So, what do you say? Will you help me?"

"Do I have a choice?"

"You always have a choice."

I wanted to believe him, just as I wanted to believe in so many other things. "Does it have to be me?"

"I have a backup plan, but I want it to be you. For things to be seamless, for Sihai not to have evidence or a way to turn peace into violence, it has to be you."

A pause. "Let me think about it."

Antony could be right, that these stories were just false legends, broad strokes of fiction masquerading as facts. Even if they were true, I was already going to hell. As he said, what was one more life at this point?

A drop in the ocean.

My hands were so red I'd never be able to tell an Emperor's blood from the blood of that minister on New Year's, or the young man from the glass box, or Hushan, the boy whose cruel prank had cost him everything.

I curled and uncurled my hands, an involuntary twitch that had turned into a habit whenever I tried to shake away the memories, quiet Death's insatiable whispers to take more, to want more. A held breath in my lungs. I was about to turn and walk away when Antony covered both of my hands with his and brought them up to his lips, to breathe warm air against my cold skin.

His hands cradled mine, his touch soft and hot, and I wanted to inch closer, to let his heat climb up my arms, envelop me like a hot bath on a winter's day

A temptation as haunting as Death. "I will get you some gloves if you're cold," he said, words quiet and tender, just for me.

There was that ache in my chest again. I tore my hands from his, almost regretfully. I could still hear Baihu's taunt and Meiya's rage in the back of my head. Coming at me from all directions until I could no longer hear myself think.

"I heard you have been coughing up blood after your kills," said Antony. "Are you okay?"

"I'm fine," I murmured. "It's the price of magic. And it only happens occasionally, not after every kill."

"It shouldn't be happening at all. Those stories your Emperors tell: They are rumors and lies made up to fool children. My people have conducted experiments on your kind. Magic shouldn't hurt the way yours is hurting you. It shouldn't—"

"Magic takes from us in different ways," I whispered, not looking at him even when I felt his gaze burning at my peripheral vision.

Antony shook his head. There was more he wanted to say, but

something held him back. "If that's true, then I will find a way to slow it down, to stop it altogether."

"Whether Xianlings live or die is not up to us. Our lives are dictated by Fate, by the will of heaven. You can't play God with your science. It doesn't work like that. I can cut my life short by exhausting the *qi* that tethers me to the mortal realm, but I cannot extend it. Life has its orders, and this is one of them."

A muscle in his jaw twitched as if he wanted to argue with me. Something that happened often when we clashed in opinions, in thoughts and beliefs. "No harm will come to you," he simply said after a pause. "As long as I am your protector, nothing—not Fate and not your mysterious Gods—will take you from me."

With that, he took a step back and walked away.

When he was gone, I cast my eyes to the ocean and thought of Meiya, Grandma, Taohua. The people of Jing-City, of Er-Lang.

Blood of my blood. Blood of my soul.

The shame in my sister's eyes the last time our paths crossed.

Baihu, who had let the world curse him as a traitor for what he believed in.

What did I believe in?

I heard Grandma's voice: *Do the right thing.* She wanted me to be good, to be the best version of myself I could possibly be.

I wanted to be good, do the right thing, too.

I wanted to make them proud.

But . . .

33

A PARADE OF MEN STOOD at the harbor to greet us.

I recognized the Emperor by his golden dragon robes, and Sihai Feng—the Emperor's eldest son and heir—from the paintings Grandma had shown me long ago.

Dark curls, smooth sun-bronzed skin, and striking blue eyes the color of the four oceans. Sihai Feng was as beautiful as his paintings. Once, he was the dream of all unwed maidens' parents and guardians.

But ten thousand maidens were offered and ten thousand were rejected. It turned out the prince of dreams didn't have the slightest interest in the daughters offered to him.

"Your Highness." The Emperor greeted Antony in the Roman language, followed by a firm handshake, per Roman traditions. The Emperor and his heir's smiles were warm, with eyes that were ice-cold like the winds creeping up our backs.

The eyes of cautious warriors.

Still, they welcomed Antony with open arms and lavish compliments, unaware of what the Roman prince was planning.

"请, *please*," said the Emperor, gesturing toward the fleet of waiting carriages. "You must be exhausted from your travels. Talk of politics can wait. First, let's get you and your companions settled in at the palace."

It pained me to watch the Emperor treat a man who wanted him dead with such courtesy, to witness a descendant of dragons bow his head like a humble servant to Antony.

If even the royals of our world lowered their dignity for Rome, what did this portend for our future?

For a fleeting moment, I understood why people rallied behind the Phantom, why Baihu risked his life for a dream of revolution, why Meiya painted posters and snuck out at midnight, willing to die for a flickering hope.

Maybe Baihu was right.

Maybe I was on the wrong side of this fight. A thought that gathered pressure behind my eyes until I blinked it away.

Antony, the Emperor, and Prince Feng rode in a horse-drawn carriage flanked by guards. I marched at Antony's immediate right. A position of power. To be so close to Antony meant that he trusted me enough to count on as his last line of defense if chaos broke out.

Inside the carriage the three talked, but I couldn't hear a single word. A Xianling somewhere had to be shielding their conversation with magic.

I was about to look away when the Emperor's eyes caught mine. Dark blue like the depths of the sea, pooled with kindness. When he offered me a small smile, something inside melted warm like honey, making me want to smile back.

I never got to meet my grandfather, who died before I was born. But I felt like I knew him from Grandma's stories. A warrior who died too young, too proud to step down from combat even when his bones became weak and his body a mantle of scars that he treasured like medals of honor.

Little was said about the war that killed him. My kin didn't like to talk of the humiliating rebellion that lasted a single day, nor the rain of hellfire the Romans unleashed that day, leaving countless permanently injured and traumatized—if they were lucky enough to survive.

That was the day many realized that every supposed God we'd once knelt for had forsaken us.

As children, Meiya and I liked to imagine what kind of man Grandpa would have become if he'd gotten the chance to grow old like the people he'd sacrificed his life to protect.

I liked to think he and Sihai's Emperor would be similar. Kind eyes and gentle smiles—such a rare trait among men of power. Though I had heard Grandma's stories and knew my grandfather was as cruel as he was kind. Ruthless in his ambitions, carelessly sacrificed his men as long as he could claim victory battle after battle.

An ability to sacrifice the few, for the many.

Maybe he and I were more alike than I was willing to admit. Looking at the Sihai Emperor now, knowing why he had invited Antony to his land, perhaps all three of us were more alike than we realized.

I'd never get to find out, though. Because tomorrow, I would kill this great Emperor. Feel his *qi* bleed through my fingers, tear it from his body until his flesh and bone became a hollowed shell without a twinge of life.

I would be the one to banish his benevolent smile from this world.

One more life, added to my tally of sins.

Sihai would mourn.

The world would change.

And I would forever be remembered as a traitor. Whether Rome won the war or lost, whether history got to be victoriously told by us or them, I would always be known as the traitor who'd killed the Sihai Emperor and plunged the continent into whatever chaos Antony thought best for our two worlds.

Or perhaps not two worlds . . . Maybe only what was best for his world, not mine.

A slow ache between my ribs, the soft hiss of the snakes that had infested my insides.

34

SIHAI'S IMPERIAL PALACE WAS A city in its own right, a maze of grand pavilions for the Emperor's concubines and children and state visitors like Antony.

Slow streams meandered beside the walkways, bordered by stones bearing intricate carvings of dragons and other mythical creatures rumored to reside deep in the ocean. Statues of marble and jade that cast fair shadows, and silk screens with hand-sewn embroideries were scattered around the imperial gardens.

Among them, I recognized vital scenes from the Great War with the Qin Emperor retold in decadent detail. Stories, bright with colors, trapped within silk panels or etched into frozen stones. It was a sight to behold—one I would have enjoyed more if my heart wasn't a heavy condemnation.

Antony nodded and smiled that princely smile, and all I wanted was for the ground to swallow me whole, for time to pause in this moment so that tomorrow would never come, the treaty would never be signed, and I would never have to . . .

After a brief tour, the Emperor led us to a section of the palace divided into several pavilions for envoys and guests. Close to the Dragon Pavilion, where the Emperor spent his nights.

Keep your friends close, but enemies closer, as the proverbs say.

Tapestries hung from the walls, and more jade statues decorated every corner. As per Sihai tradition, most depicted dragons emerging from the oceans.

Legends had it that a dragon's roar was capable of summoning thunder and commanding rain. Their scales could scrape lightning powerful enough to split the world open, and their breaths were the wind that caressed our mortal skins.

Some believed dragons lived deep in our oceans still, but it had been centuries since one was spotted.

Some claimed the Sihai Dynasty could still transform themselves into the dragons of their past if they wished. And in their dragon form, they had the power over wind and water and storms of the most violent kind, just like their ancestors.

If they had held on to the old magic, the dynasty was doing a good job of keeping it a secret. I hoped the legends were just legends. Because if they were true, Valentin Augustus and the Roman Emperor would stop at nothing to control such power.

Rome had already crushed Er-Lang under its feet. Did they plan the same fate for Sihai?

If the people of Sihai—of the other Empires and the small tribute dynasties—were smart, they would heed Er-Lang's last decade as a warning.

The Romans might disguise themselves as Gods of fables, descended from the skies, but they were not so benevolent as we'd once believed, and they were not here to save us.

If we wanted change, we had to rescue ourselves.

After the Emperor and Prince Feng left, Antony summoned me to the pavilion's library.

"You're hesitating," he announced once we were alone.

Nothing escaped his eyes. Even when his eyes were on other people, smiled for other people, a part of his attention was on me. He watched me, understood me. Perhaps a little too much for comfort. Then again, I watched him, too. Understood him, too. Perhaps a little too much for comfort.

"They seem kind," was all I said.

"Many are kind, but that does not mean they can outrun Death when the moment comes."

I bit my lip, not knowing what I should say. I had crossed the line once today, and I feared to do it a second time. Would this be the day I plucked one too many whiskers from the tiger?

Antony exhaled, rubbing his temple. "Don't look at me like that."

"Like what?"

"Like I'm the bad guy."

Maybe you are the bad guy, I thought, but I didn't say it.

Another deep breath. Antony regained his composure. "You still want to know why I need him dead, don't you?"

"It would help. With the other murders, I knew what was at stake. Peace between our lands. But the Sihai Emperor is your ally."

"This can't leave the room."

"It won't."

"I mean it, Ruying. If Valentin finds out that I've told you this, he's going to kill you. He doesn't trust you as it is, and there are only so many ways I can protect you from him."

"I won't say anything. I *promise.*"

Antony gestured at the seat across the table from him, and I took it. "This mission isn't about killing the Sihai Emperor, it is about killing him at the precisely right time. If he dies before he signs the treaty, then the power of the four oceans passes to his son, who is young and ambitious and untested with power, which will throw everything into uncertainty. But if the Emperor dies tomorrow *after* he signs the treaty, then that treaty will be his last decree. I don't think I have to explain what that means for the future of our nations, do I?"

I swallowed the lump in my throat. He didn't.

When Sihai Feng ascended the throne, he'd have no choice but to honor the treaty as his father's last decree. If he ever overturned his father's decree, it would be an attack on the late Emperor's legacy—something no filial son would contemplate.

If this was Sihai Feng's first decree, it would still hold weight, but be as breakable as all other hollowed oaths.

His father's legacy would be a chain, capable of controlling the young Dragon Heir for years to come.

Rome wanted to force Sihai into a corner, bind their hands behind their backs with not just words and politics, but our culture of Pangu.

A plan too smart for it to have come from Valentin, or their grandfather—two people who didn't understand our world half as well as Antony did.

"Sihai Feng is young, hungry, and proud," Antony added. "He doesn't have his father's patience, nor ability to sacrifice. A volatile young Emperor puts my people's future in peril, because as powerful as Rome is, we can't fight enemies from both land and sea. I've only heard rumors of what the Sihai navy is capable of, and I don't want to put those stories to the test."

"You are preparing for war."

"My grandfather is preparing for war."

"But you said you would stop it, keep the peace. That is why I'm here, doing your dirty work for you, eliminating your enemies, clearing the board so you can keep both sides alive."

"I said I would *try*," Antony replied, his voice a little too harsh, too defensive.

"What would happen if your grandfather decided enough is enough, that he's sick of waiting? Would you disobey him if he ordered an attack on Er-Lang?"

A pause. His eyes met mine and I caught a flicker of indecision. Over my question or over whether he should answer truthfully? It didn't matter because the answer was the same. "No, I would not disobey him."

"Then you're not on our side."

"Ruying . . ."

"You're just a coward who likes to think he's doing good for this world but doesn't have the courage to do what is actually right."

Like me.

"Everything I've worked to accomplish since I came to Pangu has been for your world, your people. I'm doing my best, but sometimes my best only goes so far. If it weren't for me, my grandfather would have exterminated your people years ago."

What difference did this make, prolonging tragedy when it was inevitable? A brutal fate, already written in the stars.

We could run, we could hide, but Fate would catch up with everyone eventually.

Perhaps Baihu was right. Perhaps I should have listened to my sister.

If war had come sooner, before the Romans planted their roots and readied themselves, would our chances of victory have been higher? If we had not knelt for science so easily during that humiliating war, would things be different now? Did magic have a fighting chance, against science?

Could we still chase them out, like we should have done twenty-something years ago when they first descended from the skies?

I'd promised to kill for Antony in order to prolong peace, but this wasn't prolonging peace. This was buying them time.

This was me giving in to temptation, slashing my country at the heels because I was afraid. Of uncertainty, of revolution, of a future where Er-Lang might not exist.

Though I hated violence, it always managed to find me no matter how fast I ran. Stalked me from the shadows and stirred Death from his lulling slumbers. They said some magic was given by chance, some given for a purpose.

When I let myself look into Antony Augustus's eyes six months earlier and saw not a prince but a broken boy who wanted to do good by both our worlds, I thought I had found my purpose.

It wasn't a permanent solution, but it was the best solution we had.

Now, I saw things clearer.

I was wrong.

I was *so* wrong.

"Do you want to back out of our deal?" he asked.

"No," I lied.

Victory gleamed bright in his eyes as he handed me a supple leather file, fingertips brushing mine when I took it from him.

"The plan is inside. Everything you need to know about tomorrow. It's just one life, Ruying. It shouldn't be that difficult."

35

THAT NIGHT, I TOSSED AND turned in the silence of my room, clutching tight to memories of Meiya and Grandma in an attempt to remember why I was there.

I thought I had to do this for them.

For us.

For survival.

But if I was really doing this for them, I wouldn't fight on the side of our enemy.

Meiya would happily die for freedom, and so would Grandma.

As a child, I dreamt of the world Mama grew up in. A time of languishing peace, before the Romans came from the skies and ruined it all. For so long, I wished I was born in her time instead of mine. A life where I could want more than just survival.

Now, I wondered, would the next generation envy me, envy this tentative era between peace and chaos like I did Mama's?

One didn't have to die to suffer.

Sometimes, to live was a much worse fate.

I stared down at my hands.

If I killed the Emperor, I'd grant Rome the confidence to invade Er-Lang without fearing Sihai's interference. His death would ripple into millions more until they piled high like a tsunami, sparking trauma that would last generations. A war unlike any other—one that might turn the entire continent of Pangu into a vast battlefield and ruin the land for thousands of years to come.

I wanted so desperately to believe in the things Antony said, in the world he envisioned, the peace he claimed to cherish.

I didn't know when this wave of doubt had soaked itself into every thought of him. The hate that had once coiled like a strangling serpent was now supple and delicate—rose petals and shimmering silk. Jade cold and green as his eyes. My chest contracted and expanded, that thudding heartbeat a traitor I would never acknowledge.

So I turned away.

He is as evil as his brother, I reminded myself. The only difference was that he was an evil who could protect those I loved.

A trickster who used me the same way I used him.

Nothing more. Nothing less.

He would always be Antony Augustus.

As I would always be Yang Ruying.

Two people who were not of the same world.

Who would *never* walk the same path.

Our tentative friendship was fragile. All his lingering glances and delicate smiles couldn't protect me from his wrath.

Heroes die. Cowards live. These familiar words echoed like a taunt, urging me to close the window and go to bed. *These lives are not mine to save; their pain is not my pain. The only people I have to worry about are myself and my family.*

Six months earlier, I would have swayed under these thoughts, caved like brambles under pressure.

Not this time.

I didn't realize what I was doing until I had one foot on the windowsill, ready to climb out.

My better judgment repeated the same four words: *This is a mistake, this is a mistake, this is a mistake . . .*

If I climbed out of this window and tried to warn the Emperor, would he believe me? Or would he call me a liar and slay me on the spot? Even if the Emperor didn't . . . If Antony ever found out, *he* would kill me, personally.

But Death was not something one could take back—I knew this too well.

If I killed the Emperor tomorrow, I would throw a crackling match to summer hay and ignite something more than me, more than my family.

A blaze I couldn't live with the consequences of.

I didn't want to die, but maybe Meiya was right. Maybe freedom was worth dying for.

There was a limit to how far I would corrupt myself for survival. There had to be.

36

GRANDMA INSISTED THAT, AS CHILDREN, Meiya and I learn *qing gong:* the art of moving swiftly and lightly. She taught us how to leap from roof to roof, soundless, like wraiths in the night, and scale the smoothest of walls.

You never know when you'll need it.

I didn't know what her words meant at the time, but I knew now. It was always better for a girl to know how to get out of a situation she no longer wanted to be in. Escape in the night, slip into the darkness, a chance to leave the past behind.

苦海无涯, 回头是岸. *The sea of bitter misery is endless, but if you turn around, the shore will be right behind you.* It was never too late to change and start anew.

As a child, I hated Grandma's stern lessons, her insistence on perfection.

Tonight, I was grateful.

She had raised us well. Her unrelenting aspirations for us to be the best versions of ourselves, to always strive to be better, made us strong.

It was almost midnight when I leaped from roof to roof across the palace to the Emperor's pavilion, climbed in through the unlocked window of his study, and found father and son around a candlelit desk, hunched over an unfurled piece of scripture.

The room was dark, and I was quiet, steps light from practice. I hesitated at the window for a heartbeat. The room was empty of guards, and the Emperor and Prince Feng were too consumed by whatever they were reading to notice me.

Their security was lax tonight. I guessed they'd sent their best guards to protect Antony.

Rightfully so. If anything happened to Antony Augustus on Sihai soil, it would be perilous not just for Sihai, but for the whole continent. It would give Rome the perfect excuse to start a war with Pangu.

Prince Feng was the first to notice me when I stepped through the window, my shadow distorting the still room, catching his attention. The Prince's hand was quick to the blade at his hip, but I was quicker to kneel, hands outstretched and in clear view so that they knew I wasn't a threat.

I bowed until my forehead touched the ground. Respect. This was how one should greet the Emperor and his heir. Not a measly handshake like Antony had chosen that morning.

If we let Rome wash away our customs with theirs, all that would be left would be a husk of a world, a culture forgotten. Thousands of years of traditions, perished in a single breath of the wind.

When I looked up, the Emperor wore a smile so wide it touched his watering eyes, which remained kind and trusting. Shame burbled up as I remembered how I'd considered killing him just this morning.

"Feng'er." A wave of the Emperor's hand and Prince Feng reluctantly sheathed his sword.

But the prince put away the blade only to draw another. Eyes like daggers, there was a low warning to the way he watched me, ready to cut me down if I dared to overstep.

"What are you doing here?" The prince had a voice like furling thunderclouds, rumbling with a quiet promise of violence.

"I'm here to save your father's life, your highness."

"Save me?" The Emperor chuckled, stepped forward, and lowered himself to one knee so that we were eye to eye.

Sihai Feng edged forward, too, close at his father's heels, hand resting at his sword. If I made a sudden move, the prince would sever my head from my neck.

I kept still, head slightly bowed. I expected nothing but the best swordsmanship from the Heir of Sihai. I couldn't blame his vigilance, either. I did just climb through their window like a wraith come to collect souls. It actually warmed me, seeing how much the prince cared for his father.

I wish I shared that same love for my own father.

"And how do you propose to save me from Antony Augustus, young one?" the Emperor asked. There was a slight smile at his lips, amused. Not shocked or rattled with fear as I had anticipated.

"You knew?" I gasped. The expression on his face was all the answer I needed.

"That Antony Augustus will kill me tomorrow after we sign the treaty? How could I not?" The smile wilted, his eyes left mine. There was a serenity to his tone, the voice of a man ready to meet Death. "The Augustus family doesn't trust anyone, not even their own kin. They are not people who take chances. I know they'd never risk letting me live and potentially overturning the treaty one day. I have to die to secure their trust, to protect my people from war."

I bit the inside of my cheek. How naïve I was, thinking the Emperor would be unsuspecting.

He knew. Of course he knew.

Only a fool would trust the Romans blindly.

"Come." The Emperor helped me to my feet and offered me a seat at the table. "You must be freezing. Feng'*er,* pour the girl some tea. Now, tell me what you came here to say."

I drew a deep breath. There was no point in withholding information. I had already risked everything by coming here. So I told him everything. From the kidnappings to the dungeons under Jing-City and Rome's plan to divide and conquer after this new treaty with Sihai.

I talked and talked. When I was done, the Emperor nodded and exchanged a look with his son.

"Thank you for coming here, Yang Ruying. The four oceans will remember what you did tonight. You don't have to do anything tomorrow. If I have to die for my people, I will die by my own hands, on my own terms."

"Father," Prince Feng pleaded. "If we sit idle as they slaughter our neighbors, there would be nobody left when they turn their greed on Sihai. Tyrants like these will never be satisfied."

"We can fight, yes. But at what cost? By retaliating, we will mark ourselves as enemies of Rome and make these oceans a war zone. I cannot risk the destruction of our home for centuries to come. We are not the only ones who inhabit the oceans; you'll have to remember this when you are Emperor, Feng'er. This world does not belong to just us, it belongs to all life, and we are merely its keeper. I made the oceans a promise when I ascended the throne. One I must keep. Even if it costs me my life."

"And if they lied when they said they'd spare Sihai?"

"Then at least I would have bought our people a few more years of peace with my old bones," he replied without looking at his son. There were tears in the Emperor's eyes, a tremor at his lips. I felt like I was interrupting a deeply private moment between father and son—one of their last. "When I'm gone, Sihai is going to need a good Emperor, the best Emperor the four oceans have ever seen, to lead them out of these dark times."

"Father . . ."

"I need you to be that someone, Feng'er. Be the kind, just ruler I know you can be."

"You don't have to do this, Father." Prince Feng dropped to his knees, clinging to the Emperor's hands, trying to get him to listen, pleading in a way only a child could with their parent. "We can find other ways of gaining their trust. We can—"

"No. This is the sacrifice they want. We must oblige. My life in exchange for your peaceful reign is a worthy bargain."

"This isn't fair," the prince rasped, his voice breaking as tears gathered heavy between lashes, threatening to spill from those hurricane-blue eyes.

"I know."

"Why should we kneel? Why should we bend to their will? This is *our* world, *our* land. Why must we offer everything to them on a silver platter? Those men are not Gods. They are demons who have escaped hell."

"We kneel because a war between magic and science might destroy us all, son. Sometimes, surrender is better than senseless slaughter. Freedom and pride are worth fighting for, but only peace is worth *dying* for."

The same words I had told myself months earlier.

Between the Emperor and the prince, who was right?

The tension grew taut, their words reminded me of the conversations I'd had a thousand times with Meiya.

"Your death isn't going to bring us peace, Father. This treaty won't save us. It will only chain us to Rome's commands, make us their lapdog while they claim our continent, inch by inch, massacre by massacre." Prince Feng's rising voice was thunder.

I flinched, waited for the Emperor's lightning to strike and shatter the sky. But instead of raising his voice, the Emperor gently reached for his son's hand and held it tight. "This is my decision, Son. This is a risk I'm willing to take, a sacrifice I'm willing to make."

Droplets of tears finally spilled from the prince's eyes just as he jerked away, turned his back on his father so the Emperor couldn't see him weep.

With his other hand, the Emperor reached across the table and held mine. "Fate brought you to me for a reason, Yang Ruying. My stargazers once said Death only blesses a mortal when the world is at the verge of chaos, and his protégé will either save the world, or destroy it."

"I'm no hero," was all I managed to say.

"Then let's hope you're not a villain, either."

37

I PERCHED BY THE WINDOW before dawn to watch sunrise paint the sky a deep shade of red and promised Death I wouldn't cry today, no matter what happened.

The Emperor had made his choice. I had no right to judge his decision because I couldn't see the future, couldn't predict how his choice would play out.

I could only hope a good man doing what he believed was right would be enough. That he had chosen the right path.

The signing of the treaty would be held at a prosperous hour, a little before noon. The Emperor wanted to show Antony the city beforehand, let him witness its beauty and the joy of his people. So, after breakfast, we sailed from the palace rivers on a lavish boat carved in the shape of a roaring dragon, painted in red and decorated in silk, made to cruise through the city's canals in luxury.

A piece of the palace, floating on water.

On the top deck was a tiny pavilion complete with swallow-tailed roofs, supported by thick gilded pillars, draped with silk curtains so thin they were almost transparent—to better appreciate views of the city and to maintain privacy at the same time.

Around a carved table, the Emperor sipped tea with Antony and Prince Feng. Four Roman guards and four Sihai guards surrounded them. I was one of them, permitted to be here by Antony himself. It should be an honor, being in the room where futures would be decided.

Except I didn't want to be here, to take part in any of this. I wanted to leave, go home. Close my eyes and erase the past six months from my mind.

I pulled Death's magic close in order to feel some sense of control.

The Emperor's words from the previous night echoed in my mind. *Death only blesses a mortal when the world is at the verge of chaos, and his protégé will either save the world, or destroy it.*

If this was Death's intention, if he had any intentions at all, then why not bless someone who had the will to lead? Someone like Baihu? Who would listen to a girl in the presence of princes and emperors?

What power did I have here?

Did Death ever consider what I wanted?

"The boat would be safer if you replaced these curtains with bulletproof glass," Antony mused, lips downturned at the edges. He clutched the table every time the boat swayed over a rippling wave.

He didn't like the water.

"That's your way of doing things, not ours," Prince Feng replied in a low voice that demanded respect.

Something Antony would never give him, if only out of pettiness.

The air turned heavy.

Both princes wore frowns at their brows and hatred like daggers in their eyes.

If the Emperor wasn't wedged between them, his aura the only sense of calm on this trembling ship, Prince Feng might very well kill Antony Augustus and wash his hands in these rivers before noon.

Even if it did spark a war to end all wars, I doubted Prince Feng would regret it. He wanted Antony's blood, justice for all that Rome had done to Pangu.

Just like Baihu.

"Sihai rules the four oceans. Our ships have been built like this for thousands of years. They need no modification, nor do we need advice from the likes of you."

"Everything needs to be updated eventually. Everything can be improved. That is how humans evolve."

"You keep telling yourself that. But the people of Pangu like how things are—*were,* even. You—"

"Feng'*er,*" the Emperor interrupted, his voice stern. "Please excuse my son, Prince Antony. Youth breeds pride, and pride breeds arrogance. I'm still working on that with him. Hopefully by the time he inherits the throne, he'll be rid of these bad habits."

As we sailed out of the palace and into the city's wider canals, where water was deeper and rougher, the ship swayed more violently than before.

Antony's face was beginning to turn green. This ship was smaller than the Roman one, small enough that we felt every colliding wave and burbling ripple.

Prince Feng smiled, his hands hidden under the table. I smelled magic in the air as I tucked myself closer to the beam for support, my own stomach growing nauseous, unused to the unsteady waves.

"You don't look so well, my prince," Prince Feng mused.

Antony faked a grin. "It must be your rickety boat. Back home, our ships are so sturdy and well made that you can barely tell the difference between water and land."

"You little—"

"Prince Antony," the Emperor interjected, "boats may be the main source of travel in Donghai, but if you prefer the land, we can easily summon a fleet of carriages."

"No, it's fine. Just give me a few minutes to adjust."

A lie. I knew fear when I saw it.

I cast my attention outside, tired of the two princes' childish squabbling.

We were flanked by smaller ships now, each one carrying dozens of soldiers, watching, waiting, ready.

Donghai had the nickname of the City of Ten Thousand Rivers and Ten Thousand Bridges.

It lived up to its name.

Rivers streamed in hues of blue and green between the streets, and slender willows curved through the air and washed their leaves against the crisp waters.

Beyond the waters were streets full of shops displaying fluttering signs, selling rice soup, dumplings, roasted duck, and a hundred different varieties of mouthwatering food. In the corner, a Xianling roasted chestnuts with his own hands, and a puppeteer made paper dolls dance with slight gusts of wind.

The air in Donghai felt different, and magic felt more abundant here than it was back home. Was it the water, or was it something else?

Above us, a thousand lanterns cast an eerie glow over the river, illuminating the waters in the color of blood.

While the city was beautiful, the people of Donghai were the truest treasure. They threw flowers and sweet words of greeting as we passed, cheering and showering Antony with kindness he didn't deserve.

I searched the crowd for hollowed cheeks and darkened veins and found none gathered around the canal. This didn't mean opian hadn't infiltrated Donghai, or any of its tens of thousands of islands, scattered across the four oceans.

Even if it had, its claim over the people was still light. If Sihai Feng was vigilant after he inherited the throne, he might save his people from this venomous drug after all.

I hated that more people might fall prey to opian, though it was inevitable.

The only question was how many.

Prince Feng was right. Rome wouldn't be satisfied with just Er-Lang. This treaty might protect Sihai for now, but not forever.

"I heard Donghai's water system is a thing of legends, one of Pangu's great wonders," said Antony. "I've noticed none of your boats have oars. Most boats in Pangu are powered by men, but this boat is different, isn't it? It's powered by magic."

The Emperor smiled. "It's not the boat that's powered by magic, but these rivers. An intricate system of tunnels and water passages hides beneath the city, its motions controlled by those who have dominion over water. This is how our boats sail without oars and without wind."

"The reason these rivers are considered a wonder is because they are Donghai's greatest defense against invaders," Prince Feng added, chin jutted with pride. "Throughout history, many have tried to invade us. Our enemies think that just because our people are scattered across the four oceans, our capital will be poorly manned and poorly defended."

"Is it?" Antony asked.

Prince Feng flashed a crooked smile.

I remembered what Grandma once said about the canals of Donghai. Deep beneath the surface, its riverbed was stacked with the corpses and bones of all who'd tried to take the city.

If I focused, I could feel Death in these waters, following us like a hunter waiting to strike.

"It doesn't matter if Donghai is guarded by one hundred men or one hundred thousand men; no man who attempts to siege this city has lived to tell the tale. Water nourishes these streets like blood through veins, and our city is mightier than any army that has walked Pangu. This must be a foreign concept to you." Prince Feng's tone was cold, and his blue eyes a sharp blade tilted toward Antony. "To live in harmony with your world, respecting the land which you inhabit."

The air stretched tight, like the string of a bow before a fatal shot.

"Feng'*er*," the Emperor warned, but the Heir just pressed harder, his eyes furious.

"Tell me, Antony Augustus, is everyone from your world as cruel as you and your brother? Do your people even know what love is?

Have you ever cared for a life that's not your own?" The Heir's tone was sharp with resentment, his eyes locked with Antony's.

I couldn't blame him for his pain.

This was a young man who would soon lose his father and inherit an uncertain future where he'd have to shoulder the responsibilities of an Emperor before he was ready.

"I have," Antony replied.

I snickered without realizing, then instantly regretted it when Antony's attention turned toward me.

The corner of his lips twitched. Head tilted, eyes inquisitive like our first meeting. Like I was a puzzle he wished to solve. "Do you not believe me, Yang Ruying?"

"I . . ." Words lumped in my throat, and I choked on their sounds.

This only made Antony's grin grow wider. He enjoyed watching me flounder.

"If you would excuse me, I think I need some air." Without waiting for the Emperor's response, Antony rose to his feet and motioned me to follow.

Cheeks still warm, I trailed him outside to the head of the ship where winter winds beat at our clothes and I shuddered, pulling my coat tighter.

We passed a series of Sihai guards patrolling the deck. They eyed me with curiosity and disdain.

I could hear their unspoken curses.

Traitor.

"I'm sorry for laughing," I said when we reached the edge of the deck. Better to get it out of the way before Antony pried it out of me.

"I didn't bring you outside to scold you." Antony hesitated for a beat. "I wanted to see if you were okay." His voice was quiet, almost lost in the howling wind.

A shiver ran down my back, and it wasn't from the cold. "I'm fine." A lie.

My voice must have betrayed me because Antony's brows tightened. His hand twitched. For the briefest of moments, I thought he would reach for me, close the distance between our bodies and pull me into an embrace.

He didn't.

"I'm sorry," was all he said.

"Me too."

"Ruying, it's not too late to back out. I don't want you to do anything you don't want to."

"That's never stopped you before," I snapped, remembering the time he'd threatened my family in that car, pulled a gun on me and made me choose.

As if recalling the same memories, his face fell in shame. "I was wrong. Those mistakes from before I got to know you were . . ."

I took a step closer, and Antony froze mid-sentence, eyes wide. I could have sworn his cheeks darkened into a blush. It could have been the wind, but something told me it wasn't.

He liked to see me flustered, so it felt good knowing I could fluster him, too. Make his body tense because I was a little too close. "Do you have to kill him?" I asked, my voice a whisper only he could hear.

I wanted him to say no. I wanted him to see the wonders of Sihai and the good of our people and know that there was so much more to Pangu than he first thought. I wanted him to love this land the way he loved his own. I wanted him to fight for us, to convince his brothers and grandfather that my people deserved the chance to live.

I hoped that despite everything, Antony was good, that he would do the right thing, be my ally as he'd promised.

If there was a moment that could change things, it was now.

By letting the Sihai Emperor live, he could—

Antony's thumb brushed my cheek, his touch so warm against my frigid skin.

I swallowed the lump in my throat, tried to ignore the thudding of my own heart.

This fire could burn us to ashes if I wasn't careful.

"I'm sorry," he said.

I flinched, and tears pricked the back of my eyes. I should have known this was coming, shouldn't have felt so disappointed. Antony was a prince of Rome. His allegiance was with his own world, his grandfather.

It didn't matter how much things felt otherwise; the two of us would always be separated by Rome and Pangu. "He doesn't deserve to die."

"I know."

"No, Antony. You don't." I took a step forward, closed some of the distance between us until our bodies almost touched.

Antony was so much taller than I was. My eyes came to his lips, and if he wanted to, he could tuck his chin over my head and cradle me like something fragile.

"He knows," I whispered. Antony would find this out sooner or later. If I told him now, maybe it could change his mind and . . . "The Emperor knows that you plan to kill him, and he's going to let you. That's how much he loves his Empire, his people. He's willing to buy your trust with his blood, buy Sihai a few years of peace with his life. He's not going to betray you, Antony. *Please.* He's a good man. Call off the assassination. Let him live."

Antony's eyes didn't turn kind like I'd expected. Instead, they hardened, brewed into something like anger, like rage. I should have feared him, should step back and look away, bow my head in submission like Father said girls should in the presence of angry men.

I didn't.

I held my head high and kept my eyes locked with his, waiting.

"Good," he murmured, finally. "If he wants to die, then let him die. Come on." He reached for me. "You're cold. Let's go back."

I pushed him away before he could touch me. "Didn't you hear what I just said? He's not going to rebel! Cancel the assassination, Antony. Why should a good man die just because your family doesn't know how to trust people?"

A shadow crossed his face. "Do I want to know how you found out about all of this?"

My courage dropped through a trapdoor, and everything stopped.

I saw Meiya's and Grandma's faces.

I saw blood and Death and corpses littering the streets like autumn leaves.

"Ruying, I'm willing to keep one eye open and one eye closed when it comes to you, but don't ever tell me what I can and cannot do. Remember who I am, and who *you* are. We—"

"Watch out!"

An arrow whizzed through the air.

Without thinking, I pushed Antony out of the way just in time. The arrow zipped past where his head should have been.

More arrows followed the first, poured from the roofs at either side of the riverbank like summer rain, sudden and violent.

"Get down!"

I reached for Death's magic, but before I could grasp it, Antony grabbed me and pushed me back down. His body covered mine like a shield. I heard the grunt he made when an arrow struck his shoulder, its impact sending him hurtling toward the ground and me with him.

"Protect the prince!"

As I fell, the world tilted farther and farther off its axis until I saw the men perched atop the swallow-tailed houses on either side of the canal. Clad in black, they wore the painted masks of opera performers and flew a blood-red flag bearing the same mask at its center.

The Phantom.

38

SHIELDS COVERED US BEFORE MORE arrows found their mark. Soldiers blessed with affinities for wind rushed forward and launched violent volleys of air at the arrows to divert them.

Men surrounded us, some trying to help Antony to his feet, others shouting for aid.

Antony's eyes were on me and me alone. "Are you okay?" he asked, one hand cradling the back of my head and the other holding on to my shoulder. I didn't notice when or how we'd become entangled in each other's arms.

"Y—you're bleeding," I stuttered, and tried to press my hands against his wound. He saw the second arrow before I did and could have run, dodged, done something—anything. But he didn't. Instead of only thinking about himself in the face of danger, he'd reached for me, protected me with his body. "You idiot! Why didn't you run?"

Before Antony could provide an answer, one of his guards grabbed us by the shoulders and pushed us toward the pavilion. The deck was packed with soldiers now.

As soon as the gunshots started, Death seeped into the air.

Once we were inside, iron curtains fell over the silk ones; then they were nailed down by half a dozen soldiers with alarming speed until we were safe inside a cocoon of plated metal, strung together like a near-seamless armor.

"We might not have bulletproof glass, but we have things that are just as good," Prince Feng remarked, his expression oddly calm, his voice quiet enough that I wasn't sure anyone but me heard him over the commotion. "Who needs science when we have magic?"

Healers quickly encircled Antony, pressed hands to his wound to stop the blood as they cut away his clothes. They extracted the arrow and quickly began tending to his wound, applying balm and bandages—and all before he had the chance to sit down. Their movements were smooth and organized. As expected. They were imperial healers; they had trained their whole lives for moments like these.

Antony's shirt was half off, and I tried not to look, but out of the corner of my eye, I couldn't help but notice the silver scars that marred his body. Slash after slash, covering his back like the marks of a vicious whip.

My stomach dropped, remembering all that he'd told me about his childhood, his life on the streets before he was adopted as a prince. And those brief mentions of the grandfather who seemed as cruel as the streets that raised him.

"Is he going to be okay?" the Emperor and I asked at the same time.

"Give me space," one of the healers grumbled.

"Check her for injuries, too," Antony ordered. When his eyes met mine, he flashed a smile as if trying to comfort me.

Like a traitor, my heart fluttered like a swarm of butterflies.

I looked away. I didn't want this terrifying feeling inside me, and I didn't want to owe him a life. I'd rather take that arrow myself than owe Antony Augustus anything.

"Ruying?" I didn't realize his hand was holding mine until he squeezed it.

Immediately, I tore my hand from his. I pretended I didn't notice how his face fell, or the way my chest suddenly felt so tight it was hard to breathe.

"Why didn't you run?" I asked.

"And watch you get injured instead?"

Magic woke suddenly at his words. From a slow simmer to a hungry gasp.

But I don't want to see you hurt, either. These words weighed heavy on my tongue. I clenched my jaw. I couldn't say them out loud, couldn't let Antony know.

So I turned my back to him, paced toward the edge of the boat, backed against a pillar for cover, and prepared to do what I did best: kill.

Right now, I owed him my life. It was only fair that I saved his in return.

Beneath us, the current raged faster and the boat rocked violently, its waters pulled from all sides by the Phantom's Ghosts and the Sihai soldiers who wished to utilize it. But the soldiers couldn't turn these canals into a weapon without endangering us. These waters were deep and violent. If the currents became wild enough to overturn the ship, it would be a death sentence for us all.

If it were just the Emperor and his men on the boat, maybe it would be fine. They had spent their whole lives commanding water, sailing these streams; they could save themselves. But there were too many Romans who didn't have magic to protect them, and an enemy prince who didn't look like he could swim well enough to survive.

This wasn't going to end in our favor.

I peered through the tiny seams between armored curtains. Arrows against arrows, blades clashing. Sihai soldiers tried to scale the buildings that surrounded us, but the Ghosts picked them off one by one with mortal weapons and blasts of magic. Bodies fell, from all sides.

Blood was everywhere.

Already, we sailed in a river of blood. Mayhem reigned on all sides as the tidal wave of crowds surged and shrieked. Panic was a burning smoke, dark and drowning and—

Among the chaos I saw a red-faced child, no older than five, balancing on the barricade at the edge of the water to avoid getting trampled by the madness, clinging on to the pillar for dear life, crying. Weeping. "Mama! Mama!"

My grip tightened on the pillar. My body moved by instinct, but before I had the chance to even stumble forward, a stray arrow slashed the air. From a Ghost or Sihai soldier, I couldn't tell.

The arrow punctured the hollow of the child's throat and immediately the screaming was replaced by gouts of blood. His face distorted. He gasped for breath.

Before my body remembered how to move, the boy collapsed onto the ground and disappeared under the trampling feet of terrified people. Nobody stopped to help him. I wasn't even sure if anyone else saw him fall.

His soul was the orange of a rising sun. The color of a flame snuffed too soon.

Bullets and arrows continued to fly, and more colors followed the boy's soul.

Greens,

yellows,

golds,

silvers,

lilacs,

and blues . . .

Swirls and swirls of color rising through the air as souls left bodies, lives slipping into oblivion one by one.

Color upon color, they blinded my senses.

I could taste their lives in the air.

Sweet and bitter and spicy and sour. Happiness and pain and fury and loneliness.

I tore my eyes away as innocent souls bled into stark colors faster and faster, and I remembered my last conversation with Baihu.

"The Phantom is after Antony," I told the Emperor. "They want to kill him so that the Roman monarch will blame Sihai for his death—to wreck this treaty maybe, or to force Sihai into war with

Rome. I don't know. But we have to get Antony out of here. We have to keep him safe, and—"

Before I could finish, an explosion blasted open the iron curtains, knocked everyone to the ground in a dizzying wreckage of splintered wood and fractured metal.

Magic tasted tangy in the air. Six Ghosts leaped in through the cloud of debris, blades drawn, their eyes focused on Antony.

I tried to stand, but my head was spinning. Everything was spinning.

Silence rang too loud in my ears.

In the corner of my vision, Antony's guards reached for their guns just as Sihai guards reached for their swords. But the Ghosts were ready and they were fast. The clash of metals, souls perishing from both sides with such startling speed and efficiency that I shrank back as blood sprayed the wreckage like burning raindrops.

"Take care of her," someone in a gold mask ordered, gesturing toward where I lay crumpled under a wreckage of splintered wood. "Remember, the Phantom wants the girl alive."

Before he had finished talking, I threw out Death's magic and wrapped it around the men closest to me. But when I pulled, their qi clung to their mortal bodies, stubborn as a sash of silk knotted tight around a protruding hook. Only a shimmer of what I intended to take ended up trickling into my body.

Their resistance was enough to make me recoil. The ones who had the most to live for were always the hardest to kill.

Six months earlier, I wouldn't have stood a chance, but as the moon bloomed and withered, my command over Death's magic had improved. It was strong, like a well-used muscle.

If I couldn't take down all of them at once, I would pacify them one by one.

Clenching my jaw, I focused everything on the Ghost closest to me.

He stumbled, his energy fighting hard, clinging on with everything it had.

But I was stronger, my grip tighter. Within seconds, his *qi* yielded and poured into me reluctantly. I took enough to make him fall unconscious, letting go just in time—something I had been practicing.

When his body hit the ground, I reached for the next Ghost.

I tugged fast and hard, and he, too, collapsed. I immediately moved on to the next target, who was already in motion.

He dashed toward me. I reached for his currents of *qi,* but my heart burned from exhaustion, and I felt my vision beginning to blur, the familiar feeling of clotted blood climbing up my throat. There was a numbness at my fingertips, washing fast over me like heavy waves, soaking my limbs and making everything feel that much heavier.

One moment of pause—enough for my target to smash through the broken table I was hiding behind with a violent swipe. So fast I barely had time to roll out of the way.

I tried to tug at his *qi,* but my grip was loose, my mind unfocused and exhausted, energy fizzing through my body as they trickled into Death's realm. When I snapped back into focus, my hands grasping his *qi,* I wasn't strong enough to make him fall. He merely stumbled, with a slight sway of dizziness.

An opportunity.

I found the knife I kept in my boot. If I couldn't fight him with magic, then I would do it the old-fashioned way.

"I don't want to kill you," he hissed. A warning.

"Me neither." I kicked out my leg and swiped him off his feet, then drove my blade through his chest.

Another man charged at me from behind. His sword swung forward; I caught him too late.

But before metal mangled flesh, the thunder of a gunshot pulled everything to a stop.

Coppery blood sprayed my face, and the man collapsed at my feet.

I looked up and saw Antony leaning against the wall, just behind the Emperor, a smoking gun in his hand.

Antony fired another bullet at Gold Mask, but the willowy figure at his side raised her hand and swiped it off course with a motion of her fingers. Toward me.

The bullet missed the mark by millimeters, grazing my hair as it flew past.

I rolled behind a pillar for cover, gasping for breath, still checking my head for a wound.

"All of you are going to regret protecting this leech," Gold Mask snarled.

The Emperor pushed Antony behind him like a tiger protecting his cub. One of his hands danced in the air, a blue glow gathering at his fingertips. "Call off the attack, or I will show you what real regret is."

"Father, no!"

"The Empires are stronger together than apart!" the Gold Mask cried. "If you won't fight with us, then we have to make you. The Phantom prefers the Roman prince alive, but he doesn't *need* him alive . . ."

With that, the Gold Mask conjured a blade of fire out of thin air and hurled it toward the Emperor and Antony.

The Emperor twisted his wrist, and water gathered before him to form a heavy shield.

Fire evaporated water, but the shield held the flames back for a heartbeat—enough time for the Emperor to push Antony out of the way.

Gold Mask hit the Emperor with another blast of fire, but this time the Emperor didn't even try to fight back. He merely offered Antony a small smile as he closed his eyes, and—

By the time Gold Mask realized what was happening and tried to pull back, it was too late.

The shot of flame cut through the Emperor's chest, seared his flesh until it blistered and darkened.

"Father!" Prince Feng cried from beneath the rubble.

In the stunned silence, Antony raised a gun and tried to put a bullet through the Gold Mask, but was not quick enough.

"*Che!*" Gold Mask barked. *Retreat.* With that, every remaining Ghost leaped from the wreckage.

Whatever they had planned, it was not this.

"Father . . ." Prince Feng cried as he crawled to his father's side.

I held my breath. Death hovered over the Emperor's dying body. I saw shades of blue surfacing as his *qi* struggled to hold on.

He put his hand in his son's.

"Father . . ." Prince Feng collapsed, cradling the Emperor in his arms, but the Emperor wasn't looking at his son. He was looking at Antony.

"I saved you," he said. "Please, no more fighting. Let my death solidify the peace between Sihai and Rome for the years to come. If my life can buy peace and prosperity for my people, I'll die happy."

Antony looked down at the Emperor and said nothing. He didn't even have the audacity to lie.

"Feng'*er*," the Emperor choked.

"Help!" the prince cried. "Help!"

Nobody moved. They knew what I knew.

"Promise me that you will sign the treaty, Feng'*er*. Promise me that you will honor your first decree as if it were my last. Sihai needs this. *I* need this. Don't let me die in vain," the Emperor croaked, his voice faint as a whisper, delicate like a vanishing storm.

"Father, nothing is going to happen to you. We'll fix this. It's going to be okay." Prince Feng stared at the healers who cowered in the corner. "Do something! Save him!"

I looked away to give Prince Feng privacy in these last moments. Death had made his mark, and he would not be denied.

There was no use in begging.

Death didn't discriminate, and he didn't play favorites. No matter how much unfinished business we had to leave behind. We could fight with Death all we wanted, but when it was our time, he would come sure as the seasons.

And he would not be denied.

"Feng'*er*, promise me that you won't start a war with Rome."

"Father . . ."

"Promise me, Feng'*er*!" the Emperor begged, his voice raspy now, a man running out of breaths, running out of time.

"I—I promise."

Colors bled into the air.

The Emperor's soul was the peaceful blue of the sky before a storm.

"Father!" Prince Feng's cry was ear-splitting.

I sensed the magic before it happened: a rancorous torrent that thundered from the prince.

Water sloshed at the ship, rising high like giant claws, obliterating everything in its path.

The water was fast. It swept enemies from rooftops in swift slashes, and the world echoed with muffled shrieks and cracks of bones. I barely had time to get to Antony before a wall of water slammed us into the canal.

Bitter cold tides enveloped us, the current merciless as it clung tight to every soul in its grasp, dragging us down, down, down . . .

Blood for blood. The water sought vengeance for the Emperor, guided by the Heir's magic.

Caught in its grip, I gasped for air that wasn't there and clawed for help.

39

LIFE WAS A FICKLE THING.

A slender string.

A whisker of a flame.

Fragile porcelain, wisp thin and in need of protection.

I knew what it felt like to drown—knew the burning lungs and the flailing limbs.

Memories of that day under the waterfall scarred me still.

I gasped for air but swallowed only the water that filled my lungs gulp after gulp.

First came fear, then pain, and finally the euphoria and the peace.

Sihai's water system was intricate, its current fast, too strong for mortals to fight. In the darkness, I saw flashes of green against deep blues.

An arm around my waist.

Please, Death. I don't want to die.

40

I TRIED TO SWIM, BUT something pulled me down.
I tried to breathe, but there was no air.
I tried to fight, but—

41

LIKE DRIFTWOOD, I ROSE AND ebbed at the edge of consciousness.

I drowned and resurfaced a hundred times, each flash of reality brief and blurred, rolling into each other until I couldn't tell them apart.

Wintry water oozed down my throat, flooded my lungs.

Hands on my back.

The weight of the world held me down.

"Ruying! Wake up!" A voice burbled through the waters. "Get up!"

The bank of a frozen river. The currents had finally relinquished their hold, leaving me with my lungs burning but my heart still beating.

Icy mud beneath my hand as I tried to stand.

"Go." My own voice.

Clothes heavy with water, their iciness clinging to my skin, freezing me to the bone.

"I won't leave you."

Cold blue tones. The sun dying in the distance.

"I won't leave you."

Death hovered over me.

"I won't leave you . . ."

I don't want to die.

42

I WINCED WHEN I WOKE; my hand grazed the bandage around my abdomen, wrapped tightly and neatly but not enough to prevent an infection, because my skin felt hot. A fever was settling in.

"You're awake." A deep murmur drew me to open my eyes through the haze.

Antony sat at the edge of the bed, a threadbare blanket over his shoulders. The fire in the corner was dying, the room growing colder. His lips had lost their color.

"You saved me?" An uncomfortable feeling twitched in my chest. The snakes strangled my ribs, making it hard to breathe, hard to look at him.

"Of course I saved you. What was I going to do, let you drown or leave you on the riverbank to freeze to death?"

"But you can't swim." I remembered the way he'd clung to the table whenever the boat had swayed, the fear in his eyes. It could have been general water sickness, but when he frowned, I knew I had touched a sore point.

"I wasn't going to let you die," he repeated. The same words he had said on the boat. "It doesn't matter whether I swim or drown, I will not let you die."

The feeling in my chest grew tighter. He's risked his own life for me, again.

Two life debts I owed him now. This trip was more expensive than I had originally imagined.

"Where are we?" The four bare walls around us were a far cry from the luxuries of Donghai's imperial palace.

An abandoned cottage, veiled in heavy dust—overgrown with mold and wilderness that crept in through the scarcely papered windows and the cracks lining the walls. Everything smelled faintly of dirt and damp, but there was a roof over our heads, sheltering us from the cold that would otherwise have devoured us like a famished beast.

It seemed nobody had lived here for a long time, at least, so we weren't in danger of trespassing. The furs that kept me warm were moth-eaten, and the threadbare Pangu robes Antony now wore were of linen and a world away from his tailored suits and silk ties.

At least we were dry.

At least we were alive.

Flashes of rabid currents and never-ending darkness flashed behind my eyes. I remembered gasping for air, and the thick, icy water, currents too strong to fight, that pulled me down, down, down.

I shivered.

"I had to change you out of your wet clothes," Antony added, hesitant, not quite looking at me. There was a slight shadow staining his cheeks. Was he blushing? "I hope you're okay with that. You would have caught your death if I had left you in those robes, and I needed to bandage your wound. You were bleeding and I—"

"Thank you," I murmured, resisting a half smile at the way he stumbled over his words. It gave his stern, princely face a human touch, reminding me that beneath all his pensive frowns, moments lost in deep thoughts of duty, was a young man of just twenty. Merely a few months older than I—something so easily forgotten, given the way he carried himself.

"Don't thank me. You did the same for me, back on the boat. When you saw that first arrow, you didn't run or protect yourself.

Instead, the first thing you thought of was me. If you didn't push me out of the way, I might not be alive right now."

Something caught in my throat. He was right, I did push him out of the way. An instinct, an action without thought.

But him covering my body with his like a human shield, and carrying me through the frozen wilderness when he himself was wounded . . . This was something else entirely.

If the roles were reversed, would I do the same?

Maybe I would and was too scared to admit it.

Or maybe his feelings were unrequited, and his sacrifice would ultimately be met with betrayal.

As long as Jing-City suffered under Rome's tyranny, Antony was Er-Lang's mortal enemy. It didn't matter how much I liked him— and like him I did. Nothing could erase this truth.

A thought that dug deep and bit hard, like the tiny fangs of rabid bugs thirsty for blood.

With the corners of my eyes, I let myself look at him and felt the kindness of his gaze like a slow pour of tender sunlight. A kind of warmth that crept up my neck and sank deep beneath my flesh, soothing the wrinkles of my indecisions and making everything a little more bearable.

When his lips twitched, when he flashed that half-dimpled smile that seemed to enchant me more and more each time, a piece of me wanted to lean toward the light, let it surround me, lose myself in him.

A desire that I tried to kill quickly.

No matter how much I wanted to give air to this thing that bloomed between us, I couldn't. For I knew this fire would burn us to ashes if we weren't careful.

If I leaned too close, it wouldn't hesitate to consume what little I had left of the girl I once was. The sister and the granddaughter and the friend that those I loved remembered me as.

But here, far from the glimmering palaces and Rome's politics, we were alone.

Here, just for tonight, he didn't have to be Antony Augustus and I didn't have to be Yang Ruying. Instead, we could simply be a girl and a boy. I shifted in the bed, made room for him. "It's cold," I whispered, relenting to temptation. I knew the consequences of such invitation, of such words.

The hope that would spark in him, and the future I'd never let myself entertain.

Meiya and Grandma would be ashamed if they knew, but I'd already done too many things that would bring them shame. This was nothing compared to some of my heavier sins.

For tonight, for a glimmer of precious warmth, nobody had to know.

Antony hesitated, a knot between his brows. "I've read that it's shameful for an Er-Lang girl to be alone in the same room as a man after sunset, let alone . . ."

"After all the people you made me kill, *this* is where you draw the line?" I huffed a laugh. "We will be warmer together. I don't want to die of hypothermia, and I don't want *you* to die of hypothermia, either. Not after everything we went through to keep you alive. We will concern ourselves with matters of honor after we've survived the night."

Plus, after all that I had done these past six months—working for Rome, murdering my own kin—my reputation and prospects of a respectable marriage had long ago been tarnished by the blood that soaked my hands.

When Antony's lips parted, I wasn't sure if he'd protest further or apologize.

In the end, he did neither, but simply climbed into the bed beside me. In the brief moment when he slid under the blankets, I shivered from the cold that he brought, but soon, everything turned warmer. Two bodies heated this small cocoon of blankets faster than one.

This bed was what we called a 坑—essentially a long stretch of mattress over the fireplace, big enough to fit a whole family. At some point this house might have housed six or more. Three generations living under the same roof wasn't uncommon in rural parts of the Empires. The center of the bed was warmest, reserved for the eldest—the grandparents of the family—with the sides left for the young and the healthy.

I wondered where the cottage's former inhabitants were now.

In theory, if Antony really wanted to stay warm, he should have lit the fire under the bed, but I doubt he knew there was a fireplace under here.

Beside me, Antony's breaths turned shallow, every inhale and exhale thunderingly loud against the silence. He was close enough that I could feel his tense heartbeats, but still far enough that it wouldn't be considered indecent. Even now, he was careful; the distance between us not to be crossed.

"I was so scared when I saw you passed out on the riverbank," he whispered into the darkness, so quiet I wondered if these were words meant to be heard. "I thought you were going to die."

I felt his eyes on me, and flickering flames climbed up my neck as I kept mine on the ceiling, on anything but him.

I felt like I was drowning all over again. Except this time, I was tempted to let the water take me.

"How did we survive the canals?"

Antony snickered. "Luck? The water was fast—a blast of energy rather than an intentionally manipulated current. I wondered if the prince's raw power overwhelmed anyone else who tried to control the water and drown me. I don't know. And I can swim, I'm just . . . not very good at it. But the water carried us faster through the secret underwater passageways than I could ever swim. And before I knew it, we were spat out onto a river where the tide was slower, where I dragged you to shore."

"Why did you save me?" I asked, my voice as quiet as his. "You could have left me on the riverbank, but you didn't."

"I saved you because I wanted to." If he knew what I had done just the night before, how I had warned the Emperor of his plans, would he still want me alive? "Because I had to . . . Because I can't bear the thought of you dead."

"Because of my Gift? Because you don't like to waste talents?"

"If that's what you want to believe."

A beat of silence. We both understood his words, but neither were willing to say it out loud, to be the first to admit the knotted butterflies suffocating deep in the confines of our chests, the fluttering wings in tempo with our fevered hearts.

"Years ago, I heard of a Pangu prophecy, that those blessed by Death can either save the world one day or destroy it."

The same faithless prophecy the Emperor had mentioned last night.

"There are a lot of prophecies in my world. Don't take them so seriously. If they are all true, then lots of people are destined to save the world. Most of these prophecies don't come true, and the ones that do are often vague strokes of luck." I paused, considered my next words carefully. "Is this why you recruited me, because you think I will destroy my world?"

"Or save it, whether that be your world or mine," he murmured. "And I'd be lying if I say that never crossed my mind."

"This is why you're kind to me?"

"In the beginning, maybe."

"Not anymore?"

"Not anymore."

A pause. I let go of the breath I was holding. "Am I a fool, Antony? For thinking that, beneath everything, you're a good person and not the monster everyone else believes you to be?"

From across the narrow chasm that divided us, Antony reached out and touched my hand.

He was the one who reached out, but I was the one who let our fingers entwine under the covers.

"Thank you," was all he said. Two words that held too much heartbreak, too much trauma.

"You too," I whispered, "for seeing me, for understanding me. I think you might be the first person who looks at me and sees something to be admired and not something to be feared."

"People will always revile what they don't understand. I promise you, Ruying, history won't remember you as anything other than a hero. A legend whose magnificence shall be sung and recited and retold for eras to come."

"I don't think that's something you or I can dictate. History chooses how our stories are told."

"You forget that history is written by the victors, and I intend to be victorious. The world will remember you as a hero, Ruying, because *I* will remember you as a hero. Always."

His words lured me like sweet lies. I wanted these melodies to sing true. I wanted to linger in the world he painted, so badly.

But Antony couldn't make me a hero.

If I stayed loyal to him, I would never be a hero to my people. Not after what I did. And I doubted his people would ever see a Xianling as anything other than a savage whose Empire perished under the might of science.

He could lie for me, but the truth would live eternal in whispers.

And I didn't want to be remembered by lies. If a thousand years from now, this world still remembered my name, I wanted them to remember me for my truths. I didn't want a tale smoothed over and coated in gold.

I wanted to be remembered for who I was.

The good, the bad, and everything in between.

"The world is vast, and you are capable of so much, Ruying," he mused. "When all fades to ashes and dust, you will be remembered by the stars. I will make sure of this. Power is the most beautiful of all, and you are more powerful than you know. Embrace the magic Death has bestowed on you and be proud of it. *Own* it. You and I, we could be Gods if we wished. If we are strong enough to unshackle ourselves from these mortal morals that bind us to mediocrity."

"You mean the morals that bind us to humanity?"

The morals that slipped between my fingers with every kill, like sand, like water. The harder I held on to them, the quicker they perished.

And soon, they would run out and I would be left with nothing.

What happens then? A question that had raced through my mind for six months.

"Goodnight," I murmured before one of us crossed a line that might change everything.

"Goodnight," he echoed. But neither of us moved. Two heart-beats thudding in rhythm. We were so close it would be too easy to kiss him, to reach across this canyon dividing us even though we were supposed to be on the same side. Allies. Friends . . .

If just for tonight. If just in this moment, perhaps . . .

Antony was the first to cross the invisible line. He leaned in, gingerly, as if to give me time to push him away, to run.

I didn't.

When he came close, I leaned forward, too.

Just like that, in the murmuring dark, our lips brushed lightly, like the graze of two falling feathers. The touch of a match against firestone: spark, heat, hunger, pulling me forward, forward, forward like a gravity I had never felt. Like a want not even Death could coerce from my cold heart.

But just as Antony's hand reached for me, as his lips pressed harder against mine for something more than what I was willing to risk in this abandoned cottage with a prince of Rome—a prince of the very Empire that built its ivory streets on the bones of my ancestors . . .

I pulled back, cheeks flushed.

Antony didn't lean in harder or hold me closer like a part of me wanted him to.

He let me go, as if he'd expected this all along.

Silence.

My thumping heart, lungs heavy for the breaths I held in order not to make a sound.

"Goodnight," I murmured, finally.

In the dark, I could have sworn Antony smiled. "Goodnight, my love."

I closed my eyes. Whatever I felt for him, it had to die. I couldn't entertain these thoughts or feelings, and neither could he.

Power was a dangerous game. Those who wished to be strong couldn't have feelings like these, couldn't love. Because as soon as you cared for something, it became your weakness.

For my sake, for his sake, these delicate moments far from the world should forever remain here, in this decaying cottage.

When tomorrow came, we could never be this close again.

Because Antony Augustus was my people's enemy. Nothing would ever change this.

I peeked from beneath my lashes, watched his face fall in the darkness. When he finally turned away, he released one last whisper into the night. "Maybe one day I'll deserve you."

And maybe one day, I'll learn to forgive.

Maybe one day, our two worlds would learn to coexist, as my world had with magic.

43

ANTONY

DAWN CAME SLOWLY THAT MORNING, its golden light filtering through the tattered paper windows.

Antony couldn't sleep, so he lay on his side and watched Ruying beside him. Watching the steady rise and fall of her chest, her face so peaceful in the dim light, made Antony wish he could freeze time and stay in this moment forever.

Once upon a time, Antony's grandfather had told him that love was a weakness. Because of love, his father had to die. Antony's grandfather had refused to leave the future of his people in the hands of a weak man.

Ever since then, Antony had promised himself that he'd never be weak, that he'd make his grandfather proud. He'd promised himself that he'd never love anyone or anything aside from Rome and its people, like a good monarch should. And at the dawn of apocalypse, his world needed a good monarch now more than ever—one who could lead them back to prosperity.

For almost a decade, Antony had kept that promise. He'd starved himself of love, laughed at the Romeos and Juliets of his world, the love songs that echoed on the radios. Now, in this bed with Ruying beside him, Antony finally understood what his grandfather meant when he said love was a weakness.

Why they fought the wars.

Why poets dedicated their lives to putting this feeling into words.

His gaze traced her eyes, her cheeks, her nose, her lips.

Antony didn't know how Ruying had forced her way into his heart, circled a spot, and claimed it like a dragon with her treasure.

All he knew was that when he saw that arrow coming for her on the ship, he'd moved without thinking, without even a beat of hesitation. And when he saw her bleeding on the riverbank, when he thought she might be dead, nothing else mattered.

If anything happened to her, Antony would burn this whole world to the ground.

He would start wars to keep her safe.

Which was why he had to let her go. *Soon*. He didn't want to watch fury illuminate her face like a wildfire sweeping across crisp autumn trees if she ever found out about the horrors he was capable of, about the crimes he'd committed.

What he planned for her world.

He didn't want to see disappointment bloom to hate.

And she would hate him.

Forever.

If she saw him for who he was, his mistakes and his flaws, she would never understand.

Antony didn't want to get his heart broken.

Yet, at the same time, he couldn't bear to let her go.

He wanted to remember her like this, for an eternity. A moment frozen behind glass.

Even if she broke his heart, he would remember her in this moment.

Beautiful, magnificent. Antony Augustus was not a religious man, but he would worship at her altar, kneel for her until the stars perished, until both of their worlds were nothing but forgotten particles lost in the universe. Even if they one day became enemies, he would remember tonight. Remember the softness of her hand in his, how she'd smiled for him once upon a time.

44

My wound was infected. Pus festered around the raw flesh. I cleaned it out as best I could the way Grandma had taught me, but we were in the middle of nowhere; I didn't have the right herbs or ingredients to treat it. I could only do my best and hope Antony's men found us before the infection turned worse.

"Does it hurt?" he asked as he reapplied the freshly washed makeshift bandages that were just torn bedsheets—the closest substitute we had right now.

"A little," I said, keeping my shirt rolled up. "You're good at this." I gestured at the bandages, his fingers moving meticulously; it was as if he'd done this a thousand times.

"I've had practice," he said, and I remembered the scars I saw when the healers tended to him with magic. "The streets of Rome are a special kind of evil. And so is my grandfather."

This was all the explanation I needed, all the explanation he would ever give.

"Can you tell me a story?" he asked once he was done. "One from your world."

"What kind of stories do you want to hear?"

"Your favorite."

I smiled. "Have you ever heard of the Goddess Nüwa?"

"The Celestial Goddess of the Wucai Mountain?"

I nodded. "Grandma said she was a serpent Goddess who'd lived at the dawn of time. She was the mother of men, and the protector of our realm. Traces of her legacy can be found in every fragment of our history, our legends. Her descendants guided the Great Gods to victory against the Qin Emperor millennia ago. Some still believe that her descendants will rise again and . . ."

"And rescue your people from mine?"

"It's a street rumor."

"Don't look down on street rumors, Ruying. Rumors lead to hope, and hope is the spark of all things great and terrible."

"This story has nothing to do with the rebellions. This story began long ago when the world was first made, when Nüwa lived alone in this great land, among echoes of silence, the burden of loneliness heavy on her shoulders. It was this loneliness that drove her to make things from the earth. People and animals, whom she loved so much that she gave them the Gift of Life by breathing on them.

"Of her creations, she loved humans the most. She loved us so much that she couldn't make us fast enough. So she dipped a vine into a pool of mud, and wherever its splatters touched ground, humans rose like sprouts in spring, perfect and beautiful. They say the ones she made by hand inherited her magic and became Xianlings. The ones made from vines and mud did not inherit her magic, but they were so grateful for life that they didn't care.

"For a long time, Nüwa lived in harmony with her creations, tending to us as if we were her children. She watched as we prospered and learned to gather, hunt, farm, and fashion marvelous creations of our own. This peace didn't last long, though. One day, under a sky of thunder and lightning, two battling dragons emerged from the ocean and broke the sky, flooded the world, and wreaked such havoc upon the land that it drowned the humans she loved so much. To save us, she had to mend the sky. So she took a blade to her hand and made a cut so deep that blood flowed like a river. From her blood, five colored stones solidified. She melted these stones down and poured them over the parts of the sky broken by the dragons. But the process took too long, and she couldn't bear to watch us suffer.

"In the end, she sacrificed herself—used her own body and blood and magic to mend the sky. For us. Grandma told me that in the place where the sky once collapsed, where Nüwa melted the Wucai stones, rose the Wucai Mountain, where her children gathered to worship her. For thousands of years, we studied under the Monks to harness our magic. To remember where we came from and what Nüwa sacrificed for us so that we might live . . . Well, until your people came and claimed the mountain and the temples as your own, and the Monks vanished from our world."

"What happened to the Wucai stones that were left over?"

The question caught me off guard. "What?"

"I read it in a book somewhere," he said casually. "I'm curious. The book never mentioned where the stones went. Do you know?"

"That depends on what kind of legends you believe in," I replied, cautiously. "Some say the stones were scattered across the sky and became stars. Some say they returned to blood and melted into the ground when Nüwa died. Some say they grew into Wucai Mountain. Grandma told me only one Wucai stone was left in the aftermath. Bestowed with Nüwa's magic, the single stone was too dangerous to keep. Wucai means *five colors,* so the Monks divided it into five smaller stones, each one a different color, each holding a piece of Nüwa's magic."

"Where are these stones now?"

"We don't know." I laughed. "Some people claim each of the Emperors hold a single piece of the stone, but I think if the stones are real, they would have been lost long ago among the fallen Empires and mad men who wished for more power than anyone should possess."

"When the treaty was signed twenty years ago, the Emperors of Pangu supposedly gifted us fragments of the five colored stones, one from each Empire, each possessing a different hue. I have always wondered if those stones are real."

I arched a brow. "I had no idea."

Another thing the Emperors never relayed to their citizens. Whatever the truth was, it was not something mortals like me would ever know.

Antony's expression turned thoughtful at my response. "Regardless, it's a beautiful story."

"I've always loved Nüwa for what she represents. She was a serpent deity, and serpents are so often associated with evil and danger. I sometimes wonder if Nüwa was shunned by the other Gods for her serpent body, hence her loneliness and love for humans, who worshipped her instead of fearing her. Those born with evil don't always have to be evil. Those born to destroy don't always have to destroy. Nüwa escaped her destiny of becoming a demon, so it gave me hope that . . ."

"That you might one day escape your own powers?" Antony watched me for a moment, as if contemplating what to say next. "Back home, our sky is broken, too. Not by a war between dragons, although that would have been cool. Our sky was broken by the greed of my people—our pollution and our recklessness. Our greed for luxury and comfort." A bitter, hollow laugh. "If Nüwa was of our world, if she'd made us the way she made your people, I wonder what she'd think of us. Would she be ashamed? Would she still love us enough to give her life for us?"

"Nüwa loves all of her children."

Antony's smile was empty. "She would not love me. She would not love my grandfather. She would not love the people of Rome." His hand touched the spot behind his ribs where I assumed his scars stretched to. "Do you want to know my greatest fear?"

Death? I almost said, but a man who feared Death would never jump in front of an arrow for a girl.

"Your grandfather's wrath?"

"Close—though I'm not afraid of him. I'm only afraid of *becoming* him." His smile wilted. "I don't think I need to tell you where my scars came from . . . Every time Valentin and I made a mistake, disappointed him, or did something he deemed weak, he hurt us. He thinks everything is a weakness, and the only way to be strong is to be cold and cruel and heartless as the winter wind. He raised us in his image, thinking it would make us strong, but I never wanted to be like him."

His hand touched mine, and I let our fingertips entwine and lace like last night.

"You don't have to be like him," I whispered. "苦海无涯, 回头是岸. *The sea of bitter misery is endless, but if you turn around, the shore will be right behind you.*"

"苦海无涯," he repeated—*the bitter sea is endless*—his eyes somewhere far, somewhere I couldn't reach. "Can I ask you a question?" Antony said, his hand still holding mine, his thumb brushing the back of my hand, tenderly, hesitantly. As if one sudden move and I would pull away like last night.

"Yes."

"Why are some souls harder for you to harvest than others?"

I smiled. "I don't harvest souls. I pull the *qi* that exists all around us and is what anchors our souls to our mortal bodies. I think, at least. They don't exactly teach us these kind of things in schools."

"Why not?"

"Because every form of magic is different. Because it is impossible to understand magic as there are so many variations of the same powers. Because magic is rare. And above all, because magic is dangerous. It is a curse that haunts us, a demon we must resist, always."

"That's a lie. The royal families know more than they let on. If they weren't so scared of their own people's potential and trained Xianlings like you from the moment you discovered your Gifts, helped you ascend to your highest of possibilities instead of just learning how to tame and control your powers like something that needs to be suppressed, maybe Er-Lang would stand a chance in a war. Progress is difficult to make when humans are too busy drowning in fears of their own potentials. Your kind could have—*should have*—lived like Gods. Rome should have been the one to kneel. Now look at us. Look at you, terrified of your own blessings, of your own shadow."

I frowned. "What are you talking about?"

Antony shook his head. "Nothing. Please, continue. Why are some *qi* harder to take than others?"

My lips thinned, and I withdrew my hand from his. I hated when he did this, said something I didn't understand in that righteous tone then refuse to explain it to me. He didn't trust me. Not yet. "Like I said, I don't have any real answers. These are not the sort of things that are studied or can be learned, for every Gift is unique in its own way. My theory, however, is that it depends on one's will to live. The more things that tether someone to the mortal realm, the harder they fight to hold on to their *qi*. It's survival instinct. If I tried to kill you now, you would fight back."

Again, his lips twitched. "But what if—"

An arrow zoomed into the cottage, piercing the paper windows and narrowly missing Antony's neck.

"Get down!" he cried.

I was already moving, scuttling across the room to latch the door closed—though I doubted this piece of rotten wood could protect us for long.

I ducked against the wall and peeked through the window. Across the river stood men in painted masks—the Phantom's Ghosts.

I cursed. I'd hoped Sihai Feng took care of them back in the canals, and I didn't think they would be foolish enough to patrol these forests and risk clashing with the Roman soldiers searching for Antony.

But I guess if they wanted Antony captured or dead, this was the perfect time. And perhaps their last opportunity.

"How many?" Antony asked, coming to kneel by me.

"Twenty," I said, counting the glimmering souls in the distance.

"Can you take care of them?"

"I don't know. There are too many of them. I can't take all of them out before they kill us."

"I believe in you."

My heart swelled at his words, but his faith meant nothing. Not if I didn't have the strength to pull this off.

I peeked out of the window. The men at the edge of the river had stopped moving. They were hundreds of yards away. Just out of reach, as if they knew the limits of my magic.

"Yang Ruying!" a voice called from outside. A man wearing a red mask, standing at the front of the formation leader. "That's your name, right?"

Baihu?

No. His voice was similar, but it wasn't him. And Baihu would never risk his position among the high Roman ranks for a mission like this. Even if he was desperate, he was not reckless. His position as Valentin's right hand was too valuable to lose.

"We don't want to hurt you, Yang Ruying. Just give us the prince and we'll let you go free. Don't you want to go home? See your family?"

My jaw tightened. We didn't have guns or swords, only the knife still strapped to my leg, and the magic in my veins. I curled and uncurled my hands.

"Do you have a plan?" Antony asked.

"Not a good one." I drew my blade and pressed it to his throat.

45

WE EMERGED WITH ANTONY'S HANDS behind his back and the tip of my blade dangerously close to his throat. One irrational move and I could pierce his jugular, easy as popping a berry.

We approached the Ghosts with slow, measured steps, but my hands were shaking.

Antony had saved my life. I couldn't abandon him. Not before I repaid this debt.

He only had one chance to escape, and if he was fast enough and lucky enough, he might outrun the Ghosts while I bought him some time.

There had to be a Roman search party somewhere in this forest. If the Gods blessed him, they would find him before the Ghosts chased him down.

Red Mask clapped. "I knew you would choose the right path. A child of Pangu will always be a child of Pangu."

Antony said nothing, didn't protest. I wondered if he thought I was selling him out, selfishly trading his life for mine after all that he had done for me.

Step-by-step, we moved closer to the Ghosts but also edged toward the wilderness of the forest. There was endless foliage and canopies and shadows for Antony to hide in. He would survive this. He was too clever and too ambitious to die before he toppled his brothers and inherited the throne.

I guess this was my answer. In the end, I would save him. Because he was a prince of Rome. Because if he died at the wrong place at the wrong time, it would spark a war, render the sacrifice of a good man, a good Emperor, useless.

This wasn't the only reason, though. In my heart, even if I refused to admit it, I knew I wanted him to live—despite knowing I shouldn't, despite the ever-growing doubts of whether he deserved to live.

Maybe this was the best ending for both of us.

If I died for him, he'd always be indebted to me, to a daughter of Pangu. And in death, I wouldn't have to hurt my people, and Antony would take care of my loved ones out of guilt for as long as he lived.

And I selfishly couldn't bear the thought of letting him die.

Just as he couldn't bear letting me die.

"They won't kill me," I whispered. The forest was so close now. If he was fast . . . "Run!"

I pushed him toward the direction of the forest and threw out my magic, ready to run into the jaws of the beasts to see how many precious minutes I could buy him. But before I could take a single step, Antony grabbed my hand.

"要死一起死," he hissed. *If we die, we die together.* With that, he pulled me into a run.

"Antony, no!" I cried, but we were already running. "I can hold them back. I can buy you time."

"Do you know how hard it was to carry you to that cottage? I won't run for my life and leave you!" Antony countered, his mind made up.

His hand gripped mine so tight, as if his life depended on it—as if he were afraid I'd pull myself from him, run back toward the Ghosts.

An arrow whizzed past us.

"If we can get to the forest and find somewhere to hide we might be able to lose them, or at least buy time until your men find you."

There were too many of them and only two of us. We didn't stand a chance.

"Until they find *us*."

"If you die, it means war. If I die, it means nothing." I should make him let go. I should push him away and tell him to save himself.

Yet . . .

"Your life doesn't mean nothing to me," he snarled, tightening his grip until it hurt. "And if you die, it will mean war, too. I will start it myself and—"

A spiral of red shot onto our path, and as soon as it touched grass, flames exploded in a wild blaze, so fast we barely had time to scuttle to a halt before it enveloped us in a perfect circle. A blaze so fast and vicious it had to be guided by magic.

Antony and I stood back-to-back in an attempt to stay clear of the flames that raged so hot I felt my lungs scorch from the sizzling air.

This is it. I waited for the fire to consume us, for heat to turn everything into pain. Antony's fingers weaved through mine one last time and squeezed.

"If we go to hell, at least we will go together," he said, echoing what he had said on the ship, not knowing then that our end would be so close.

But Death didn't come.

Instead, the fire quietened. I had the sudden urge to test faith and run through the flames, but something told me it wouldn't be that easy. If this fire was guided by magic, then it could grow and burn at its master's will. I searched the Ghosts for a sign of the fire wielder, a telltale brow or a tense hand. "I'll get us out of this," I murmured.

I couldn't let these life debts go unpaid. The Sihai Emperor didn't sacrifice himself just for Antony to die before he could repay Sihai.

I raised my hand to gather magic, but Antony stopped me.

A shake of his head, squeeze of his hand.

"Do you trust me?" he whispered.

"I do." The answer came too easily.

"Good. Then do as I say."

"It's such a shame," Red Mask announced as the Ghosts slithered toward us, serpents with their heads reared, fangs bared. "A talent like yours would have served the Phantom well. It pains me to see a descendant of the legendary Yang Clan degrading herself to live as Rome's dog. Your grandfather would turn over in his grave if he knew."

"There's nothing shameful about wanting to live." Antony spoke with that sultry, princely voice of his. "And if you're here to take me as hostage, it won't work. My grandfather won't relinquish Pangu for me. He won't do it for anyone. If you take me, it will only inspire more violence, more bloodshed. Think carefully before you make your next move."

"Oh, that's precisely our plan, dear prince. We *want* war. We *want* bloodshed. We want your kidnapping to force your grandfather to drop his pretenses of peace. We want him to attack, shatter Pangu's fantasies of kind Gods and treaties that hold weight in the face of greed."

"That's your plan? Use violence to unite all of Pangu's empires and the little dynasties calling themselves kingdoms because the Great Empires couldn't be bothered to wipe them out?" Antony sneered. "If your world were to witness the might of science, it would be everyone for themselves. No one would come to Er-Lang's or Sihai's rescue, I assure you."

"Bold words for a losing man."

"It doesn't have to be like that, though," Antony added. "If you let the girl go, I will not only come to you willingly, I will also tell you everything you want to know about Rome. All of its scientific secrets that your spies will never gather in a hundred years. I will tell you how everything works, give you the power to make this a fair fight of mortals against mortals, not Gods against mortals."

"You're willing to betray your Empire for a girl?" Red Mask laughed. "英雄难过美人关啊." *All heroes fail to pass the test of love.* "I didn't take you for a lovesick puppy, Antony Augustus."

"Just let her go."

"Fine. A weapon like her is too rare to kill anyway. It would have been a shame."

The fire died around us.

"Go," Antony told me.

"What? No. I'm not going to leave you."

"Trust me, Ruying."

"Antony . . ."

He leaned in, and as he placed a kiss on my cheek, he slipped the blade from my hand and into his, tucked it into his sleeve. "Trust me, Ruying."

With that, he pushed me away and I stumbled, not knowing what to do. I could fight, but it would be useless. The Ghosts would kill me before I killed them. I had no idea what kind of Gifts they had. It would only be a fair fight if Antony and I had our guns, but he had lost his in the water and I wasn't permitted to carry them.

"Go!" Antony snapped. "Run, and don't look back. Trust me, Ruying. *Run.*"

There was something feral in his eyes. A desperation. My feet felt like they were glued to the ground. I couldn't leave him like this. What kind of coward would that make me?

But what use did I have here?

Maybe it was better for me to run, to get help. Find the Roman soldiers and bring backup.

When my feet began moving, Antony finally smiled. "Goodbye, my love."

As I ran, I kept looking over my shoulder.

I watched Antony approach the Red Mask.

"Come, my prince. You have much to tell us."

"I certainly do." They stood face-to-face. Close enough that when Antony brandished the blade, stabbed it straight into Red Mask's throat, it was too late for him to fight. "You want the secrets of Rome? You will have to pry them out of my cold, dead hands."

With that, Antony turned the blade on himself and plunged it into his chest.

No!

He fell before a scream was ripped from my throat. The Red Mask lay motionless on the ground, and the other Ghosts were frozen in place. Nobody moved.

Then everything happened fast. The only thing I heard was the thudding of my own heartbeat. The only thing I saw was Antony's slumped body, the blotch of red that seeped fast through his tattered robes.

Run, the last thing he asked of me.

I did run, but not for the forest.

I ran for him.

"Stay with me," I whimpered as I collapsed next to him. "Please, stay with me."

Muffled screams sounded in the distance, the echo of chaos through heavy water that drowned me with every shuddered breath.

"Please!" I begged for Antony to hold on, for Death to spare him.

Blood spread too fast. It burned my hand as I tried to apply pressure, to make it stop.

Gunshots echoed in the distance.

"I told you to run," Antony choked, his voice hard and tainted by rage, but when his hand reached out to touch my face, it was gentle.

Death lingered in the air. I tried to push him away with all that I had within me. "No. You can't take him; I won't let you!"

"Retreat!" somebody bellowed in the distance.

"Antony . . ."

"Your Majesty!" A pair of hands covered mine. "We've got him."

Someone gently pulled me away, and I let them.

Doctors in white coats swarmed Antony as Death lingered over him, waiting, waiting, waiting.

PART 4

苦海无涯，回头是岸.

The sea of bitter misery is endless,
but if you turn around,
the shore will be right behind you

46

WE FLEW BACK TO ROME'S side of Jing-City on a helicopter like the ones that hovered near the portal. A bird without wings, faster than what ought to be possible. As soon as we got back, they rushed Antony into an emergency room under the city to perform surgery.

I stayed in the hallway and waited.

An operation. The doctor tried to explain it to me but there were too many things I didn't understand. Too many Roman terminologies of science I didn't know.

All I knew was that he could have abandoned me and saved himself, but he chose to stay. He traded his life for mine. But why did he plunge that knife into his own chest? Was it to give the Ghosts what they wanted so they wouldn't chase after me, or was the thought of living as their prisoner so painful he'd rather die—

No. He's going to be okay. He has to be okay. I owe him too many life debts now. He has to live, so he can collect these debts. So I can repay him.

But while the Roman doctors tried to save him, all I could do was wait.

Hand against my chin, I did the only thing I could in a time like this.

I prayed.

To the Gods of old legends.

To the celestials of my bedtime stories.

312

MOLLY X. CHANG

To Death, the patron of my Gift.

To the north that was supposed to love its children and protect us with all of its power. I prayed to every God who would listen.

Please, I thought into the abyss, hoping Death would hear me. *If you take his life, I'll never forgive you. And Antony Augustus, until I repay you for saving me without my permission, you can't die.*

"You can't die . . ." I whimpered through the tears that drenched my clothes. Over and over and over and over . . .

You can't die.

After a while, a young doctor treated my wound, which I had forgotten about, but he refused to let me stay in the hallway any longer or let me see Antony.

"Go get some rest," he told me after handing me some medicine that was supposed to help me heal.

I wanted to protest, but the guards who stood behind him made me pause.

"We will notify you if anything happens to the prince. He is going to be all right."

He is going to be all right.

In the end, I nodded, made my way back to the apartment I kept at the edge of the princely estates, close to the barracks that housed their guards, and close to the well-hidden hospital that promised to take care of Antony.

47

THERE WAS A VISITOR IN my apartment when I got back.

Baihu held a finger to his lips when I stepped through the door. Shock shuddered and faded from my consciousness in the same breath.

I closed the door behind me but didn't lock it.

My eyes darted left and right, checking whether others hid in the shadows. If Meiya was . . .

"I'm alone," he said, mistaking my vigilance for unease.

I wavered at the familiarity of his voice that reminded me so much of home. A comforting blanket of warm fleece against my worn skin. My feet staggered forward, and I almost threw myself into what I knew would be a familiar embrace before I remembered that Baihu was the Phantom's spy.

Someone who had, directly or indirectly, played a part in Antony's attempted assassination.

One of the reasons Antony was in that operating room, fighting for his life.

"Are you okay?" Baihu kept his distance, but his eyes searched me for wounds. Worry masked his face in the watery light. His half-extended hand hovered between us, as though he wanted to reach out but feared how I might react.

When he finally gathered the courage, moved toward me, reached for me, I shoved him away, hard.

"You tried to kill him," I choked, my breath hitching.

I didn't know I was crying until I felt the sobs in my throat, sorrow ripping my heart to tatters and shreds. Did I just start crying, or have I been crying ever since Sihai, since Antony plunged that blade into his own chest, choosing death rather than being a traitor to Rome? "It's your fault. Everything is your fault."

"What happened?" He had the audacity to ask.

"What happened? You tell me, Er-Lang Baihu. You planned the attack in Sihai, didn't you? You sent those Ghosts to kill Antony and the Emperor because you didn't want them to sign the treaty. You killed a good Emperor who cared about his people simply because he had the fortitude to choose peace over war, sacrifice over decimation."

Baihu's eyes turned hard, as if he'd finally realized whose side I was on. I expected his face to morph into wrath and fury. Instead, he simply laughed and gave a subtle shake of his head. Just like that, all pretenses were dropped. The concern he had shown for me a second earlier vanished like tears under storm.

"He really got to you, didn't he? Do you have any idea what you've done, Ru?" His voice was quiet as a breath, in case these walls had ears. "Do you know, if you had helped the Ghosts, let them take him instead of protecting him, you could have helped us turn the tide of this conflict? Instead . . ."

Baihu closed his eyes, the planes of his face half-pinched by disappointment.

"I've told you once already; I'm not going to let you kill him."

"We had no plans to kill him! Not unless it was the last option available. Trust me, if taking his life was our priority, he would already be dead. You are not the only assassin who walks this land, Ruying. Your powers might be rare, but there are killers as strong as you, as subtle as you, and who have trained their whole lives to be better than you. We wanted to kidnap and interrogate him. The prince is more use to us alive than dead. And do you honestly think we'd give him an end as easy as death? He deserves pain. A lifetime of it, to avenge the millions of blood siblings we lost because of Antony and his science and his claims of peace . . ." Baihu's mouth trembled, a strained smile.

He was biting back the words he knew would hurt me, but his silence was louder than any words. And in his silence, shame burned me in singeing embers.

"I don't regret what I did," I whispered. Half truth, half lie. A twisted shade of gray between the black and white. "I had to save him. I couldn't let the Sihai Emperor die in vain."

At this, Baihu's face turned soft. "The Emperor was collateral damage we didn't expect to pay." Perhaps the closest thing I would get to an apology.

I could still hear echoes of Prince Feng's cries as he held his father's corpse, could see the Emperor's vivid shade of blue explode into air when Death took him from this realm.

Magic sang at my fingertips. My bracelets were still unlocked. I could end Baihu if I wanted to. Avenge the Emperor, pay him back for what he did to Antony, for everything that he made me feel by just seeing him, this shame that continued to gnaw at my insides though I was doing my best, doing what I believed was right.

"Do you know how many people will become your so-called 'collateral damage' if war does come? Countless lives with names and thoughts and wants and fears and tens of thousands of reasons to live. Like all the people I watched die at Sihai. Innocent people, Baihu." I stared at him, waited for some fragment of penitence to cross his face. It never did. "I know you want the best for Er-Lang, for Pangu, but war isn't the answer. It can't be."

"War is the *only* answer. Peace might have been an option in the early years, but not anymore." Baihu took a step forward, closing the distance between us. "Tell me Ruying, are you willing to turn your back on your own blood for him?"

"No." The answer came easily. "But I won't let you kill him, either."

"Because he saved your life? Because he is kind to you, looks at you with tender admiration instead of fear? Is that what it takes to win your trust, your loyalty . . . your heart? Tell me, how much do you actually know about Antony Augustus? Do you know how he wishes to achieve this so-called peace he keeps talking about? Do you know what happens to the Xianlings whom they don't deem worthy of keeping? Do you know of the laboratories they keep deep underground?"

My heart jolted to a stop. "Laboratories?"

"Antony waxes poetic and is willing to put his life on the line for you, but he does not treat all lives in Pangu with such reverence."

Dread rolled in my stomach, scorching hot and acidic.

When I said nothing, Baihu's eyes softened further, and every muscle in my body shuddered at the way he looked at me. With such sorrow—the kind of pity I had always hated, as if I were a clueless, helpless girl who needed to be taught and protected. A girl too frail to brave these storms and wild winter winds.

"What happens in these laboratories?"

"Antony's father discovered the portal between our worlds and began his research into magic, but it is Antony who broke the limits, dug our graves, and nailed our coffins."

"What are you trying to say?"

"Valentin might be a warmonger who has more power than brains, but what Antony has done—*continues* to do—is ten thousand times worse. He's been experimenting on our people with his father since he was a child, and continued to do so even after his father's death."

My stomach dropped. "Opian?"

Baihu shook his head. "That was his father's doing, a way to bargain with our people. We have everything that they wanted, and they had nothing that we wanted. The scale of power wasn't in their favor, so Rome chose to ruin lives in order to change that. Opian is just the tip of the iceberg."

What's worse than opian?

"Show me. I want to see it with my own eyes."

48

I was prepared to scale walls, break windows, and paint my hands red with rivulets of blood to gain access to the laboratory.

Reality turned out to be much simpler.

Being the right hand of Valentin Augustus, Baihu enjoyed a long list of privileges. One of them was unchallenged access to almost every corner of Rome's territories, which included their underground network of endless corridors and dungeons and rooms of science.

I followed at Baihu's heels, playing the role of obedient guard as he led us past electronic doorways, round and ivory white and unlike anything I'd ever seen. They parted diagonally down the middle and opened only for the keys worn around certain guards' necks. Each time they parted with an electronic buzz, chills dripped down my spine.

My steps were light, hesitant like a thief waiting to be caught. I waited for someone to grab me, ask for identification, but nobody dared under Baihu's imposing shadow. The guards bowed to him, showing him the respect I had never been shown.

My insides twisted with every tedious step, fear of what I might find in these corridors climbing up my throat. The coward inside me wanted to pause, to stop, never know the secrets they kept.

But I was so tired of the dark, of treading on thin ice with my eyes closed just because it helped me sleep at night.

Now, I wanted the truth—to stop living with one eye open and one eye closed.

"Do you come here often?" I asked Baihu, my voice no louder than a sigh. I kept my head low for fear there were security cameras hidden overhead. Though I couldn't see any, this didn't mean they weren't there. If Antony truly hid secrets between these walls, he wouldn't let these corridors go unmonitored.

"Only once, and once was enough." As if sensing my paranoia, Baihu added, "Tiny little cameras dot the ceiling, almost undetectable, but don't worry—they don't have audio, so as long as you talk quietly and subtly, they won't be able to read our lips."

"You know a lot about this place."

"It's part of my job. Valentin thinks I learned the layout of the city and all of its secrets to better help him scheme against Antony."

My lips twitched. Baihu was far from the mindless pawn he'd let everyone believe. He was a player in the game, making decisions, causing reactions, the oil poured over the growing flames.

Another flight of stairs took us down a darkened hallway with exposed brick walls, lined with what must have been hundreds of iron-doored cells.

Screams tore through the air, sharp and piercing—a sound that made my bones tremble.

I remembered these screams. A memory that felt like a lifetime ago.

After the kindness Antony had shown me, I had almost forgotten everything the Romans did in those initial days after I was kidnapped.

"I know this place."

"It's where I found you, months ago, where Rome keeps the Xianlings whose Gifts they haven't assessed, or they don't deem worthy. Locked in here like mice in cages, waiting to serve their final purpose."

"And what is that final purpose? What does Rome want from us, from Pangu?" The questions I had tried to ask Antony time and time again and received only meaningless answers or silence.

Baihu was no different. Once again, my questions went unanswered as he led me down a heavily guarded corridor where cell doors became few and far between and seemed to be made of an entirely different material than the ones we'd passed.

When we came to a stop, Baihu was no longer looking at me.

"I remember you wanted to know what happened to Princess Helei." He made a gesture with his hand, the silent guard pressed something into the glass panel beside the door, and an image flickered onto the screen.

Unlike the cells where I was kept in stale air and the haunting dark, this one was illuminated by electric lights. Its walls looked soft and padded, and there were stacks and stacks of books, carved furniture, and drapes of silk too fine for an ordinary captive.

The girl inside sat cross-legged in a corner, focused on the stark white ceiling. The Princess was as beautiful as the legends said. Sun-bronzed skin and dark hair, her face delicate as a raindrop. Perfect nose, pillowy lips, and dark eyes so ethereal they had to be made by Nüwa herself.

When her head turned, when those midnight eyes met mine, I stumbled back at their intensity. Even though it was through a camera and a screen, something about them made me feel as if she saw right through Rome's technologies and into my soul.

In that moment, I could have sworn I saw recognition on her face.

With a subtle furrow of her brow, the princess rose from the ground, lips parted as if she had something to say. A secret kept for too long, waiting for the right person to share it with.

I leaned in, just as she moved closer toward the camera, as her lips began to move . . .

The screen went black.

"Come," said Baihu. "We're going to be late for the main event."

His hand curved against mine. I was about to protest when he shook his head in warning. We were still among enemies. And unlike the cameras, these guards had ears, and everything we said would be relayed back to the princes.

I swallowed the lump in my throat. Baihu did everything for a reason. The whole way here, he had made no attempt to keep a low profile, choosing to wander the hallways with his head held high instead of keeping to the shadows. He wanted people to see us. He wanted the princes to know about this visit.

Why?

We can't leave her here. The words weighed heavy on my tongue.

"We have no choice," he whispered, as if sensing what I wanted to say. "And the princess doesn't want to be rescued. Despite the rumors of how the Roman princes lusted after her beauty and forced the Emperor to give up his only surviving daughter, no one forced Helei to sacrifice herself. When Rome asked for a hostage as a sign of goodwill from my uncle, none of my useless, princely cousins wanted to do their duty. Rome didn't want those addicts anyway; they knew most of them would not live longer than a handful of years at the rate they consumed opian and burned up their *qi*. In the end, it was either her or the then-Prince Yongle, my uncle's heir and the only somewhat competent son he had." Baihu's face twisted under the stark lights into something hideous, full of bitter spite. "My uncle didn't deserve her sacrifice, but this is what she wants. Filiality and all that crap."

At this, I had nothing to say. It was a daughter's duty to sacrifice for her father, for her brothers. It seemed even princesses couldn't escape this fate.

We moved through more doors, more corridors drowning in translucent white lights, but a darkness laced these hallways, too—one that made the hairs on my neck stand to attention. The air smelled of bleach, tainted by the lingering shades of Death. A coldness lurked behind the walls, and I felt its presence grow with every step. If Baihu's hand didn't find mine, didn't squeeze and urge me to keep moving, my feet might have faltered. I might have turned back.

Whatever they hid down here, it couldn't be worse than the terrors my imagination conjured. Or maybe it was as wicked as I knew it would be, but I was too spineless to admit it, to accept that I served a cruel master in disguise.

"You see it, don't you? Death, lingering like an intruder who refuses to leave."

"How did you . . ."

"You told me once, before my mother died, before I left Jing-City and became . . ." A half smile.

I remembered it now, a confession in whispers when his mother was going through her worst withdrawal yet. I had sensed Death lingering near his home, a viper ready to strike.

"She did it for me," Baihu said.

"What?"

"On her deathbed, she told me the real reason she started taking opian. It wasn't to ease the pain of her body or the pain of heartbreak after my father abandoned us. She took opian for me. Some lowlife sold her on the fiction that opian could procure longevity, and my mother was desperate to live for as long as her tumor-ridden body would allow her. She was the only one I had left in this world. Without her, I would be an orphan, alone in this cruel city. She wanted to live so that she could watch me grow up, become strong enough to withstand the city's vultures. She never would have guessed that the sacred medicine she thought was her savior would end up becoming the very thing that took her from me."

"I'm sorry . . ."

"Don't be. I will wash my hands with their blood soon enough."

An image of Baihu standing over Antony's corpse crossed my mind just as we paused outside of a locked door in a lonely corridor.

Baihu took a key from his pocket and led us into a dim room

with a wall of illuminated glass at the farthest end. I moved closer, peered down at the huge room below, occupied by men and women in white coats, filled with computers and screens, graphs and glistening test tubes. With machines I didn't know the names of.

"It's one of his research rooms. One of many. You see those people down there?" Baihu pointed at the white coats, so far down that they looked more like puppets than people. "They are Antony's scientists, here to carry out his experiments—among other things."

"What are we doing here?"

"Just wait." He took a seat by the window. The room was built like the balcony that overlooked the arena, where the princes had lounged while Xianlings like me fought for our lives.

Not a minute later, two guards dragged a bloodied young woman toward a round glass pod in the center of the room. Her hair was cropped short, and there were scars marring the whole of her exposed back. Battle wounds, cuts deep and jagged. A permanent reminder of the enemy blades she had survived.

Like a true warrior, she fought the scientists with every step, but it wasn't enough. There were too many of them and only one of her.

It wasn't until they began strapping the young woman down in the pod that I got a good view of her face.

My hand flew to my mouth.

Taohua.

I couldn't hear her shrieks through the layers of glass, but she thrashed against her restraints so frantically I feared she might break her own arm just to get out. Her eyes were wide like those of a wild animal. She had lost weight. Her once slight form now no more than wisps of flesh and bone.

A woman plugged a tube into Taohua's right arm as a man injected something into her other arm.

I was on my feet before I knew it, running toward the door until Baihu seized me at the waist, pulled me back like I was a kid throwing a tantrum.

"Let me go!" I cried. "She's not supposed to be here! Antony said he'd let her go. He promised—"

Baihu's hand clapped over my mouth before I could make another sound. He grabbed me, an arm wrapped so tightly around my waist I could scarcely breathe. "Stop, Ruying. Getting emotional isn't going to help anyone."

"Let me go!" I cried, my voice muffled. "Let me go! I have to get her out! I have to—"

"Think of Meiya and your grandmother, Ru. Antony might be lenient with you, but this is different. If you do anything to interrupt their experiments, Antony won't hesitate to punish you, teach you a lesson using those you love the most. Trust me, I have seen him do worse for less."

Meiya.

Grandma.

My family. I clung to them with everything I had. But with each act of horror I witnessed at Antony's hand, these thoughts of family, of survival, became worn, frail, like strands of unraveled silk.

Taohua was family, too. My closest friend. A sister not in blood but in honor, in memories and loyalty.

"No . . . This can't be. Antony promised to let her go!" I whimpered. Tears burned my eyes and everything inside quaked with a sort of rage unlike anything I had ever felt.

I should have asked about her, checked up on her the way I did with my family. But like with my family, I was too consumed by my own shame to face her. Now, seeing Taohua was like tearing open the stitches of still healing wounds.

Baihu sighed. His hold loosened, just a little. "This is Rome's world now, and there's nothing we can do to change it. It's too late. Taohua is going to die. She's been dying since the moment they took her in here and started injecting her with those serums that were supposed to make her strong. She has served her purpose. Now that her organs are failing, her days are numbered. Death is an act of mercy, a way to finally put her out of her misery. But not before they exploit her one last time."

"No. That's not true! We can do something. Help me, Baihu! Help me save her! Help me—"

"It's too late for Taohua, but it's not too late for the thousands of people who might face the same fate as her, Ruying." Baihu put a hand on my shoulder to comfort me, but I didn't want comfort.

I wanted Antony to have kept his promise. I wanted Taohua safe and healthy, at home with her mother and father who had already gone through the great tragedy of losing son after son until Taohua and her sister were the only two left. "When I pledged my loyalty to him, he promised he'd let her go."

"This is what Antony does. He lies."

My eyes trailed down to the room below once more. As my dearest friend cried for her life, a piece of me burned from ashes to ember, and ember to flame. The deceptions that had once clouded my eyes dispersed. The more I saw, the harder it was to look away.

"What are they doing to her?" My voice trembled. The girl down there wasn't a stranger I could turn a blind eye to, wasn't a target I could force myself to dismiss.

That was Ma Taohua. My friend, someone who was there for me during the loneliest times of my life. I knew her. I had grown up with her. I'd laughed and cried with her, shared my hopes and dreams with her. She was someone I never thought I'd lose. Never . . .

Magic seethed and boiled, coaxed to blaze in fury. My hands clenched into fists, pressed hard at the glass, and willed it to break, willed this moment to shatter like an interrupted nightmare.

The sight before me didn't change, the world around me didn't change.

But a piece of me did.

"Ruying," Baihu uttered my name softly, gently. I could hear his own heart breaking. Taohua had been his friend, too, once upon a time. His hand covered mine, cradled it as if it was something delicate and breakable. "Your Gift won't work here. The entire chamber is protected by a forcefield that interferes with magic, designed by Antony's leading scientists. If magic worked here, someone would have broken out a long time ago, burned this place to the ground and Rome with it."

Above us, the laboratory's overhead lights dimmed.

"I'm sorry you have to see this, I really am," Baihu whispered as the scientists stepped away from the pod. He squeezed my hand, too tight, like a wrangler minding a kept predator. "I'm sorry it's Taohua . . . But you have to know what Rome is doing. What kind of savagery Antony keeps from you."

An explosion of blue lights slashed the dark. Baihu's arm went around my waist and held me close to him. To comfort or restrain me, I wasn't sure.

"Every day, they take Xianlings here to drain their life force." He kept talking as the lights grew brighter and brighter. Taohua screamed harder and harder, the veins in her neck bulging so hard I feared they might burst.

Blood trickled from Taohua's veins through a tube, then was collected by a container.

I wept.

"If you want this to stop, then you have to fight, Ruying," Baihu said. "This is what they do to our kind once we've served our purpose. We are not humans to them, just *things* they can dispose of. Like wood for a fire, or silk for clothes."

Blood poured and poured, and Taohua's struggles died. The tension of her cries eased into nothing. Through Death's dimmed eyes, I saw energy leave her, slowly. Her soul wavered and fluttered, ready to spread its wings and fly into the next realm.

I closed my eyes. I wanted to go home, back in time to days of ignorant bliss, when I could pretend not to see all that was in front of me. Not notice how the Romans killed us for sport, hunted us like wild animals at the outskirts of the city, and slaughtered families just so they could make pretty maidens and strong boys their orphaned servants.

I tasted the salted tears that rolled down my cheeks.

"You can look away from the horrors of the world, but that doesn't erase their existence," said Baihu, gently. "Open your eyes, Ruying. Open your eyes and see. Stop running away from the truth."

Beyond the edge of my senses, I felt Taohua's color.

Her Death was a shimmering gold, vibrant and beautiful, a shade brighter than *qi*, the life's essence that existed in all of us. The color of happiness, of joy, of kindness and glory and the brilliant hope of dawn.

"*No!*" I cried, tried to reach into the room below and hold on to her *qi* before it evaporated into nothingness.

But beyond the glass Death's magic was thin like spun sugar that melted in my hands. I grasped and grasped but nothing materialized. Death was my patron. I could call him like a friend, an ally, but I could not stop him. He was not mine to command. I was never his master, merely a tool to be used. A vessel for him to claim what he believed was his.

Death didn't discriminate, nor did he play favorites.

And when anger ceased, when Taohua's eyes were empty, I clenched my jaw and wiped the tears away.

Pain hardened to courage.

Antony would pay for this. I would make Rome regret the day they set foot on our land and thought they could mistake our kindness for weakness.

"Taohua isn't the first person who's died like this," I said. My breath hitched, and I ceased crying. Not because the pain had faded, but because crying wouldn't change anything. My sorrow wouldn't change anything.

Just as looking the other way didn't change anything, either.

"Countless victims of their failed experiments were strapped down to that same pod, countless Xianlings had their blood harvested in this very room," said Baihu.

Every single one of those souls were my people. Kin who shared my blood, made by Nüwa in her love for us, whether by hand or from nature's vines, it didn't matter.

Blood of my kin. Blood of my soul.

Every single one of them was someone's friend, child, parent, or sibling. They had loved, and they were loved.

Here, deep beneath Rome's halved city, they were nothing.

Pawns in a game.

Toys for Antony and Valentin Augustus to play with. Just like the multiplier I had killed in the cage all those moons ago to prove my worth to Antony.

He was dying. This was what Antony had meant.

"He promised he'd let Taohua go," I echoed, and wanted to laugh at my stupidity. I knew I couldn't trust him, yet I did anyway. And look where it got me, what it had cost me. "He promised . . ."

"I don't know what kind of tales Antony has told you, what kind of promises he's made, but they are all lies. The only thing Antony cares about is himself. His ambitions and his hunger for power. You've only known him for a few short months, but I've known him for three years. He doesn't care about us. He only wants to use us, possess us. Salvage his wretched world with the magic of our people. Do you remember when I said the raid that took you never should have happened? Valentin is not reckless enough to conduct such a high-risk operation right under the Emperor's nose. The peace between Rome and Er-Lang might be a smokescreen, but this smokescreen is something both sides are invested in maintaining. For now, at least. The Emperor knows about Rome's activities, how they are stealing Xianlings to conduct these experiments. It is just one of the many prices my uncle paid for this false sense of peace. The Romans do whatever they want whenever they want, and Er-Lang Empire keeps one eye open and one eye closed . . ."

Baihu kept talking, but all I could think about was Taohua.

I've heard reports of corpses washed up on the shore, their blood drained, their bodies like shriveled husks: one of the last things Taohua had ever said to me.

"Taohua didn't know what was happening, right? She was investigating the bodies drained of blood. She—"

"It was a private investigation. Her father knew the truth and had tried to urge Taohua off the scent for months, but you know how she is. Stubborn, just like you. How could she just forget about this, when her people were going missing and turning up as corpses thousands of miles away? Taohua was young. Her father wanted to protect her, but it wasn't enough."

"Why did Rome conduct a raid in the capital? Was it only an exercise of their power, to remind the Emperor and every Er-Lang martyr of our place?"

"I wish that's what had happened." Baihu handed me a few sheets of folded paper from his jacket pocket. "Read it."

The pages were heavy in my hand, and upon unfolding, my belly tightened in a dead knot that could never be untangled.

It was a long list of names, and mine was at the very top. And on the end of it all, was Antony's signature. His familiar, cursive penmanship and the gold-inked emblem I had seen countless times. The same one he used to sign off on all of my missions.

My heart stopped in that moment, clutched by shame, by grief, by a thousand different emotions I didn't know how to put into words.

"Antony was the one who ordered that raid, Ruying. Not Valentin."

"Why?"

"For you. He conducted that raid to get his hands on *you*. A power as godly as yours, Antony was willing to risk everything for it. Even war. He knew the consequences of such an act in the capital itself, but he didn't care. All of his talk of peace, of tolerance and mercy, none of it applies to him—especially when there's something he wants at stake. Antony is not who you think he is. He is not the guardian of peace you so desperately wanted him to be. He wants to rule, and will do anything to prove to his grandfather that he can govern us better than his brothers. He's never cared about the good of our two worlds. The only thing he wants is power, and the easiest way to amass such power is by becoming his grandfather's heir apparent."

"All of those people . . . They died. Because of me. *Taohua* . . . died, because of *me*."

"It wasn't your fault. When Antony sees something he wants, he will take it—regardless of the consequences, regardless of the collateral damage." Baihu's hands took mine again and squeezed tight. "Join me, Ru. Help me end this tragedy and make things right. Kill Antony, kill Valentin, and together we can start a war between Rome and Pangu. Together, we can free our people from the oppression they try to sell as peace. It's time we end these decades of humiliation."

I didn't answer.

Instead, I glanced down at the scientists again, at the blood they'd gathered. "Why did they collect Taohua's blood?"

"It's not our blood they want," Baihu replied. "But this is a question you should ask Antony yourself."

49

I DIDN'T CRY AGAIN UNTIL I got back to my room and crawled into my bed—except it wasn't *my* room or *my* bed. None of this was mine.

I was in a cage.

No matter how many pretty things Antony filled it with, a cage was still a cage, and I must not forget it.

Still, this gray room was the closest thing I had to safety. Here, I allowed myself to be weak, to break and cry and muffle my screeching sorrows into the pillow.

Tears burned until they didn't.

Hearts were broken until time healed.

I let myself shatter just so I could put the pieces back together, stronger than before.

If an afterlife existed, I hoped Taohua found peace.

If reincarnation was real, I hoped that in her next lifetime she'd be blessed with parents who told her they were proud so she would always know how much she was loved.

In the silence of twilight, in the loneliness of my room, I thought I could hear echoes of Taohua's laughter, feel a piece of her lingering close.

Her hand on my shoulder, breath against my skin, the scent of persimmons and lemongrass in the air. I didn't know if I imagined it, but I swore I felt Death tugging at her from the other side, and

Taohua holding on, because she didn't want to leave me here all alone. Just like as kids, she hated for us to be apart, hated it when I had to walk back into that house and face my father's wrath.

It should have been me.

I deserved to die, not Taohua. My soul was wicked, and my hands tainted. Taohua gave love like the sun, and her kindness knew no bounds. All she wanted was to make her father proud, to prove that daughters were as good as sons.

"I'm sorry," I whimpered, my breath catching on the sobs, the tears, the fractured shards of my own beating heart. "I never should have trusted Antony. I should have known this would happen. I . . ."

My voice broke, and I clutched my chest because something was breaking beneath flesh and bone. A part of me that I couldn't bandage or balm fissured slowly like thin ice cracking under weight, and the frigid blue waters beneath waited eagerly to drown me in their bitter depths.

I curled my hands to fists, and welcomed Death's magic, invited it to flow through me like winter's sunrise, its heat simmering like tiny flames that burned over sorrow.

Crying wouldn't bring Taohua back.

I clenched my hands till eight bloodied half-moons marred my palms.

"A life for a life," I whispered into the cold air, wiping away the tears, the cold cotton of my sleeves rough against skin. My eyes stung from the crying; my vision blurred.

Antony broke his promise first.

The Gods wouldn't punish me for breaking mine, too.

"Go," I whispered into the dark, empty room. "I won't let you die in vain, Taohua. You'll be remembered. As the hero I always knew you were."

50

ANTONY WOKE TWO DAYS LATER. By the time I got to the infirmary, he was surrounded by advisors—a room of pale old men with stern frowns and biting stares. A different sight from what I had anticipated.

I thought these initial lucid moments would be spent with Valentin at Antony's bedside, holding his hand, eyes red from crying.

Valentin and Antony might be at odds, but they were still brothers, right? If not in blood then in spirit. If anything like this happened to Meiya, I would stay with her, no matter what the doctors said.

Valentin *was* there, just at the back, arms crossed, a sour expression on his face, as if displeased that his brother had lived to see another day.

I also expected to find Antony weak and fragile, but while he was paler than usual, otherwise he didn't look any different. If I hadn't felt his fading pulse, watched blood pour like a crimson river from his chest, felt Death settle beside him, I never would have known how close he'd come to losing his life.

The pungent smell of Roman chemicals stung the air. I knew science was capable of impossible things, but this—stealing a man from Death's waiting arms—was something else. No man should have survived that wound. When Death came to claim a soul, he was not to be denied.

Yet . . .

Antony looked up when I stepped into the room. "Leave us," he told the advisors and Valentin.

I stood in the corner until they filed out, one by one.

Even in those hideous infirmary garments, Antony looked beautiful. A sight breathtakingly haunting, as the best of liars were.

It was easy to trust a beautiful face, and Antony always had a way of making me trust him despite my better instincts.

Valentin was the last to leave. Before he did, he whispered something into Antony's ear. Something that made Antony's jaw go tight, a slight frown between his brows.

Valentin winked when he passed me but didn't say anything.

"How's your wound?" Antony asked once we were alone.

He tried to sit up straighter. There was a slowness to his movement, a slight wince of pain. A part of me wanted to rush to his side, but I stopped myself. Despite everything, what I felt for him on the island persisted, like the lasting cold of a long winter, regardless of the piercing spring light.

In that brief moment, his pain hurt me as much as it hurt him.

I pushed away the remorse prickling at my neck, stayed close to the now-closed door.

Antony flashed the kind of smile that would have swept the air from my lungs and left me fluttering with butterflies just two days earlier.

Now it made my stomach turn.

Memories of Taohua's pale corpse, her face frozen in an eternal scream, haunted me every time I closed my eyes. A memory I'd never forget, one that kindled a kind of hate that would never perish.

As if sensing the change in me, Antony sat a little straighter. I thought he might climb out of the infirmary bed and stumble over to me.

He didn't.

His mouth parted, words at lips' edge, yet none materialized.

He knew that I had been to the laboratory. He had to. I knew guilt when I saw it. This had to be what Valentin had whispered before he left.

The silence stretched until his half smile hardened into a grimace, until the air went cold. "I dreamt of you while I was unconscious."

"Really?"

"It was a dream of us. In a different place, a different time. Another universe where you didn't look at me with hate in your eyes, where I wasn't a prince chained to my duties." He took a deep breath, braced himself. "Valentin sent Baihu to you. He wants to—"

"Don't try to manipulate me. It doesn't matter why Baihu showed me the laboratories. What matters is what I saw."

His expression was like the sky before a storm, calm but deadly. "Would you listen if I explained?"

"Go ahead," I replied, curt. I didn't have the patience for his mind games, but if he wanted to explain himself, I'd entertain his lies.

"I didn't want to deceive you, Ruying."

"You told me you'd let Taohua go."

"I know." He winced, his voice cracking.

If I didn't know better, I'd think he was about to cry, but I was done putting faith in a man who couldn't be trusted. I was a fool to think he was a good man when he was as vicious as the monsters who swarmed him.

Here and now, the sight of him felt like knives slicing at my heart. Whatever had bloomed between us had wilted, petal by petal, ruined by mold and rot and a kind of hate that couldn't be swept away by charming smiles and lulling words.

"You said we were friends, but friends don't break promises like this. Friends don't . . . ." My voice cracked. I swallowed the lump in my throat as memories of Taohua swelled behind my eyes. "Why didn't you let her go, like you promised?"

"They started experimenting on her before we made the deal," he explained. "Her Gift was strength, and her body was capable of gathering energy at impossible rates. There was more energy in a single drop of her blood than most Xianlings have in their entire body. The scientists thought if they could unlock the code to her genetics, they might find the answer to all of our problems."

"Don't try to shift the blame, Antony. Those scientists follow *your* orders. If you had told them to stop, they would have. Don't try to wash yourself clean of her blood, because you're not clean. Is this what it means to be a prince? Making mistakes only to have others suffer the consequences? Claiming praise when it pleases you, and pushing off blame when you don't want to admit your wrongs?"

"Ruying—"

"I should have trusted my instincts." I laughed, my voice trembling, my chest shaking. Every part of me was tense and fragile all at once, and at any moment I might shatter under the slightest of touch. "After you saved me in Sihai, I thought you were different from your grandfather and your brother. I was wrong. You're just like them, if not worse. Valentin might be the one my people weave tales of terror from, but at least he's genuine about who he is. You? You're a wolf in sheep's clothing. A snake in slumber, and I can't believe that I once clung to your every word and believed despite . . ."

A shuffle of sheets. Soft footsteps.

When Antony came to stand before me, there were tears in his eyes and remorse painted across his face.

Those tears might not look fake, but I knew they were. He knew how to lie and deceive and justify his sins as acts of honor.

I could almost hear his honey-coated words, ready to pierce this heavy air. I'd been here before. I believed him the first time; I wouldn't be manipulated a second time.

"I was going to tell you the truth," he said quietly, like a boy admitting something he didn't want to be found out. "Eventually."

"But you didn't."

"I didn't want you to hate me."

When I laughed, he flinched like I'd plunged a knife in his chest. "The scientists took Taohua's blood," I said. Antony's mask of guilt and shame vanished into something cold, something that resembled fear, as if he knew the question that would follow. "Why?"

"You wouldn't understand."

"Tell me the truth, Antony."

He sighed, admitting defeat, backing away. "Your people think we're here to exploit your powers. They're wrong. We are not here for your magic—or at least not in the way you think. Inside your body, there are these tiny cells that contain unholy amounts of energy—so much it shouldn't be scientifically possible. We have many names for these cells, but the one I finally settled on a few months ago is *qi*-cell, named after the force behind your powers. They exist and reproduce in your body just like any other cells, and store energy the same way blood cells store oxygen. We think this energy is how your people came to possess supernatural abilities. Either by contamination in the ways of radiation, or it is the source of your so-called 'magic.' But how it may or may not have manifested your abilities is irrelevant. The key is the unfathomable amount of energy each cell holds. It may be the solution to all of Rome's problems. My father wholeheartedly believed these tiny little cells will save my entire world, and upon investigation, I think he was right."

"What does any of this have to do with saving your world?"

51

"My world is dying," Antony said quietly. "It's been dying for centuries now. For too long, my people have lived beyond our means. We overmined, polluted, and exploited our planet in every way. We were greedy. We wanted everything, and then more. We took and took and took till Mother Nature retaliated. We knew what we were doing, knew the damage we were causing, yet generation after generation maintained lifestyles of unsustainable luxury. Like Kings and Queens on borrowed time, stealing from the generations yet to come. Everybody knew the consequences, but nobody did anything because they thought these were problems of another generation." Antony smiled. "Well, the time has finally come for us to pay for the crimes of my ancestors, and the generation that price falls upon is mine. Thanks to the humans who lived before me, my world is on the brink of chaos."

"What does any of this have to do with us? Your world is dying? That's your problem, not Pangu's."

"My world's past has everything to do with your world's present—and future. You see, the scientists of my world are looking for solutions. A way to power our cities, maintain our standard of living, without further damaging our world. Yet, despite all of their PhDs and accolades, nobody could come up with a viable solution until my father discovered the portals. Until we discovered Xianlings, and the energy that exists inside you."

Dots connected, one by one by one.

"*Qi*-cells are a special thing. Once harvested, a single cell can hold a hundred times more energy than the fuel that powers our cities without the dangerous by-products that have polluted our rivers and air."

"So you train the ones you deem worthy as good soldiers, then kill the rest just to reap their cells like grains for winter?"

We were just a harvest to them, nothing more. Our lives were as worthless as the fruits in their baskets and rice in their bowls.

"Where does opian come into all of this?" I persisted, before he could answer. "Your people spread the drug for a reason."

"Initially, my father thought we could establish trade with your people in exchange for building factories here and disposing of our garbage—all the things my world can no longer withstand—but we soon discovered there's nothing you want that this world and its magic can't provide. We could have traded weapons with you, but you were already so powerful with magic, you'd be unstoppable with science. So, we gave you opian—a drug that was originally developed as a stimulant to enhance magic in those who already had it, or even grant magic to those who did not. It was intended as a gift, a solution for your dying magic. But along the way, we discovered the power that exists within you, and how opian works by stimulating the growth of *qi*-cells, therefore creating more energy within your bodies. We didn't lie when we said it can make your Gifts stronger, and even awaken magic from those with dormant cells. But it also has other effects. The ethereal highs generated as a result of this process was an unexpected bonus when it came to creating something your people craved."

"But opian also kills us. If we take too much, we die. If we take too little, we die. You are playing God with our bodies, something mortals were never meant to do."

"As I said, there are . . . side effects. The overproduction of *qi*-cells can sometimes . . . cause less than desirable outcomes when the body does not have enough energy to sustain that reproduction.

Energy is a finite thing. One cannot create energy, just as one cannot destroy it. Like magic, the laws of science give with one hand and take with the other. We don't know where these cells are harvesting their energy from. My scientists believe it is from the sun, from the air around us, from the energy that exists in all things, as it can't possibly be just from your bodies. But when there are too many cells and they can't gather enough energy from what's around them, then they start attacking the body like rabid vermin demanding to be fed. It's kind of like gravity, or how blackholes are created, and if you think of it like—"

I laughed—a sound that stopped him mid-sentence. "My magic-less father used to praise opian and Rome. *They are Gods,* he used to say, *and opian is their Gift for everyone to enjoy, not just the Xianlings.* If he had known that your people fed us opian like pigs being fattened for slaughter . . . How stupid he was for believing in your fabricated truths. Did you ever see my people as humans, or were we always just *things* to you? Our lives nothing but fuel for your world's greed?"

Antony had the audacity to shake his head, as if he could defend his indefensible actions. "My father never intended for any of this to happen, Ruying. You have to believe me. He set out to create something that would make Xianlings strong, so that we'd have something to offer you. All he wanted was to *help* your people, have our two worlds live in harmony."

Antony reached for me, but I pushed him away. His words were just sounds now. They meant nothing.

I could smell the corpses scattered in Jing-City's streets, the gnawing stench as my father drifted away from us in his high, the smoke that constantly filled the foyer.

Grandma's tears. My sister's bruises.

All of this because of the greed of people who lived a world away.

They murdered their world, but in the end, mine was the one that paid the price.

My family's demise. Countless deaths. These cuffs around my wrists.

Everything my people were forced to live through these last two decades, happened because of them.

"We didn't intend any of this, Ruying. Please believe me." Antony's voice was breaking, desperate for me to hear him.

But the only thing I could hear were my ancient cries for the father who abandoned us for the highs of opian and worshipped the Romans like supreme beings.

"If you never intended for any of this to happen, then prove it. *Do* something."

Antony's face fell. "It's not that easy."

"Really?"

"This is beyond me, Ruying. Even if I want to stop it, my grandfather won't let me. My world won't last long without your people's energy; their sacrifices are buying time for a whole *civilization*. This isn't a permanent solution, just until we find a better one. Give me some time, I—"

"And how many will die before you find that better solution?" Taohua's face flashed again, her bone-white skin, her mouth frozen in an eternal scream. "How many of my people have died so far to buy time for your kind? Do you even know? Do you know all of their names, because those people had names, as well as mothers and fathers, whole lives ahead of them before you stole them from us. They were *people,* Antony . . . And you killed them in cold blood. You and everyone from your world are monsters."

He turned away, cheeks tainted by shame, his fists clenched tight as if he could make this moment vanish with the force of those mighty hands.

"And the raid, it was done under your orders, right? You took me from my family so I could become your butcher."

A muscle tightened in the prince's jaw. Anger, frustration, strained like an archer's bow. "I know you are angry with me right now,

Ruying. But I swear, everything I do is for the greater good. For *both* our worlds."

"If you truly cared about peace, you would not have raided the city that night and risked a war with Er-Lang because you saw a toy that you wanted, and you didn't care what it took to get it. You kept me in a cage, and you almost let me die in that cell to coerce me into believing in you, into depending on you. So that you could use me as a weapon."

"I patched things up with the Emperor. Sometimes, in order to win the war, we must take risks. And you were a risk worth taking."

Win the war. This was what he wanted.

Not peace, but victory for Rome at all costs. He didn't care what happened to my people, as long as his got what they wanted. Stealing magic from our bodies so that they could live on borrowed luxuries, just like their ancestors.

He wanted the Empire weak, so if Rome ever wished to invade, they could. He didn't care about people like me.

He never had.

And never would.

"What other secrets are you keeping?" I asked. If Antony lied to me about this, then he had to be lying about other things, too. "Are my family—"

He cut me off. "They are safe. I may have kept things from you, but your family is as safe as can be. And will continue to be, for as long as I live. I'm sorry, Ruying. Just give me time. I can fix all of this if you'd just *trust* me. Sometimes people have to die for others to live. To sacrifice the few for the lives of the many isn't an easy decision, but it's a decision rulers must make. And I was born to rule. I thought you out of all people would understand this. The weight of power, the strength it takes to kill, to decide who lives and who dies. We are the same, Ruying, can't you see? You are the only person in the world who understands—"

He reached for me once more, and I jerked away. "I am nothing like you, Antony Augustus. You say you're here because your world is dying? Well, my world is dying, too. It's being killed by your drug, and your experiments, and your greed. You are not a God."

His mouth opened, but nothing came out.

A charged silence fell.

I closed my eyes. I didn't know what else to say to make him listen. He'd made up his mind, and nothing I said could change it, could make him understand.

"I'm doing what I have to do," he said. "Just as you did when you pledged your allegiance to me to save your family."

"That's not the same."

"It's *exactly* the same. We *are* the same, whether you want to admit it or not. Two people doing bad things for the right reasons. This is why we are here. Pulled together by fate because you and I were destined to be equals. Together, we can right all of the wrongs that came before us. But to make new rules, we must be brave enough to break everything that came before us. And upon their ashes, we can build something new and better in its place. A benevolent ruler cannot save the world. Peace comes at the price of blood. Stand by me, and I promise I'll build you a better tomorrow. For both of us."

He stepped forward, and I fought not to take a step back. I didn't want to cower in front of him, didn't want him to think I was scared.

"Together." He reached for my hand. This time, I let him take it. "We can save everyone."

The only thing my world needs to be saved from is you.

"It's this, or watch Valentin and Cassius bring apocalypse to Pangu. I destroy with the intent to rebuild, but they do not. I want both sides to make compromises, but Valentin and Cassius want domination. They want to conquer your world and turn Pangu into a second Rome. If they succeed, everyone you've ever known will die in the process. Another world for my people to ruin," he said, voice slow and cold.

My bracelets were still deactivated. I could kill him. I wouldn't walk out of this room alive, but I could end his life, avenge Taohua and Father and everyone who died because of the Romans.

But revenge wasn't enough.

And Antony was right. This was above him. Above all of us, now.

Even if I killed him, it wouldn't bring Taohua back to life or turn back time to the days before Rome infiltrated Er-Lang. If Antony died, his grandfather would still harvest my people's blood to power their cities.

Choose your fights, Grandma's teaching echoed. *It's okay to lose a battle, as long as you win the war.*

"Do you trust me, Ruying?"

"I trust you," I lied.

Relief flooded his face and illuminated the room in his wicked, brazen light.

I tried to smile back.

Baihu was right, it was time for us to take a stand.

If it was us, or them . . .

I chose us.

52

WHEN I KNOCKED ON BAIHU'S door, he was expecting me. Two cups of tea were poured, steam puffing, still hot. He gave me one and sipped from the other.

"When I first found out about everything, I couldn't believe it, either. I remember the feelings that buried me: the anger, hate, frustration . . . I don't think I've ever wanted to kill anyone more than I wanted to kill the Augustus family that day, but alas I had to wait."

"Because to avenge the dead isn't the same as protecting the living." I sighed. "Why isn't anyone doing anything?"

"The Phantom—"

"I'm not talking about him. I mean the Emperors, the royals. Those whose job is to protect us. Er-Lang's people have been dying since the Romans arrived. Sihai is going behind everybody's backs to sign another treaty. What about Lei-Zhen, Ne-Zha, and Jiang Empire?"

"They are scared. For now, none of this is their problem. So they stay out of it, keep their hands clean of trouble that doesn't involve them."

"But their duty is to *protect* us. This is why Emperors exist, right? To protect people?"

"Take it from someone who shares blood with these supposed descendants of Gods; the royals aren't as great as you think. Bloodlines don't make us good people. My father's very existence can attest to that, Ruying, and my cousins are just as rotten as their fathers. The only person with half a decent soul is Helei, and look where that got her. A prisoner of Rome, her life held hostage in case Yongle ever rebels." Baihu shook his head. "It's time that we put our faith in something new. The Romans are the greatest threat our world has ever faced, and the Gods aren't coming to save us. They won't descend from the heavens to fight for us like the legends claim. They won't reincarnate into mortal bodies like those who saved us from the Qin Emperor a thousand years ago. It's up to us now. If we don't do something, they won't ever stop." He offered me his hand. "Join us, Ruying. The Ghosts need you. *I* need you."

This time, I didn't hesitate. I placed my hand in Baihu's and asked, "What's the plan?"

53

My mother named me Ruying because she wanted me to be brave.

My father thought girls should be meek and gentle. He said courage was a luxury only men could afford.

For too many years, I believed him.

Bow.

Kneel.

Obey.

Stay out of trouble.

That was the life Father wanted me to live.

But I wasn't born to be a perfect, docile daughter.

No girl was ever born meek and afraid, as men claimed.

Father told me to scream in the face of danger and seek the kindness of a good man for protection.

I didn't want to scream. I wanted to look danger in the eyes and make it tremble.

Courage in boys was bravery.

Courage in girls was foolishness.

From this day forward, I wished to be foolish.

ACKNOWLEDGMENTS

To Anne Groell, who was the first to believe in this book: I will forever be grateful for the opportunities you offered me. This book took almost eight years to publish, and I contemplated giving up so many times over the years, but something stubborn (or incredibly foolish) in me always pushed me to keep trying, keep believing. In hindsight, all of the tears and heartbreak over the years were worth it, because I ended up with you and the best team in publishing, including Scott Shannon, Keith Clayton, Tricia Narwani, Ayesha Shibli, Bree Gary, Alex Larned, Ashleigh Heaton, Tori Henson, Sabrina Shen, David Moench, Jordan Pace, Adaobi Maduka, Maya Fenter, Abby Oladipo, Rob Guzman, Ellen Folan, Brittanie Black, Elizabeth Fabian, and everyone at Del Rey and Random House whose hands have touched this book.

To Carmen McCullough, Alicia Ingram, Harriet Venn, Chessanie Vincent, Stevie Hopwood, Adam Webling, Bella Haigh, Andrea Kearney, Becki Wells, Kat Baker, and the entire team at Puffin/ Penguin UK: Thank you for making my dreams come true. Over the years, I was told too many times that books like mine, about people who look like me, would never sell in the United Kingdom, but you proved them wrong. I will forever be grateful for the faith and passion all of you have in this little book.

To Xiran Jay Zhao: Thank you for being my emotional support human, executive art director, friend, cheerleader, and therapist, for staying up with me until 6 A.M. while I cried, and for pulling me through the worst days, weeks, and months.

Thank you to the incredible authors who agreed to read this book early and offer kind words. Thank you to the friends who saw me through the storms and who held my hand when I wanted to give up. And for always believing in me, for offering wisdom and kind words, and for being my inspiration when I seemed to have lost all hope, thanks goes to: Thea Guanzon, Joelle Wellington, Adalyn Grace, Namina Forna, Natasha Bowen, Anissa De Gomery, Hannah Whitten, Chloe Gong, J. Elle, Alyssa Earthly, Daphne Lao Tonge, Ciannon Smart, Sam Soar, Amy Andrawos, Emily Russell, Maeeda Khan, Andrea Stewart, Ann Liang, Alina Khawaja, Isabel Cañas, Lydia Gregovic, Sydney Shields, Joel Rochester, Rebecca Ross, Gabriela Romero Lacruz, Jordan Lynch, Ariana Godoy, Rebecca Schaeffer, Sarah Rees Brennan, and so many more.

To the amazing booktokers, bookstagramers, reviewers and bloggers, thanks for all of the support. Thanks to the entire Illumicrate Team for all of their hard work, and for putting this battered book of my heart in the hands of so, so many people. Thanks to Sija Hong, for this amazing cover illustration, and to Regina Flath, for designing the cover of my dreams.

Thanks go to all of my writer friends who pushed me forward and cheered me on and believed in me over the years—even when I didn't believe in myself. To Kari, for not giving up. To Thao, for taking a chance on me. To Suzie, for her kindness and knowledge and for everything she taught me. To the foreign rights team and to the foreign publishers, for pushing this book into every corner of the world.

To the readers who have been here since the beginning: Thank you. To the readers who discovered me through this book: It took eight years for this book to knock down the iron doors of the publishing machine and end up in your hand. and I hope you love this tear-soaked story as much as I do.

To my grandparents: Thank you for your stories, your love, your jokes and warm hands, your morning porridge and evening walks. I love you. I miss you. I would make the same horrible choices as Ruying if it meant I could turn back time and be with you for your twilight years. I began writing this book in that terrible summer when I lost 奶奶和姥姥. I would do anything to get ten more years with all of you. I would do anything to turn back time. . . .

For eight years, I cut myself open over and over again, because I refused to give up on this book about a girl who would do anything to protect her family, who missed out on the final years of those she loved the most because she was in a far-off land, fighting for a better life. *To Gaze Upon Wicked Gods* is many things, but at its core, especially in its earliest versions, it is about a girl who loves her grandparents, who misses her grandparents, and would do anything to give them a better life. . . . Every day, I wish all of you were still here. I wish all of you could hold this book in your hands.

ABOUT THE AUTHOR

MOLLY X. CHANG is a first-generation immigrant born in Harbin, China, and currently living in the U.K. *To Gaze Upon Wicked Gods* is her debut novel.

Twitter: @mollyxchang
Instagram: @mollyxchang

ABOUT THE TYPE

This book was set in Sabon, a typeface designed by the well-known German typographer Jan Tschichold (1902–74). Sabon's design is based upon the original letterforms of sixteenth-century French type designer Claude Garamond and was created specifically to be used for three sources: foundry type for hand composition, Linotype, and Monotype. Tschichsold named his typeface for the famous Frankfurt typefounder Jacques Sabon (c. 1520–80).